13/4/2018

The Lyra and the Cross

Ты, София, первый
мне благославенный
плод Боже. Эта
книга — вторая.
Вы обе дали жизни
моей больше
значительности, чем
представилось мне,
даже в мечтах.
Спасибо, о, спасибо!

The Lyra and the Cross

Elizabeth L. Sammons

DLD Books
Editing and Self–Publishing Services
www.dldbooks.com

Editing, print layout, e-book conversion, and cover design by
DLD Books, www.dldbooks.com

ISBN: 1986571297
ISBN-13: 978-1986571296

Dedication

Thank you, valiant translators of myth and holy writ from every nation, from every generation! From your mind, through your ink, and sometimes with your very blood, you have allowed us to keep faith and hold memory.

Foreword

"As my brother Stephanos walks, the dust barely parts." The opening to this novel sums up the traces of Stephen that have come down to us after 2,000 years. Nothing is known of this man beyond seven mentions in the Bible, primarily from Acts Chapters 6 and 7. But the fragments we glimpse are as enticing as any in scripture: "Stephen, a man full of faith and of the Holy Spirit ... But there arose certain of them that were of the synagogue called the synagogue of the libertines ... disputing with Stephen. And they were not able to withstand the wisdom and the Spirit by which he spoke." (Acts Chapter 6) And his unforgettable final action and words: "And he kneeled down, and cried with a loud voice, 'Lord, lay not this sin to their charge.'" (End of Acts Chapter 7)

Stephen's final mention in scripture (Acts 22:20) is worthy of particular note, and it stands central to this writing. Speaking to his fellow Jerusalemites just before they intended to stone him like Stephen, the now–converted Saul of Tarsus recounts his trance. "I said, Lord, they themselves know that I imprisoned and beat in every synagogue the ones who believed in you: and when the blood of Stephen your witness was shed, I also was standing by, and consenting, and keeping the garments of those who killed him." Saul enters the Bible doing just what he confesses here—anything but a fetching debut for the man known later as Saint Paul. Indeed, Saul stands out amidst Christianity's first martyrdom like a darkened figure amidst the flames of faith soon to ignite the Jewish and the Hellenic world alike.

This man is far from the later Paul we know as instigator of so many dramas, dangers, and dispositions as Christianity spread around the eastern end of the Roman Empire. Saul, even if young, was not a man to stand to the side and hold the garments of those closely involved in matters of faith. This novel hinges on the question, why did Saul of Tarsus take such a stance at Stephen's martyrdom?

Some have speculated that Saul had a physical disability. In 2 Corinthians 12:7–10, he prays three times for "this burden to be lifted from me." Whether his readers are aware of the burden, or whether by some private concern he chose to allow it to remain a platonic silhouette of burden, it is obvious that he was facing a heavy and difficult challenge. In another passage, he refers to "what large letters I use as I write to you with my own hand." (Galatians 6:11) We see his contemporary, Rome's Emperor Claudius, who for all his stammering, limp, and awkwardness drew not just the respect of his fellow Romans, but even their admiration and love. When Claudius laughed at his own embattled body, the Romans laughed with him. Surely a man of Saul's charisma could preach likewise and find acceptance with his peers, but was he capable of casting heavy stones?

As I planted the few verses we have concerning Stephen in my heart, another question occurred to me. Physical conditions aside, did Saul have personal reasons holding him back from casting the first stone? What if Stephen and Saul, two brilliant minds of Israel, knew each other? And what if they were friends? Thus the seeds for this novel were sown, and a story was born.

Better said, part of this story was born. What about these bypassed congregations in the temple of the "libertines"? They were mostly Greek-speaking freedmen, or "Hellenisti," as they are labeled in Acts Chapter 6 and in a few later New Testament passages. Many Hellenisti were Jews, but Jews under Greek influence. We see them by the 3rd century B.C. as they began to flourish in Alexandria, spreading around the eastern Mediterranean. Over centuries of warfare, Jews were among those taken into slavery. But a remnant of the freedmen, hungering for what we would call today "our roots," straggled into Jerusalem in search of faith and fathers. By the time of Christ, this was a large enough faction to have its own community. While the zeal of these Hellenisti for things Judaic may have been strong, the Greek of their recent past lived on, as seen with the discovery of Greek temple signs from the Jerusalem area.

Was Stephen one of them? What his quintessentially Greek name and his actions reveal were the nuances, the many shades and levels of piety straggling between orthodox Judaism of the type portrayed when Jesus addressed the Pharisees and Sadducees, and the wild chaos of Greek explanations of the making of the earth, the many humanlike gods dominating its destiny, and the role of mortal to Olympian. The diversity of Stephen's ministry, the weaving of Hellenist and Hebraic thought, was the challenge that delighted me in addressing his shifting world.

References

Numerous friends and even strangers encouraged me through five years of tilling my heart, mind, and soul in preparation for writing *The Lyra and the Cross*. I pray God's hand and blessing upon each one of these thinkers, though many will never know the depth of their contributions.

Years ago, the magnificent work *A God Against the Gods*, by Allen Drury, revealed to me the power of a historical novel written through multiple witnesses. I remain forever grateful to this author for his boldness of conception.

Some of the many works consulted during this writing include the following:

Coming out Christian in the Roman World, by Douglas Boin

The Poems of Catullus, by Gaius Valerius Catullus, translated by Peter Green

On the Natural Faculties, by Claudius Galenus (Galen), translated by Arthur John Brock

Greek Gods and Heroes, by Robert Graves

The Gods of Olympus, by Barbara Graziosi

The Grammar of God: A Journey into the Words and Worlds of the Bible, by Aviya Kushner

Hymns of Orpheus, translated by Thomas Taylor

Pontius Pilate, by Ann Wroe

Final Notes

We lack a definitive birth date for Jesus of Nazareth, as well as for many other historical events depicted in this book, such as the popular protest portrayed at the end of Part I. My timeline of 11 A.D. to 35 A.D. assumes Jesus' birth in 1 B.C.

Modern-day Jerusalem has a gate on its eastern side called "Saint Stephen's Gate" or "The Lion's Gate." While many faiths mark this site as the place of Stephen's martyrdom, an older tradition holds that it took place at the Sheep Gate to the north of the city. I have chosen the older interpretation, while recognizing that as with much else about this city, era, and people, we know little with certainty.

Both Hebrew and Aramaic were spoken in Palestine in the days depicted in this novel. Hebrew was the more literary language, but Aramaic held much in common with its sister tongue. Because readers are already dealing with Greek and the local languages of Jerusalem purveyed through English in this book, I have labeled all Jerusalem speech as "Hebrew" merely for the sake of simplicity.

Similarly, I have chosen names for some minor characters that are easy enough to recognize without using all original names. Saul's Greek name was "Pavlos," but in common speech, it becomes "Pavlo" when he is summoned or spoken to directly.

We have no evidence that Stephanos ever penned writings regarding Jesus Christ. However, the depth of his sermon to the council in Acts Chapter 7, combined with his persuasion of

Greek–speaking listeners, indicates great ability to convey important truths. Given his pivotal role in promoting Christianity before the faith had an identity or a name, I have granted this possibility.

I have selected a range of Bible translations interwoven in this novel. My preferred verses used for this book come from the New King James Version, thanks to its grace but modernity of phrasing. I have also made minimal adjustments to nuance or abbreviate the text, and in one case, to change the possible speaker.

Finally, some readers may find ending this novel at the lowest point in Saul of Tarsus' spiritual road disturbing, given the events of Acts Chapter 9 and later. But Saul never forgot the initial persecution of Jesus' followers, for which he was the primary instigator. Just as Stephanos hears the words "Saul is a chosen vessel of my own," we do well to remember, even faulty vessels such as Saul of Tarsus may be transformed in grace. And like a star, this grace crosses the centuries to meet your soul and mine.

Table of Contents

Part III—The Deliverance

Questions for Thought and Discussion

Part I
The Promise

1. The Boy and the Dove

Witness of Irini, Jerusalem, A.D. 11

As my brother Stephanos walks, the dust barely parts, but Saul's feet make the whole earth shake. So when Saul kicks a stone in my way, it bruises my heel.

I cling to my brother's hand and walk as straight as I can. If I fall, I could be lost in five steps. All three of us are complete strangers in Jerusalem, and here we are, stuck like dates in honey right in the middle of this crowd hurrying toward the great Temple. Stephanos says our road has led us even farther than the brave Odysseus, and like my favorite hero, I refuse to stumble here at the end of our journey!

Far above my head, my big brother is talking to Saul. I am already in my eighth year, so I am proud to still my cry of pain, even though I start falling behind. But Stephanos feels my hand flinch. Mid–sentence, he swings me high onto his shoulders. And my eyes are amazed. No more robes or tunics or sleeves block my sight. Instead, my whole head is bathed in the light of Apollo's chariot wheel swinging upward, the rising sun in my face. The blue sky reminds me of our River Cydnus, water from home in Tarsus that flows to the sea nearby at the middle of the world. Now that I am above the crowd, I am safe and happy again, even though my heel is throbbing.

"Just look at it, Irini!" my brother says. He points toward the stone face of the new Temple on top of the hill we are climbing.

But I look down instead. The men around us are not talking

and gesturing like our friends at home. They walk as though their bodies are made of sticks. Even their eyes are straight. They avoid gazing into this beautiful Cydnus–blue sky far away, or even greeting the people close by. They remind me of arrows aimed straight toward a target.

But what I stare at are the women. At home in Cilicia, the girls braid and ornament their hair like all the Greeks. Even young girls like me wear gold earrings, or silver and bronze for the poor. Here I cannot tell one woman from another with their silly covered heads, milling around like a flock of pigeons in the market. So I laugh.

When my eyes turn upward, I see why our father, whom we call Baba, has dreamed so long of coming here. Just like me, sitting on my brother's shoulders, this heavy–walled building is strong and safe on its stony rise. I believe it is something built to last forever, and I feel proud. My eyes dart like swallows to memorize absolutely every detail to tell Baba later.

Still, my brother was right when he whispered along the way not to expect this temple to be as mighty and graceful as our marble palaces, our colonnaded libraries, or our great Tarsian University along the banks of the River Cydnus at home. On our entire walk through this city, I have not even seen any statues. Jerusalem feels lonely without them. In Tarsus, my favorite is the huge and beautiful new flying horse, Pegasus, who stands before our library. My brother reminds me I am older than that horse, and I always will be. So I say, "Hello, baby colt!" whenever we pass by. Then I laugh, and Baba and Stephanos laugh, and even Saul laughs, and it happens every time we walk there together.

But as we climb these Temple steps, the bellowing of frightened animals comes from inside. The sound breaks the peace and joy I imagined from Baba's stories of how this place is the greatest house of our Lord in the whole world.

"Do you want me to take her for a while?" Saul asks

Stephanos while we stand in a long line to buy a Passover dove. We already had to wait in another line. They made us change our good Cilician silver, because here they say it is unclean. Instead, we got Temple money, and the coins are not even big like ours.

I am bored with the wait and annoyed with Saul for his question. So inside my mind I start what I call the "if" game my brother plays with me sometimes. Only he calls it "logika." Saul and Stephanos often use big, needless words to explain things. But here is how the game is played. It's easy. You just have to start with a question and count how many ifs are hidden inside it.

Today's "if" question is this: "How many ifs made Saul just ask about taking me onto his shoulders?" After all, Saul doesn't even know why Stephanos picked me up. I count on my fingers and find all the ifs that he doesn't know about. If he hadn't kicked the stone my way, and if my hand hadn't flinched, and if Stephanos hadn't noticed, I wouldn't be on anybody's shoulders in the first place. That is three ifs. And here's another if: Stephanos would laugh with me if Saul weren't standing right beside us and I could talk about all those ifs I just figured out. But Saul can't help the way God created him, to walk with uneven feet, or to speak with a gusty voice, or to touch with fingers that tremble a little. And it would be very cruel to take away all those funny ifs and put in a real if to say, "If you walked like my brother and other boys walk, your foot would not have kicked the stone that bruised me, my heel would feel fine now, and I would be walking on my own."

Instead, I think up another if that seems even bigger than the three ifs I already found. I wonder if just for a minute, Saul has forgotten how awkward he is. Doesn't he know it would be like riding an angry camel to clasp his solid neck and sway on his shoulders, even though they are broader than my brother's? But high up here with Stephanos, as I rock back and forth above the crowd, I am reminded of the ship we sailed on our way from Tarsus, the days when the waters were safe and the wind was still.

Since my brother can't hear any of those ifs buzzing around in my head like gadflies, he passes Saul's offer off to me, looking up and grinning. "I suppose that would be up to Irini."

When Saul looks up at me, too, I can feel my face turning red, because I have to bite back all the "logikas" I just figured out. "I'll just walk on my own if you two don't stop talking about me like a tent bag," I answer, even though my heel still stings, and I like being up so high.

Saul laughs. "Better the bag than the contents of the bag!" He says this because he let me sleep in one of the tent pouches his father sells as we were traveling. Then, twice, when I did not want to get up as early as the men, he tipped me out right onto the sand. He becomes serious again as he notices unfriendly glances from all these stiff Jerusalemite men crowding around us. "It's safer for you to stay up there with your brother than with me, I guess."

Stephanos and I pretend not to notice Saul's reddening face. I see now that Saul has recognized the big if, his earthshaking limp that started all the other ifs in the first place. This "if" makes him sad.

I feel sad, too. But if Saul's sad is like the cloud always around the top of Mount Olympus to hide the gods, mine is quick and windy, like a sandstorm in the desert we have crossed to come here. This day wasn't going at all the way we wanted, and neither was this whole trip.

The good began this way. For as long as I can remember, our Baba has talked about wanting to see Jerusalem. After our Ima died, he decided it was time, and he would bring us along. He knows how curious my brother and I are to visit every place we hear about from the Odyssey and from scripture, and I think he was trying to cheer us up. He promised Stephanos and me again and again that Passover in Jerusalem would be wonderful. He reminded me of this when the sea made me feel sick and when the sand along the desert paths got in my eyes and made me cry. I believed him then.

Saul's father and Baba are best friends, just like Saul and Stephanos. So it made sense when Saul's father said he would bring the tents he makes to sell in Judaea, and Baba decided to join him.

The bad began this way. We delayed our travels back in the wilderness. Saul's father remained there to trade and sell tents to the wanderers passing through. His goat–hair cloth called cilicium, named for our province in Asia, is the most sought-after material in the whole desert, and he was commanding high prices. But when Baba told him we must go on to arrive in Jerusalem for the feast of the Passover, I was proud of him, because he decided to keep his word to us, even though I know he wanted to be with his best friend. I was proud of Saul, too, because he asked his father if he could go with us, even though I could hear in his voice that he was afraid of the answer he was likely to get as eldest son, learning his father's trade. And I was proud of myself for hurrying on with the men and not snuggling in the tent bag too long, not even one single time after Saul's father said that Saul could come along.

Maybe the boys were bored along the way after that, without all the stops to spread tents wide and attract people from the mud–built villages and wilderness around. Anyhow, they decided it would be a good game to see who could teach me the alphabet faster. Stephanos helped me memorize sixteen letters, but even though Saul only taught me eight, he also taught me to write my name in secret, so I showed Stephanos. I told them I thought they both won, and they agreed with me. Then I taught myself to write the name "Pavlo," which is almost Saul's entire Greek name, "Pavlos," that I like to call him.

I think Saul was glad I started getting up on time and

stopped slowing them down. Anyhow, after that, he started telling me stories along the road that he says I should know. These are stories of our people. Sometimes Stephanos interrupted him, and the boys would argue. Then they would unroll a scroll and find the words. But still, they would argue on, and I would listen.

Only once, I interrupted them and showed my own logika. It was after Saul told me the story of a foreign soldier. His name was Naaman. He came to Israel and was healed. The prophet Elisha ordered him to wash seven times in the River Jordan. My brother argued that the Lord himself healed Naaman through Elisha, but Saul said it was his action of going to the holy river.

But I had listened to the entire story, and it began this way: "Now bands of raiders from Aram had gone out and had taken captive a young girl from Israel, and she served Naaman's wife. She said to her mistress, 'If only my master would see the prophet who is in Samaria! He would cure him of his leprosy.'" So with my logika, I told them Naaman would still be a leper if a faithful slave girl had not hoped and believed and spoken up.

The boys laughed at me and made me angry. So I went to Baba and Saul's father, who were behind us, to ask them who was right. And both of them agreed with me. Baba repeated words to the boys I often hear him say. "Most of us grow up, and as we do, our eyes learn to see what they wish and our ears begin to hear what they expect. Never lose your keen eye and your listening ear, Irini," my Baba went on.

"You might learn something today from a child's listening ear," Saul's father added, and Baba nodded in approval. Ever since then, the young slave girl who spoke bravely is my other favorite hero alongside Odysseus, even though I will never know her name.

The boys shuffled and stayed silent the rest of the morning. Then Stephanos brought out his small, wonderful lyra, starting to strum as we walked, and I sang some hymns of Orpheus, and

Saul picked up two small stones to beat together, and the music reunited us.

Even though Saul does not seem to like the wonderful heroes and the horrible monsters of the Greeks that my brother talks about, I am full of joy whenever Stephanos begins his songs or poems or stories. At least the boys never argue about them. Most of all, I love nimble, wonderful Odysseus, who could slay monsters and outwit any man. And even though I beg Stephanos to tell me everything about the stories he knows when the sun is shining, at night, sometimes I am afraid when I remember Cerberus, the three-headed guard dog dividing the living from the dead beyond the River Styx, or Medusa, the snake-haired gorgon. But Stephanos' stories are usually more exciting than the ancestors and sad things Saul speaks about, or maybe it is just that my brother is a better storyteller.

Some days of our journey, we even made up our own stories. I imagine the three of us growing up, and as long as we live, how we will explore the wide world together. The boys like to laugh when I make up wild adventures about when we are big like our fathers and we can go anywhere we wish, but it is the same laughter they have when I call our new statue of Pegasus "baby colt" in Tarsus, so I don't mind.

All these stories made the dusty days short along our road. But the bad air, or the bloodsucking insects, or just our speed of travel turned our Baba's health. His cough became worse every day. A fever began to burn in his eyes, and when I kissed him, the skin of his forehead felt as thin and dry as the best Egyptian papyrus at home in our little writing shop. But he urged us to continue toward Jerusalem. Stephanos insisted that we rest an additional day beyond last Sabbath, and then another day. By then all of us knew that we could not arrive in time for the feast marking the first day, and today is already the end of Passover. But here we are, even though it is nothing like all we hoped for.

I expected to stay at the inn with the servants while

Stephanos, Saul, and my father went to the Temple. Last night, Baba told the boys, "You are old enough to go there without me." None of us wanted to leave him, but all of us knew that he could not walk up the steep road to the Temple through the crowds. It took all his strength just to arrive here. But the more we objected, the harder he insisted that today was the day. "And take Irini with you," Baba told my brother at dawn. "She will tell me everything when you return tonight. She will be my little witness." This is why when Stephanos told me to look up toward the great Temple, I also looked down to see the people, so that I could tell Baba absolutely everything and not disappoint him.

I worry, because no one is there in the inn to bring our Baba water or healing things—certainly not all those uncaring strangers. But Baba insisted. "You will always be our Irenikon," he said. "That is more important."   They all use this family nickname, calling me a symbol of peace.

"You must especially remember to call me Saul while we are here," Pavlos whispers. "That is my real name, you know." He has corrected me several times since we have entered Jerusalem, even though I always called him by his Greek name in Tarsus, and he will always be Pavlo in my heart.

I nod in agreement, but at the same time, I feel another sad. I have only my Greek name of Irini. Names are something I must ask Baba about when we talk in the evening.

Stephanos and Saul are studying things in the academy at Tarsus that I only know by name, like "rhetoric" and "the arts of war." How is war like art, I ask them. Usually they just laugh at me. But when they are bored, or in a good mood, they talk of other things, even with me sometimes, like poetry or music. Mostly they are friends when they discuss these things they learn. But after the Sabbath meetings of our little Jewish community, studying what they call "the Torah," our Jewish scripture, their words often grow hot under their tongues. And here we are, coming right into a real temple, not like our borrowed room in the city library. So I knew what Baba really meant—I needed to distract them from their quarrels and bring them together, since he was too ill to do so. I think this is why I am here.

We have finally reached the head of the line and paid for a dove. She is jammed into a cage so small she cannot even spread her wings. She looks very white in Saul's hand. "This will be enough to bless us," Saul says. And he lifts the cage close to my face. "You, Irini, hold it up so it doesn't get dropped."

A real Passover dove, much better than the new robes the boys are wearing. It is the best present I could ever ask for! I will take good care of her, and I can't wait to show her to Baba!

Even through the bars made of twigs, I feel the dove trembling. Fear blazes through her ruby eyes. Her tiny beak opens, then closes. I am glad I have thought to bring a small loaf of bread in my sleeve. I break off a crumb from the end, put it on my hand, and then slide my finger through the bars. The dove's beak feels like a kiss, and the crumb is gone. She seems calmer now that I am holding the cage, and I try to keep it steady as we walk forward.

Near the next portal, I see a big sign. "Look, Greek!" I say. Just to show how much I have learned in our travel, I sound it out. "Foreigners may not pass this gate." But the sign doesn't make sense, even when I read it again, so I ask, "Why would foreigners want to come to our Temple?"

And the boys look at each other and say nothing, so I go on. "Isn't everybody in Jerusalem a Jew except the Romans? Romans don't want to come here anyhow, do they?"

A man standing behind us approaches, frowning and pointing to the sign. He says something in Hebrew and laughs when Stephanos replies.

"What did he say?" I ask when he walks away.

Saul does not look at me, and my brother stoops down, a gentle way of letting me know I am getting too heavy. "He thought we were Greeks. But he said that sign is even to keep the Hellenisti, the Jews like us who speak Greek and don't come from Judaea, out of the inner Temple, like the Romans. He called us even more ignorant than the Hebrew women," he whispers.

"But you answered him in Hebrew. What is wrong with us, just because we speak Greek?" I search my brother and his friend head to toe, and I find nothing lacking. How wonderful they look in those new sandals and robes they have bought with special money for Passover that Baba gave them. Other than being so fresh and clean, they look no different from anyone else around us.

For a little while, all of us just stand there at the gate. We don't know what to do. "Kicking at the pricks," Stephanos mumbles, using a phrase he often repeats when they argue about Jewish law and other things I don't understand. I am trying to use my "if" game, and this is what I think, but I don't say this, and I can't finish it. "If I spoke Hebrew, and if I were a boy, and if we lived here."

"After all our travels—strangers in a strange land," Saul says. His voice, with the slight stuttering he sometimes gets when he is angry, sounds as stiff as his feet. And I can hardly believe it when I see tears on Saul's cheeks. "We aren't supposed to go in—even though all of us in this Temple are sons of Abraham!"

Then Stephanos smiles and takes my hand. "Amen, Saul. Even Irini is a son of Abraham today."

"But Irini—" Saul continues.

It is like he is playing the "if" game. I know what he is thinking, that I am not even a Hebrew speaker, and actually, not even a woman yet. I bite my lip and tell myself to be brave like my hero Odysseus and not to cry. But I am almost sure that now Saul's sad and my sad are the same.

Meanwhile, the crowd of men is moving in from behind, pushing us closer to the steps rising behind the sign and the portal. Saul wipes his tears with a sleeve, and looking down, his sad eyes meet my sad eyes. And he grasps my other hand so I am walking ahead, divided from the pushing men by him and my brother as the men press us from behind.

He has given in, either to Stephanos or to the crowd. One more quarrel started and stopped, and this time I didn't have to say anything! But Saul bends his head low to my ear. "Then be our witness, not our tongue!" he whispers.

I laugh and nod as the dove flicks her wings. I know Saul is serious, but I stick my tongue out at him, and he begins to smile, despite himself. "Our Irenikon," he manages as we move forward. I think that is when I love Saul most, when I can overtake his spirit and make him smile that way.

This inner space is still open to the sky, but darker, since the sun chariot has not climbed high enough to shine inside the stone walls surrounding us. And I am happy now that Baba insisted I put on my brother's golden-tinged robe and head wrap that Ima made him a long time ago. The robe is too large for me, but it keeps me very warm draped over the fancy Grecian dress I had for Passover, even late Passover.

Did he already know about this unfair Temple rule keeping us out, and especially me? All he said this morning was, "Stephanos' cloak will keep you warmer."

Now, looking at me, it wouldn't be obvious that I was any different from the boys inside. But the sign behind us has made all of us feel unwanted.

This place is quieter than the outer square where we bought the dove. In one corner, some boys sitting in a circle on the stones of the courtyard have fuzz on their faces. As we approach them, I quiver with the excitement of a new adventure. I can hardly wait to tell Baba how I will hide and pretend to be one of them today.

Two bright-robed men are standing in front of this group of big boys. One of them is almost as young as the oldest boys, and the other one is even older than Baba.

"Be small, very small and still," Stephanos whispers.

I know what he means—that as a child, I am welcome here, but not as a girl. Saul and my brother find a place in the middle of the learners, and almost as one, they spread the ends of their robes wide to make a soft little nest, where I settle on the floor right between them. The tunics around us smell of sand and of unwashed wool, and I pinch my nose to kill a sneeze.

As I settle on the ground, it is as though men on horses are riding close. "Why are the flagstones quivering?" I ask my brother.

He shakes his head, but then he whispers, "I believe it is because we are on holy ground."

"Shouldn't we take off our sandals, then?" I reply.

But Saul shushes us. "No Greek here! Just listen."

It's true that at home, we speak nothing but Greek. But I have heard the Jewish tongue all my life. Baba discusses trade with fellow merchants from Palestine in his writing shop where I am always welcome, and Stephanos sometimes practices with Saul. I just cannot answer. So I open my ears expecting nothing. But I become the princess Ariadne; I feel as if I am walking step by step through her father's deadly labyrinth, but weaving a string of yarn to show me the way home. That is, I can go through the labyrinth, but not without something to guide my mind. This is how it feels to hear things you understand, but you know that you can't reply. From my ears to my mind, I focus on weaving a thread of concentration. And like the sand, these words build and shiver in my ears and crackle with meaning.

When I close my eyes, something wonderful happens! A kind of living air surrounds me like the moment when Stephanos is swinging me up on his shoulders, or when I run as fast as I can up the steps of the hill leading to our home in Tarsus. It is something that makes our hearts beat, yet it keeps us still, like sunlight on my dove's back. Everything—the sounds around us, even the light—absolutely everything has disappeared. But the darkness in front of my eyes is restful, like Stephanos' warm old cloak wrapping my shoulders. And even my heel has stopped hurting.

I want to know if Saul and Stephanos don't see and don't hear like me, and if they feel the breath of motionless wind as I do. I look up to question them, but they have faded, too. I feel their warmth and their hands flat on the ground alongside mine, and I am not afraid. The teacher's gentle voice is weaving into my skin, taking all my movement away, like a windless leaf with its story. "God's promise" are the first words I know from him. And following, "Many things man means for evil, but God means them for good."

Saul's hand trembling softly is just like my dove, and it is the only thing that reminds me of things that are here. And I hear a thing inside the young teacher's voice, and it is that labyrinth thread to my heart, and then I can see. From the blackness, light—stars in what was the blue morning sky a few minutes ago. They swirl above my head, forming into the shapes of animals, birds, and a sword. Their points sing with color in the blackness. "More stars than you can count," I thread from the teacher's voice, like a song. My heart is beating fast, to fly among the stars shining through the teacher's story.

As the teacher continues telling, the sky lightens behind my eyes. I see a tent taken up and folded, women, camels, travel. They are leaving one place and going to a new land that God promised them.

And though I have promised silence, I must speak to Saul now, who knows these stories best. "Pavlo! Can you see the tent?" I whisper. "I can see the teacher's words right in the air!"

To my joy, he whispers back. "Oh, yes, Irini. Let us look at this work of our Lord together!"

And when he says this, I know that as much as I love my brother's stories, Saul's stories are the ones that are real.

I feel Stephanos' warmth as he leans closer to hear us, and I hope he understands these wonderful things, too. I bite my tongue. I will ask him later.

And the teacher's words keep unthreading around us. A child is holding the hand of an old woman, then this child, "Isaac," Saul whispers to me, as the teacher is reminding us, he grew to manhood and had two wives. One has twins. I watch as the boys fight in front of me, as small as I.

As the teacher's voice travels on, the air stiffens as my heart races. Saul and I are traveling up steps, and more steps in his words.

This man the other boys address as Rabboni Gamaliel asks us to name Isaac's sons.

"Jacob and Esau!" they chorus all around. Even I know these names. I whisper them a half breath behind the others.

This Jacob goes on to have twelve sons. One of them shines with many dreams until his brothers tear off his bright robe and sell him to foreign people.

"Joseph!" the boys chorus.

"And where does Joseph go next?"

"Egypt!" I chorus with the others, and both Saul and Stephanos press my hands. Even my dove gives a little hop in her cage, and I smile as the real courtyard reappears in front of us.

Still holding Saul's hand, I turn all my heart and soul and mind to keep understanding. All the stones beneath us and around us disappear again, and instead, there are the green fields turning moist and bright, then brown and dry, a sky blazing above. I am walking along the road with the same brothers that stole Joseph's robe. And I hear them begging for food in front of Joseph, and I turn with him as he leaves them and weeps. I begin to weep also, but stop myself before Stephanos or Saul can notice. And I see from far away a long line of people, Joseph's family. They are coming to him from their hunger and being fed. "You meant it for evil against me," Joseph is saying, "but God meant it for good."

"A promise," Rabboni Gamaliel ends, and I hear and understand. "God's promise to guard our people, even in Egypt." The dove shuffles her wings, because she is agreeing with the rabboni.

The teacher tells us that after this, other kings made our people slaves in Egypt. I cannot believe what I think I hear next, but I don't want Saul to think I am wrong or that I do not see the words with him. So instead, I ask my brother. "Did he just say they had to give away their baby boys?"

My brother nods. I see a tear in his right eye as he lays a finger against my Greek voice. I am not sure if he is really seeing these things like Saul and me, or just using his ears.

I see a basket close to a river, and some women walking. "Is it baby Moses?" I ask Saul. He smiles and squeezes my hand, because I remember this story he told me.

The baby is taken to a palace, and as he grows up, both Hebrews and Egyptians surround him. When he walks away from the palace, I see what he sees. They are slaves working. When one man is beaten, I feel the spring in my own arms as Moses takes a heavy stick and kills the foreigner. I am shaking, and Stephanos cradles me in his arms. "Don't cry, Irini," he whispers. "It is the story of our people, and it is all in the past."

As Stephanos rocks me, the Hebrew words surround me like sand in the wind, and my ears lose things strange, running too fast. Then I watch Moses, older now and alone, as he walks toward a bush, burning. I am afraid along with him. That promise in the words again; I can feel it like hot wind. He will return to Egypt, and he will show his people signs, and he will take them away and free them. Around me the boys sigh, as all of us share the relief. And I am back in the courtyard.

"Think about all your fathers and the fathers of our fathers who came before us," Rabboni Gamaliel ends. "Every single generation had to teach the next one. And even one of them not teaching would crack the steps and make the promise to our people to be broken and forgotten. This is why you come to the Temple, to learn and to be pure."

Some of the boys shuffle. My brother and Saul nod at each other.

As the teacher reaches out for a scroll, a voice interrupts from our circle. And a red–haired boy in a shabby tunic stands up just behind us. "But what does it mean to be pure, Rabboni Gamaliel?"

I am proud of this brave boy, because I am hungry with the same question.

The speaker smiles. "Being pure is doing everything we have learned from our ancestors. We honor our God and our parents, we do not murder or steal, we eat no unclean animals, and our hands are washed at table."

The boy is younger than most of them there except me. He remains standing. "I know those are the things we do." Then his gaze meets the elder teacher's. "But I can hate my brother without killing him. Or I can want something day and night without stealing it. How can I be pure inside?"

What wonderful logika this boy has spoken!

My brother's hand tightens on mine, and Saul's foot brushes one of my sandals. Some of the other boys were whispering before. Now everyone falls silent. Is this boy standing up daring to correct our teacher?

"Through fasting and through prayer," Rabboni Gamaliel answers after a pause, "you should set your mind on the Lord."

This ruddy boy still does not sit down. "And what should I pray for? How should I fast?"

Stephanos emits a small "Yes" in Greek, as Saul breathes out.

The older teacher takes the scroll from the rabboni's hand, and he sighs. "We are here today to learn and to memorize the laws of our people," he replies. I can hear the same disappointment in his voice as when I give Stephanos the wrong answer in logika. "You are too young to understand all the reasons why we do such things."

My dove fidgets in her cage as the boy behind me sits down. But Rabboni Gamaliel continues looking at the boy, and even at me, I think. "My little children, if you set your hearts on the Lord when you pray to him," he says, "I believe that you will find him."

A woman's high scream from behind us makes all of us jump. "Jesus, oh, my son!"

The boy from behind us stands up and turns toward the gate. "Ima!"

The woman runs toward us. "Your father and I have been looking for you for three days, now. Why have you done this?" Her voice is broken with sobbing.

In the silence after her question, the boy's stomach growls, making me laugh, but he does not move. "Why did you even look for me? You know how I love my father's house."

I tap the boy's arm, and I slide him the bread from my sleeve, smiling. Nobody notices. He smiles back as he takes it with a word of thanks. By then his mother has nearly reached us.

"Woman!" The older teacher shoots this word like an arrow. "You have no place here. Take your son and leave."

But Rabboni Gamaliel raises his hand. And his eyes shine toward the woman's face. And he says, "I believe you come here each year to Jerusalem."

Through her tears, the woman nods toward this teacher, with his wonderful words that I could see just a few sentences ago.

"It is my joy to spend Passover with our youngest students, and not at my school. Your son Jesus has a mind full of questions," he says, and then, turning toward the second teacher, "and a heart toward the Lord. He has already memorized all he will need for his bar mitzvah, but he seeks more from us. Who knows? Perhaps he shall be one who can move the people of Israel."

After he takes a bite of our bread, Jesus' smile becomes a grin. "See you next year, Rabboni Gamaliel," he says before turning to embrace his mother.

"Let's go with them and take the dove," Stephanos whispers to Saul over my head.

"You and Irini go. I want to listen more and speak with Rabboni Gamaliel," Saul answers.

Stephanos has already started moving toward a gate behind the mother and Jesus, and I follow.

In a different court, I feel the hubbub around me even more than before, because I am walking now. We stand in a shabby line, each family with a Passover dove, just like us. After it is blessed, I hope it will bring Baba back from his sickness.

I feel the cage tremble in my hand as our dove grows anxious. Cupping my hands around the cage, I bring it close to my mouth and whisper reassuring words into the darkness through my fingers, and the bird quiets. "You'll be blessed soon," I tell her.

"We should have bought an animal," my brother says. "Baba gave us enough money." Then he asks me for some bread.

"I don't have it," I answer, not wanting to lie.

"Where is it? What did you do, feed it to the bird?"

We are near the front of the line now. And I feel a raindrop on my chest, only when I look down, it is red, like blood. Then I hear the priest speaking words, and his knife rises, falls, shears the throat of someone else's dove.

"Our turn soon," Stephanos whispers down. "Give me the cage."

But I freeze in place. "You and Saul said the dove would bless us!" I can hardly say the words, because I am choking back a sob. "You lied to me, Stephanos!"

"Shhh!"

But I won't stop, even as his hand reaches for the cage. "Why did you tell me that? She's mine!"

Now Stephanos' right arm is around me, and his left hand encircles my fingers clasping the cage over the blood spot on my robe. His reach is gentle, but I push him away. "Let her be mine, mine!" I say. And the line moves forward another step. "Baba will be happy. I'll take care of her. Please."

Stephanos is still whispering. His face is close to mine, now. "I'm sorry, Irini. But it's what we have to do to give God the weight of our sins. Without this, we can't honor our people's freedom."

I shrink back, since his arm has lifted. Oh, I wish I were Perseus! I would hold the gorgon Medusa's head that no man can look on and live. I would pull it out of its bag and turn every one of these men right to stone, forever, maybe even my brother! Instead, I scream. "Then I don't want to be part of our people! I want to be Greek!"

No one around us understands, but they stare at us. "Does your brother have a demon?" one man asks my brother, stepping in front of us in line to proffer his bird to the horrible, bloody knife ready to rise.

My brother's face is as crimson as the altar in front of us now. "She is too young to know what she is saying," he manages. "She has no unclean spirit, I promise you."

Again, I understand this answer more from something I hear inside than from words I can translate.

The man questioning frowns. "She?" he begins, and I recall that I should not be here as a girl.

A shape moves between me and my brother, and a warm hand closes over mine as I hold the cage. "No, there is no unclean spirit here."

To stay calm, I focus all the strength of my eyes on the

whiteness of our dove. Now I look up and my eyes recognize what my ear already knew. It is that boy I'd given bread to. "Come with me," he says.

Stephanos does not argue, and to my amazement, he steps aside, out of line. Some kind of power rings in this boy's voice like a hammer, even though his head is a full hand's length lower than my brother's. We follow him to a corner of the courtyard. I try to wipe my tears, but I feel a stickiness on my cheek instead. The drop of blood is out from my robe, on my hand, and now smeared on my face.

And the boy Jesus spits on his sleeve, then wipes my cheek. "All clean," he says, as gently as Rabboni Gamaliel. "You were marked by blood today. Your heart is pure and ready for our Lord." Then he wipes my brother's hand, which is also marked with blood.

Stephanos is just looking at us.

"And you," the Jesus boy tells him, "you believe in sin, and you believe in freedom. Remember, our Lord provided the ram to our father Abraham."

"But even the ram was sacrificed," Stephanos begins.

The Jesus boy has persuaded my hands open, and the small cage slides through them like water over logs. "A stream of justice," I think for some reason, remembering words from Baba, or maybe from Saul.

"You have sacrificed enough today," the Jesus boy continues. His eyes meet my brother's.

With a deft flick of his thumb, the boy opens the cage. And our dove springs upwards. One wing just grazes the boy's hair as she rustles into the river–blue sky, circles us twice, and then disappears over the Temple wall. "God provided the ram," the boy repeats. And turning to me, he smiles. "And you provided the bread, too. I was so hungry." Then he turns away, and with long strides, he disappears into the crowd.

"God has provided," Stephanos is repeating slowly, his

Hebrew echoing the deep vowels of the boy's.

I smile. "Yes, see? Now all of us can be happy!" I realize the boy took the cage with him in parting, but on the ground, I see a white feather. I pick it up and tickle my brother's hand. "Look, it is Pegasus!"

My brother frowns. "You should not talk about the Greek stories here. They are unholy," he begins. "But I know—I miss Tarsus, too."

Both of us are remembering one of the ancient stories about our city in Cilicia by the sea far away. The king of the Greek gods, Zeus, had in his service a mighty, winged horse he loved and named Pegasus. When the horse was old and ready to die, Zeus honored him by transforming him into a cluster of stars in the night sky. But on that final day of Pegasus' life, Zeus allowed a single feather from his wing to fall near our city. Since that day, we in Tarsus are blessed with Pegasus' strength and courage, and that is why my "baby colt" has been carved in marble for us to remember him by. That is something else for me to be proud of.

I give a whinny, and Stephanos laughs. "Come on. Let's find Saul and eat something!"

He takes my hand as we walk out from the horrible courtyard where the knife is still flashing and slashing out the life of many. "Let this stay between us," he whispers as we hear Saul stamping toward us. And I know three new things today. God's promise is real, my brother will protect me, and the flight of Pegasus will always remain our secret.

2. The Pileus and the Passover

Witness of Baba, Jerusalem, A.D. 11

"The stones themselves cry out." This strange turn of phrase springs from my head and even to my murmuring lips, like newborn Aphrodite from Zeus' splitting skull. I lie here between the sleep that pursues me like the Furies and the wakefulness I desire. Nightmares evoking the past I dare not speak of with my children have tormented me all day since they went to the Temple, and I long for their return as I sweep between drenching sweats and desert-night chills. I fix my will and sit upright on my couch when the uneven echo of Saul's footsteps springs from the "talking stones," all his strength, roughened with the shuffle he cannot avoid. I hear closer now the laughter of Stephanos, my son.

A small shadow streaks the floor just a moment before Irini leads the way and all three of the young people I love step inside our chamber. I am glad I have washed my face and oiled my hair in their absence, though the effort wore me down to this baffling exhaustion. As Irini kisses my cheek, her hand caresses my brow, and I know she is testing for the fever I want to hide. She sends Stephanos a quick glance that I am not supposed to see as they settle on the floor in front of me like doves.

"It was so beautiful," Irini starts, but the boys interrupt.

It is difficult for me to focus on their three-way words, and I want to hide my lack of concentration, so I, too, voice and interrupt. "The sacrifice was acceptable?" I ask.

Saul, who would know best, simply nods, while Irini and Stephanos look down.

"Or perhaps it was not acceptable?" I go on.

"It was a dove," Irini said. "Pegasus the dove."

I laugh despite my misgivings. This tiny, last fruit of my loins can make me happy without even trying.

"Let's go find a meal," Saul says to my son.

"Come on, Irini," Stephanos says, turning away from me.

But Irini shakes her head. "I am staying with Baba."

Perhaps I should chide her for turning against her older brother's words. But a knot of loneliness stops me. "She may stay here," I answer. "You boys go with my blessing and eat for all of us."

Saul laughs, as do the others, knowing his huge appetite. But as the boys' shapes turn black at the door, I hear Stephanos' phrase "a doctor," and see Saul nod.

I want to distract my youngest. "You, Irini," I continue, "you can tell me all about what you saw. Come, I want to hear you. Come, sit, and stay with me."

Irini takes my hand, and then whispers, "I'm going to get something for you and me to eat, too. I'm hungry. You and I get to feast on our own."

I do not have the heart to tell her to bring me nothing. Swifter than any servant, she returns with a tray of bread, fish, and olives, which she puts on my knees, seating herself at my right hand with her head on my thigh.

"So," I begin, as we recline side by side and Irini starts eating the olives and spitting pits into her hand, "tell me about this Pegasus."

From her sleeve, my daughter pulls something white. "Look! Pegasus left a feather for us," she answers. "It reminded me of home." The tears in her moist, brown eyes remind me of the eyes of another.

I am not sure whether the shudder that racks me next

comes from my fever or my sorrow. In the sphere of my mind's eye appears Irini's mother, departed from us in her quick death from plague that seized so many of us in Tarsus.

"I miss home, too," I tell Irini, but I leave unvoiced that the true home I miss is this woman who gave birth to my children, the woman whose love set my entangled spirit free. "We must learn that where our people are is our home always." Taking the feather from my daughter, I use it to wipe her cheeks, which have reddened.

"Pegasus is alive, she is my dove, and she is in the sky," she says, "and we are still here."

I laugh, then break into a cough at the thought of some female dove being named for a godlike stallion in the sky. "Yes, we're here, just you and me." And I wonder, can I outlive this current illness to put off the inevitable fate for us all? Would telling the story to such a small girl, the story blazing in my feverish mind and haunting my dreams, in fact bring on the end, but free my soul toward peace?

No. It is better for us to talk of other things, I decide, shaking off memories of those departed from this life. Summoning all my willpower, I ask, "What did you witness in the Temple, my Irenikon?"

After some hesitation as she debones her fish, Irini responds. "A boy ran away, and the dove flew," she starts.

I respect the quiet as she savors her food, and when she has nearly finished, after I have refused her small, morsel-filled hand swaying toward my own lips several times, I say, "There is nothing I want more than your little witness. So, tell me everything you saw and about this flyaway dove and this runaway boy."

"The boy's name there was Jesus." As soon as she says this, the skin of Irini's face burns hot under my finger.

"Jesus?"

Irini nods.

I lie completely down and beckon Irini to join me, now that the pile of fish bones and olive pits is larger than the scraps remaining on the platter. "Who is this Jesus? Why are you remembering him?"

"Because," Irini begins, "just because. He had red hair and skin, and his stomach growled." She lies close by my feet, sucking a juicy olive.

"Ah, perhaps a boy of the house of David," I say, but I know she will not understand the joke, since she has not read of the ruddy shepherd boy before he became king of Israel. So I set my mind to closer things. "Did he say something, or did he do something that you remember?" I encourage her.

Once she spits a final olive pit far into a corner of the room and crawls up beside me, she answers. "He did something, and he said something, too."

I stroke her hair.

"Your hand feels like Saul's," she says, laughing.

Only then I realize how my fingers are trembling. The solidity of her flesh rests my hand. "Let's start with what he said." Behind my daughter's gaze, I see some kind of confusion, beyond my grasp.

"The teachers were talking about our traditions," she starts. "And how some things that people mean for evil, God means for good. They told us how important it is to believe the Lord's promise and keep all the teachings. Every father needs to teach every son, because if he doesn't, the stairway will break. And I felt like I was walking up some steps. I know now that if you miss even one step, you will fall down, and you can't ever get up the stairs, because you have to keep passing every step and walking up the same way, and staying pure and righteous and believing in a promise. And also, sometimes what people mean for evil, God turns into a promise of good."

The earnestness in my daughter's voice compels me to remember the pull of generations that I, too, have lived. I need to understand her better. "Slow down," I say. "Your words are tumbling out like grains of wheat from a sack." I make my fingers jump in front of Irini's eyes, and she smiles. Then I go on. "This Jesus boy did not say this, did he? Was he there with you?"

"Yes," Irini manages, while chewing a bite of bread. "He was."

"Well?"

"I mean, he was there, but he didn't say all that. A teacher did. The teacher was talking about Abraham and Moses and the Temple."

I listen amazed as Irini goes on with Hebrew words, such as "pure" and "righteous" amidst her Greek. "You speak as though you hear these Hebrew words again in this very room," I interrupt her.

Irini sighs. "Baba, I heard the words then, not now. But I understood them like Greek. And I also saw the things Raboni Gamaliel said. The words were alive in front of my eyes."

"How so?" I manage to ask her as I shiver, not only from the cold.

She goes on to speak even of Joseph and Moses, names she has scarcely heard in our house. "Joseph was thrown into a pit and then sold as a slave. Then he served a king and brought his family to Egypt to save them. Moses was a tiny baby taken by the princess of Egypt; I saw his basket. Then he grew up and killed a man who was beating a Hebrew slave. I saw all this in front of my eyes, and Pavlos saw it, too."

Surely only our Lord could put such words in my daughter's mouth and draw such visions before her eyes for her to speak of. But my breath is not even enough to interrupt her or speak aloud to praise what my ears record.

When Irini finally ceases the repetition of what she has heard, I turn back to the topic at hand. "Did this ruddy Jesus talk to you?"

"Not then. He talked to the teachers."

"And he said?" I stroke some hair that has wandered down onto her forehead.

"Well, he asked about what it is to be pure and to be righteous."

"Those are good questions."

Irini nods. "Saul says if we do what is written by our ancestors, it's done. But Jesus thinks it depends on what is inside your heart. The teacher told him to fast and to pray. I think it's like those steps you can't see that you have to go up without anybody else knowing what you're doing."

I smile despite myself, knowing Saul and his family, their zeal to follow the old ways, and that Stephanos will learn so much being with his friend, things I cannot teach. "There are many things in life that we can't see, and we still have to know about them and do them," I say to my daughter. "Jesus was right."

But Irini is not done. "And then his mother came and found him because he ran away. And she said they were looking for him for three days. But he just said he was in his father's house. Maybe his parents don't live together. And he was hungry, so I gave him our bread," she concludes.

Sleep and a heaviness are again tugging at my eyes and at my chest as we lie there, and the quiet expands. But recalling the strange reactions to my earlier questions, there is more to ask, and this keeps me awake. "Tell me about the sacrifice," I venture.

"You will be angry, Baba," Irini says.

I rest my hand on her cheek. "I will not be angry," I hear myself saying.

"That's what Stephanos meant to do," she whispers. "But Jesus came back. He started to talk about being free, and then he took the dove away from me and he opened the cage."

I nod.

"I didn't know they were going to kill the dove," she says. "It isn't fair. I don't want to go back to that Temple again."

In my illness and in my son's ignorance, of course, everyone had neglected to tell Irini what to expect. My heart throbs as I think of her mother, of all the life and the ways this child would now never learn from a woman as she should, and my throat, already aching, swells with pity. "I am glad the boy freed your dove," I say at last. "I am happy you saw her fly free."

"You're not mad, Baba?"

She feels my head shake no. "It was a special blessing," I manage.

"Pavlos—Saul, I mean—doesn't know about that, because he was in the Temple. It was just me and Stephanos. But my brother saw it, too."

I cannot speak for a long time. Irini's breathing quiets with mine. "It was a day of many things you did not expect," I manage eventually.

With more relief than pain, I feel something like a dove in the depths of my own body struggling to free itself from inside my chest. It is time to entrust her with things too large for her young mind, words that if not spoken will be lost. "Come, Irini. I am going to tell you a story about Passover, our own story, and about freedom." My eyes are closed, and I feel her heat from the other side of the robe wrapping us both.

"When I was as small as you are, I lived in Alexandria," I begin. Startled now, I can see the rooms of my father's house, even smell the grassy papyrus and bitter ink. "You have seen the library we have at home in Tarsus."

I feel Irini stir in agreement, but she is concentrating so hard that her breath scarcely rises under my hand on her back.

"At home in Alexandria, our books are even more than in Tarsus. There is no library like the one we have there."

"What books?" Irini asks.

"Some very special books," I continue, laying my hand on her lips. "Even our Jewish laws, and they are written in Greek."

My daughter laughs. "In Greek? Well, then, I can almost read them."

I shudder with cold, but I smile. "I know the boys have taught you well. Sometimes you even listen to Stephanos' lessons. This is a good thing that you are learning, and I am proud of you. I was also full of watching and learning in my house when I was small."

"Did your baba have a tutor for you?"

I smile again, despite myself. "No tutor," I said. "But my baba had a very important business. He made the papyrus and scrolls and tablets people needed for messages, and he sold the ink and the styli and everything else for writing."

Irini sighs. "Why didn't you ever tell me about this, Baba?"

I turn from my side, where I had been cradling Irini, to my back, and I feel her shift and lay her head just over my heart, her body draping along my ribs. Resolving to tell on, I draw in all the breath I can.

"Because, when you were small, this would have been only a tale. Now you are a little bit big. Now you will know that it is the truth," I tell her. "Passover is a truth, not a tale. It is one of those steps you talked about that we pass through our hearts and minds and spirits and remember forever."

"Oh." She shifts to burrow wormlike deeper into my robe, and her tiny pool of warmth comforts me.

"My baba wanted to make a strong house, a rich house. I also learned his trade."

"Why doesn't Stephanos learn more about it from you, instead of spending all his time in the academia?"

Would this girl never stop interrupting? I want to reproach her. Then I realize her questions are saving me enough air to pause, then go on. I cut back the chiding remark I would make.

"Stephanos understands enough because he spent all his time with me, just like you, before he studied with the Greek boys. And he also knows a more important thing, which is how to obtain the things people need from one place to another, and how to convey these library things," I tell her. "He also knows now through our travels how to judge good things from bad, which papyrus is cut straight, which leather will endure. He will not be just a shop owner. I believe he will be a translator of these goods from one man to another."

Irini's head rises along with my chest as I draw in the air I need to continue, though my breath burns in my throat. "Once upon a time, when I was older than you but younger than your brother, my baba took me to follow a great army. We sailed from Alexandria with the ships. We crossed wine–dark water that I thought would never end. Finally we arrived in a little Greek port called Actium."

No motion from Irini, not even a question now. She is not yet aware of what I want to tell her, of what she needs to know. Actium is no name to her mind. Meanwhile, ship–like, the couch seems to sway beneath me. I can feel my pulse quicken and my stomach lurch in the remembered waters of my youth, the storm. Lights are dancing before my eyes like the winking waves on brighter days of our voyage.

Then Irini's voice cuts through my memories. "What army, Baba?"

It is hard to rouse myself for an answer, but I must. "The army of Egypt. The army of our queen, Cleopatra, led by a Roman. His name was Marcus Antonius."

"Did you know them, Baba?"

I shrug slightly, and my daughter adjusts her head to a more comfortable position above my heart. I must not dwell on these questions of hers; with the breath remaining to me, I need to tell her more important things.

"No, little one. I did not know them. There were hundreds of ships," I whisper. "But the queen's vessel had beautiful silver oars and a gilded stern and purple sails that caught all the sunlight. They even stayed in our port at Tarsus, building many ships to go along with hers."

"Who won the battle? What did your father do?"

Well, now, in fact Irini's questions have arrived at the heart of this matter, and I must tell her.

"It was a battle of terrible things. Ships sank like stones and the waves were red with blood for three days," I say. "But my father and I were not the soldiers. We were on land to witness, to write and to pass messages."

"With your styli and your tablets?"

"And not only that, Irini, even with some doves like Pegasus," I tell her. "They could fly to our home faster than any horse or ship or runner."

"Well? What then?"

"When it was clear our forces were lost, the Romans also came on land, and we were captured."

I still feel the thud of the soldiers' feet, hear their piercing Latin words, and just like that day, I cannot run.

"My father, your grandfather, he was an important man, you see."

"Because he passed on messages, Baba?"

I pat Irini's shoulder. "Good girl. You understand."

"So did they want him to pass on messages back to Rome then?"

I hear a sound like shearing linen as I draw my next breath. "Ah, no, little one. If it could be that simple!"

I see again the binding of Baba's hands, the terror in his face, his gesture for me to flee, and my body turning to wood, my face to flint.

"They wanted to kill my baba," I go on. "He was no friend to these Romans, and he helped their enemies from Egypt."

Irini is motionless, and so am I. I cannot help but stop here. It is the heart of the Passover for me; it is my silent and unspoken Passover.

"Yes, and it was my own Passover, then," I voice. "I became

the lamb."

Irini sits up. "Baba, you said you were telling me the truth, not a story."

I cannot say in the dimming light whether she is happy or a little angry. I take her hand and draw her back down. "No, Irini—no story," I answer. "I was indeed the lamb."

"You were a boy, not a lamb," she responds, and I hear a ripple of laughter in her voice.

Taking her hand, I raise it to my left ear lobe. "Feel this," I say. "Squeeze it."

Irini laughs again. "My lobe is like a little dried apricot. Yours is like a squished olive with its stone still inside, Baba." She is giggling aloud as she lifts my hand that is not holding hers and places it on her ear.

I stroke her ear, her cheek. How fresh-skinned and cool this little fruit of mine is, and how I wish not to tell her what comes next. "My olive pit, as you call it, is a scar, Irenikon."

Irini is silent. How I wish she were a little older—just a few more years, and she would divine my meaning on her own, without my needing to put it in words.

"A scar?" she asks. "What from?"

I can hardly draw in all the air I need to reply. "It is a scar from an earring."

"An earring?" Irini asks, then repeats. "An earring. But you don't wear an earring."

"Not anymore," I say. "Thank God, no more." And from her silence, I am sure she still doesn't understand. Can I guide her there? "Who wears earrings, Irini?" I ask her. "Do you know?"

"Women," she says, and she laughs again.

Her breath is so soft on my face, cooling my fever for a moment. I can still feel the sea breeze from my time aboard ships, and the image of oceans swims in front of my gaze, replacing what I can still see of Irini's figure in the gathering shadows.

"Women, yes. And who else, daughter?"

"Slaves in the market. Oh, Baba?"

Irini's last words are whispered. Our gasps are both audible this time. "Baba—Baba? Do you mean you used to be a slave?"

I nod, then nod again. "I was the Passover lamb, for my father, for our family," I said. "When they captured my baba, I fell to my knees; I grasped the knees of the man who had captured my baba. I told him I could read, write, I knew all the craft my father had taught me. 'May you have many sons, and may I teach them the ways of the Greeks!'"

I can still see the hardened face of my father's captor above me, almost black, backed as it was by the burning sun of that autumn. I feel his eyes pulling themselves away from my father, his regard picking me over as a dog fastens to a bone. I feel his tunic rise as he shrugs his shoulders. His rough Latin voice is saying, "I could kill your father and take you captive as well. What difference is it to me?"

Then, another voice, high but penetrating. "It is enough, Marcellus. Let this merchant go, and keep his son as he proposes. That is punishment enough for his house. Bringing a slave like this boy to your family will educate your sons, but they could do far worse than learning from his example of courage as well as benefiting from his Greek."

This second speaker comes to me and lifts me by the shoulders. "And you, boy—yes, you shall serve in the house of Marcellus Victorinus. But when his sons grow as noble as you, ripen to your age, you shall be free. This is my command."

I cannot tell my own child these things, nor of the piercing of my lobe, the bestiality of the trip, the years of service. So this is the truth I say: "My father was freed, and he returned to Alexandria. I became the lamb, Irini, the slave in a household of three sons. But you learned well today. Sometimes we must remember the words of our forefather Joseph. What men intend for evil, our Lord intends for good. That day, a man offered me hope that I would not remain a slave forever."

"Who was this man that offered you hope?" Irini's voice rises, eager, as she presses her face into my chest.

"His name was Octavian," I reply. "He allowed Marcellus to use me, to train his sons. But after this service, he promised, I would be free to go."

"Octavian? Was he the head over Marcellus?"

I smile despite myself. "The head, indeed. Indeed, Irini. He was the winner of this war with Antonius and Cleopatra of Egypt, and you know him as our emperor, Augustus."

Except for the slow rising and falling of her breath that I feel almost like my own body, Irini is motionless. So close she has cuddled to my chest. "This is why you have always spoken of Caesar Augustus gently, not like our friends, isn't it, Baba?" she whispers.

I nod, clear my constricting throat with difficulty, then voice my, "Yes. Indeed it is, Irini. Go to my storage chest," I whisper. "Go and reach deep, deep inside, and you will feel, in among the linen and the Egypt cotton, a little, rough shape. like a mushroom top."

My entire body shudders with cold as Irini's light warmth moves away. As from a distance, I hear her small hands opening the chest so much larger than herself, and soon she returns to me.

She places an object, small and round, into my waiting hands. "It really is just like a big mushroom top, Baba!" Her laughter is as warm around me as her returning presence clinging close.

I breathe out too shallow for laughter. "Yes, it is," I manage. "Quite like one."

We smile together.

"I also think it looks like the cap of darkness that the Greek gods wore when they wanted no one to see them," she goes on. "Is it a little like that, Baba? Why don't you wear it?"

My throat wants to laugh, but the bellows in my chest do not obey by giving me wind. "Yes, Irenikon, I imagine that in fact it is a little like a cap of darkness, as you say. But for me, it was a cap of freedom and a blessing of light and hope."

"Oh," she answers. "I'm glad, but I think a cap of darkness would be much more exciting, wouldn't it?"

"You ask why you have never seen it on my head, daughter. I do not wear it here, because I have no need of it in this place," I respond with all my remaining force of effort. "It is named a pileus. It is my cap of freedom following the years when I was slave to the Roman."

"A pileus," Irini repeats, giving the proper Latin intonation.

I am so proud of this, my youngest, my girl child, her gentleness and her loyalty. I would like to explain it to her—this token of liberty given to slaves at the end of their service—my wearing it until I had crossed the sea from Rome to return to what I thought would be my home again in Alexandria. I would like her to know the joy of removing this cap arriving in Alexandria, and then the sorrow of learning that no one awaited me. My father dead, my remaining family dispersed, no one knew where. Yet this cap gave me the determination to move on to Cilicia and start my freedman's trade, to marry unabashed, though Irini's mother knew my story.

"Give this to Stephanos. We are a freedman's house, and you and your brother are free forever," is all I can voice.

Some kind of motionless wind, a power with no sound or viewing, yet a mighty force, overwhelms me. A gentle tug, as from a thread separating from the weave of its garment, frees me to arise. No more—no air, no breath, no weight, no chills, no heat nor pain, as my soul drifts and watches me. I see Irini and feel more than I hear her speak "Baba!" then, my name. I do not respond and realize I cannot do so.

Oh, my dear, dear girl! I do not want to abandon you, orphan you, pileus cradled in your tiny hands. I have left you only the symbol, not the whole story for you and Stephanos to know. And your lives must break today, and your feet must tread the continual earth with no mother, and henceforth, with no father, either. How can I bear it, but more, how can you bear it, my children?

Yet sure as my rising spirit, I see the good of God's promise surrounding my daughter and my son, strong as a shield in battle. "Protect them, Lord, as I cannot," I pray as I release them to His will; I can only call upon His mercy.

Tiny Irini cries my name again, and then shakes my shoulders below my upper self watching on. But this girl does not weep or shout as a woman would. She is as brave as my Naomi was in birthing, in grieving our three dead children, even in her pale slipping to the Almighty One during the plague.

Is my girl tearing her garments? No, but her hand has sunk deep inside her sleeve, pulling at the secret pouch my wife so cleverly designed as part of Stephanos' old yellowish robe. A coin emerges in her hand, and I know it is a Temple coin as I enter her mind to see. She returns to my couch.

"Good–bye, Baba," she whispers. "I will remember your story, and I will keep your pileus safe for Stephanos. I will tell him exactly your words. And I will remember you every time I see a lamb of Passover. Here."

She opens my voiceless mouth, laying the coin beneath my tongue. "For your passage to the next world."

The form of my Irini melts into the luminosity ahead of me, the beaconing of my beloved wife across a passage, where I proceed with joy.

3. The Tablet and the Light
Witness of Stephanos, Tarsus, A.D. 12

How is it that the full moon turns everything it touches to silver—from the leaves on the olive tree, to the stones of the floor of this chamber, even reaching to the Egypt cat pretending to bathe in the light? While my eyes and my mind know the guile of this silver, yet my heart must call it a miracle. At synagogue, I have voiced the prescribed prayers for my father at Kaddish, but the weeks and months marking his passing are behind us. This very night completes an entire year since his death. My spirit opens in a way put upon me not by my elders, nor by my school, never even by my sorrow. I want to believe that this moonlight is my father's blessing, his farewell. As a freeborn boy still in far-off Alexandria, surely the man who gave me life once gazed for the first time into the wonder of this silvering moon. As I contemplate this, my spirit walks with his memory.

The Egypt cat scrambles away as something dark crosses the patch of courtyard beyond the open door of this chamber where I share my sleep with the younger brothers of Saul. Any veil of dreams blows from my mind like wind. I stiffen as a small figure creeps inside our room and reaches my couch; it does not move like a man.

"Brother?"

The word blows so softly that if my ears were not straining, I would not hear, even knowing the figure is there.

Drawing my heavy sleeping wrap tight around me, I rise,

making as little sound as possible. Irini grasps my hand and pulls me to the courtyard.

"Irenikon, are you sick?" I whisper back to her once we have cleared the sleeping quarters of men and women. We move onward, into the spacious garden at the back of Saul's family residence.

My little sister shakes her head.

My heart gentles as she remains silent. "But you would not wake me unless this were important, would you?"

"No, never."

We sit down on a bench under an olive tree whose aspect is made new in the light around us. Then Irini climbs onto my lap, something she has not done in many months. But instead of resting there, she turns her head to face me, back arching away from my chest. Though she has scarcely grown since I last took her on my knees, her aspect has changed from open trust to shrewdness too great for her nine years. But her sweet, sweet scent, the oils of rose and laurel once created by our Ima and whose making was passed on to her, reminds me of our past.

"Do you remember Orpheus and Eurydice, Stephanos?" she asks. Her voice is low, though given our distance from the large house, we have no need to guard our words or our voices.

I nod. "Of course," I reply. "Of course. It is a story I told you myself as we went to Jerusalem last year with Saul. I thought you were old enough then to learn not just the happy stories and the adventures, but also the sad ones."

Irini sighs. "I miss Pavlos. I wish he had come home with us."

"Sometimes I wish so, too. But how could Saul refuse the invitation Rabboni Gamaliel gave him to study in Jerusalem?"

Without his presence, it has taken a long time for me to feel welcome in his family. For while our father respected Jewish custom, with his business to run, he had little time to show us things that are second nature to this traditional household of wealthy Pharisees.

Irini nods, but then she turns her head away. "They lived together happily for a year and a day."

"Who did?" I ask.

"Orpheus and his wife, Eurydice, until she died."

The start of this conversation was overridden in my heart with the sadness of missing my best friend, now so far away. But as Irini trembles after her words, I pull my sleeping cloth around her. Either she is cold, or I was wrong to tell her such a sad story when her height rises not yet to my elbow.

Then Irini stands up to face me. "A year and a day," she repeats.

My sister's memory for details and numbers continually surprises me. "Yes, that's right," I answer.

When she is silent, I go on. "Why did you bring me out here? Surely not to confirm this."

My sister draws a deep breath. "Eurydice died, even though she was happy," she says. "Tomorrow it will be a year and a day since Baba died."

I nod. "Yes. A year and a day."

Irini sighs. "I was punished tonight."

I click my tongue. Irini is constantly being chastised for this or that. But between my life at the academy and at the synagogue studying Torah, I have not paid attention. It is a normal thing, one boys and girls endure until they are old enough to marry. Still, it is a worse thing for girls, too weak to withstand what I can tolerate with a sigh or a shrug.

"Try not to take all of this so close to your heart," I reassure her. "In just a few years, when I am at the university, I am certain to find you a husband, and I will find no man that you dislike. I will stay here with you and not leave until you live the life you want as a fine Jewish woman."

"I cried. I cry every day. Only the doves see my tears," Irini replies as if she has not heard my promise to care for her.

The tending of these doves is something my sister asked to do as soon as she returned to Tarsus. The old servant who had that dirty job was all too glad to end the hard climb to the roof and let Irini do it instead. I thought then that all would go well with us in the house of Saul our friend.

Like our own baba, Saul's father keeps the doves in order to send them with fellow merchants, who tie tiny messages on their feet and release them on the road as they travel to alert him to opportunities and other news. Twice, a dove has even survived to Jerusalem and brought back a few words from Saul.

"I also cried today. But I cried for Baba," I answer. "But now the year is ended, and it is time for us to put away our tears."

But in my heart, I take pity as I consider the plenitude of boys and the few girls and female servants in the house, and the coldness of Saul's mother toward both of us as unexpected fosterlings. Irini has learned a first share of womanly things this year, some starts at weaving she has shown me, along with many rules of cleanliness any Jewish woman must observe, and some cooking with the servants.

"I cried for Baba today, too." Irini presses close. "I was punished, because I was not found to do the carding of wool Saul's mother told me to complete."

I recall the bleeding of Irini's fingers when she first showed me this task. "Did you refuse?" I ask. "It is tiresome, but it is something girls must learn to prepare the yarn we use for winter garments."

"Stephanos, I know that!" Irini interrupts. "But that is not what I said to you. I said I was not found."

"Did you hide when she called you?" I ask, half laughing.

Irini stamps her foot on an olive root, and this stops my laughter short. "No, Stephanos. I did not hide. It is not a game, and I am not a fool to create my own punishment for doing stupid things. But I am reproached for speaking Greek when I should use Hebrew. I am chastised again when I speak Hebrew and use the wrong words. And I am disciplined for certain words, even when they are full of logika, if Pavlos' mother disagrees with me."

I clasp her by the shoulders, and to calm her, I resort to the exercise of "logika," which she loves most. Several Sabbaths have gone by since I have invited her to sit with me as we used to sit and master this game, choosing instead the company of my fellow Torah students. "So, this means using deduction, sister. If you are no fool, as you say, then you must have done a wise thing."

"Yes. Using your logika, you have guessed correctly," she responds with the clear articulation of the Greek teachers she hears me imitating as I rehearse speeches to give before my classmates. "Well done. And will you use more logika to tell me what is wise?"

I laugh. "If we speak as Greeks with the words of Socrates, we will ask, 'What is wisdom?' But if we speak as the Jews we are, in the words of Solomon, then I should answer you that the fear of the Lord is the beginning of all wisdom. So since we are Jews, I should deduce from this truth that you were approaching the house of the Lord."

I expect this twisting of logika into sophistry to make her laugh, or at least to calm her from what I sense is a great heaviness at her punishment.

But my sister neither smiles nor laughs; instead, she nods. "Again, brother, your logika has prevailed." She steps back, then forward, her shadow rippling as it crosses uneven stones on the path.

"So?" I demand, but in a soft voice, so she knows that my word is not impatient.

"Tell me who was at synagogue today," she says in a quick breath.

"Perhaps just twenty men," I answer. "It is not Sabbath."

"Twenty men?"

I hesitate. "Or seventeen, or two dozen."

"Only men?"

"Our boys were at work or in the academy, except for me, since it is an ordinary workday, as you know. And there were no strangers visiting. I attended to mark this year of our father's return to our Lord. Saul's father attended along with me."

"Yes, I know," she returns. "But you say there were no boys at all?"

I shake my head. "Not a single boy."

"But there was someone there besides a man," she continues.

I do not know if she is mocking me, or whether perhaps she is beginning to create one of her own stories, like those she used to tell along the road to Jerusalem.

"Say on, sister. Was it some spirit with the blood of a horse and the wings of a dove, like Pegasus?"

"No," Irini replies, then pauses. "Do you remember Hermes, and Athena, and Perseus and their cap of darkness?"

"Of course I do," I reply. "I am the one who has told you how the gods and heroes of the Greeks became invisible using this cap as a disguise, to trick their enemies or to learn secrets from their friends."

"Yes," Irini replies. "But what you told me are only stories, I know this. But what I have to say to you is the truth."

I laugh. "Well, sister, go on. I am listening."

"When I say there was someone besides a man in the synagogue today, it was a soul with flesh and blood over it," she goes on. "It is a soul who can tell you that there were twenty-one men present, that Pavlos' father sneezed five times, that Rabbi Samuel coughed during final prayer, and that your tears were more vigorous than your prayers."

I grasp her by the shoulders. "Do you mean, you—yourself?"

Irini nods. "I was draped like a beggar, just a shabby little boy no one would mind or attend, or even see by the door of the library room you call synagogue when you pray there. This is what I have learned to do in the house where we live; I know how to walk and not be seen. I remember our baba telling us many times to keep our eyes open wide and our ears keen, since our eyes learn to see what they wish and our ears hear what they expect. I know now that this is the truth. The last time he said this was when I was right about the miracle of Naaman the leper and his healing, do you remember, along the road to Jerusalem?"

I find myself recalling along with her, though my throat has gone dry.

"I prayed this morning, and I heard the voice of our Lord. I had to go to the synagogue today, because Baba is also my father. I needed to speak words there with you, though no man would hear, but our Lord would listen."

"Irini!" I cry. When I hear the echo of fright in my voice, I lower my words to a whisper. "You could be not merely punished for this. You could be stoned, even as young as you are, under our law. It is an abomination for any woman, even a child, to enter in the places of men and to pretend manhood!"

"But Baba himself approved this," she replies. Her calm makes me all the angrier.

"What are you saying? Have you lost your reason?" It is the first time I have heard my voice hiss since telling her of monsters like Medusa and speaking as though through tongues of the snakes that were her hair. If only this talk could be a child's tale, not this revelation in the night!

Irini replies softly. "In Jerusalem, Baba told me to wear your old yellow cloak and head cloth to look like a boy. And surely, using my logika again, brother, which you are lacking right now, he gave his blessing on this. Why else would he have packed this cloak in the first place when we left Tarsus?"

"Enough!" I cut her off. "You must never even think of

accusing our father of a sin like wanting you to take on the appearance of a boy."

Irini sighs. "I was not playing at being a boy; I was simply making myself invisible to all men with the help of our Lord."

"Do not ever put a Greek story like wearing the cap of darkness into your prayers, sister. It is yet another abomination," I say, but now my voice is under control.

"Stephanos, I believe if our Lord made the sun stand still when Joshua called on him in battle, or if he permitted the sea to part for our people to cross from Egypt, it is a very small thing if he allows the eyes of others not to see me," she replies. "And it is certainly not impossible. Don't you believe this?"

Could she be speaking the truth? I search my mind for the times I have seen my little sister since our return from Jerusalem. What memories I find come only when I have looked for her, such as when we sit together at Sabbath or I have something to bring to her.

"I pray every morning and each evening to our Lord for help, but I think that I will disappear for everyone if I must continue my life in this family," she adds. "I have nobody to cry with when you are away, and nobody to laugh with, either, except the poor doves on the rooftop. I think this is why he allows me to disappear."

My heart twists with the truth of her words. As I remain silent, she goes on. "Tomorrow, if we do not change our life here, I will die like Eurydice. A year and a day is too long to live and be sad."

Most of what my sister says is spoken like a child. Even the day she was with Baba at his death, her words were small and soft. But now her voice is as hard as a judge giving sentence.

Perhaps from the very shock of such words, I laugh. "Sister!" I say. Then I reach a hand toward her. "Oh, sister. Do you see the beggars in the street? Surely more than one of them asked money even from you as the shabby little boy they thought you were on your way to our prayers—if the Most High let them see you, that is."

Irini nods.

"So, come, let us use our logika together again. If it were not for Saul's family, we could be just like those beggars. We have no one to turn to except this household of our father's friend. Without living here, we really would die."

"No!" Irini says, interrupting me. "Stephanos, we will not die. We will live. I have a plan."

From her sleeve, Irini draws a wooden tablet coated in wax. "I inscribed this tablet this evening in the girls' room when everyone else was away and I had to stay there for being absent when they sought me for carding the wool."

The tablet, too, turns silver in the moonlight. The words are engraved so deeply, their shadows strike my eyes like ink.

REQUEST FROM YOUR SISTER IRINI:
TO MY BROTHER STEPHANOS OF TARSUS

You shall demand the return of the shop from Saul's father which he took from us after Baba's death.

We shall leave this house forever and live there in the room over the shop.

I shall prepare food for us on the roof.

I shall dress as a boy wearing Ima's old robe, the one she made for you, and I shall act in all ways as your younger brother.

My name shall be called not Irini but Aaron.

You shall turn to the traders you know through Baba to procure goods for sale. I shall also help you with the making of ink, scrolls, styli, pens, and all other common goods I can learn from you.

You shall continue your schooling, and I shall sell in the day and scribe in the night for more money if we need it.

We shall ask our friend Pavlos to pray for us,
and we shall also pray for him.

When we grow up, we will be like Odysseus and travel everywhere
we want to go. We will leave this city forever like our Baba left
Alexandria, and we will venture to the ends of the earth
and never, ever look back.

I remove the small tablet from her hands. Though the childish slant of her letters is evident, so is the grace of her stylus as it touched this wax. "I did not teach you to write so well," I say. Of course, even in our Sabbath talks, showing her the art of writing was out of the question, since this is labor forbidden on our day of rest.

"I have observed your hand, your lettering, and your touch. You and the other boys see nothing else as you write, but I have gazed on you a hundred times when you were not watching," she replies. "I enter the room where the scrolls are kept to read what I can. I have taken styli and traced in the dust, in the sand, onto my own hand every day until I was certain. And I will continue with your help, and I will become as strong as you are with this skill."

I laugh. "I have no doubt, seeing what you have done here." Then I look at her seriously. "But what you propose on this tablet is too difficult, both for you and for me, sister. If you lived such a life with me, combine your imagination and your logika to picture it. There would be no time for anything but work, and no thought but maintaining secrecy to anyone but me. It would be like slavery for you, and not much easier for me, since I would worry for you each day when I am in the academy."

My sister says nothing for a long time, still standing in front of me. Then she seems to decide on her words. "Saul's sisters call me a dirty little Hellenist."

My throat tightens with anger, but I hide it as I steady my

mind and my voice to reply. "Perhaps they are jealous of your knowledge of things they do not know, and that you traveled to Jerusalem. You must not take them seriously, sister. I promise you, life will become better when you grow up. Just withstand it like your hero Odysseus for a little longer, and always know I am ready to listen, whenever you wish. Most of all, do not worry about it, because this will do nothing to help you."

"You speak of slavery. I live already as a slave. It will be your turn to worry if I remain here. To convince you, I have used both my words and my logika, and I did not want to show you this, but I must," she replies. Then she lifts the edge of her robe. Her bare feet turn to silver in the light above our heads. Lacing her calves and ankles are lines of shadow.

"What is this, Irini?" I ask, though in my heart, I know.

"They are my punishment," she replies. "I want to die if I am struck again."

I reach my hand to what my eyes see, my finger confirming the lash marks. They rise, hard as the ribs of a fish. My mind travels like a man pursued by hounds and not knowing where to turn. To confront Saul's father with this cruelty would bring shame to his house, and possibly even more ill treatment upon my sister. Nor would life become any easier for me, since knowing this would shape the entire atmosphere of living here. To say nothing and remain as we have would curse my soul and kill any joy I have in the studies I pursue, bought at the price of Irini's grief and suffering.

"Yes," I hear my voice speak aloud. "You have thought well, and we must indeed leave this house."

Irini clasps my hands. "I promise you, Stephanos of Tarsus, I will do anything to help you, anything. It is not right for you to give up your studies or your scripture lessons because of me. I will be with you, and I will learn everything I must, and we can make it possible to live a different life. I will not even allow myself to miss the doves who nest here."

As the breeze sways Irini's robe, and I cannot turn away from the marks on her feet, it is as though my father is speaking the familiar words Irini said once more deep in my heart: "Most of us grow up, and as we do, our eyes learn to see what they wish, and our ears begin to hear what they expect."

I nod in gratitude, both for Baba's remembered voice, and for Irini's trust that I will hear it.

I realize why I have seen the moonlight and thought of my father. Though I was made a man three years ago at my bar mitzvah, this night, my father's moonlight demands that I live no longer as a young scholar considering only his own thoughts, but as a man protecting his only family. For who else can stand at Irini's side to defend her but me? The fear in my heart at leaving this house for the uncertainty ahead is nothing beside the sacrifice our baba made to save his own father.

"Sister, there will always be doves for you wherever you live, as long as we are together," I reply.

A small sound from the sky, indeed almost like the wings of a dove, makes me look upwards. Far over the moon, directly above our heads, shines the constellation we call Lyra, the instrument of Orpheus, the great poet and musician. Five stars outline his harp—placed there by the gods, it is said, to mark his memory.

My sister's eyes follow mine. "Sometimes, when I look at the lyra in the sky, I can almost hear its music aloud," she says.

"So can I," I reply. "I thought that I alone heard music from the stars until I asked Baba. He said it is a gift from our Lord for those who keep their eyes and ears open to His wonders."

"Yes. He was right. And the Lyra brings me hope," she replies. "The gods did not make this lyra in the sky, but perhaps our Lord set it there for us to remember what is beautiful. Your own lyra also gives me happiness when you play it. We must bring it with us so we can keep our songs alive together."

I raise a silent prayer to the Most High for wisdom to say

what I must to Saul's father tomorrow. Like wind without motion, a great peace, silent yet real as the light around us, wraps my soul in reply as the light blurs with my tears.

"Sister, before this very time tomorrow, we will make our own home together. This is my promise to you as your older brother. From this day forward, you will never be invisible to me again."

4. The Crown and the Flint
Witness of Saul, Tarsus, A.D. 16

"Better for me to be the lonely shepherd boy David, tossing stones from his slingshot, than to sit here on the eve of the Sabbath in this happy crowd!" I must choke back these words, bitter as the waters of the Dead Sea, because here she sits at my side, my little Irini, now jumping up, shouting out the blessings she knows—"May you fly with the sandals of all the winds!" and then, tossing her head like a horse, "Stephanos! Flee the ground like feather–footed Perseus!"

To hear her, Irini is no different from the Greek spectators lining the stadium, and to see her, not one thing distinguishes her from all the boys around us. Yet I know what no one here perceives—that this boy-girl is almost a woman, and that though her tongue spews Greek in public, her real voice should be that of a daughter of our people. How different she looks from how I imagined her on the way home to Tarsus after my years studying with Rabboni Gamaliel in Jerusalem. Only my pity for her overrides the shame of being with her in her current condition.

Stephanos' old garment she is wearing brings me back to the day that has marked all our lives. It was when all three of us first visited the great Temple together. For me, that day was above all days in my life, since it was then when I met the doctor of the law Gamaliel, and he gave his blessing for me to study at his feet. Five years of my learning, and the relief they have brought from facing the Greeks at our academy, have barred that day from this one.

How can it be that a single day can bless my life with such purpose, when the same day broke the life of my closest friend and his sister as they became orphans? This is a question for which perhaps even Rabboni Gamaliel would have no reply beyond the hidden purposes of the Most High, but I resolve to ask him when I return to Palestine.

My best friend's sister has hardly changed since I last saw her five years ago when she and Stephanos left Jerusalem to return here with my father. A hand's length taller, perhaps, or maybe just a hand's breadth. Still, gazing at her in that old, boyish garb, I cannot help seeing in my mind exactly how she looked in the Jerusalem Temple. Her appearance in my memory shines as golden as the sun on her robe today. I still envision the inner light from her face when she asked me if I could see the wonders before us springing from the stories of my teacher's lips, and then as I whispered the ancient names to remind her of our forefathers when we first heard and saw the words of my blessed rabboni. I was certain that first day at the Temple that the Lord gave Gamaliel's voice not only to me; Irini's eyes, too, were full of the vision.

But I cannot remind her of that day's wonder of Rabboni Gamaliel's words coming to life as we witnessed together the household of Abraham and the tents, not when this same boy's robe recalls Irini's face as it was robbed of its blood, stricken as she ran to find us after her father's passing that same evening. Like my dismay at her vain-tongued Greek blessings, I must withhold these memories from her. Instead, I breathe a prayer to our Lord to forgive Irini in her ignorance of our customs. If Stephanos had not insisted with such force that they leave our household to run their father's shop, this gentle Irini would have a far better life in my family. At least she would live as a woman and not in abomination of everything we hold true about a girl.

But I seem unable to convince Stephanos of this.

Yet it is solely because of Irini that I find myself here, surrounded by all this dust and vanity. Every day since I arrived home, she has sent me scrolls no larger than the first joint of my thumb, tied to the feet of doves that nest on the roof of my house and on the roof of Stephanos' store. The lettering on these tiny bits of parchment is as graceful and perfect as any Greek I have seen in my travels. First she informs me, then she asks me, and finally beseeches me to attend Stephanos' race. I lacked the heart to write a reply.

Then yesterday, Irini called to me as I passed out from my family's gate. She stood there alone like a beggar boy, and I did not know her until she smiled up at me, just as she used to do when she wanted a sweet fig or an almond on the road to Jerusalem. I could not speak a single word.

"Pavlo," she said, using my Greek name, "I know you and everyone in your house consider me disgraced as I am dressed, and I will not go to the races tomorrow alone, yet I will go if you come with me. It is a kind of mitzvah for us both."

I was not entirely astonished that Stephanos was racing, for my father had made it clear that this young man should go his own way. But for Irini to ask this favor of me—even to think she could ask me was close to abomination. As I inhaled to protest, dust, or my own spittle too quickly breathed in, choked my answer. I shook my head, coughing.

But she said on as I spluttered. "Do not kick against the pricks."

I could not rule my spirit then, as I remembered the favorite phrase uttered so many times between Stephanos and me—merely whispered when the weight of our Jewish law seemed too heavy for our child shoulders. To hear it from this unstudied girl choked me with laughter.

Irini clasped my hands as she looked up at me and laughed along. I knew that all my protests had been beaten, mine that I could not help, hers full of ignorance and relief.

Ah, this girl—one side of her tongue more Grecian than the Hellenists, the other a faltering daughter of Abraham, rising on the wave of teachings my family should show her. "It is a mitzvah," she repeats, and to reassure herself in Greek, "a good deed."

"Then we will go together," I managed, though in my heart I was already begging my Lord for forgiveness, and wishing the impossibility of avoiding my father's harsh reproaches.

As though she read my mind, she continued, "No one will know us."

No young girl must go to the stadium, let alone one small enough for any man to snatch away like a cluster of grapes. Is this why she had spoken of a good deed in asking me to join her? Yesterday, I was unsure if she merely wanted male protection, or if she guessed something more, which is the very anger prickling sourness on my neck today amidst these unholy Greeks.

As I staggered up the rows and now sit beside her on the stony step drenched in sun, my bitterness has mounted. I feel to my bones the real reason she chose to wear the boy's garb. No child, not even as young as a girl before her first monthly blood, wants to be seen with me. I am the shadow that crosses the sun and makes a guest shiver with my shuffle, the wind that disquiets the still waters as I snort out certain words too hard for my heavy tongue to say. In fact, this is why Irini calls me "Pavlo." My own father–given name, "Saul," wheezes out like a double flute when I say it. "Pavlos," however, that is a name I can say perfectly. When I use that name Irini gave me years ago, my voice can guide a listener to what I can say, instead of what I cannot. Irenikon is the only person who would think of that, and only she would care to give me this gift of a name that now sometimes I use when introducing myself.

"Are you too hot?" she asks me now in the Hebrew she is

trying to master. Her wide sleeve stretches toward me as she fans her arm to cool my face.

"No. I'm fine. And you–girl will get even hotter if you try to cool me," I reply.

"But I'm you–boy," she whispers, giving the man's form of address in Hebrew. "I use the name of Aaron. Don't forget!"

I shall speak harsh words to Stephanos about this in private, but for now, I must smile at her pretense of being a little man. "Your Hebrew is good today, Aaron," I reply, finding the closest boy's name to hers coming to my tongue far too naturally. Warmer than the sun, I feel a wash of tenderness for both the dove-tending girl Irini and the studious boy "Aaron." But loneliness pierces me. He–you, she–you, it doesn't matter here. In this Greek stadium, what difference does it make? We're the only ones who would know.

For a moment, Irini looks down. I have overshadowed her with the bitterness of these words that I wish I could bite back. Then she turns from me to scream with the rest of them as the seven runners line up behind the banded gate that will spring open at the sounding of a horn, one not dissimilar to our shofar, I think, allowing myself some scant amusement amidst my discomfort.

The stony track stretches wide before our seats. The sun is in our eyes, but I can count the poles at each end of the rectangular course marking one stada, a distance equaling the burst of speed as I draw perhaps five full breaths. These athletes will run end to end to complete twenty-four stadia today.

Though I have seen Stephanos nearly each day since my arrival home, he said nothing to me to give me thought of attending his running. Yet how radiant he gleams after his bath, his olive oil–coated skin sweating from his practices in the gymnasium, glorying in the temple of his own body. He is the tallest man in our tiny synagogue when he takes time to visit. The joy in his words as he describes running through sand to make his legs and feet strong, the quickening tempo of the double flute exhorting all the young men to test their pace ever faster, the ecstasy of his increasing triumphs, first in our academy, then in our entire Tarsus, all these I endured hearing, and like a sheep led to slaughter, I have said nothing, not even when he has spoken of "the wonder of the creation of our Lord" allowing him this freedom.

I wonder, is this creation he has in mind the sun and sky around us, the sea salt soaking the breeze, or is it his own body? The thought that he may be mocking me, or even worse, breaking our traditions for the sake of his pride—this is all too painful to voice.

When the gate springs upward from its hooks and the track resounds with the sandals pounding, I must close my eyes. I hear them, like drums losing rhythm. The vigor, the power of them, all this nearly conquers my spirit. It is not enough that this "Aaron" has persuaded me with guile to be in an unholy place on the eve of our holy day. Now these sure-footed runners, nimble as goats on the mountain, all of them mock my very existence. How light and easy this run of theirs sounds, some sandals skipping like stones over water, others shaking the wind with their thudding. In my lashes, through the tears I do not shed, I can feel the vibration of their energy, the perfection of their footfalls.

"The Quail," I whisper. Yes. The Holy One has sent me punishment through this noise as I remember my stumbling childhood feet, and the ignominy of that word. The Greek boys remembered their idol-god Zeus, who threw his own infant son Hephaestus off the mountain because of his ugliness. The baby's leg was broken, leaving him forever to walk like a quail dancing in its spring courtship. And ever after, that cruel name born of a crueler father was how the Greeks supposed the other Olympian gods spoke of Hephaestus in secret. For the academy boys, it was only a short leap of their Grecian minds to turn this horrible name upon me.

In the pounding of this race, I feel anew their shattering mirth—the torments they inflicted every day as I suffered in my Hellenic studies of vain learning. Their feet sounded just like this when they ran off, hurling their taunts back on me like sparks, knowing that I could pursue not even the slowest of them. I shudder anew with the shaming of my body.

But I also remember Stephanos' words, once he heard of this "Quail."

"It is a noble bird, and one sent from the Lord," he said to me in private. To the boys in our academy, he said, "Our Lord, who is far greater than Zeus, sent quail to save our people when they were hungry in the desert." And to some boys, he said, "Your Hephaestus is by far the cleverest of your gods, as you know, with his smithy and his wheel. Saul can outthink any one of you here who outruns him!"

I am sure this was the only time during our years together in the academy that Stephanos said anything of our faith or theirs.

I shrug my shoulders to clear my mind of these things, and force my eyes open to look down on the track. At first, it is difficult to distinguish the men, because each of them has garbed sand over olive oil as protection from the sun. But every one of them has some distinctive mark—one a silver amulet, another a golden wrist band, and—"There!" Irini points directly at her brother.

I see now what I could not notice from afar. On my friend's head is perched some round, peculiar cap. It looks too heavy for the lightness of his steps, a dark, woven thing of no decorative beauty.

"What is that?" I ask her. "Is he making some kind of fun with such an ugly cap?"

Irini smiles, but she says nothing.

"Would you like some water?" Irini's question pierces my

thoughts, as I have bowed my head into my hands.

Her voice forces me to look up. Only to please her, I take the clay bottle she offers. It is shaped like an owl.

"I saved money to buy this vessel to give my brother for running practice," Irini says. "Come on, stand up and yell, he might see us!" she says as Stephanos hurtles around the end post and back toward us on the third or fourth stada.

I shake my head. "He'll never know," I answer.

What I mean in my heart is this: "God, forgive my envy of these runners. Let me release this pain of my own deformity. Do not allow this brother and sister to see my breaking of your commandment, as I covet the perfect forms you have given the runners, and which you have withheld from me."

As the racers reach midpoint on each stada, closest to our seats, their breath ripples their chests and swells their backs. The flame is hot inside their bodies.

I have become used to the pounding feet, the shrieking crowd, and the glaring sun, now, or perhaps Irini's water has done me good with its trace of something tart—pomegranate, perhaps—that she put in the bottle against the heat.

"They're finishing the tenth stada right now," Irini says after a few minutes of shouting as her brother passes and repasses our seats. "But Stephanos only has nine."

At that moment, the lead runner falls just before our place. One of his sandals flies through the air all the way to the first row of spectators. Helpless to continue one–footed, the young man lays his head in his hands as I had done before, stepping to the side away from his fellow runners.

"Poor Menelaus of Sebaste!" Irini says quietly. "He was said never to be lucky."

Even though Irini continues in her imperfect Hebrew, she leans close to my ear. "The men from all the seven cities running here have sponsors," she says. "The winner will receive a bag of gold from Archipos of Salamis. Stephanos was told that some men here are all for Rufus of Ayas. But I think my brother is fooling them all, like the slow one, until they tire at the sixteenth or eighteenth stada, and then"—she whirls her hands—"he'll skim the earth like Boreas." She blows her cheeks out like the wind god of the Greeks she is set on imitating.

They thump on, these light runners under our Tarsian sunlight. I force my eyes to take in all six young men remaining. My gaze seems to bend between their shifting legs that dazzle me with their speed. I catch a shred of joy from the crowd as the young men pass the halfway point of twelve stadia, like the thrill of receiving a sprinkling of blood that has more than once hit me at a temple sacrifice. But I refuse to shriek with those around me.

Passing the halfway point, a second runner leaves the race, hurtling to the side and losing the contents of his guts on the parched ground.

Many in the crowd laugh, but Irini sighs. "Hector of Salamis," she tells me. "Stephanos told me he refused to observe the diet the trainers advise them to keep before a race."

Soon Irini grasps my forearm and pulls my sleeve almost strongly enough to tear it. "Pavlo, Pavlo, look! He's gaining on them all!"

Then, lifting her high voice above the crowd as a man would launch a javelin, she cries, "Stefani ya ton Stefano!" ("A crown for Stephanos!") The name of Stephanos and the word for crown in Greek are the same word. She continues to chant. Then around me in the crowd, I hear her phrase repeated and swelling tall as a tidal wave by stada 19—"Stefani ya ton Stefano! Stefani ya ton Stefano!"

But my friend is thudding next-to-last of the five remaining runners strung along stada 20. All of them are breathing wide, sand and sweat falling from their bodies, uncovering the shame of their nakedness in streaks of sweat down their heaving torsos and legs—their strong and rhythmic legs. As the call turns into a chant, Stephanos continues gaining ground. At stada 21, he has become the third runner, and at stada 22, already the second.

Why is my voice silent, my breath like the still night air amidst this gasping out of speed in my fellow native city dwellers?

If not for your friend, call out for your Tarsus! I tell myself as Irini keeps shaking my arm, though she seems oblivious to my silence in her ecstasy. And if not for your city, why not for your dearest friend? Or even—I stop the thought short before it can find final voice under my tongue—he is your fellow Jewish brother!

But I cannot, and I will not ever call out. This voice of mine would be harsh even to my own ears. "Thtefanoth!" And anyhow, it would certainly not be heard above anyone else's in this mass of thousands of spectators. I am lost without my voice, lost without reason. No one knows or cares if I cry out, or if I do not.

In stada 23, "The Crown" levels with a runner who has been in first position most of the time till then, silver pendent gleaming.

"That's Phillipos of Adana," Irini points out.

Their feet lap up the space and the dust in near unity. How beautiful it would be just to hold this blur of healthy feet in my vision now, like dancers, if they could stay so harmonious, so impersonal in their forward motion.

Then they turn the posts to take the twenty-fourth stada, their final stretch. "Stefani ya ton Stefano!" every son of Tarsus is shrieking now. Even many others from cities destined to lose have taken up the chant.

One-third of the way down the stada, approaching our place, my friend stumbles groundward. The crowd gasps, but quick as the lowering of their shriek, he launches a leg forward, bent-kneed, springing straight upward. If he has been grazed by the earth, that near fall seems to give him the final push he needs, for now instead of rising like hammers, his legs extend nearly parallel with the ground, shooting forward to devour the dusty earth beneath. He arrives a full two strides before Phillipos.

As the crowd roars, both men tumble to the earth as though stretched forth after cruel battle, forearms touching. Longer than it takes the final runners to cross the finish line, they continue to pant in the dust like fallen horses. Then almost as one, Phillipos and Stephanos push against each other to rise. The crowd waits in silence until the two men face us and salute.

As Stephanos stands, a redness streaking his sandal starts to pool around his left foot. The crowd gasps, and I have no time to say that it is probably just a light flesh wound before Irini shouts, rising from our seat. Respecting the space of no man, she pushes straight forward through the rows separating her from her brother.

But as Stephanos remains standing tall, she stops before the first row as the three judges approach her brother. "Stefani ya ton Stefano indeed," says the leader, arms outstretched. "Remove this silly hat, Stephanos of Tarsus, and be crowned victor!"

But Stephanos makes no move to obey. Instead, he steps back from the crowd to survey us, and then he begins to speak. "My fathers and my brothers of Tarsus!"

Murmuring that began when Stephanos stepped away from the bearers of the laurel crown dies down. He repeats his call. Besides his voice, we can hear only the jagged panting of the defeated runners. Stephanos allows his own breathing to quiet.

"This silly hat, as you call it, belonged to my father."

Irini covers her face with her hands. The front–row men have allowed her a place. They hardly need to move for her to fit.

"My father, some of you remember him, came to our city alone more than thirty years ago. You welcomed him here as a son. Here he continued his father's own trade of papyrus, scrolls, and tablets that he learned in Alexandria. It is the trade he taught to me, and which I have continued."

"None better!" a spectator shouts, and the crowd begins to laugh.

"Say on, Stephanos, and grow rich! No better audience to tell!" another man exclaims, bringing on additional chuckles, which spread back from the front rows as humor passes mouth to mouth.

Stephanos does not join in the mirth. "This cap," he calls, quieting the crowd "it is a Roman thing, and it marks my father's life, and mine as well. It marks, too, the life of my people, the Jews."

The sun makes sweat run into all eyes. The stink of us rises as a thousand arms wipe their brows.

"Yes, my father, like my people, lived first as a slave, but he died as a freedman. That is what this cap signifies."

A craning of necks to see the cap better follows these words along with our stench. And a wave of surprised throats raise murmuring of bafflement or shock as those who have not heard catch the news from the audience closer to the track.

Stephanos pauses again, whether to regain his breath or to let his words take root. The crowd is so silent now that nothing but the breeze passes through our ears. Irini's face is still sheltered behind her fingers. Stephanos' father—a slave turned freedman? Until today, I believed that my oldest friend held no secrets from my family, and most of all, none from me.

After looking toward Irini, Stephanos goes on. His sharp voice splits the silence like Moses' rod smiting the stone to bring forth a spring of water for our thirsty people traveling to the Promised Land through the desert. "You think I ran this race for the glory of my youth and for our city's fame. I would deceive you if I said no. 'Stefani ya ton Stefano!' sounds the sweetest of any words this crown-head has ever heard."

I find myself laughing with the crowd.

Then Stephanos' gaze shifts down the stadium, and he fixes his regard straight on me. "But I have not run for myself today. I have run this race for my people, the Jews, once enslaved in Egypt, and now free. I have thought of them with every footfall. But also, as I prepared for this race and felt the rhythm of my feet, and smelled the unguents of oil on my skin, and sweated as my legs led me, and scraped my skin clean in the baths, there is one man of my faith for whom I have done this. He is here with us today."

I wish I were as small as Irini. To make it worse, Stephanos is motioning to his sister, and she returns to me, pulling me up amidst this silent crowd.

"This is our Saul, of a house that gave me shelter when first my mother, then my father, returned to their fathers. I wanted to win this race for the sake of this brother of faith and for his household. I thank our God for the victory." Stephanos' voice falters as he ends. "But his is a different kind of enslavement, from which he will receive no freedom."

Like contagion, these words of Stephanos spread further and further back until everyone in the crowd is devouring me with their sweat-beaded gaze. Irini balances my gait as I step down along the seats and move forward. Through my entire body, my awkwardness before this crowd burns like nakedness. But I hear no jeers, no laughter, as I struggle downward. Rather, here a forearm rises to steady me, there a robe pulls wide to clear the way before me. There are whispers and sighs.

It takes all my concentration to descend without stumbling, but Stephanos has walked to the front row to meet me. He takes first Irini's hand, then mine as we arrive at the final step to the track.

His arm is around me, and we step back as he addresses the crowd again. "I will not yield my father's pileus, for it makes us remember our past, both the past of our people and that of my family. But I will pass on my victor's crown to Saul, my friend and my brother in faith."

Irini is whimpering as she kneels at her brother's feet. Someone has torn a strip of cloth, and she has tied it to his ankle. The blood has stopped. But I am confronted with this sea of faces—a few I recognize from our own academy, but most I do not know. They are smiling and waving at me, and they are kind.

Of course, I know it is Stephanos and not me bringing this victory of goodwill. But my heart swells almost to bursting. For the first time in my life, a warmth of countenance shines toward me. How far this is from the eyes lowered, sneers half uttered, or sighs of pity surrounding me—not only in Tarsus, but even in Jerusalem. The three of us stand with the sun to our backs, this sea of goodwill waving and turning before our eyes. Even the judges bow as they encircle me, their faces sincere. A disordering in my locks, the deep scent of fresh laurel, and I am the one wearing the victor's crown. Meanwhile, Stephanos' ugly, little, round slave's cap broods on his head, while the crown adorns me and the people look on.

What robs me of words is not my shame; it is my amazement. I am lifted in the air by the judges. Meanwhile, someone wraps Stephanos in a scarlet cloak. No one minds the sand and sweat still flecking his body that will streak the garment even before they move forward. The crowd rises as Stephanos, too, is lifted high on the shoulders of many men. Even the beaten athletes are applauding now as our cap and our crown rise above them all. "To the feast! To the celebration!" they call out together.

I cannot see where Irini has disappeared to, but as I gesture to Stephanos, he smiles at me and points behind us. She is slipping through the crowd as only the small and the young can do. It looks as though she is digging in the dirt, squatting alone as the rest of the crowd follows us.

We proceed to our old academia, and I try to shield my

mind from the memories of the past that Stephanos and I share there. At the victory feast, I scarcely allow the Cyprian wine to touch my lips, yet Stephanos weaves me into the celebration. I have not been in the company of Greeks since leaving this very academy, where I was allowed to associate with gentiles to gain the learning I would need. But this is quite a different matter, unexpected, an impure feast among godless men, and I am utterly defiled, shamed. Even the victory crown prickles my head.

Almost, I envy Stephanos' smooth freedom cap, his pileus, as he calls it, which must be less uncomfortable. I envy, too, the courage he showed today in speaking aloud the shame of being the son of a freedman, turning it somehow into a victory. Irini, still thought to be "Aaron," stays close to us, but she is quiet. The athletes and their friends turn little notice on her. I watch her to assure her wellbeing, but there is little need as she slips through the large-bodied celebrants to find the olives she loves, and a few times, to whisper something to her brother as he bends low to hear.

A few of our former peers from the academy ask me all about my learning, now that Stephanos has announced my studies in Jerusalem.

But what should I tell? Besides my family here, I have put away childish things and all the bitterness of my Tarsian past. Their talk holds no meaning for me; their words are empty. What I have learned to cling to in Jerusalem is the law of the Lord, which gives my breath its air, my life its meaning. None of these young men around us have any interest in and less awareness of the one true God, whose word is my daily milk and honey, my life, my breath, my love. The wine they drink roughens their voices and tatters their respect. And tomorrow I will be forgotten, and Stephanos will wear the crown of olive leaves in their minds, not I. Some of them, in a tussle, seek to yank the pileus from my friend's head, but his smile fades and his hands reach up in reproach, halting the play they intend.

As the time comes to give the victor's purse, the flutes and the lyra fall silent, and men reclining on their couches or standing near one another grow still. To our surprise, Phillipos, the second–place runner, accompanies Archipos of Salamis, the sponsor, to stand before the assembly.

"A question has arisen regarding the victory," Archipos begins.

The stone hall of the academia where we are celebrating stirs with laughter, but then with nervous murmuring as Archipos of Salamis fails to join in what we first believe to be a half-drunken joke.

"Better to say, Stephanos, you gained the victory, but yours was not the victory to gain," Phillipos adds.

Stephanos steps forward, his freedom cap on a level with Phillipos' dishevelled locks. "What question do you have for me, Phillipos?" he inquires.

The room has fallen utterly silent.

"The question is this," says Archipos. "Are you a man, a whole man?"

Surely no one in the room but myself has grasped his intent. Even Stephanos appears at a loss. But I suck in my breath as Irini turns to me. I recall horrible stories whispered in Jerusalem, tales of our own fellow Jews who have undergone the circumcision knife not once, upon their eighth day of life, but twice. The second cutting is intended to hide their circumcision and allow them to join such races in certain provinces of this empire under Rome where their participation in competitions is not otherwise allowed. At least my friend has not committed this sin, may our Lord spare me from the very thought!

As the silence lingers, Phillipos points to Stephanos' victory robe. "Beneath your robe, there is not a whole man's parts."

Stephanos attempts to laugh, but weakly. "Phillipos and all of you have seen me in the baths each day when I have run with you. What makes you say this? Even you agree, Phillipos, that I ran the fastest."

"But this is not the question," Archipos repeats, voice cracking as he raises his tone. "The question is, are you worthy to win when you are not a whole man?"

Irini grasps my hand. "Pavlo, what do they mean? Please, help my brother. Only you can help him."

I long to be gone from all of this, but Irini's sweet voice and gentle gaze draw me in. Despite my better judgment, I rise. The laurel crown crackles with my motion. I must look high to meet the eyes of Phillipos and Archipos of Salamis as I step forward. The men around leave the four of us in a bare circle.

"Brothers," I force my lips to speak, and every eye is turned on me. Now the former smiles are hesitant at best. "It is a true thing that Phillipos has said regarding our bodies as Jewish men. We are cut to become men of our people on our eighth day of life. It is a mark to remind us that we belong to our god the Lord of all the earth."

Archipos laughs. "Or to make you not quite a man, and certainly not someone to run with those of us who are whole." His eyes pierce mine as he takes in the short bulk of my stance, perhaps even the shifting of my knees in order to keep me as tall as I can rise.

I ignore his taunt and go on. "If we worshipped your gods, we would have no need of this, but as we are a people freed from captivity and called to our god, we would surely be wrong to ignore the command of our Lord."

"Tell me, Stephanos, does your command include the call to run with the rest of us?" Phillipos' face has twisted into a sneer.

"No, indeed it does not," I reply before Stephanos can draw breath. "But keeping the commandments of our people does allow us to keep our honor."

The murmuring in the room arises like dust after a running camel. "And to keep your own honor," I continue, "you would do well to respect the victory that all your eyes have seen today, and which the judges have already considered, though they have looked upon every one of the runners as our Lord created them, each one."

"Remember! Pavlos the Quail always could use his logika to win," a shrill voice calls from the back of the room. "But he is right. One honor must respect another. The Greek honor must bow to the Jewish honor today."

The room tingles first with whispers, then with laughter that burns me to the very soul.

"But—" Phillipos tries to protest.

Archipos sighs. "What a backwater your Tarsus is if you fail to disqualify a man like that one!" He waves a hand to Stephanos as though to dismiss a stray dog.

But Archipos' wine or his anger has turned his tongue to words far too rash, and in a place far too full of Tarsians. His remark spawns hissing all around.

One of the judges rises and comes forward. "Do not insult the city hosting these races, Archipos!" he says sternly. "There were three judges, and none of us come from this city. Our word is final. As we have judged, in front of Tarsus and now before you, we repeat," he intones. "Stephanos the Crown is our winner today. Phillipos ran well, but not so well as this one."

He stands directly in front of Archipos. "And I believe you to be a man of honor as well. As the runners turned the final stada, you were heard by all three of us to say that your pledge of a purse would not be the twenty gold coins you had promised earlier to the winner, but fifty. You even told us to announce this amount before you give it. Now it is time for you to honor your own city by keeping your word.""

Irini gasps, as do the men around her. This is the work of many years for a scribe or a builder. The weight of it makes music as it now passes from the hand of Archipos of Salamis to the judge, since Archipos is too angry or too shamed to hand it directly to our winner. Then comes new applause, again for Stephanos, but many eyes look to me as well. And though he accepts the purse with gracious words of thanks, Stephanos quickly transfers it to his little sister as others begin to eat and drink once more.

Almost too late, I realize that only a hand's width separates the sun from setting, and with it, the start of our Sabbath. "I must leave now; I should have already left," I say to Stephanos and Irini.

On one hand, I am dismayed when my friend interrupts the merrymakers to announce his departure along with me, for he is expected to remain well into the night. Yet I am also relieved that despite his defilement among the Greeks, and despite their laughter now, he shows at least this respect for our tradition.

As I walk with Stephanos and Irini, returning toward my father's house, the shadows stride ahead of us. Stephanos' form is swaying slightly, though whether because of the wine he has drunk or from his foot wound, I do not want to know.

"The victors!" a porne calls out to us from a side street, her robe more crimson than the sunset. "Ah, hail to the victors! Come taste some victory sweeter than honey between my breasts!"

Irini stamps up to the smiling woman. "Look out! I'm a little bee that is going to sting you for stealing my honey! And we are not whole men!"

The porne shrieks with giggles and Irini flounces after us.

Stephanos grins. "She would have given you the whole hive if she knew how much gold is in your sleeve, sister," he says in Hebrew. "You may give it back to me now."

My face is burning as I stamp along at my fastest.

Irini starts jumping up and down and grabs Stephanos' hand. "Brother, now we can do what we've always dreamed of, can't we?" she asks. "With the gold, we can go all over the world, maybe even to Athens!"

I laugh. "You always loved the stories of travel, both the Hebrew and the Greek ones."

Irini smiles. "I still love them, and I will live them out. You will see, Pavlo!"

"Well, before you make your way to Mount Olympus, you need to have dinner, and you should join us in our house tonight," I reply.

The smile fades from Stephanos' face. "Neither Irini nor I can enter your home, Saul. You know that we are not clean as your family regards the laws of purity. I am sorry that even you have violated many rules by being with us today."

I nod. "This is true, and I will go to purify myself in the synagogue before returning to my family's home."

Stephanos nods but says nothing. Then he opens the victor's purse that Irini has given back to him and counts ten coins into my hand. "This is a fifth part of what I received today. Please take these to the synagogue on my behalf."

"You need to give only five for tithing," I reply, then stop as Irini looks at me.

"It is our gratitude to give more, Pavlo," Stephanos replies.

"And I know how to prepare many foods now," Irini adds. "You should come to eat with us above our shop when you come to market." Then she runs ahead of us.

I look above her head to meet her brother's eyes. "She does all she can to honor cleanliness, but it is not as it would be in your father's home or in Jerusalem," Stephanos says in a quiet voice. "I am sorry."

"Look, Stephanos," I begin, "this gold you have won is ample for the rest of your learning, even in university if you wish to study on. If you live simply, it should even allow for the bride price you will need someday. But it will not buy your sister's life back as the girl she is and the boy you force her to be. Please let her return to our house so she can rejoin our traditions."

Stephanos turns to face me. "I would have no gold without

your coming today," he says quietly.

"Then honor your people even more than you did at the stadium today by giving Irini the life of a girl!" I splutter with emotion and turn my face away as I cough.

Stephanos takes my arm. "Saul," he says, then sighs and lowers his gaze. After several steps, he continues. "The decision to leave your family was taken not only by me. I must ask you not to speak of this with me again."

Since my father has mentioned no rift with Stephanos beyond his shock at Irini's treatment, I wonder what made my father favor this decision. But I will honor Stephanos' request in light of our friendship, and I resolve to say no more.

Meanwhile, Irini runs back to us and opens her hand. "Do you know what made you fall today as you ran?" she asks her brother, blocking our way.

"A stone flew up and struck my foot," Stephanos replies. "I felt it cut me, and I breathed a word of thanks to the Lord that it was not on the heel, like Achilles' weakness, or perhaps I could never run again. It was only the breath of my prayer that lifted me up and let me win."

"No. Look here!" Irini raises one palm. "This is what struck you, brother."

Stephanos removes the object from her fingers. There is no mistaking it—a flint-edged razor stone, one gray tip flecked with blood.

"The broken sandal, and now this!" Stephanos exclaims.

"It was not a fair race," Irini continues. "At the party, I heard two boys talking about the gold offered by Archipos of Salamis. He fully expected his lover, Phillipos, to win. He laid plans for others to fall or to be hurt. Menelaus says his sandal strap was weakened. They think Hector's wine was spiced. But it can't be proven."

"The stone only made me faster," Stephanos replies. "I am in fact grateful for its sting. Let's keep this flint to remember the day."

I must say something, though I do not know how to begin. I remove the olive leaves from my head and lay them in Stephanos' arms. "You paid for the victory with your own blood. And the crown," I add, "is yours, not mine." I draw a deep breath, preparing for truth–telling. "I did not want to come to your race. And when I came, I did not want to watch you. You are too strong and too fast for me to behold. In my heart, I have coveted your strength and your speed all my life. I am not worthy of even holding your crown. I have done wrong to you and to our Lord. But now, please take my sincere congratulations."

The childhood name I hate most comes back to me, only now the quail is hobbling my tongue, not my legs, flapping in empty words. My voice rings hollow, like the rhetoric we spoke before our classes in the academy. Better for me to grasp Stephanos' knees and beseech him to pardon my inner weakness. But this is not a thing any man can do. And thus, banded in my chest, the shame lives on and stings my spirit, sharper than any razor flint.

Stephanos meets my gaze and presses my shoulders. "Pavlo, do you think a single day has passed that I have not desired to sit with you in Jerusalem and learn from Rabboni Gamaliel?" he asks. "Is this envy of mine less than yours? But you will bless the earth with your learning, and I will always run for you."

5. The Purse and the Beef
Witness of Timon, Athens, A.D. 26

A coin clinking on the cobblestones catches my ear, but what makes me turn my head is the misplaced scent of a woman. Nose on alert, I spot her at once. The breath of roses, spiced with laurel no man would wear, wafts out from her boy's robe.

She sweeps to the ground and catches the bouncing gold piece I heard, her reach so deft that the men around her scarcely notice. Her tiny size is all the more remarkable beside the tall man who must be her husband. She laughs as she tosses the money into his palm.

Satisfied no thievery has taken place, I could turn my attention elsewhere, but my amusement keeps me watching.

Though this little coin catcher may not be a criminal, she is no Athenian. But around me, even the junior guardsmen under my orders will never notice her. They are simple men. They half fear, half revere the powers of my eyes, my ears, and even my nose as something that slipped out of their lineage. The careful mastery of these so-called animal gifts of mine have finally earned me status as senior guard at this year's festival of Dionysus.

Yet what a simple thing if the men around only looked, to observe the feminine proportion of "Rose's" hands, or at least the empty earring holes through her lobes. But close observation is scarcely likely here as the men hurry to this festival play. If guards or spectators look her way at all, what they will notice is the weave and absurd sun-yellow of her garb. It reveals near barbarity to the gaze of any self-respecting Athenian as surely as her foreign perfume. The man with her, while better dressed, has a fascination in his shifting gaze unbecoming to our citizenry.

True, it would be within my rights to stop the two of them and turn the woman back, but I decide to watch and wait. After all, the day is hot, the crowd is thick, and I need to be on guard for more important things. This couple from afar is showing not only ignorance, but a boldness that makes me smile. There is no law against Little Rose attending this play, just a deep-seated custom. It will bring me amusement beyond the skills of any actor to see what happens if she is found out. Even if she isn't, I want to witness how this tiny foreigner will react to what she beholds on stage, along with the only other women attending, those sitting in a few rows dedicated to whores.

With more men than you find in two armies, the crowd is stuffing the curving maw of our Theater of Dionysus below our great Acropolis. Not even a Roman eagle could watch them all. But "The Eagle" is what my fellow guards call me. What point would there be in divulging my name of Timon? My gaze is sharp enough to keep all my junior colleagues busy following my gestures of command when the crowd is thick, if the action becomes unruly. It is seldom that a wrongdoer goes missing on my watch. Like a captive eagle on the hunt, I am given just enough food money to hold me a hair's breadth from the edge of hunger, despite this rank that I have earned through years of honesty and diligence. My tongue is bitter with this condition of half starvation.

Today's play is among our greatest, enduring all the years since Aristophanes first won a prize for its production many generations ago. Like all our great dramas, it refreshes our souls, because even though the actors will recreate the interminable Peloponnesian War between Athens and Sparta, we are reminded of much more recent events, most notably the Roman intrusion and the triumph of our spirit over the order they impose.

Yes, "Little Rose" deserves to see this play all about women and what they tried to do to win the peace. But what could they do with no armor and no money, with children to tend and meals to cook? The one thing a woman can do when she really wants something—giving or withholding her love.

I select my observation place to the side to get a broad view of several hundred spectators nearest the seats Rose and her husband have chosen.

Our stage is built in clear sightline for all the viewers, with sound travelling naturally upward and inward around the huge semicircle of stone rows. Today's heroine is being played by Alexander of Crete. Now, that's a man who can quite convince you of his female persuasion through his high voice, soft tone, and even his delicate gestures.

Today, Alexander is in rare form as he begins Lysistrata's lines. I think, if he borrowed Rose's perfume, his disguise would be complete.

After just a few lines, as Lysistrata exclaims, "Greece saved by the women!" a sound like gagging wrests my attention. It is no scoff of amusement. I follow my ears to a Roman fallen from his seat, flailing around with a violence making him a risk to other audience members.

I have no need to sign to my companions; a junior guard leaps several rows through the air to catch the fellow. Unfortunately for the Roman, this help does not arrive in time to avoid his head smashing against the stone base of his seat. My colleague's chest is soaked in blood as he holds the unconscious man's head, shoves his own staff in the man's mouth to keep him from biting his tongue, and then picks the fellow up with the help of another Roman. The two of them ascend the steps and leave the play.

"It happens in the heat with him sometimes when it is very bright," I hear the Latin apologizing in execrable Greek to my junior guard, who is offering to help him find a doctor. Besides the spectators sitting closest to those Romans, no one's enjoyment has been disturbed, which is as it should be if we follow our duties.

By now a bevy of women have arrived on stage, representing all parts of our war–torn land. Lysistrata reminds them of their soldier husbands' needless absence, and how to get them back. "We must refrain from the male entirely."

I glimpse the exotic yellow of Rose's sleeve rising, brushing her husband's shoulder in an altogether playful gesture. Catching my breath at their closeness, I set my gaze to scope the audience as he whispers something to Rose at the same time as the actors in front of them resist the very idea of abstinence. But women are frail. The idea of swearing together and emptying a great bowl of strong wine pleases them all, and onstage, they drink up.

As the women triumph over a waning group of soldiers, and Lysistrata explains, "We propose to administer the treasury ourselves," I note three pairs of flying hands, then voices raised in a middle row.

Like our actors, these men have imbibed, but the drink makes them angry instead of happy. I signal, three of my guards race down the rows, each seizing an offender, and they are up and out. We have no tolerance of such behavior here.

As the women triumph on stage over the male forces seeking to reclaim the treasure, I look each of the men in the eye. "If you appear again in our theater, I will see to it personally that you are fined and humiliated. I never forget a face."

Now more sober, the men slink away. Meanwhile, I laugh with the rest of the audience as the old women's chorus soaks the old men bumbling to storm the gates of the Acropolis where the treasure is stored.

All in all, things are going well with our audience through the next scenes, where the manly Argos plays the much–beleaguered magistrate as he attempts to impose the order of men. He plays against his stage colleague Alexander as Lysistrata, who defends the ways of women and how their spinning of wool is like the good governance of Athens. Argos' exasperation at being dressed up first as a woman, then as a corpse, ripples through the audience. My Rose gives her rapt attention to the scenes, along with her wide–eyed husband, as the magistrate is bound up in wool. An ordinary day at the theater, perhaps, but even to me, guarding performances here these twenty years, these men are making a fine show today, Alexander most of all.

I keep my watch keen, but it is beyond me not to look at the scene to come, the best of them all. I know it nearly word for word. My eagle's ear and my memory equal the lettering educated men depend on to learn things and to rehearse such lines. Sometimes I can hear nearly a whole play inside my ear, and it is a matter of pride for me that I do not use the coarse, common speech of the streets, but at will, I can adopt the beautiful language that has surrounded me in these plays over the years.

Certain that their womenfolk share their desires, and hungering for the pleasures they have lost since the women's oath, men try to convince their wives to return to their beds.

Cinesias, the young husband of Myrrhine, appears. His desperation is made manifest. "Alas! Alas! How I am tortured by spasm and rigid convulsion! Oh! I am racked on the wheel!" He hobbles like a quail before his wife Myrrhine, while grasping a stiff leather cock.

As the audience sways with laughter, the thud of many back slaps is loud enough to echo. But Rose, who has sat motionless, responds with upswept hands as Myrrhine replies, "No, at least not till a sound treaty puts an end to the war."

Then Myrrhine appears to cater to her husband, first agreeing to meet in the Cave of Pan, but asking how she can purify herself in secret before returning to the other women and their oath. A bed would be better, she says, dismissing Cinesias' appeal to come together then and there. "Bad man as you are, I don't like your lying on the bare earth."

Some secret bellows Alexander pumps make his cock swell with each of his lines. Rose laughs loudly, then throws both hands over her open mouth with Cinesias' reply. "Ah! How the dear girl loves me!"

I see her husband's face turn red and his attempts to quiet her as the scene unrolls further with Myrrhine's arrival, first with the bed, then insisting on a mattress and pillow for her husband's comfort.

Cinesias' "I don't want a pillow, no, no!" is followed by Myrrhine's reply, "But I do."

Rose buries her entire head in her husband's shoulder, shaking all over, so great is her effort to block her laughter from distracting others. Most of the audience is in the same state. But seeing an honest woman laughing in public at what the men find funny in private makes me smile.

Something sliding behind Rose's robe sets my eyes back to her. Yes, a shadow—a figure even smaller than hers. That shape is reaching up to her sleeve. A flash, a slash, and the shade disappears between the benches.

This takes place in the time it takes to say the lines I have virtually memorized:

Myrrhine: "Would you like me to scent you?"

Cinesias: "No, by Apollo, no, please!"

Myrrhine: "Yes, by Aphrodite, but I will, whether you like it or not."

There is no time for me to signal; my eyes track the flying little shape, which by good chance is headed in my direction. I crouch, ready to spring, as it makes the end of a row. But all I must do is rise and spread my arms wide, because the form that emerges is not even as high as my belt.

I grasp it by its scruffy hair. "You!" I mouth in its face, more spit than sound on my breath. "Thief!" The revolting smell of it will mark me for hours, but I tighten my hold.

The creature does not even struggle; instead, it grows limp as I heft it up like a sack of wool.

"Where is your father?"

Its hand points to the stage.

My urge is to strike it, but I humiliate it instead. "And you want to watch the play, do you?" I continue in a hiss. "You'll see your play, all right, up here on the very top of the wall!"

Drawing a rope out of my pocket made from the tough cilicium from Tarsus, I knot the child's wrist to mine. It trembles as I heft it up and its backside thumps onto the stone of my surveying place.

"The money!" I snarl. It just shakes its head. Angry now, I uncurl each of its fingers, open its mouth, and finally shake the whole body like a dog with a piece of meat. From somewhere inside the ragged garment it is wearing, a tiny blade slips to the stone below, and a purse.

"Ah ha!" I say, pointing to Yellow Rose. "I know whose purse this is, and you shall give it back yourself." The little bag is made of the self-same stuff as her robe.

Its eyes grow wide as the choruses of old men and women merge to dance together, the naked form of Reconciliation pleases men from Athens and Sparta alike, and peace terms are hammered out with the promise of mighty celebrations at the Acropolis.

Meanwhile, I contemplate proper punishment. These foreigners do not have the right of Athenians to take someone before our judges. Perhaps Rose will simply demand compensation from the sire of this creature, which would be both just and permitted.

With the little thief burdening my wrist, it's fortunate that I note no further misadventures in the audience as I look on to play's end. True to his talent, Alexander tumbles in a womanly faint as the audience acknowledges his acting, and the rest of the thespians carry him aloft offstage, laughing.

I emerge from my place to stand close to the dividing aisle where the foreign couple will exit. When the child tries to hide, I shove it in front of me instead and broadcast, "Anyone who has lost a child or a purse, this way." This is more to humiliate the thief than to draw claimants, but I hope the father hears me.

I see neither shrinking nor recognition as hundreds of men file past. Yellow Rose is one of the last, since she and her husband continue their pointing, naïve gesturing, and open-mouthed laughter as lines from *Lysistrata* leap from mouth to mouth around the circle. When she is close, I attract Rose's attention with a gesture, and the couple stops, perplexed.

"Are you lacking anything?" I ask. That scent of hers is almost but not quite strong enough to override the stench of my captive charge.

Laughter returns to Rose's tiny mouth. "Oh, no, the play lacked nothing; it was wonderful!" she says in Greek that surprises me by its lovely tone and purity, but like the perfume, laced with a lilt of places far away.

"Are you sure?"

As the couple begins to show apprehension, I shove the thieving thing forward. It almost tumbles. Rose reaches out a hand to steady it.

"What is this?" It is the man talking now.

I yank the little thief's hands holding her purse upward toward Rose's face, though they come barely to her shoulder. "Look!"

The husband regards Rose with brows raised.

"Ah! I must have dropped this, because I saw how the

threads were fraying on this old robe of mine, and I did not repair them."

Is it possible she is trying to defend the vile little vessel of flesh below her, with its verminous head sunken to its chest?

"No," I bark, both to Rose and to the child. "Head up, you thief, and give this lady—er, this lord his possession!"

With no struggle, the thief's hands rise up and dangle the purse for Rose to take. If the woman inhales its stench—and she must—she makes no sign of it. Instead of slapping or cursing the child as any proper man would do, Rose reacts as a woman, of course. Oblivious of the remains of our crowd still straggling past and the dirt they leave behind on our stonework, Rose falls to her knees. Those tiny hands of hers take the child by both jaws and coax its face to look up. "Are you hungry?" she asks.

The child nods, which is its first response besides pointing to the stage earlier.

Even this foreign fellow has dropped to his knees now beside Rose, and he speaks calmly as Rose did. "Where is your father?"

Once more, it just points toward the stage.

As the eyes of this man and woman meet, again I must guard my aching breath as I witness the human awareness they have of one another, a language beyond my grasp.

"Do you mean your father is a thespian?" Rose asks.

The child nods again. Women—they may not win wars, but they usually win arguments, like a frightened child's silence.

"Come along, and let's find your father," the man murmurs.

Again, the thief nods.

Rose looks up at me as her husband grasps her arm to help her rise. "We will take care of this," she says.

But I shake my head and tug the rope to make the child's wrist jerk. "I will come with you. As guards here, we must resolve this matter."

Without argument, the couple nods.

"Well, go on!" I say to my little charge that has started all this trouble. "Lead us to your father."

The rope does not hinder our small criminal as it half runs, half crabs down the considerable hill toward the stage and the actors' building.

The couple walks behind me, purse swinging in Rose's hand. "Did you have anything in the purse?" I ask her, but she has not heard me.

Arriving without any introduction, I enter the lower stage, invisible to the audience. A man is lying there with others around him.

A tug at my wrist, and then the child runs ahead as a metal object clatters to the ground. By Zeus, this stinking little snatcher has managed to get the blade it had before out of my robe and to cut the rope.

But instead of fleeing, it is falling on top of the man lying on the stonework. My astonished eyes take him in—it is Alexander, today's main player.

"He's dead," one man states. "Died right there on the stage in front of the world, and carrying him off, we did not even know it."

"I told you there was a thing gnawing Alexander's guts," a second man adds. "When he has gone missing, he was not seeing a woman or getting drunk. Even the child could tell you that. He would have preferred no other death. Here's his little Cassandra. Hello, child! Come here. I'll give you your father's share."

A gasp from behind me, and as I turn, Rose is leaning on her husband. "Oh, I know it—the death smell!" Her date-brown eyes are spilling tears like olive oil from an amphora.

I ignore her outburst. "Where is its mother, then?" I ask the thespians.

"Dead, if she's not still rotting in her brothel. That whore pursued Alexander all the way to Athens to drop her baby and disappear," the same man who pronounced Alexander dead replies. "Oh, well, you're stuck with all of us now, my girl. Bitter fates lie on you to match your bitter name as prophetess of doom!" He laughs with a sharp breath.

The child's eyes widen and reach out to Rose and her husband, then to the man addressing her, and finally to me. "Unless, of course," the man goes on, and he smiles at me, "maybe you want to make a reasonable offer?"

Even if I had money, and even it were possible, it would be folly to take in some stinking, thieving little nose runner like this one. I shake my head.

"An offer?" the husband asks. "What do you need for Cassandra?"

The group of actors look at each other and now, they are smiling not as actors, but as hungry men in front of a table. But before they can answer, Rose steps forward, uncoiling the cloth wrapping her head. Night-sky beauty gleams dark from the oiled braids whose shape I had surmised. "No! I will protect Cassandra," she says in a voice bold enough for any thespian. "No one will buy her, now or ever."

All the thespians are so startled recognizing Rose's womanliness that they fall voiceless. She confronts them like an actor herself and looks each of them in the face. "My brother and I lost first our mother and then our father when I was not much larger than this girl. We will provide for her."

With a clearing of a throat to my left, I see her husband biting back tears, but nodding.

These foreigners have bewitched our attention and with it, any reply. Rose is settling down on the floor by the corpse and cradling the child on her knees. She swings her purse before the child. "Cassandra," she says several times until the girl's gaze turns from its father to her. "Take the purse," she says. "This was my Ima's work, and it will be yours. Your purse will not be empty, and you will know no hunger with Uncle Stephanos and Aunt Irini."

The child hesitates, then takes the purse and huddles into Rose/Irini's robe, almost hidden.

The man has approached and stooped low. "We can all be orphans together, all right?"

His words reveal to me the roots between them whose harmony clawed at my throat like an Egypt cat when I first observed them. This is no man and wife; they are brother and sister. True, I know no brother in the world who would bring his own sister to such a play as this one—but this is not my matter.

Meanwhile, all the actors remain motionless, speechless. I see tears in the eyes of more than one man, whether at the death of their fallen Alexander, or from the words just spoken.

"Then take her, and the gods be with you," says the leader, the man who was going to give Cassandra her father's share. "And have this, too," he adds, voice low with sorrow. He removes a ring from Alexander's finger and gives it to the woman. She whispers a word of thanks and drops it in the purse Cassandra has now draped around her neck. Then he returns to the corpse, opening Alexander's mouth to lay a coin beneath his tongue to see him across the river to the afterlife—if there exists an afterlife.

The four of us walk away from the heart of the amphitheater as Irini hastens to cover her head against prying eyes in the folds of yellow cloth matching her robe.

"You are a watchful guardsman," Stephanos remarks when we are nearly at the edge. "How can we thank you?"

I snort. "Wash off that little bundle of thievery and never let her run wild again."

Irini stops and meets my eyes. "Sir, attending today's play as I have dreamed of for so long, and now finding this child, make this the happiest day of my life. Without you, it would not have been possible. May I thank you in any other way?"

Because of my public position, I ignore her offer of money, which is yet another example of her ignorance and barbarity, like the Romans. But questions intrigue me about this peculiar couple, so I nod. "There is not far from the Agora a small taverna called 'Cattle of Hermes.' At this time of the theater festival, it serves the best wine and beef in Athens," I reply. "Any Athenian can tell you where it is, if your nose doesn't take you there first. Would you like to meet there tomorrow evening?"

Brother and sister nod as one, smiling. They understand that in my invitation, though they shall pay, they are also my guests as I introduce them to this wonderful locale—a fair enough trade, I convince myself. The thought of meat already has my mouth watering; just when was the last time I had any?

Stephanos swings a fearful, then laughing, Cassandra high on his shoulders. "Let's go, and we'll see the whole city now, little one!"

The next evening is cool and ocean-aired, just as I had hoped. I wait only a short time before the foreigners approach.

Tonight, Cassandra is clad in a proper dress of dove-colored silk, complete with dainty sandals. She swings between the brother's and sister's outstretched arms like a bag of apples. However, Irini comes as a man, since no respectable woman would visit a public place like this one. But again, her betraying breath of roses surrounds me.

I am grateful that the air holds no pollution from Cassandra this time. Tonight's only competition with Rose's scent is the delicious savor of the meat being cooked over huge fires here, making the place famous. In this taverna, we'll enjoy all the beef we could desire, along with all the drink our throats can swallow.

The Romans call men like me "triumviri nocturne," or "judges of the night." We police are expected to sound a man through and through with stern eye, ready action, and grasping questions. I am a master of this when performing my duties as "The Eagle." Rare is the time, however, for me to hold any idle conversation with Athenian citizens when not on watch—let alone with foreigners. Perhaps for this reason, my tongue runs away with me, as I hear myself say "So, who are you?"

Irini blushes. "Well, a woman."

All of us laugh, untying the awkward knot of how to speak together. Even Cassandra guffaws.

I make bold to look Irini in the face. She is not in the white-powdered disguise of our Athenian women, and no kohl edges her eyes. But even clad as this shabby boy, she carries a beauty as striking and as foreign as her perfume. All I can say, however, is this: "And a brave woman at that."

Meanwhile, the little one starts crawling under the surrounding tables with the zeal of a stray dog.

"Tell me this," Irini goes on. "You already knew before we descended to the stage. I heard your slip of tongue. You are the first man in all our travels to recognize that I am in fact a woman."

She is both observant and polite not to ask me her question directly, but I will not give away the pleasurable secret of her perfume. I counter with a limited truth. "Other men have the luxury of seeing what they expect and hearing what they wish to hear, but not a guardsman."

The woman laughs. "Listen, Stephanos, this man speaks almost with Baba's own tongue. The last time he said that was on our way to Jerusalem. Do you remember when I won an argument with you and Saul about the cure of Naaman the leper?"

The man nods, blushing. "You still remember winning over us, even back to the time of Emperor Augustus, sister, and he is gone these dozen years!"

I wonder what wager it was that allowed a girl to defeat her older brother, and what peculiar father would speak of the thing and make her proud of winning. There is no room for asking these foreign strangers, of course.

"And who are you?" Irini counters before I think of what to

say next.

"I am Timon, but I am called 'The Eagle.'" If these strangers wonder at this introduction, they are too polite to ask.

"If you wonder where we are from and why we are here, I will gladly tell you," Stephanos continues. He speaks of his time first in an academy and running the writing shop left to him by his father, then continuation at the university in Tarsus. "Irini is my right hand," he finishes. "You could find no better scribe in Tarsus than she is." And turning to her, he takes her hand. "I could never have lived the life of a student without your diligent pen and your patient hand to keep us alive. You richly deserve this time in Athens that you have always dreamed of."

"There are no books and writing things more beautiful than here in Athens," Irini adds, as though completing her brother's thought. "We promised each other we would come here some day to see your great city."

I am amazed at this distant Asian province of theirs where brothers take sisters to plays like *Lysistrata*, people beyond marrying age remain single, and women are scribes. But it is much better to rejoice in these lavish hunks of beef than to ask questions that could reveal my ignorance.

Meanwhile, Irini beckons to Cassandra and scolds her, but in a soft voice. The girl has stuffed not only her cheeks, but the entire front of her bodice with meat handed to her by fellow diners, staining the dress and swelling her shape. With reluctance, she picks the bones and marrow from inside her garment. She and Irini are well matched; for such small creatures, both these females certainly enjoy their meat!

"And you, have you guarded Athens all your life?" Irini manages between bites. "Is it a thing you enjoy?"

"Twenty years, and the festival of plays each year," I reply. "I've seen a lot."

"The soldiers serve twenty-five years. What about you?" Irini asks. "Anything must be boring by comparison to your surveying the theater. You'll miss such wonderful work someday, won't you? I have never seen anything so fine!"

The sheer simplicity of this girl's opinions and question leave me speechless. How can such a one be entrusted with copy work or writing composition of another's words?

"You don't understand," I reply. "I have not always been a guard, but I have been a slave all my life."

Brother and sister cast each other a peculiar regard. If they speak another tongue—and I suspect they do—it is sheer courtesy that keeps them silent in front of me. Of course, now that they know me for my lowly rank, this meal will come to a comfortless end.

This being the case, I speak on, making no effort to hide the bitterness beneath my tongue. Let them see the other side of Athens! "Oh, yes. It's the way we do things here. For an Athenian, it would be a humiliation to be arrested, or to stop someone of his own rank. But we slaves are below their high-born humanity, so it makes it tolerable to have us do their secret and not so pretty work." I gesture toward the gorging Cassandra. "At my birth, I was like this child, only I was left outside the city gate. For me, there was not even a whore to chase a father down like she had. I do not know who gave me my very name."

Each of us chews several more bites of this savory beef. At least there is this consolation. Cassandra has once more left her place at table to circle others sitting near us, smiling up at them. And though I listen on, I keep the girl's wanderings well within the corner of one eye.

"But—" Irini begins. I can almost feel her working out the "ifs" inasmuch as I can comprehend such a foreign mind. "At home in Tarsus, many people own slaves. But you are here doing the will of this city, not of one master."

"Athens is my master," I reply. "I report to a magistrate." That wide-eyed gaze of Stephanos that I first saw yesterday at the theater both amuses and annoys me. So I continue. "We slaves who are owned this way by the city that all of you who walk free consider so grand, well, we are bound and married to this city of Athena, you could say. We can take no bride, have no child, and use no money but what is given to us for food. That is why I refused your money yesterday."

Irini blushes redder than the setting sun tinting our cheeks. "I did not know. I only wanted to thank you."

Stephanos nods.

Meanwhile, Cassandra pulls Irini's sleeve. Glimmering in the child's hand are a bracelet and a coin. She tries now to slip them to her newfound mother.

Stephanos sees this, too, but before he can react, I lay a hand on his arm as my Judge of the Night mind springs into action. Rising, I scoop the pilfered items from Irini's palm.

"Friends of Athens," I call out, "we have our own little Hermes among us tonight. Yes, you will see, dear guests. Even as our beloved messenger god stole Apollo's cattle when he was only one day old, this little one," and I lift the trembling Cassandra high on the table like a statue, "this small one has pilfered from some of you. Now, have a look to your things. Who is missing something?"

"An earring," cries one well-known porne with her garish face, and everyone laughs as Cassandra shakes her head.

"My ring," another diner calls, raising a bare hand. Sure enough, out pops the object from Cassandra's mouth onto my palm.

Irini and Stephanos are frozen like men who have seen the gorgon Medusa.

Laying the ring back in Cassandra's hand, I say to her, "Go to the nice man and give him back this ring, little Hermes."

The man, who looks annoyed at first, must smile as Cassandra puts the heavy thing on his finger and bows with all the grace of a messenger. She does the same with the bracelet and the coin. Her subtlety dispels any doubt that this girl is the true flesh and blood of Alexander of Crete. After their laughing subsides, the guests pay no more attention.

When Cassandra returns to our table, grinning, I take her by the shoulders, lock my gaze deep into hers, and use the hissing voice of yesterday. "If you want to stay with your Aunt Irini and your Uncle Stephanos, you will never, ever steal a single thing again. Do you understand?"

"Yes."

I figure that since this is the first word I have ever heard her say, she means it.

Stephanos tries to dispel the discomfort Cassandra has created by returning to our earlier theme. "And tell us how it could be possible for you to become a free man." He cannot understand that this question for me is as agonizing as the memory of their orphaning that I saw in their eyes yesterday as they claimed the child.

"It is not allowed for a person to buy himself," I snap. Seeing either pity or misunderstanding in Stephanos' gaze, my bitterness nearly overrides my speaking of these hopeless matters. I have tried never to dwell on them. "The fates have woven my thread tight in the fabric."

At last, sleepy from the mouthfuls of meat she has consumed or frightened by my threat, Cassandra is acting almost human, laying her head on Irini's knees and her feet on Stephanos' thighs.

None of us meets one another's gaze, but trying to consume more meat is nearly impossible by now.

"It was brilliant to call Cassandra Hermes and to make the other guests laugh and avert their anger," Irini ventures finally. "Surely the name of this tavern, Cattle of Hermes, gave you this idea."

I smile, since telling the background of this witty name will remove from us the distress of our earlier conversation.

"Because the cattle we are enjoying are in fact stolen from the gods," I reply. "It is the choicest beef from the finest animals. But you will see, when you pay, you will need just a little silver, no gold. The meat is what our priests have laid on the altars as sacrifice to the gods in the temples yesterday. Afterwards, this taverna procures it for a very low cost, and we have more than we can eat here, as you see." I smack my lips with a fullness I have not enjoyed in months—or years.

The transformation on the foreign faces banishes my laughter. Stephanos rises with abrupt words uttered in their guttural, rough-tongued speech of barbarians. He cannot make it to the street before all the beef he has consumed erupts from his mouth. Irini looks scarcely better, with a face turned ashen. My bafflement is complete.

To add to the chaos, Cassandra springs up, shouting. With no mind to the bile around Stephanos, she grabs the shawl of an unsuspecting diner, snaking onto the top of a dividing wall and swiping at her new guardian's mouth to clean his beard.

Casting coins enough for ten of us to eat again tomorrow onto the table, Irini rises. My sheer perplexity leads me to follow her as she staggers out from Cattle of Hermes, Stephanos striding ahead of her and Cassandra tagging at her heels. "Uncle is sick, like Papa was sick," I hear the girl whimpering.

Stooping, Stephanos takes the girl in his arms. "No, Cassandra. I just ate too much," he murmurs, and I am close enough to hear the sadness in his voice. "I am not sick like your papa."

Then he turns to me. "We need no doctor!" He is striding ever faster once we are away from the crowd.

But Irini clasps his arm. "No," she says. "You know he has not intended any offense to us or to our Lord. Let me tell The Eagle what concerns us."

Still shaking from his retching, Stephanos sighs and sits down along the path. "Tell on, then," he says in a voice like a cracked tile.

Irini gestures for me to sit beside her brother, but she remains standing. Even so, her head is scarcely above ours. "We worship the god of Abraham, and of Isaac, and of Jacob. These are our father's generations from Israel. We know the Lord our God is the only true god."

Cassandra is sitting on Stephanos' knees, her gaze on Irini like an Egypt cat's on a bird.

"Eating anything that is unclean is forbidden to us, but something given to idols is unthinkable for us to even be near," she concludes. "It is an abomination. But you know nothing of our people, so you could never have understood this when you asked us to eat with you there."

"Our laws do not even allow us to eat meat of animals that are killed as Greeks kill," Stephanos says, raising his head. "But as we are here in Athens, we agreed to live as the Greeks. But to consume meat of idols..." Swiping Cassandra off his leg, Stephanos bows his head and retches again between his knees.

Looking at his bloodless face, I envision just how the ancient King Thyestes must have paled when he learned that he had just eaten his two baby sons in a stew, and I shiver at his recompense, exiled, old, alone. May the god of this undeserving Stephanos not repay him with such cruelty as our gods visited upon the king!

Stephanos manages to rise, and the three of them begin to walk away.

I cannot bear to have this human conversation end so badly, and perhaps the unaccustomed wine lends me courage. Raising my voice, I call out. "Wait, please. Do your people from Israel own slaves?"

Stephanos turns back and nods. "Some of them," he replies. "But in our law, no man may be a slave all his life."

As I catch up with them, Irini looks up at her brother, and he inclines his head with that wordless way they have. "We know this situation, and we think nothing the worse of you for your slavery. Our beloved father was himself a slave captured in Greece."

Now it is my turn to gaze in astonishment at these foreigners. "Freedmen?" I manage.

"For you in Athens, yes, we would be called that," Irini says. "In our city, it is less important."

An idea occurs to me to protect these odd but kind strangers after dealing them such a blow and offending their god. Perhaps I can avoid losing their company just yet. "Come, and I will show you something that perhaps will not be an abomination to you," I say.

As they follow me downwards through flights of steps along some winding pathways, I half turn to explain. "Many generations ago, even before the time of our great plays and the thinkers, Athens had a terrible plague. Our priests sacrificed to all the gods, but people continued to die. Finally, one thinker from Crete came here. He ordered sheep to be freed all over Athens, and where they lay to rest, they sacrificed each one."

When we reached the destination I had in mind, I point. "I have been told that on this altar it is written, 'To an unknown god.' Perhaps this is an altar to your own god. Perhaps you can make sacrifice here and free yourselves from your god's anger."

Cassandra has climbed the altar and is spreading her arms. "I'm Hermes, Hermes!"

Stephanos sweeps her down. If I had been another man's baby, would someone have picked me up to carry me around the hearth in welcome after my birth with such gentleness as this?

Brother and sister stand before the altar. "I believe," the brother starts, then he falters, looking to Irini.

"The Lord has put you in our path, Timon," Irini echoes in that peculiar manner of theirs, finishing each other's thought.

"Yes," her brother goes on. "It is no small thing to have this child, thanks to you."

"And it is no small thing that you live with no hope of liberty," Irini adds. "Is there any way we can help you to get your freedom?"

Every rule rises that I have ever learned as "The Eagle" to silence my tongue. But if I do not trust them and speak, I am certain that in my life, there will be no other chance like the one opening before this obscure altar. What more can I lose, even if they ignore or betray me? They have merely asked me a question, after all.

I weigh my words and say them slowly. "I have heard of it done, though almost never," I begin. My tightening throat has become as dry as Stephanos' bile-burned gorge. "Only another man can—can give certain people certain gifts, and I can die, so to say, in the accounts of the city and then leave Athens forever."

"Do you mean, one could go to your magistrate with such gifts, and you could leave the city?" Irini asks.

I nod at this woman obviously used to thinking in terms of bribes and payments, as she did yesterday at the theater.

Brother and sister survey each other, and Irini nods.

"Our lord has told us not to murder, and we have more silver than gold, but I believe we would have gifts enough to kill you on the Athenian scrolls," Stephanos says.

My ears must be deceiving me, or I must be dreaming after the great amount of meat and wine I have just enjoyed. I shake my head to clear it.

"Yes. If you are willing," Irini concludes, "you can have a different life."

As though a motionless wind descends from the altar, I feel and see this city where I have always lived, attending, but invisible. I picture the students here from around the world, shabby or splendid, lusty or studious—ears tingling after the stuff-headed philosophers arguing their pointless thoughts each day in the Agora—the crumbling of cobblestones and marble worn away by the centuries. And as much as this city is beloved home to many, I realize that I will live now and die later with no portion; my life will ripple like water into sand, leaving no trace. I shake my head at this realization.

Stephanos lays one hand on my shoulder. "If you decide this thing, meet us here tomorrow at this time," he says as they turn away. "And if not, may the Lord our God always overshadow you with his loving kindness for the faithful guard you remain."

Their footfalls die away in the young night, each treading its own beat. The spicy rose scent disappears on the breeze. I lay my hands on this obscure altar, then my head. An alien thing beats in my chest. It reminds me of my earlier anticipation of watching "Rose" at the play, and later, stronger, my appetite for the meat to come.

"Hope," I whisper. "This is what it means, then."

And my mind forges a prayer to the nameless god of these peculiar barbarians: "If I walk free, you shall become my god." Knowing that no prayer of request can go without a promise, I gird my thoughts by speaking aloud. "And I shall become this family's eagle, to my last breath!"

6. The River and the Aqueduct
Witness of Saul, River Jordan, A.D. 28

What a hard thing to set my ears on words spoken from this river as my eyes follow the chaos of flying stones! The child Cassandra has joined other children on the embankment upstream, and already she has attracted a following. Looking down from the top of this embankment, I cannot avoid watching.

After her pebbles race beyond the rest, she stops throwing. Like a Roman commander, she arranges all the other children into a line. Then she grasps their hands one by one, hooks her fingers to their wrists, and slings their arms to help them skip the rocks. Their yells of glee pierce the crowd around this place like an amphitheater, but one created by the wind and water of our Lord. We sit and stand and creep toward the teacher striding to and fro in the Jordan below us.

As all Jerusalem began twittering about this preacher, Rabboni Gamaliel spoke with me privately. He urged me to be his eyes and ears and learn the truth about the river man. I was honored by his final words: "You, Saul, above all students of mine, seek the truth, and you will see this man with justice, not with other men's eyes. This is why I have asked you."

It came to pass that as I prepared to depart, Stephanos and Irini returned from their years of traveling the world together, just before last Sabbath, and learning of my plans and purpose, they decided to join me.

If it were within my rights, I would have forbidden them to bring along gentiles, this stone-slinging child and an Athenian whom they call "The Eagle." But my joy at their visit after these years apart, and the patience I strive for like my teacher Gamaliel, and the child's clinging to them, made my desire impossible. As we left Jerusalem, Cassandra took glee in running around us. I soon grew tired of the delays her antics caused, and I insisted that she ride the donkey carrying our supplies.

This victory was short-lived, as the child continually complained from above our heads. On our second day, Stephanos let her down, but Irini became worried, as the child gained an oddness in her stride. When Stephanos offered to take her a while, however, the girl looked up at him and smiled. "Don't you know? I am walking this way because I don't want Uncle Thaul to be alone in the way he has to walk. People can look at me instead of him." Yes, she even said my name "Thaul," as I do.

As Stephanos' face burned, and Irini struggled for words to chide the girl, Cassandra looked up at me. "The people are not nice to stare at you, are they?"

I swooped down on this little bundle of defiance, and for the peace of Stephanos and Irini, I lied. "Don't worry. I don't care about people staring at me." Then I spoke on with truth. "But as for you, Cassandra, you are like a weed in the desert," I heard my voice proclaiming, "that reminds us of hope and of life. But don't walk that way. It will make your leg hurt soon, and it might ruin your new sandals, too."

"But what about your sandals?"

I shrugged. "Mine are much bigger and tougher than Little Weed's."

It was in this peculiar fashion that Cassandra made me her friend, for after this, she hardly left my side. "I'm Uncle Thaul's Little Weed, Little Weed, Little Weed!" She made a song of what any normal child would have found a curse.

Irini and Stephanos have shown an odd reserve when I ask about this Greek child and her Athenian guardian, though they promise me, when the time is right, they will say on.

Now that the sun is high, even more people are edging into the crowd. We have been here, sweating and swaying, since morning. Like my teacher, I must admit to itching ears after hearing so many rumors that have spread about this man John.

He is, they say, a desert dweller, removing himself from all the comforts of his household of the priestly order of Abijah after the death of his mother Elizabeth, who bore him in her old age. The desert brothers we call the Essenes exist childless, comfortless, with hearts fixed on God, living in caves and wrapping themselves in robes of a whiteness rivaling the toga of Pontius Pilatus, the new Roman governor.

But this John has no look of an Essene. True, the sinewy limbs dangling from his garment reveal a diet less than worldly—honey and dry food, it is said. He refuses any bread or wine the crowd wishes to ply on him. Rather, after each day, he and his disciples find a secret place to rest and pray. The bronzed ruddiness of his face and the red streaking his hair and beard indicate long days in places shadeless and arid. But his robe, barely belted in leather, is a coarse, meager scrap of camel hair. My tentmaker eyes recognize it for the cheapest stuff available, something that even the desert dwellers would cast aside at first chance.

John is repeating familiar words. "I am a voice of one crying in the wilderness, 'Make straight the way of the Lord.'"

Irini and Stephanos take turns whispering in Greek to the attentive Athenian.

Led by John's disciples, some in the crowd take up a chant repeating his words. Irini's voice edges into my ears with a sweetness I had forgotten. Her singing unlocks memories from our days as children. The three of us sometimes made music together, Stephanos on his lyra, I beating a drum, and little Irini intoning hymns of Orpheus or verses of Homer. The purity of her voice has scarcely changed in all these years.

A peace surrounds me as my eyes continue following the children on the beach below. I have lost all meaning of the ancient Hebrew words in the labyrinth of her song. Not in all the years at the Temple and nowhere in Jerusalem has a single voice pierced me to the heart in this peculiar way. The word "family" rises to my lips unbidden, though no one can hear me.

I only realize how far my spirit moved when the song ends, and John adds, "People of Israel, how crooked and rough is our road today!"

Murmurings like the river itself flow through the crowd. "He is surely Elijah!"

My earlier peace fades like smoke as I shudder at the ignorance around us. Why these people would think such a man is a prophet come back to life is beyond me. I tap Stephanos on the shoulder. "I thought even the simplest Jew among us would know he is using words from the prophet Isaiah, not Elijah."

Stephanos turns his eyes away from John with reluctance, but then he laughs. "Oh, Saul—you have lived in Jerusalem too long. If you had traveled with us to Greece, you would have tugged your locks from your head at the ignorance of the Jewry we saw, when we could detect a Jew in the first place!"

Irini nods in agreement before both of them turn back toward the river.

Meanwhile, others are responding to the name of Elijah. "No, not Elijah, but he is a prophet, like one of the prophets of old. What a blessed thing to hear words from his lips!"

Who is he, then? This question builds and rustles around us like a breeze before the storm, until one man raises his voice above the rest. "River man, tell us, please, are you our Christ?"

The entire crowd falls so silent that the croak of a stork flying overhead blunders into our ears like thunder. Quick-breathed expectation rises like clouds before the rain as every eye fixes below.

Throwing his arms wide, John draws a deep breath to reply as the children's stones continue plunking in the distance. "You ask who I am—" he begins, and cannot continue until he calms himself, gasping.

Even a child could see this man's heart written on his face. I shall surely tell Rabboni Gamaliel that John is a poor and simple man without a claim in the world to call himself "Messiah" and assuage the hope of these ignorant, needy followers.

Lowering his hands, he continues with less emotion, gazing into our faces. "Now hear this, and be my witnesses, and say this clearly to your neighbors and your houses. I am not the Christ, but I have been sent ahead of Him. I must become lesser, and He shall become greater."

At least the man has spoken harmless truth simply and clearly. But this is no consolation to those around us. Sleeves are raised to wipe tears, and knees are bent to hide many heads.

John sees this, and he sighs. "Do not be heavy-hearted. Remember, my children, the friend of the bridegroom, who stands and hears him, rejoices greatly because of the bridegroom's voice. My own joy has been made full at the very thought of our Christ. The One we all await is coming soon, soon now. He is mightier than I. His works will speak far louder than my poor words. I tell you, I am not even fit to untie one thong of His sandals. I baptize you with water, but He will baptize you with the Holy Spirit and with fire!"

While he speaks, the voice of John has grown in power until it echoes as though the stones themselves cry out. Simple as he is, I feel a stirring of wonder at the iron joy in his belief. What is Israel without such men of hope? If this joy brushes me like a breeze, it ignites the crowd like fire as they chorus with "Amen!" "Let the words of your mouth be written in our hearts!" Or simply, as Irini murmurs beside me, "Truth!"

But as I look down upon her, Irini's eyes are full of more

sorrow than I understand. Stephanos has not noticed, as his gaze burns on John with the rest of them.

The river man is weeping into the water, but his voice is strong. "I am here and must tell you, my people, the axe is already laid at the root of the trees; so every tree that does not bear good fruit is cut down and thrown into the fire. It begins even with those in high places." He lowers his gaze to the water, pondering. "What I say now, I have already spoken in private to Herod the Tetrarch. He has taken Herodias, his brother Phillip's wife. What law is there to justify this, can you tell me?"

"Roman law," the same man shouts who asked earlier, "Are you the Christ?"

John shakes his head. "The law of our God allows no such thing, and this is our law. I tell you, with the sin in such high places, our Lord's winnowing fork is in His hand to thoroughly clear His threshing floor and to gather the wheat into His barn; but He will burn up the chaff with unquenchable fire, unquenchable fire!"

Again, a song rises, led by John's followers. The water flowing around him seems to magnify their music as it swells and rises in the crowd. "Unquenchable fire, unquenchable fire!"

The loud-voiced man cries out again amidst the singing. "Curses on the amphitheater of Herod at the very gates of our holy city. Curses on the beasts that fight there, the wrestlers who struggle there, the musicians who play, and the horses that race there, for all is done in honor of the dead Augustus they call God!" He lifts his hand high above our heads with something glinting in the sunlight. "Look! Even these coins forged by governor Pilatus show Roman vessels to pour out oblation on the altar of their idols, and their divining wand!"

He throws two coins to the crowd, who shake their heads and pass them hand to hand.

The Eagle has slipped away from my friends, who stand transfixed by the chant "Gather the wheat into His barn! Gather the wheat into His barn!" wavering around us, drowning the coin man's angry words.

Can Stephanos and Irini possibly rejoice with this chanting of scripture turned nonsense? I cannot tell their thoughts as brother bends low to sister, and they whisper. Irini's sorrow continues in the very slope of her shoulders. I barely brush her sleeve with my thumb, but Irini feels the motion. Then, ignoring our custom, she joins hands with me as in younger days, and she clasps, as I clasp back.

How many days have come and gone since anyone has touched me with willing fingers, me, the cripple not allowed even to approach an altar of sacrifice? Again, the word "family" comes to my mind, and I must speak the word aloud above the chant around me to calm my spirit. May my Lord forgive me!

After some time, John's voice breaks the chant. "What does our Lord ask of us? Only this—to act justly, and to love mercy, and to walk humbly."

The cry "Amen! Amen!" choruses from the lips of Irini, Stephanos, and the throng.

The crowd presses to river's edge, and John meets them in his dripping, water–shrunk rags. "Come, confess your sins and be clean," he calls. "What else has the Lord asked of you?"

As I glimpse The Eagle moving ahead in the crowd, I wonder what John will say when he spots his Grecian clothing and style of hair.

Meanwhile, John turns to a group of Temple men, several of whom I recognize. As leaders, they are at the head of the crowd. But instead of stretching his arm in welcome, John seems to turn to stone. I see his eyes searching each face.

Our Pharisees are humbling themselves by attending and wetting their robes in this water, even if it is the holy Jordan. Like John, they have frozen in place.

"Do you bear fruits in keeping with repentance?" he asks them. Though his voice is soft, it carries in the breeze to the rest of us.

The men turn to one another, not to him. They do not meet his eyes in their astonishment.

John's voice rises again like the priest whose household he came from. "Men, do not begin to say to yourselves, 'We have Abraham for our father,' for I say to you that from these stones—" and turning, he gestures to the children on the beach "—God is able to raise up children to Abraham."

I see the group step aside, leaning toward the water and whispering. Though I cannot hear the words, my years in Jerusalem make me witness to their thoughts. The insult John has just thrown at them is as sharp as a stone itself, after all. Who but we are children of Abraham? To whom has our Lord shown mercy? To the Egyptians who pursued us out of bondage, or perhaps to their horses, drowned as they rode them into the sea? I think not!

As they turn away, one rends his garments. Seeming not to notice, John bellows to their backs, "You brood of vipers, who warned you to flee from the wrath to come?"

As I imagine Gamaliel in their midst, I am full of relief that my teacher will not need to bear this volley of insults, and that he will only hear of it truly from me.

The rest of the crowd hesitates until the Temple men have ascended the embankment and passed me by. Then John extends his hand. "Come!" he intones, voice low and tender as that of a father. "Confess your sins, repent, and be clean. Come for baptism!"

So tight has been my concentration as I am frozen here like a graven image, I failed to notice that Stephanos and Irini have followed the crowd forward. As John clasps the shoulders of each one in line, whispering something, each man and woman in the crowd who desires dips beneath the water, only to rise up again between his steady hands.

I find myself nearly alone on this part of the embankment.

Wafting up are cries of all emotions, from grief, to fear, to joy. I am reminded of sheep without a shepherd.

The children on the beach have wandered into the Jordan as Cassandra copies the river man, mouthing words, then pushing the other children beneath the water and pulling them by the shoulders above the surface again, with a gentleness I had not expected.

From behind my back, a voice startles me. "You did not come here to be baptized." It is the same loud man from before.

I turn. "I am a disciple of the teacher Gamaliel from Jerusalem. I have come to learn the truth about this man," I reply, knowing nothing else to say.

He waves his hands at the crowd shoving and shuffling below us. "And all of them need to know the truth, too." He pauses, and as though reviewing my words, he repeats them. "A disciple of the teacher Gamaliel."

"Yes, these more than a dozen years, now," I answer, expecting his courtesy.

But he does not smile. "Then you must know the other abomination this new Roman governor Pilatus has contrived, within the priestly order of our very great Temple."

Turning away from the crowd to face the man, I shake my head.

"You do not know? Tell me the truth, man! Aren't you in the Temple every day?"

Trying to moderate my voice from anger at his sneering, I reply, "I must make my own bread, too; I sell cloth from Cilicia many days each month. And I am not a priest or from the order of priests."

He shakes his head and seems calmer. "But have you seen the start of stone cutting and laying for Jerusalem to get her water?"

I have heard of the thing, but I shake my head.

"Oh, a fine project from our caring Roman governor, a noble

tribute to his power, with the collusion of Herod the Tetrarch," the man sneers. "It will be a labor of years and of thousands of men."

I nod. "Such aqueducts always are, sir." The term of respect comes out of my mouth before I can stop it.

"Indeed," he answers. "Indeed. But you do not know where the money is coming from."

When I do not reply, he goes on. "Not from our taxes, though those are certainly great—and certainly not from Italy. No, man. You really do not know, do you?"

Biting my annoyance, I snap, "I told you already, I do not know of this thing."

If John speaks with the strength of a shepherd, this man hisses with the power of a viper. "Well, then, let me tell you, sir," the man replies. "This so-called kindness from the rulers is financed with our own corban money."

I do not think I have heard him right, so I repeat his phrase. "Corban?"

"Indeed," he snaps. "The very money our widows, our Jerusalemites, our people from all over the world pour into our Temple treasury for things devoted to God. This is our recompense, what our very high priests," he spits on the ground "have done to appease the rulers. They sell their power at a high price to the governor by letting him use our corban for his Roman project."

"Corban money," I repeat in disbelief. "Our own Jewish corban, our charity."

In my heart, I feel two beatings. There is the horror of this accusation, if it is true. And there comes a second horror—I imagine this man's spittle on my own face, were he to know that I, too, am a citizen of Rome.

The man's laugh is bitter. "Charity indeed!"

A cry from behind me and rising above the rest of the crowd makes me turn away from our conversation. Someone with a stick is slashing his way through the people, past the believers milling and weaving to receive baptism. I hear shrieks as his staff strikes those standing in his way toward the water.

It is the Greek voice I know, The Eagle. Now past the watery crowd, he is swimming with fast, smooth strokes, having flung his robe on the bank. I glimpse something dark floating in front of him before it disappears below the water. A child? Calling a Greek oath, he swings across the troubled current like a fist. His stick flashes in front of him, and in a moment, emerging on the other end, Cassandra's head rises. He tugs the stick to safety, grasping the limp bundle of sopping clothes to his chest and releasing his staff into the current.

"Cassandra!" he cries as he swings her high, throws her face down onto the bank, cleared now that the crowd has seen what has happened, and beats her on the back. Even John has stopped his dipping as he looks toward the figures.

The child's tight cough is audible as the crowd draws a breath of relief. Stephanos and Irini, wet from their baptism, emerge to kneel beside the child with one man from the crowd, gesticulating with The Eagle as they exchange words. But she sits up, shaking herself off like a dog, then clings to The Eagle, retching and trembling.

My feet trudge their own way down the slope toward my friends and the Greeks. While I am still at a distance, Stephanos walks directly to the river man, who inclines his attention as my friend speaks into his ear. With a gesture, John motions The Eagle toward himself. "See how our Lord raises servants from the Greeks, from the slaves, from the ones we sometimes curse," he calls to the crowd. "See how a man has put down his life in the river for a small child, and not his own child."

As Stephanos turns to The Eagle to make him understand, the Athenian turns to face us all. "Today, your god will become my god," he calls. "I am the smallest servant of your people."

"Servant of the Lord," Stephanos corrects in warm-voiced

Greek before he speaks The Eagle's words to the mystified crowd.

"Today is the day of our salvation, and indeed, the day of salvation for this man!" John calls as he dips The Eagle beneath the water and raises him up like a child. Again, his disciples lead the crowd as it sways and lifts hands high and sings this refrain with joy.

In the evening, I pull out the old tent bag slept in by Irini when we first traveled together to Jerusalem. I wave it in front of Cassandra. "Sleep here. But only if you promise to stay there all night and not to sleep late when we leave in the morning."

She nods, smiling, as she grasps the tent bag, twisting like a locust as she squeezes tight inside it. The Eagle curls close beside her, no stranger to the roughness of the ground.

Desiring to have words with my friends, I have built a fire a distance from our tent, where the cool air can warm as we speak and the others sleep. "After the events of today, I believe it is the time to tell me of these Greeks of yours," I begin, with no introduction.

"Sing to me of the man, Muse, the man of twists and turns driven time and again off course," Irini begins.

All of us laugh at her artful rendition of the first words of the Odyssey that humor our talk. As my eyes turn heavenward, I can imagine music from the beautiful constellation that the Greeks call Lyra shining in the night sky.

"These twists and turns have taken you far indeed, my friends," I reply.

Stephanos speaks of our years apart, beginning with the purse of gold he won at his great race, but which Irini insisted on saving for the future. She persisted in being not only the right hand of Stephanos' trade, but the one who won bread by the careful tracings from her inkwell into the night, as she copied writings for his studies and for his fellow students who lacked her diligence.

I still long to judge him, using Irini so, until I remember myself in Jerusalem as I devoured the law, supported in turn by the labor of my father and brothers. But these are men who take work upon themselves willingly, while Irini should have turned to gentler things. My heart clenches within me.

"And at last, we began to tread the edges of the world, as we both longed to do ever since our trip to Jerusalem with you as children," Stephanos concludes. "It is what my sister's work and my book trade have freed us to do."

The firelight does not allow the expression of Irini's gaze to reach my eyes, but I recognize again that same sorrowful slope of her shoulders as during the day, when she stood below me in the crowd. It was when John clearly spoke that he is not the chosen one. When she remains silent, I voice what I must know. "Was this not a tiresome thing to you, and a burden, Irini?"

"Not a hard thing," Irini says. Turning to Stephanos, she sighs. "In fact, it is a harder thing for me being a woman."

But at last, she looks like who she is. The fire gleams from her hair, now parted and well oiled, from her nut-brown eyes and straight, white teeth, even from a ring of beaten gold on her finger. This is not the boy-clad "Aaron" of the Temple or from the writing shop, or even from the races of our youth. Instead, my eyes know the appearance of a woman whose head rises just to the height of my own heart. My lips long to unbar words to reassure her that the you-boy of the past need not cast any shadow between us now. But from a man marked imperfect of limb by our Lord, it is a mockery even to think of this thing. Yet I must choose some words eager to spill from my heart in defense of this woman Irini, who fills my eyes. "But our Lord has made you a woman, not a man to stride and scribe and hide yourself behind your brother's robes," I hear my tongue reply.

Irini glances first at me, then longer at her brother. "You know well, both of you, I did not have much chance to be a woman in Tarsus after the races—even if I had wanted it. And after, what womanly arts could I learn working in our shop and traveling all over the world with you, Stephanos?"

As if I see it before me, but with new eyes, I recall even after these years, how Irini's face was bowed into her hands after the race and as Stephanos spoke of their family, and as she bound her brother's wounded foot, the cries I heard at the race. That day, I thought her tears were for her brother. Only now do I understand more, that she was weeping in shame at being found out before all the city there as the daughter of a slave.

Irini's words and my memory hang between the sparks that divide us. "The truth of our family was not a thing that I could keep unspoken that day, Irini," Stephanos whispers, and it is as though I am not present. "It was to honor our father and not to deny our family respect that I told the city of our past."

Irini nods. "I know this. I cannot disagree or take back your words, Stephanos. But in building our story, you also destroyed my prospects of living as a woman. What freedman with simple mind and dirty hands and presumption do I want as my husband? It is easier being a boy with you than a woman, as I say."

I feel her shame in my own body as smoke billowing through the door of a tent.

"Indeed," Stephanos replies. "But there are freedmen Jews here in Judaea, and many, as you know."

Irini snorts. "Freedmen from all the Hellenistic world who do not know Isaiah from Elijah!"

My heart shrinks within me as she casts back to us my earlier words.

Stephanos turns to me, as though he has not heard his sister. "I want to remain here. There are many opportunities I have seen even these few days for our trade that we have established with the Greeks and which we can well apply in Judaea, Irini and I. And we can support our new family."

Though I greet Stephanos' wish to remain here with joy, my

dismay outweighs it with his latter words. "Family?" I demand, standing up. "You insult our people, Stephanos. How can you call an uncircumcised Greek and a gentile girl family?" As often when my voice rises, I splutter, though perhaps now it is the smoke I have inhaled.

Irini replies as a woman. "The girl Cassandra was a new orphan. Even as your father took us in, Pavlo—how could we not protect her? She was with actors who would have used her like an animal. She is still a lost shadow, but she will find her way with us."

"All right, perhaps it was a good deed for the foreign girl," I start. "But this man?"

Stephanos replies. "He was the guardsman who found Cassandra thieving from Irini. He carried out his duty to catch her, to tell us, to administer justice. Later, he invited us to a place in Athens, where we talked."

As he pauses, a glance shoots between himself and Irini, and I see her shake her head as lightly as a palm leaf in the breeze.

"And later, when he believed we stood in need," my friend continues, "he showed us to an altar as it is written there 'to an unknown God' to make sacrifice."

I stamp my stronger foot. "He defiled you! What nonsense is this? We have a God we know."

Stephanos seems not to notice. "And when we learned at that altar of his hopeless slavery, and of his desire to respect our Lord—"

"Or to spare us from punishment after an abomination," Irini goes on. "He is an honorable man. We had to help him to leave his slavery."

Stephanos raises one hand, a troubled look crossing his face, which is turned toward Irini. It is his turn to shake his head.

"Leave his slavery?" I repeat.

"Yes. He was announced and written away as though he had died," Irini goes on. "He had no master but the city, and no one to mourn him. It was not such a difficult thing to purchase his official death there. Our ways are not their ways, as you know."

"Thanks be to our Lord," I snort.

Stephanos interrupts me. "And today, John showed us that there is no slave or freedman, and no Greek or Jew. Today, we were all of us one in the river, even Timon The Eagle."

But his words hardly enter my ears as Irini's face transfixes me, and with absolute certainty, I know that it is the face I beheld when she was in her eighth year, and I was twice her age. As our eyes meet, I wonder at her thought that has joined mine.

"Do you remember the Temple, Pavlo?" she asks, and her voice is hesitant.

Knowing exactly what she speaks of, my blood switches course in my veins. "The Temple, and your face then, and your face now," I answer despite myself. I bite my tongue to force silence from my blood.

Stranger to my pain, Irini only smiles and nods. "Yes. The wonder I knew today was like that day, when you and I witnessed Rabboni Gamaliel's words together. I know now what I was too small to understand then. It was a vision from our Lord."

I have wondered for all these years, and this night I know. Irini witnessed Raboni Gamaliel's words with her own eyes, along with me, then, indeed!

"But today in the river, we have both seen and heard the nearness of this promise of our Lord," she continues. "Pavlo, if you had followed us there, you would have known. The water was a living, moving, loving thing that wrapped us in its glory. I called to our God, and my body to my very hair sank down, and as I was part of the river, I saw the sky open above us. I saw..." Her voice trails away with her hand. "I have no words to tell you what I saw, Pavlo!"

Her wonder surrounds me as if a motionless wind brushes my face. But even as I cannot speak to Irini of the bond from my heart to hers, even so, nor will I be able to voice to Rabboni Gamaliel this truth that they have felt in the Jordan. Yet to remain silent before my teacher regarding their witness that is beyond my grasp will make my own witness incomplete.

"Yes. What we lived and saw today was a thing no man can say in words," Stephanos falters. "But I am certain of this: It is the promise we are waiting for."

As I behold here my oldest friends, I am not sure which of all these is greatest—my weariness, my astonishment, or, I must name it now, my love. They vie within me like snakes that fork my aching tongue. My friends are helpless to understand this silent confusion springing in me like grass in the desert at first rain, this rain being their presence. Like a swelling wound, I feel my soul this night, which is run ragged with knowledge, but wrung dry with aloneness.

When I can master my ears and their pounding once more, I hear.

"It is the way with Cassandra and with Timon," Irini continues. "Both of them have been used and taken by those who meant evil. Both of them seek truth in their hearts. God intends the evil for good, even as He did when He promised Joseph a better life, just as He promises the rest of us."

"Enough," I voice after a long quiet, when only the fire sputters its syllables into the night. "Your words are like water over my head."

I rise and begin walking toward the place where Cassandra and The Eagle lie before turning back to them. "But know this. You will be a joy on my path if you remain in Jerusalem, even if it means your living with these Greeks."

7. The Steps and the Witnesses
Witness of Many, Jerusalem, A.D. 29

1. Witness of Cassandra

Now in the house where we live, there is a courtyard, and in the courtyard is a well, and by the well there is a wall, and in the wall there is a stone with a hole. And under the stone with a hole there dwells a house snake. And beyond the well, there stands the door, and inside the door there is a room. And in the room there is a floor, and on the floor there looms a couch taller than me, and on the couch taller than me lies Uncle Timon. And Uncle Timon is sick to be a Jew. For to be a Jew, he saw a doctor, and in the doctor's hand there was a knife, and with the knife, the doctor cut Uncle Timon to make him a Jew.

But to make me a Jew, I needed no doctor, because Uncle Thaul said all I need are the talking lines, and Aunt Irini has made these talking lines, and from the lines I start to make sounds, and from the sounds I get a voice, and with the voice I make words, and in these words I can hear of the Lord of the Jews. And the Lord of the Jews is Uncle Timon's Lord, and the Lord is Uncle Stephanos' Lord, and the Lord is Aunt Irini's Lord, and now He is my Lord, too, because I read the talking lines with my voice, and I know this is true, that my God is my Lord of the Jews! Even Uncle Thaul says the Lord is my Lord, too, and he is the wisest man in the world, so now I can be two things, Uncle Thaul's desert weed and also a Jew!

But even Uncle Thaul cannot tell me everything, because only Uncle Timon can tell me stories about Athens far, far away, and only he can tell me great things about my father, Alexander of Crete. And he tells me that my father was the greatest actor in Athens. Inside my ear this morning, I want to hear Uncle Timon's voice, because I can no longer hear my father's voice. But inside my eye, I see with no shadow the stage in Athens. And on the stage is Papa Alexander, and Papa Alexander is a doctor, and the doctor holds a wooden staff, and on the staff there is this snake, and with the staff and with the snake, Papa makes men well.

Now I walk to this stone where there is the hole, and out of the hole, there is the snake, and in the bowl I bring for her, she drinks her milk, and after the milk, she sees my Doctor Asclepius stick, and on her belly she follows the stick, and on the stick, she wraps her skin, and up the stick she climbs!

Then into the door and across the floor and up to the couch I walk as Doctor Asclepius with my healing stick and my house snake. And Uncle Timon is asleep, and then Uncle Timon opens his voice, and from his voice are no talking words, but a moan like the wind around the walls. And on his face, he opens his eyes, and with his eyes he sees Doctor Asclepius, and then his talking voice is very loud from the couch on the floor, through the room and out the door, and he says these words. "Child! We are Jews. Jews do not like snakes!"

And I tell him it is a house snake who protects him, and I am Doctor Asclepius who loves him.

And he tells me to go to Aunt Irini and get the talking book. And he says in the talking book, God curses the snake, and I will see the talking lines, and I will speak words about this thing.

And I tell Uncle Timon, I cannot get the talking book from Aunt Irini today. But I will certainly care for him until Doctor Lukas returns, as Aunt Irini instructed me. I also tell him words as she told me last night before she put me in my bed. She must visit the Temple today. And I may not go with her, and many Jews will go with her, and they will go to a man who has just arrived in Jerusalem and ask him to change his heart about a certain thing.

2. Witness of Irini

Perhaps just once in my life I am first in Jerusalem to witness the beautiful Lyra of Orpheus, shining its five-starred music from heaven to my eyes. Leaving the household well before predawn, I took care to step quickly, softly. Yet it was no small thing for me to once again put on this robe the color of old saffron. I have not worn it in these many months living in Jerusalem, since the scribing I do for my brother is safe behind the walls where we live, and I never need to go out alone. Yet the nature of you–boy, along with our years of travel, all these memories surround my shoulders in its folds and wrap my mind as I shelter my flattened braids in its matching strip of cloth. Only now, while my strides lengthen as a young boy's would, and while my head raises boldly unlike a girl's through years of inhabiting this garb, my heart can never return to the small Aaron who will appear to the eyes of others once day breaks on these Jerusalem streets.

But for now, not even the cock has crowed, and I walk with assurance that I am unseen. As Lyra dwells in my eyes and in my mind, my wonder has time to expand. I ask in my heart, should I tell such stories to Cassandra of this lyra, of men like Orpheus, the noble Greek musician, who loved so deeply that he risked journeying to the underworld to spare another from death? There are many wonderful stories among our Jewish writings, but to me, none quite like this one. For what man in all our scripture would venture death for another's life?

I hurry onward, dismissing thoughts of Saul that linger like beggars too numerous to feed.

By first light, I have arrived at the tribunal, near the great Temple. Already a small crowd is standing on a sloping square before the building where the Romans conduct their court and govern our affairs. And while I have no thought of what I can do here as we make our plea to Governor Pilatus to release his hold on our corban money from the Temple, not to act would burn my soul.

With The Eagle laid up on this day after his cutting, Cassandra promising to care for him, my brother dealing with a buyer of Greek scrolls, and Saul in the Temple, my presence here will remain a secret. The doctor who came yesterday will return today to assure Timon's proper healing. He is a young Hellenist Jew named Lukas who rushed to help us last year while at the River Jordan. He tended to Cassandra and found her whole after her near drowning, examining her with such gentleness and care that the child was unafraid, and she will not fear now to let him in and follow any order he gives her until I can return home.

As rough-tongued men surprise me from behind, I realize, as in all our years of travel, how much better it is to be in my old and too-familiar manly disguise. As always, this robe removes my fear. The men seem merely bored, tense, and shiftless as they parade behind the growing crowd. Their language is not Hebrew, probably Samarian, not all of which I understand. It is an oddity that these half-Jews would pursue such a concern as ours, but their presence makes it clear that they share our cause today. My heart grows grateful to them despite their strangeness.

Ignoring them, I look ahead to the colonnaded portico dominating the square. Before my eyes take it in, a roar rises in front of me as a door swings and a man in white emerges. It is the governor. If I were taller, I could see him well. As it is, I can only glimpse and know him through the whiteness of his toga, the shortness of his hair.

Pilatus ventures to the top of the steps dividing him from

us, and as he raises his hand, we quiet. "You," he begins. Even this one word of Greek displays his Latin imperfection of tongue to my ears. A tall man beside him voices his Greek in Hebrew. "Why are you here? To thank me for my visit?"

So great is our shock at Pilatus' greeting, either its ignorance or its arrogance, that no man speaks or even stirs. Only the doves whisper through the sky above and perch on a cornice.

"Well? Speak."

The stink of our sweat rises, even so early in the morning. Then one man steps forward. In Greek more faltering than the governor's, he nonetheless voices directly to Pilatus, mistrusting the interpreter, perhaps.

"You have taken holy money, sir."

Though I curse my smallness for the blindness it creates in a crowd, I bless it whenever I move. Step by step, I succeed in worming all the way forward to have a better view and a better hearing.

"I have taken no money into my hands," Pilatus replies, and again his words reverberate in the interpreter's Hebrew after him.

The crowd rumbles until Pilatus speaks on.

"Your own Temple priests, however, have allowed money to the aid of your great city that longs for water as a deer sighs for the river."

Has this Pilatus read our holy writings to find such a phrase? I think it more likely that the Temple folk have pasted these ancient words from the Psalms of King David onto his lips. I see others like me shaking their heads.

"It is true that our people need water, sir," the spokesman replies. I am not far from his side now, just below the steps. "However, no good thing can have bad roots."

It is Pilatus' turn to appear at a loss. "Which of you Jews," he finally begins, and the interpreter slows to match his tongue, "who among you has ever tried to solve your own woe of dryness here? In our empire, we bring you culture, and comfort, and now water to give you a better life. What contradiction can you find to argue with me and call this a thing with bad roots?"

Our crowd turns on itself. No one speaks; they whisper in their sleeves and sway to tell one another their thoughts. But my eyes fasten themselves on Pilatus as they longed in the dawn to grasp the shining Lyra.

Does the governor Pilatus perhaps feel some power from my fixed regard? "Even this boy here," and he gestures to me. "Even you could tell me the benefit of water."

If only I had lowered my gaze or remained distant, but it is too late, now that many eyes turn to me. Attention is the one thing I must always avoid. Greeks like Timon would be merely amused or titillated uncovering my disguise, but here in Jerusalem, a woman clad as I am could become the subject of stoning.

I draw a deep breath, for now I must listen to our Lord. He seized me by the heart in a dream for three nights, and with words I saw like those of Rabboni Gamaliel, he bid my feet to come to this place. While I am certain of hidden guards, of spies who will hate me and who, if they ever knew me, might turn my and Stephanos' world upside down, I bow, and I climb the steps in obedience to the governor's beckoning. My weakened knees surrender as I kneel before Pilatus. I do not touch him, but my arms circle before me in Greek fashion as though to clasp his knees.

With all my heart pleading to the Lord, I find words, strong, unbidden, and unthought, rising from my soul to my lips. "Sir," I voice in Greek and repeat before the astonished interpreter in Hebrew, "perhaps you touch the Temple money with clean hands. It is a great thing that Herod began and that you continue to lace the waters and to bring them to our thirsty land."

I am no stranger to the crowds of cities around the empire,

but never before have eyes devoured me this way, both the multitudinous staring from below, and close above me now, the flint–gray gazing of the governor.

"But, sir," I continue, "the money you use comes from our Jews from around the world. They have sent it in a holy trust to assist the poor and adorn the temples of our Lord, from the wealthiest merchant to the poorest widow. Your aqueduct is new, and noble, and needed. However, it is not a holy thing."

These eyes above me pierce me like a dagger, and then the lips part. "I see we have a shabby little scholar worthy of his god."

But what Pilatus has meant for insult, the crowd takes for good as the men smile and nod. "Speak on," they seem to whisper, though the only whisper now is the wings of doves.

I remember my Passover dove, my Pegasus, and I smile and regain courage. Perhaps these birds are even her descendants.

"Sir, we pay our taxes to Rome, and we learn your ways. Please keep our way here and leave the veil drawn between your works and our holy places."

He shakes his head, not to deny my words, but in his confusion.

As I lift my heart to our Lord, a final thing that I can say to this man rises to my lips. "Do you know of our father Moses?"

Pilatus does not answer, but he nods.

"Our people wandered with Moses in the desert for forty years. They hungered, and our Lord gave them quail and manna. They thirsted in a place, and our Lord said to Moses to strike a rock, and when he did, a spring arose."

I stand, turning away from Pilatus and toward the crowd. My vision spins as I face the mass of men who look at me but will never see who I am. Then I remember Naaman's little slave girl, the one with courage to believe the good news of God's healing of lepers. Thinking of her, my fear is swallowed in joy as the full impact of the faith, hope, and love of her message overshadow me. What I say next, the Lord gives me voice to call out to my people in beautiful Hebrew worthy of dear Saul. "Whether you build your aqueduct, or whether an earthquake swallows it in the ground, our Lord shall provide for us always. It is his everlasting promise!"

The Samaritans standing at our fringes seem unmoved, but the hundreds or thousands of Jews standing below burst the air with their laughter and their joy. "Amen! Amen! It is the truth!"

Pilatus turns his attention away from me and toward the throng taking heart. As I have heard from many Latins, he launches a supposed question that is actually his passing of judgment. "What is this truth of yours?"

As though I am a mewing Egypt cat, he signals me away, then strolls to a comfortable chair in the middle of the porch. My face burns with shame at his dismissive gesture, but my heart has never beaten so proud since the day I first came to Jerusalem. I am a tiny, weak vessel, but the Lord has used me to give these men the heart they need to carry on today as they cheer and call brave words to one another.

When I descend the steps, I feel my heart slowing. I must express praise and gratitude too great for words to our Lord. Like the comb oozing its honey, my spirit is full as I turn my feet to the Temple close at hand to offer up my prayers for our people.

The morning sky has taken on the same blue of our River Cydnus that I remember from our first day in Jerusalem, and I am reassured that like the promise of our Lord, some things will never change.

It is easy for me to disappear once more. I pass through the thick of the men who as always are swaying, sweating, and swarming above my head.

3. Witness of Timon

I was glad to be cut on a day when Jerusalem has begun to hum like angry bees. I need no Hebrew to hear the rhythm of oppressed people righting their spirits and strengthening their voices, but as a foreigner, I am relieved to convalesce a while inside with good cause, as the Jewish anger builds around the city and even on the streets by this house.

While it is difficult for me to understand the idea, explained to me by Saul, of this charitable money freely given by priests to a governor, and more difficult to believe that the people consider the water he will bring to their city a thing not of the God we worship together now, I do know enough to understand the fire in their hearts. Our true God is one, not to be mixed with other things any more than gold may flow with lead.

The fire in my loins is a piercing, yelling beast of pain, though it was a small price indeed for me to pay to become a true Jew of our Lord. But Cassandra's words have unchained me from my drugged sleep—also, they have unleashed my fear for the boy–woman Irini.

The cost of rising from my couch on this first day from my cutting is one nearly too high to pay. Still, I brace myself like a Spartan, reminding myself of things far harder during my Athenian slavery. This pursuit of Irini is a thing of only a day, a few hours, perhaps, and that any real man must set himself to endure.

I am full of regret as I ask the child for help. "We need money today."

Cassandra does not hesitate. Drawing Irini's faded purse from under her new garments where she always hides it, she removes a small object. "Are you still sick? Or are you not yet cut enough to become a Jew?" she asks. "Here is something I can sell on the street, or you can give it to the doctor." Into my palm, she presses the ring of her father that the chief actor gave us that day in Athens.

I shake my head and stifle a groan as the room spins with agony before my eyes. "No, child. I will never take your only inheritance from you. But tell me this. Where does Uncle Stephanos keep his money?"

Cassandra laughs. "Not Uncle Stephanos. Aunt Irini keeps it."

"Well, where does she keep it?"

The child is silent, eyes lowered.

I continue, "I told you never to steal again, and this you remember, even after our whole year journeying and living in Jerusalem, I see."

She nods.

"You're Uncle Timon's good girl. You do not need to tell me where it is, then. But today we are not stealing, child. We are taking this money for a very special and important purpose. Now go, take away your Asclepius stick and your house snake, hide your father's ring, and bring me a little silver."

She obeys, unsmiling.

"It is a very important day," I repeat as I take the coins she brings. I try to bring her heart. "And we will not walk like simple Greeks. We will be like gods in a chariot!"

Keeping the stream of my breath as steady as my gaze, I fix my full intent on rising, then on walking to the door.

Cassandra clasps my hand. "I see you will need a chariot, Uncle," she says. There is only pity in her voice, and I manage a smile and hide my agony behind it.

It is no chariot that we find, but some poor contrivance on wheels to carry us far. I pay with a small bit of Irini's silver and promise Cassandra we will give it back.

The swell of the crowd echoes from the stone streets and walls even two stadia from the tribunal. My fears fly fully founded. Near the fringes of the throng, I see men dressed like Jews, but who are soldiers. My guardsman's eye spots each one immediately, with cudgels and swords hidden beneath their robes. The Roman governor has used guile, not force, to spy and protect himself—at least, guile thus far. Only thanks to the unbending current of my breath can I find strength to hobble on, spotting at last some steps across from the tribunal where some beggars and not so many men mill around. I set my spirit fast and manage to climb.

From this perch, I see the portico clearly, and there, seated alone, the governor in his bright white toga, trimmed in the purple reserved for rulers. I have nearly forgotten how easily I spot these proud-faced Romans, so much have I seen since leaving my so-called home city of Athens. This man is wordless, pitiless, his eyes swaying like wind in an olive tree around the people.

The crowd is something else. Even a fool standing where I do would recognize the happening. His silence goads them. Like slow-moving but unstoppable honey from a bee hive that has been pierced, they ooze first to the slabs of white marble marking the front of the tribunal, then to the bottom of the stairs, and finally, voices rising, they seep upwards, step by step. Some of the strongest, loudest men among them lead the way.

I need no Hebrew to take in the rise of the tidal wave. If I had my junior guards, I imagine how I could divert them, divide them, and assuage them with entertainment or with the promise of a meal. But as I am weakened today and a stranger in this strange land, I can only pray for the hand of our Lord to brood upon them.

Now, amidst the milling and confusion, a glint of yellow sears my gaze. I turn my full attention, and indeed, there is Rose/Irini—flashing like gold amidst the desert-like browns and olives the men wear. Not even a snake could pass through the tight throng massing between her and me.

For a moment, I raise my eyes skyward, and there the great Temple shimmers in the new sun above. And though it is like a swallow flying against a storm, I breathe a prayer to our Lord and take Cassandra by the shoulders. "If you have ever run, run now. If you have ever hidden, and slunk, and spied, you must do it now. We cannot reach your Aunt Irini in this crowd, but there is one who can call to her and perhaps make her come away from this madness in that temple there. You must find him."

"Uncle Thaul!" Cassandra cries.

I nod. "I do not know where to tell you to go there, or what you must do. But you have the gift for these things, and you will find him, and when you find him—"

"I will bring him to you and you will tell him what to do!"

Oh, Lord my God, grant me the gift of Cassandra's faith! "Yes," I reply, and my throat is thick not only with pain, but with love and fear. "Now go. Stay close to the edge of everyone. Speak to no man but your uncle. And if any man tries to snatch you," I hand her all but one of the remaining coins, "throw this money into his face and run like the wind!"

She vanishes before my words can echo from the wall.

In the meantime, this Jewish honey has spread and molded itself thicker, further. I count a dozen steps from the flagstones below to the portico of the tribunal, and the Roman, sitting like a monument, speechless, motionless, stares out at them all from above. As Cassandra departs, some of the men are at least to the seventh step. The soldiers at the fringes of the crowd shift their feet and mumble together, their eyes fixed on the Roman.

Then one man's voice, roaring in Greek, rises above the rest. "Tell us, the money, back to the Temple, yes, or no?

The Roman is untouched by his passion. Like a dog in the shade, he breathes deeply and continues his gaze lingering over the crowd.

"Ne, i ohi?" ("Yes, or no?") the man repeats. The rhythm of his voice spreads like a plague itself over the throats of the many. "Ne, i ohi? Ne, i ohi?" The Greek words bounce and echo; they hiss, they buzz, they throb through the entire square.

"Ne, i ohi? Ne, i ohi? Ne, i—"

Many breaths pass, during which I pray with open eyes—pray for the speed and skill of Cassandra's tiny feet, for the power of the tribunal to overshadow these yelling madmen! Even my pain is conquered in the ferocity of my praying.

The crowd has scaled to the eleventh step. Their shadows already cross the cracks of the porch, nearly to the magistrate's chair where the Roman sits and sways. Looking at him, I almost believe that the words around him are building his power—that he finds them not a threat, but a song.

"Yes, or no? Yes, or no?"

My single hope is this. The flash of yellow swallowed in the crowd keeps appearing like a flower in the dust, and it is heading away from the tribunal and toward the Temple. I tremble, beseeching our Lord as I have never begged any magistrate, any Athenian, any being. "Oh, God, only you can save and keep her!"

Meanwhile, the loud-voiced man has taken the lead and stands past the final step, directly on the floor of the portico, level with the Roman. I cannot see that man's face, but his shoulders are bunched in fury. If I could stand beside him, a quick twist of my rope would fell him and scatter the following, mindless mob. But I can only observe here, as the pain in my loins twists me nearly to fainting.

Then the loud man lowers his head, and before him, striking the Roman's foot and robe, he shoots arrows of well-aimed spittle.

What comes next, the most bumbling of my junior guards could have foreseen. With a single gesture, the Roman releases the soldiers edging the crowd to commit their handiwork.

The "Yes, or no!" turns to screams of terror, of dismay, of fury as the few hack down the many. While some run, others fall and are mashed down by a thousand feet. As some swordsmen pierce, others cuff, and roar, and even behead. In my many years, these eyes of an eagle have never witnessed such blood that blushes the very face of the tribunal.

"Kyrie eleison!" (Lord, have mercy!)

4. Witness of Saul

Among the other students, I am proceeding into the great Temple in the new morning, but I do not know how to pray. These ritual words clang like meaningless cymbals. Hot voices are building by the tribunal below our house of the Most High, voices of many who have worshipped here as I do. If the Romans strike—our Lord alone can deliver our people. Yet how now shall I address my Lord concerning the high priests? These men of God should rally our prayers and our faith, and they must be blessed and protected by our Lord. Yet by their own volition—I have learned this thing with listening ears and peering eyes— they have released the corban to our oppressors. When I asked the highest priest I dared, he snapped, "What business of yours is this?"

My head is pounding as I strive to follow the ritual chanting, but my ears pursue the louder and louder throng. Once I hear what sounds like "Amen!" and shouts of joy, and my heart lifts like smoke over incense. But my mind remains uneasy, and of one truth I am sure, that we will know the outcome of this thing immediately as it comes.

The sunlight crosses the floor and pinches my foot as our Pharisees and Sadducees debate on and on, as is their way. Does the soul exist only in our body as the Sadducees claim, or, as we argue back, does a spirit within us exist beyond the end of life on earth? As a Pharisee, I have pushed my thoughts toward the hope of eternal life for all my years under Gamaliel—and yet, who can force in a belief, even within his own heart?

From beyond my aimless prayers and drifting mind, I hear another thing, rhythmic as water pounding. If I could imagine the crowd using Greek, it would have the sound of "Ne, i ohi? ... Ne, i ohi?" I am diligent to set my mind away from this thing, but it seems to beat through the walls, through the air, to wrap my unwilling ears, and I sigh.

Another rhythm, soft as a raindrop at first, but edging closer, distracts me again. It is the voice of a child, sharp but sweet, piercing. "Da–da–da! Da–da–da!" The tune is something familiar, not a thing I can lay aside easily.

"Da–da–da!" ever closer. A corner is turned, or perhaps a door opened, and now it rushes on me with the force of motionless wind.

"Little Weed! Little Weed! I'm Uncle Thaul's little Jew, and I'm his Little Weed, too!"

Then as she enters. "Uncle Thaul! Uncle Thaul!" Always my name as I speak it, and twice over, as though to double the mockery of it.

In the name of our Lord, how has this creature like a demon contrived to arrive here, let alone to find me? Cassandra races toward me and clasps my knees, nearly pulling me down with her. "Come! Come right now!"

I want to strike her face, throw her to the ground. The confusion of this day is mighty enough, and now, I have no choice but to leave and take her home. My finger nearly snaps with the force of her tugging.

Perhaps it is a mood of confusion shared by my fellow students, for I hear a laugh as I depart, red–faced. I try to push her against the wall to admonish her, but she is far too slippery and rapid.

"Now!" is all she says. "Come now!"

As I nod, the grasp of her fingers is like the iron of slaves' manacles.

I gasp as we reach the outer court and I look beyond. What had been a roar has disintegrated into shrieks, groans, and unearthly howling. The money changers have abandoned their tables and fled their places, the animal sellers leaving their beasts to their own devices.

"Aunt Irini!" Cassandra shouts. "She's here, and Uncle Timon needs you to make her go home!"

"You, Little Weed, stay here, and do not even consider returning there!" I scream at her through clenched teeth, and I shove her down on the top step of our portico.

I have not had time to take in her words when standing high on these steps. I spot a familiar flash, Stephanos' yellowish old garment, and I know with certainty that Cassandra is right. Irini's small form is of course surrounded by larger men, and she is struggling to make her way toward us.

From a side street, I see a troop of legionaries. They have spilled like yolk from a broken egg out of Antonia fortress, and they are descending in force.

"Irini!" my voice shoots forth, and then, "Aaron! Irini! Irenikon! I am coming!"

The steps are too steep for me to descend quickly, so I throw myself, trusting the bodies below to safeguard me from the stones. Indeed, it is so, and I flay and fist and froth my way toward the spot where I believe I have seen her.

Just as I reach the yellow, the soldiers approach. Irini has fallen, but seeing me, she reaches her hand to mine. Knowing nothing else but to bring her up from the ground, a strength in my body I never knew rises in my veins; I snatch her like a tender fruit and pull her to my shoulders. No matter that I sway like an angry camel—no worry that the men around me are striking and scratching at me in anger as I scrabble with rage in their midst. The only real thing is this—the Temple is here, the steps have carried us upward; Irini is saved! Today is the only day in my life that my feet race like Stephanos' over every broken sandal, each torn robe, and the blood under my feet.

I force forward, as Cassandra hurls objects down at the men blocking my way, and the path clears.

Irini goes limp on my shoulders, and I lean on a money changer's table to let her descend from my back with gentleness. Even through the chaos, the long-remembered scent of rose and laurel which is hers alone anoints my heart with blessing. She slides downwards. I spin around. It is time. At last, I can, and yes, I must speak the tender words I have held for Irini so long barred within my soul.

Then Cassandra shrieks. I turn to stone.

There is a story told by the Greeks of a great musician named Orpheus. So mighty was his music, even the trees uprooted and the streams debanked to follow the sweetness of his lyra, the beauty of his song. Though Orpheus could have had any woman, he loved only one, Eurydice. Their marriage lasted one year and one day. Then an adder stung Eurydice's foot, and she descended to the underworld.

But this Orpheus loved Eurydice more than life itself. He resolved to risk all his mortal existence and dare to go, living, to this place where the spirit of his wife had cast itself. Again his lyra aided him, calming the savagery of first the boatman across the River Styx, then the three-headed guard dog, and finally even the furies and all the evil of Hades' realm. Lord of the underworld, Hades was so moved by the love in Orpheus' music, he agreed to set his wife free. Orpheus needed only to keep his eyes fixed on the upper world—on life.

Was it the doubting in his soul, perhaps some temptation to speak and hear his wife's voice and look into her eyes? Or could it have been some simple stumbling of foot that wrenched Orpheus' head to turn? For the story, this is unimportant. All that mattered was the law. When Orpheus turned, his beloved Eurydice was there—and then he saw her, in disobedience to Hades. And according to the law of the gods, as Hades had spoken, so it became. Eurydice turned to smoke; she was gone forever.

And for the man-clad woman Irini—was it the yellow of

her boy's robe that maddened a soldier to make her a target? Could it have been my own stumbling, placing her just in harm's way? Perhaps she was wounded already, only worse as we ascended the stony Temple steps.

A javelin had pierced her through and through. Her eyes, turned skyward, stream tears. My own tears mingle with hers, and with her flowing blood. Her braids unveiled unwrap like envious snakes spreading over the table. There are only a few of her breaths left.

"The Temple—the dove," she whispers. "We never told you." And then, worst of all, with more force and more tears, her brow furrows with pity. "Oh what a hard thing, dear Pavlo—to kick against the pricks as you do."

As I feel Irini's spirit unlacing toward our Lord with each breath, my years of doubt unmist into a faith beyond the mind's knowing or the eye's seeing. Irini has a spirit indeed, indeed!

I lean close, then closer, but all my words have swallowed themselves. Irini's eyes wrap into mine. Her throat rasps like dry grass in the wilderness. Her voice comes so still, the air of her words cannot even brush my face. "The promise. Always remember, we have God's promise. And Pavlo—Pavlo, I remember you."

The crowd from below is roaring and crashing. But here, only Irini. And her spirit, which departs her now.

"And I remember you," my aching lips reply.

5. Witness of Stephanos

Today, I am a sinner of sinners, a fool of fools! Saul's earlier invitation to join him in prayer for our city on this day strikes my memory like a rod. How could I think of doing commerce on this day? There was no trade and no talk of trade. With the arrival of Pilatus, all Jerusalem was first frozen, then it swayed with hope, and now it lies bathed in blood. I am a fool for ever leaving our house and then returning, finding not one soul of our family, not even The Eagle. Instead, I saw Lukas the physician coming to anoint Timon's wound, standing at our gate in distress. He said a doorman at the gate of a more prosperous house nearby claimed he had seen a Greek and a small girl departing in a cart, heading toward the fracas.

"If even a single thread catches the wrong way as he moves, he could bleed, and he could die!" the doctor told me.

Lukas offers to follow me, but I am already half down the street, pushed forward by his words. I hike my tunic and rejoice at the speed my racing days lend my feet. I make my way toward the Temple by way of the tribunal. Indeed, Timon the Eagle is there, face white like marble with pain and eyes red like coals with weeping.

He calls to me as I see the streets bathed in blood, and the steps, the gates, the walls. "They are in the Temple," he cries. "Go there!"

I cannot answer him as I stumble past Roman and Samaritan soldiers hoisting bodies onto their shoulders and tugging them away. Even the steps to the Temple are covered in wounded men, and the stink of blood pollutes our holy place. Choking back my bile, I strain and forge my way on through the throng.

At the top of the Temple steps, where first we arrived, bought our dove, where first my sister read the sign that has marked us Grecian ever since, I hear a sound like the bellowing of an ox. It is no ox, but a man. And it is not just any man, but it is Saul. And beside him, wrapped in my sister's headscarf, small Cassandra, trembling and lost-faced. And beside them, my unwilling eyes take in the yellow of our Ima's robe—and inside it, the one who was my sister.

Words from my father's voice spoken on a day of our journey to Jerusalem spring to my mind as he approved Irini and reproached us boys for ignoring a truth in the story of the healing of Naaman. "Our eyes learn to see what they wish and our ears hear what they expect." On this day of dread, as though scales fall from my eyes, I see in death what was hidden to me in life.

Irini's words, too, spoken from the night following our baptism, return to me: "In fact, it is a harder thing for me being a woman." And my own voice mocks me, the voice that spoke these words in reply: "There are freedmen Jews here, many of them, as you know." And I see inside my eye Irini's face in the firelight, there, in the desert, the day of our baptism, and how she looked at Saul. And I hear again his words to her: "But our Lord has made you a woman, not a man to stride and scribe and hide yourself behind your brother's robes."

As though rising above myself, I understand my sin. I, Stephanos of Tarsus, son of my freedman, Alexandrian father, know myself this day to be worse than a whoremonger, more severe than a slave master. True, I promised my sister to see the whole world as we had dreamed of since childhood—and I held faith with this promise—but at what price? The price is this: I have divided Irini from her womanhood; I have blistered her soul into something not yet male, but no longer female. How else would she have taken courage to come to this place in a boy's garb—and now, oh Lord my God, have mercy—this! What began as making a boy of my poor sister was protection, but later, I see how I turned it to my own uses and conceits, as I encouraged her to attend my race in manful disguise while shattering her life with our father's story. Then, later, she never complained, but rather, she listened to me and posed as my brother in building the trade we needed to live. To this day, all the nights of her scraping reed pen in her endless scribing pursue my inner ears.

She opened her mouth only once, in revealing her heart to Saul that night of our baptism, but the words will blister me forever. "In fact, it is a harder thing for me being a woman."

It was the nearest thing to love they spoke together—Irenikon, freedwoman, unworthy of becoming wife to a true Roman citizen of the respectable lineage of Saul of Tarsus, and Saul, unworthy by his faltering, earth-shaking walk, to be husband to my sister. Had my closed heart understood, would not a small word from me have opened the door to their love, and today, would not this shattered world be different?

Now Cassandra approaches the corpse. Ignoring the blood, her right hand opens the mouth of the one who was my sister, and her left hand places a coin beneath the lifeless tongue. I would stop this idol-worshiping gesture of hers, only it is a thing done in love. Would not my stopping break the child as I have already broken my sister?

Those who see the tearing of my garments next must believe it to be the rending from my grief at Irini's fresh death. I cannot deny this. But far more, this shearing of good cloth marks the bitterness I stamp onto my own spirit. One more thing I say, with lips trembling. "My Lord, I have not intended this evil, but now, what promise can there be for good?"

Part II
The Dividing

8. The Garments and the Song
Witness of Gamaliel, Bethany, A.D. 32

"You see, Cassandra, today even the lowest cobblestones of our road are clothed in splendor!" My tongue grasps for words to give this young girl heart. "And you in your new dress are as lovely as the lilies of the fields!"

The gentleness of Cassandra's "Thank you, Rabboni Gamaliel" belies the shrewdness of her eyes, which lance directly through my smile. If I knew the source of her disheartened walk, the root of her silence, I would attack it. Instead, I struggle like a man trying to read a scroll in darkness.

We have departed Jerusalem this morning on what should be a joyful walk to a house in Bethany. Today, Timon is to marry there.

Following the massacre of our people three years ago that he witnessed, Timon, this newest of our Jews, requested through Saul, who persisted to me, to be allowed to sit by our main gate each day. "Blesses to you, Rabboni. Without you, I not could to serve by this great house of our Lord!" he greets me each morning in his faltering yet heartfelt Hebrew.

As we leave the city walls behind, it is no surprise to struggle against a great crowd of incoming pilgrims fixed on the heart of our holy places. Today is just a few days before Passover. Yet I wonder at this oddity of raiment on the road that I have just remarked on to the child. Many around us are still stripping garments from their bodies and leaves from the palms, the figs, and even flowers and weeds from our road. They are casting them down or waving them above our heads.

Saul and Stephanos have disappeared ahead of us. The crowd divided us as my attention fell on guiding Cassandra rather than on following them closely.

The sheer thrust of people moving against us outweighs our best efforts to struggle forward. We find ourselves pushed to the side of the road, trapped against a close wall. The thronging flow is more and more—mostly the country poor and dispossessed, who line Jerusalem each year at this time to come to our great Temple, but also many Jews from all over the empire, as the multitude of colors and weaves of their garments attest.

I catch the glimmer of gold on Cassandra's hand. "What ring is this?" I ask her.

"It was my father's ring, from Athens," she answers. But looking to the crowd, she asks, "Rabboni, would you take it for me? I am afraid of the people."

I enclose her hand in mine, and she slips it into my fingers before a man could glance twice. "It is a good thing that you ask me to do this," I answer. But with the gold this child has laid on me, I feel a keen duty to protect her, and not only what must be her one and only treasure.

Cassandra interrupts my thought to ask what I, too, desire to know. "Why are they walking so proudly and yet throwing their clothes away, Rabboni? Her voice sounds muted as it rises through my sleeve, since I have stretched an arm in front of her to bar her from the throng and its pushing.

"It is indeed peculiar," I answer. "By tradition, the Jews sometimes welcome a mighty man this way."

Cassandra laughs. "So why don't they throw things in front of you when you walk?"

If it were a proper thing—if I were guardian of Cassandra instead of Stephanos—I would embrace her for her sheer sweetness. I join her laughter instead. "You know I am no ruler,

Cassandra."

"But you rule your students. Uncle Thaul and Uncle Stephanos always do what you say."

Again, I laugh, but I respect her serious question. "Well, there are people who rule over others as the Romans do now, and there are wise men who give you thoughts for your mind. But as King Solomon tells us, only the strongest man masters his own spirit. He is like a man who rules ten cities. And always remember, your uncles are men as great as this."

I think of Saul like a deep-rooted tree, remembering all his diligence since childhood to master each tenet of scripture. But Stephanos' zeal to learn in these last years in Jerusalem has transformed him into an unstoppable wind. The very thought of my students and their love of learning is sweet water to my spirit.

A shout has begun from well ahead, and while first we can hear only the tune, soon it turns into a song. "Hosanna! Hosanna!" It is the ancient cry of salvation all pilgrims voice to our Lord. The phrase rises around us like heat from a fire. "Hosanna! Hosanna!"

On this day, there is no fire, but biting wind instead. The people's cloaks and coats thrown down are indeed a sacrifice. However, many of them stand smiling even half stripped, clapping their hands beside us, while others march onward. I draw the shivering Cassandra closer before I notice two things; her lips, too, have taken up the song, but her eyes are spilling tears. At last I will know the cause of her fallen spirit. She can hardly say the word now for her weeping, "Hosanna!" which interpreted means "Save" or "Deliver."

I force my back to the crowd in order to look her full in the face, though the scraping at my outer cloak may tear it from the sheer force of those moving on the road. Fear is what I read in Cassandra's face—and sorrow beyond anything a girl of her years should carry. "What is this thing heavy in your heart, child?" I ask. If the crowd allowed, I would kneel to speak with her, face to face.

The sun catches her tears, but her hands do not move to wipe them away as she cuts short her call of salvation. Then her lips voice something, but I cannot hear her words. As she gestures somewhere ahead of us, I surmise that her dread involves these adopted uncles of hers. Perhaps even now she recalls a far more terrible crowd. I cannot forget her face the first time I saw her; this was on the day she became witness to the death of Stephanos' sister on the very steps of our great Temple.

I resolve not to remind her of this, hoping I am wrong. Instead, I gentle my voice. "We shall remain still here until the crowd thins a little. Do not be afraid. I will stay standing here just in front of you."

Meanwhile, a new cry has built among the people, and even more pilgrims and curious Jerusalemites are merging and swirling around us. "Blessed is he who comes in the name of the Lord! Blessed is the King of Israel!"

Many taking up this new chant have harsh Galilean accents. Some are swiveling their necks like doves, or in a few cases even walking fully backwards while peering and staring along the way. The road is soft as a carpet, leaves and raiments piling left and right as a path opens in the center.

Above those walking, I see a young man on a ridiculous mount. It is a donkey colt barely strong enough to carry him. When I lean forward, as he comes nearly upon us, I perceive several other things as mismatched as the man and the colt before us or the cloth–strewn road beneath us. The man's hands spread outward as though blessing the people—and then they fold inward, as though to gather them under his robe, as a hen would shelter her chicks. But his eyes lack the persuasion of his hands. They are sad and pensive eyes that, rather than sweeping the crowd, seem to pierce spectators along his way, one by one.

Could it be his concentration to stay astride the skittish colt that overshadows his face with worry? One thing I can say—nothing kingly marks this man, though the eyes of all the crowd follow him.

Cassandra tugs my sleeve. "Rabboni, please, let me see from your shoulders, just for a moment." Her tears are gone. Lifting her will protect her and perhaps diminish her fear, so I oblige. Her weight is hardly more than a lamb for slaughter, though I push this thought from my mind.

"He has red in his hair and his beard, Rabboni, look!" Cassandra says close to my face. "I remember this man, because when I was very little and I was with Aunt Irini and Uncle Stephanos and I met Uncle Thaul, he was there in the river, or someone who looked like him. You know, I can see things inside my eye from then and even from Athens, and I will never let myself forget them."

A prickle on the back of my neck arises, but not from the chill of the wind. I will not tell the child of the recent murder by Herod the Tetrarch of the one she calls the man in the river, nor of the popular rumors that the donkey rider is indeed this man come back to life. Saul inquired and learned that the river man and this man, if he is a wonder worker from Galilee as I suspect, are in fact from one family. So their resemblance could well be explained by this. A doctor of the law such as myself must not be moved by rumors, nor by a swaying soul.

"Blessed is the King of Israel!" the crowd's chant swells around us again.

The prickle on my neck has turned to cold sweat. Facing the wind, hearing Cassandra's words and the crowd's words, and beholding the disharmony of this man's gestures that embrace us, but his eyes that pierce us, wonder turns deep within me, though I can give it no voice.

"Save, oh, deliver!" Cassandra calls again, voice roughened from her earlier shouting.

She tugs from inside her sleeve, and from above my head, she launches something that serpents directly toward the man on the colt. It is a cloud–yellow, long rope of cloth like a headdress arching just above the ears of the colt before alighting in the rider's hand.

The man turns toward us as the cloth swells out like a sail in the wind, held by both his hand and Cassandra's. As he approaches, his heavy eyes lighten, and he smiles toward the child and me with a softness transforming his face. First, he nods to us. Then with a flick of his wrist as light as hers, he returns the cloth. The material weaves back on itself and flies back to Cassandra's outstretched arm through the wind in our faces. "Keep faith, daughter," he says, so quietly that only we can hear. "And you also, Rabboni."

How is it that he has called me teacher?

"Do you know him, Rabboni?" Cassandra echoes my question aloud.

The wind has stopped blowing. As the man and the colt come directly before us, the well–dressed road has erased every beat of a hoof, each sweep or stamp of a sandal. It seems to me that time itself has paused in the quiet, leaving only the child, myself, and this rider in the sheer silence. This stillness is surely akin to what Elijah must have known as he hid in the wake of an earthquake, before he was blessed to hear the still, small voice of our Lord.

I consider the many years that I have taught boys from all over Israel visiting our Temple for the Passover feast. For some years, one boy with ruddiness like this man visited at Passover and asked wise questions and listened with all his heart—but there have been so many boys, faces, and years.

I shake my head. "But perhaps he knows me," I murmur back to the child.

In the moment when the man's eyes fix on me, I cannot see, but I feel something sweeping my face, entering my heart. I breathe in awe and fear and whisper to the Most High as Cassandra calls again in the stillness, "Hosanna!"

Then time moves again; a cheer arises from a few in the throng around us as they have witnessed the turning of Cassandra's peculiar scarf.

"The teacher says faith the size of a mustard seed will grow into great and wonderful things," an old woman says from beside us. "Blessed is this color in our midst to remind us and give us heart again."

I am alarmed as the attention of people around us shifts from the man on the colt to us.

"Fold the cloth, Cassandra!" I order.

She slips from my shoulders, alighting on a palm leaf borne in on us with this wind, and the scarf vanishes in the sleeve of her outer cloak.

Now that the rider has passed, any attention on us shifts away as the clothing scattered along the road is gathered up, and my moment of a heart over full subsides. Once more the normal murmur of voices and the echoes of footfall emerge.

But Cassandra's face has not lightened, and her steps are faltering. "Your uncles are not lost," I reassure her. "Do not be afraid. We will find them as we keep walking ahead."

As Cassandra shakes her head, her braids lash my sleeve. "I know they will not be lost. They will be with you," she says, and then her tears come back.

It has been some years since I have witnessed the tears of my own son Simon, and thus I have nearly forgotten the violence of a child's sobs—or perhaps girls always cry this way.

I stop again beside the road. She looks into my eyes and voices her next words in Greek. "But I will be lost to them!"

I am sure I have heard her words correctly, but I repeat them. "'I will be lost to them'?"

She nods through her sobbing. "Uncle Stephanos became my father when we left Athens. And then Uncle Thaul told me many, many wonderful things to make me a Jew. Now I am going to be just a poor Grecian girl far away from them. Hosanna, Hosanna!"

This girl indeed stands in need of salvation today—but salvation from her ignorance. "Now, listen. Your Hebrew uncles will not forget you," I answer, still swaying with the crowd. "They love you as their own. But you see how they spend time with us in the Temple. You need more than a hired maid to teach you the ways of a woman."

"My Aunt Irini was my mother who taught me, no one else!" Cassandra interrupts. Her teeth are chattering with the cold, or from her heavy heart.

I smile and pat her shoulder. "But now you will have your Aunt Iphigenia to show you the things you must learn as you grow up." Her face does not lighten even now, so I add the only other thing I can think of to say to a girl. "And besides, your Uncle Timon wants you in his household to grow up and to be the most beautiful Hellenist girl of anyone in the whole wide city."

Cassandra's eyes pierce through me, almost like the eyes of the man riding the colt. "Do you believe this, Rabboni?"

I have been asked questions over many years, but almost never something challenging my sincerity. I do not know what rises greater in me now, my desire to teach this girl, or my pity for a motherless child. Since I am uncertain how to answer her, I pray silently. "Do you remember the words from the crowd, Cassandra?" I hear my voice inquire.

She nods.

"And even as they believe that the King of Israel is here on his way, so I believe that you are blessed with many who love you, both Jews and Greeks who will never forsake you."

Cassandra sighs, and we walk together in silence, her two paces matching my one.

Even as this was no normal walk out of Jerusalem for us, so

is this by no means a normal wedding day. For the union of a lone widow and a man no longer young but never married, there were no parents to consult, and no money to pay. No one would expect the pageantry of the seven-day feast, the one-year wait, or the show of blood on a bedsheet expected of the young and the moneyed. Still, even between freedmen, a wedding feast at Passover and a man moving to the established household of his wife to be is no small breach of custom.

Until last week, I did not know of Timon's wedding, let alone give any thought of attending such a thing. It would be held among the Hellenisti, whom I hardly know, and many of whose traditions run counter to our laws. But Timon softly requested a private audience with me several times as I passed through the Temple gate, until I finally agreed.

I have spoken for allowing Timon regular pay, but this has never been approved, and I felt sorry to tell him so, certain that this was at the root of his persistence.

For this I must admit: Timon has been a greater blessing to our Temple than the Temple to him. In his first month of work, he learned the names of all our regular Pharisees and Sadducees. Despite his scant Hebrew, he greets all of them with a smile, even the many who ignore him, remembering to pass on any messages and always knowing who is in attendance.

During these years, he has also improved matters in the place where we worship. His idea of bringing in "speaking signs," as he calls them, young boys stationed at fixed spots to direct the unlettered crowd, has greatly improved the order in our courts, the embarrassment of sending foreigners away, guiding confused pilgrims forward, or indicating which of the many Temple chests is meant for corban and which are intended for other kinds of donations. Stephanos told me in private that Timon's own inability to read gave him the thought for others that never crossed the minds of our priests.

On the evening I appointed, Timon came to my home,

accompanied only by this girl, perhaps in her eleventh year. Refusing to sit with me or even to taste the drink my servant offered, he launched into Greek, whose labyrinths of phrase I could not follow.

Despite myself, I imagined the beautiful Athens he left, where such Greek must be spoken even on the street. And I also remembered what Stephanos told me from time to time of this man's zeal to serve our Lord, even of his circumcision, and his bravery afterwards. Then I realized that the guard had fallen silent, and his last phrase had been a question.

I awaited Cassandra's Hebrew explanation. All she said was this: "My uncle knows how wise you are. He needs to hurry and get married so that he can finally live with the woman he loves. Can you come and say a blessing for them next week?"

When Timon looked at her to go on, she said in Hebrew, "Uncle, I told Rabboni what you want."

I hid my smile of relief and amusement behind my sleeve as I answered in Hebrew. "You are truly a Jew, now, Timon, but you are also just a man. Let me know the day of your feast, and I will certainly attend. The blessing will be mine to wish upon you the happiness our Lord has laid out for man and woman."

"He said yes, Uncle Timon!"

At least my Greek is adequate for understanding this.

"Thank you, thank you, Rabboni! I am little, little man but honor here sit nearby house of our Lord, and thank you next week you come my wed," he replied to me directly, using what Hebrew he knows.

Even today, I remain amused by this exchange.

As it becomes easier to walk away from the city in the thinning crowd, I realize that, without the other men in the wedding party, I am uncertain of our way once we reach Bethany.

As though reading my mind, Cassandra slips a small piece of wood into my palm. "We'll find the house with this symbol by the door," she tells me.

The wood is carved into the shape of a basket, inside which lies the outline of a cradled child. The inscription in both Greek and Hebrew on the opposite side reads, "From Bethany, passing on your generation."

"What is this?"

Cassandra smiles. "Do you remember when Uncle Timon began bringing you gift money?"

I nod, recalling well. Beginning last year, nearly each week, Timon presented coins to me, too abashed even to bring them to the higher priests or to offer them publicly, and never revealing the source.

"It is money from Aunt Iphigenia."

I bite back the surprise tickling my tongue, hoping Cassandra will speak on.

"These little baskets match the sign outside her door in Bethany, so people in need can find her house. She asked Uncle Timon to give them to women who are great with child, or to their husbands. She says the Greek women usually cannot pay her for her help, but the families like yours at the Temple give her generous money for her skills, and she can pay us back this way."

"Us?" I answer. "Do you mean Uncle Timon?" I know already of the business this clever gatekeeper has attracted for his friend, as he recommends what Stephanos can provide our priests and scribes, who hunger for the finest paper and scrolls.

Cassandra laughs. "No. Us means all of us who worship in our Temple at Jerusalem. She wanted to contribute corban money from her thanks to the rich people who pay her, and to the great Temple." Cassandra is smiling as she grasps my hand. "So you see, everyone helps everyone. The baskets give hope of somewhere to go and find Aunt Iphigenia for the mothers who are afraid, she helps them have healthy babies, they pay her, and the Temple is also thanked for the work she does for the people who go there."

I have never known the need to plan for business, blessed as I am by a family with money to allow me to live this life of study, and receiving gifts from Saul and other students whose families believe in years of study in my school. It takes me more than a moment to recover from Cassandra's explanation, which to her is both obvious and wonderful. It also clarifies much more of the bond between the Athenian and the freedwoman he will marry today.

Our walking warms us as we mount the way to Bethany. To my relief, I see that the groom, Saul, and Stephanos have waited for us under a fig tree near the gate to the main street.

"There you are at last!" Timon greets us with a smile. And patting Cassandra's head, he gives her a special look. "We are almost home, child!"

Any concerns about the sincerity of her welcome melt from my mind.

"That crowd of fools has made the way hard for all of us!" Saul grumbles.

"At least they were joyful fools," Stephanos retorts. "The man on the donkey lightened their feet on the way to Jerusalem."

Looking at these two men I love so well, and how they see our world, for the hundredth time I wonder, is Saul the just one, labeling the misguided hopes as folly? Or is Stephanos correct in perceiving that at least the crowd arrived in our city with the kind of light and hopeful hearts we should all have as we recall God's promise on the eve of the great feast to come. The man's unquiet gaze but welcoming embrace of the people—the silence of the road amidst the chanting—all this still impresses my heart beyond the reasoning of my mind.

"Time will tell whether their joy is justified," I say.

Like an echo of Timon's earlier greeting, another voice calls to us from at least a stada's distance. "Here you are at last!"

It is Lukas, a young Hellenist doctor whose skills are drawing respect even in Jerusalem. He is son of Iphigenia. Rather than approaching us or awaiting our arrival, however, Lukas sprints away toward the sector of town inhabited by the foreign and the poor. Within a very few minutes, a crowd of Grecian Jews lines the street, calling to us with a mix of Hebraic blessings and Grecian humor.

"Reach her house faster than Pegasus!"

"Find all the pleasures of our father Adam in the garden!"

"Timon, you'd better guard your beautiful wife like you guard the Temple!"

Or simply, "Blessings on your new house!"

While the Athenian smiles and waves, the spring in his feet lets us know that we have no time to lavish on the humor and the warm words strewing our way like the garments before the donkey rider. Sure enough, I spot the basket symbol not only on the door of the house, but even at a corner as we turn onto a narrow side street, along with an Asclepius cane, which is Lukas' marking as a doctor.

Prior to this wedding day, a marriage contract was drawn up for Timon by Stephanos as the Greek's stand-in father, and approved by Iphigenia's son and only living male family member. The couple has offered thanksgiving sacrifices in the local synagogue. Today marks the feast, the blessings, and the nuptials that will blend Timon and Iphigenia as one flesh, and tomorrow comes the day of gift-giving to bride and groom.

When I told Stephanos of my intent to bring some gift money for the new couple, however, he shook his head. "You are their guest and the man they respect most deeply. It would dishonor their Greek hospitality for you to bring anything."

As though hearing my unvoiced thought—"But these people are scarcely above slaves"—Stephanos spoke on. "All the freedmen community of Bethany knows of Timon's duties and has benefited from Iphigenia's skills. Today they will show their respect by providing them a fine wedding feast."

I resolve to press on for this freedman to receive pay for his faithful service.

The very breath from the open gate of this Hellenist house spreads otherness into my face. Spices prickle my nose, and an overstrong wafting of fish nearly makes me recoil.

Though from courtesy to me, the Hellenisti gathered inside this house shared by several families use their best Hebrew, it is a burden for them. They talk volubly to one another, but only the boldest men attempt shy phrases of welcome and greeting to me, looking to each other for support. When I manage a scant phrase or two of what Greek I know, Cassandra presses my arm, and I understand that this is not expected. So instead, I slow my Hebrew and attempt to use the kind of words I say when I am entrusted with teaching some of the young boys who visit Jerusalem.

Timon reveals no such discomfort, but only gladness. He serves as host as the men gather at one table, the women at another. Speaking through Stephanos, he seeks to reassure me. "Our rabbi will tell you, every Jewish custom has been observed; you will find nothing of unclean food in our house here. Our wheat bread is a little different in shape from yours, but it was given to us by a neighbor who did not know." He gestures to a woman so great with child that I am amazed at her presence here. "It is early for Passover, but this bread has no leaven in it, just in case a crumb might stay with you for the feast of unleavened bread. And the honeyed wine—you will not find this in Jerusalem, sir, if I may say so. Please, wash your hands, and eat, drink. Everything is plentiful and more than plentiful for you today."

Despite my apprehensions, I am moved that this couple from so far away is preparing not only for their new life, but for the best Jewish life they can provide from what they have and what they know. What could Jews and children and grandchildren of Jews enslaved to idol worshipers keep of our traditions? And yet, they have returned to us from all over the earth once freed, or converted like Timon, and they yearn to understand and follow our law.

Their rabbi, Elias, introduces himself to me with the reserve of a student about to face questions from his teacher. Like the Grecians, he smiles warmly and plies me with food whose care in preparation shows obvious love of tradition, even if the taste is rather foreign to me. It is pleasant food, and I am quick to say this both to Elias and to Iphigenia and the other Greek women who listen.

Musicians on the lyra and flute play from the inside courtyard shared by all this building's families, and we go there after prayers have been spoken by Elias. Stephanos explains that one joyful tradition of the Greeks will now combine with ours.

Clad in a dress of dove-gray silk, Iphigenia arrives with an entourage of women, including her pregnant neighbor.

As she advances to Timon, who is red like a young boy, everyone cheers and calls, "Take the veil! Take the veil!"

This veil is no simple piece of cloth worn by our women, but a fire-red drapery fine as spider web. It protects Iphigenia's face, streaming over her head and down her rod-straight back.

Lukas and Stephanos step forward, each clasping one of Iphigenia's wrists.

"Take this woman from my house to thine," Lukas speaks, first in Hebrew, then in Greek.

"And in truth she is well received!" Stephanos responds. He passes a symbolic coin into Lukas' hand. Then both men set Iphigenia free.

The courtyard falls silent as with slow but steady fingers, Timon begins to unroll the veil, his eyes locked only on his bride.

"Hurry it up, you, man!" calls one of the Hellenisti. "She's yours for the taking!"

Timon ignores everything but the sweetness of revealing the woman beneath the veil, whose face opening to our gaze from chin to brow glows red not only from the shadow of her veil, but from her heart.

All of us cheer as Timon's fingers reach the top of Iphigenia's braided head.

Then the bride gestures for Cassandra to come forward. With motions as delicate as Timon's, the girl reaches up to grasp the cloth, rolling it down Iphigenia's back with the same gentleness she showed earlier with her yellow scarf.

I have often imagined the eyes of Jacob beholding his beloved Rachael, second wife for whom he toiled not seven years as he had thought, but another seven after unknowingly wedding Leah, her older sister, whom he could not see behind the veil until it was too late. Today I have seen these eyes of love. Knowing the many fearful brides, haughty or brutal grooms, and greedy families in Jerusalem, I must pray a breath of thanks to our Lord for so blessing this humble house. In my heart, I add a prayer for small Cassandra, who has taken the burning-bright veil somewhere before reappearing among the women.

Rabbi Elias asks me to recite our blessings in his place. I want to decline this honor, but all the Hellenisti are nodding with faces proud to hear it. And so I do recite the seven ancient blessings of comfort and of peace for this new family over the honeyed wine, beginning with, "Blessed are You, Adonai our God, Ruler of the Universe, Creator of the fruit of the vine," and ending, "Blessed are You, Adonai, our God, Ruler of the universe, Who created joy and gladness, loving couples, mirth, glad song, pleasure, delight, love, fellowship, peace, and kinship."

We eat yet more delicacies as the musicians play on. Meanwhile, Iphigenia and Timon disappear to conduct the rites of marriage between a man and a woman.

Cassandra persuades a musician to lend his lyra for Stephanos to play. His fingers tune the strings with the grace of a dove's wing. I knew nothing of this man's skills, engaged as we always are among our discussion of scripture and interpretations of our forefathers' words.

Though Cassandra's voice is small, it blends with the lyra's strumming like gold with silver, and its pitch lines every wall of the courtyard like honey.

"Her singing is as fine as any Hebrew girl's," I say to Saul as she intones several psalms of David.

"Perhaps better," Saul replies, pride softening his voice.

The talk, normally so loud at these occasions, falls still as she sings. Then she lapses into something Greek which I do not understand at all for its ancient sound.

"What is she singing?" I ask Saul.

He begins to interpret.

> HEAR, golden Titan...
> Lord of the seasons, with thy fiery car
> and leaping coursers, beaming light from far:
> With thy right hand the source of morning light,
> And with thy left the father of the night.
> Agile and vigorous, venerable Sun...

"Is this something from Homer?" I interrupt his concentration of wording the song into my ear. The role of teacher and student have been reversed for me in this house

I am stunned as he breaks off, his eyes flowing with tears. "No," he manages. "It is a hymn of Orpheus as it is sung in Athens. We also know it well in Tarsus."

Perhaps my student has drunk more wine than he should. "No need to interpret anymore," I say, laying a hand on his shoulder.

But Saul shakes his head, and he speaks on in a hard voice.

Foe to the wicked, but the good man's guide,
o'er all his steps propitious you preside:
With various founding, golden lyra, 'tis mine
To fill the world with harmony divine

"Sing on, daughter of Apollo, our great musician!" one man calls. "You are so young, yet with such songs that even we the adults do not know entirely!"

Cassandra looks the man full in the face. "Apollo does not exist, but only our Lord. I am daughter of Alexander of Crete, who was the greatest actor in Athens. I remember, he would sing this song to me in the morning to wake me up, and he called me his little sunshine."

Stephanos has laid the lyra aside and drawn near. As he and Saul look at each other, tears glint in Stephanos' eyes as well.

Something beyond my grasp unifies these men so divided in their ideas. Recalling my question to Saul during the song, I realize my failure to distinguish Orpheus from Homer is as bumbling as any Jewish boy who knows no difference between the words of Moses and David. For the first time in all our years together, I see today how these Tarsian men walk nimbly through the Grecian world. And that world is perhaps as real as the one I know as I study our Lord. But this other life, so removed from Jerusalem and our teachings, is something I shall neither see with my eyes nor fathom in my mind.

"It is true," Stephanos says to Saul. "She began singing to herself when she was sad, and Irini taught her the words that she did not remember."

Perhaps Cassandra has noticed the distress on the faces of her guardians, because she leaves her singing place and approaches.

I wish to address another business. Calling Stephanos to my side while holding Cassandra's wrist, I confirm what she has told me earlier. "The child will stay here to live?"

Stephanos nods. "She is to learn the medicine of Iphigenia and Lukas for her future."

I press on. "This will be a blessing to her. But she has counted on your fatherhood during all the life she can remember. What will you say to her of this?"

Cassandra is wide-eyed and motionless as her gaze fastens to the man who brought her out of Athens, but she says nothing.

"No need to look like a sheep led to slaughter, little one," Stephanos begins. "These are your people."

Abandoning her attempt at bravery, the child crushes Stephanos' waist in clinging. With a trembling voice I can hardly hear, she replies. "Today I have no people."

Saul has moved near enough to hear us. "Remember, she is a stranger in a strange land, as we were in the Temple," he says to Stephanos.

I recall the story of their first arrival in Jerusalem in childhood, and their dismay at the sign to bar them from our midst. Saul has told me about this more than once.

Stephanos kneels to speak with the girl face to face. "Do you remember Persephone?" he asks.

Cassandra nods. "She is the woman in Greek stories who went to the underworld to be Hades' wife."

"Yes," he answers. "And she did not want to go, did she?"

Cassandra shakes her head. "That is why the Greeks say that we have cold winter, when her mother, Demeter, misses her daughter in the land of the dead."

Stephanos pats her shoulder. "You are right. And how long is that winter?"

"Six months!" Cassandra answers, no longer crying. "Half the year."

"Right again." Stephanos smiles. "And do you know that Uncle Timon loves you as much as I do? If we broke our love, it would come out exactly half and half, I think."

Cassandra pauses. "He does love me. But he loves Aunt

Iphigenia more. You don't love anyone more."

"He loves her in a different way. But she has no daughter, and she always wanted one. She wants to love you, too."

Cassandra's smile fades.

"We will call this a Persephone time," Stephanos goes on. "You will live in this house for six months. After this, we will talk again, and if you are unhappy by then—"

"I get to come back and stay with you?"

Stephanos pauses, and finally, "Yes," he replies. "We will find a way."

Cassandra looks up at Saul. "And you will still tell me about people like Noah and Naaman and Nehemiah?"

Saul picks Cassandra up off the floor. "I must also tell you more of Ruth and Rachael and Rebecca."

Then the girl whispers something into Saul's ear, and he nods. "Always, my Little Weed," he answers.

I smile along with them. My students have in fact learned well to respect even the smallest among us.

Then Cassandra draws the odd strip of yellowish cloth from her sleeve. I would think this a child's game, but both men beside me draw in breath as with a wound while she twists the cloth first around her own wrist, then into both their hands. Her solemnity reminds me of the earlier exchange of wedding promises as Iphigenia was held by both wrists. "You know, this is all I have left besides my father's ring," she says. "We are all holding it now. Do you promise me?"

The men are speechless as Cassandra repeats her question with solemnity.

"Yes, I promise," Saul finally manages.

Stephanos repeats Saul's words, his voice low with feeling.

"It is fair," Cassandra continues, and turning to me, "isn't it, Rabboni?"

Though not everything I have just seen is clear to me, I have witnessed their love for one another, and for this reason, I nod.

"The man riding the donkey today told me to keep faith. I am holding faith with our Lord, and I am holding faith with you. I will keep Aunt Irini's scarf and remember both of you in Jerusalem, and I shall never ever forget," Cassandra answers, sliding the long cloth from the men's fingers and wrapping it back into her sleeve.

Meanwhile, the guests around us raise a great cheer as the new husband and wife emerge from a narrow doorway.

"Hurrah to the newlyweds!" comes shouted in both Greek and Hebrew.

Though evening has begun to cast the sky by now, the flush on their faces, the joy in their gaze is evident to everyone. But bride and groom have hair neatly parted and garments in full good order. Timon leads his wife to sit between the women's table and the men. He takes his place beside her after filling a plate with honeyed dates and nuts to share with her.

When Stephanos approaches to offer the newlyweds libation, Timon leans close and whispers.

Stephanos nearly drops the wine cups, but Timon is laughing.

When Stephanos returns to the men's table near me, he whispers to one of the Hellenisti, who spits wine from his lips. I follow the murmuring of the men as this secret passes like fire up one side of the table and down the other. Even Rabbi Elias sitting nearby has picked it up. He turns to studious conversation with a man on the other side of our table, then rises pointedly and walks away from me.

Meanwhile, Cassandra has strayed from her place among the women. With what I am certain is pretense, she strolls among the men, straightening a plate here, or offering olives there. When she returns to the women, she whispers to one of them, after which their faces redden and mouths round in glee.

I am the only person left in ignorance. I must not take offense, but loneliness strikes me sharp as a stone, an isolation no stranger to me. While my gain is the love and respect of my many students and fellow Pharisees over the years, my loss is the closeness of confidences viewed as too worldly for law-laden ears.

Then the child Cassandra comes offering me some of the strong-smelling salted fish. As I decline, she pulls my sleeve and bends close to my ear. "Uncle Timon said, if the Greeks knew how nice it is being with a woman after becoming a Jew, the whole Greek world would become Jews—but the Romans would be too afraid for this. I do not know why this makes everyone laugh, Rabboni, but it is not fair for them to laugh and not tell you."

I have no time to raise my face before the child and her fish disappear. Today she has proven an able interpreter indeed. Tonight I shall whisper the wit of this circumcised freedman into the ear of my wife, and we shall share love together—and the last laugh will surely be ours.

The couple has just started to relax when Iphigenia's son, the doctor Lukas, runs into the courtyard. He is half dragging, half pulled by a disheveled boy, dust still on his sandals.

This youth kneels before Timon. "The Temple!" he cries as everyone falls silent. "Everything is in ruin!"

I know the messenger's husky voice very well, though his back is to me. This is Ezra of Jericho. He ranks among my nimblest young students. He is given to serving with Timon at the gate or in the Temple when he is not studying scripture in my Torah school. My shoulders tense, and the crowd draws a gasp.

With a hand still resting on Iphigenia's shoulder, Timon rises and pulls the boy up. "What is your meanings, Ezra?" he tries to ask in Hebrew.

The boy wipes the sweat from the dust on his face. "We followed every instruction of yours to help the crowds find their way and understand the order today. But then a man came in with some students. He completely ignored us, and he began overturning the moneychanger tables and the dove benches in the outer court. He and his followers even threatened scourging us when we tried to step in. He called our Lord's house a den of thieves. When I left to tell you, the children in the court were calling out that this man is the Messiah we are waiting for. Oh, sir, forgive my disorder here, but you had to know right away!"

Timon turns the boy to face us, laying a heavy hand on his shoulder.

Ezra gasps. "You are here, too, Rabboni!" he manages. His eyes are wide with amazement at finding me in a house of Hellenisti.

"These are our brothers and sisters in faith," I reply.

Timon seems either not to understand or not to notice. "You brave and right come here to me," he voices. Facing his wife, he goes on in Greek. "I was greedy to demand this marriage so soon, my love, and now the whole Temple is paying for my haste in something I surely could have prevented. Forgive me, but I must go there now to see what I can do to restore order."

Iphigenia's smile fades to concern. "Of course you must go, and if you did not want to go, I would tell you to do it anyhow," she answers. "It is your honor and your duty."

Meanwhile, a stifled gasp rises from the women's table as the pregnant neighbor writhes in her chair, turning white. "Oh, the baby!" her companion whispers, but all of us hear her words.

"I will attend her, Mother," Lukas calls, hurrying to the woman and beginning to lift her.

"No!" Iphigenia retorts. "This is a women's thing." Turning to Timon, she laughs. "I see we both have our duties to tend to this night."

Ezra has stepped back from the couple as Timon takes Iphigenia into his arms just for a moment. "I'll be back after I can clear up all this madness, my Aphrodite!" he murmurs, but the crowd can hear it clearly.

Both of them rush to their work, Iphigenia urging the women to help her neighbor to a room in this house, and Timon hurrying after Ezra, accepting the offer of another neighbor's cart and mule to speed their trip back to the city.

"You with me come, Rabboni?" Timon asks me.

Saul, Stephanos, and I all long to go with him, I see from my students' faces, but we must not slow him down. I shake my head, and excusing himself, Timon flees the room, Ezra on his heels.

With the couple so swiftly parted from this peculiar wedding and we the only remaining Hebrew speakers besides Rabbi Elias, we sense the discomfort of remaining. Elias offers us a room in his home for the night. When I refuse, he proffers a donkey. Thinking of Saul's exhaustion, I am moved to accept his kindness.

But before my departure, I call for Cassandra. I return the ring which she gave me for safety and which both of us had forgotten in all the day's goings on. "This ring is precious, but not so precious as the love of your uncles Stephanos and Saul, and of Timon, who also cares for you," I tell her. "You must keep your memories of the past, but walk into your new life here with God's blessing."

9. The Mustard and the Veil

Witness of Stephanos, Jerusalem, A.D. 32

Early clouds hang low, the color of boulders on high mountains. Then cold-fingered wind begins shearing them like garments of a man in mourning. "Take heart, Stephanos, and overcome your sorrow," I tell myself. "Would not Irini also tell you to do so? At last it is the start of Passover." Every Jew in the empire who can do so arrives this day in Jerusalem to worship and to sacrifice, and here we are, Saul and I, trudging among the many.

On the five days since his wedding, Timon has insisted on sitting at the main gates, even well into the night. Saul, Rabboni Gamaliel, and I have each reassured him that he bore no guilt in the madness seizing the outer courts on the day of his consummation, but The Eagle insists on remaining on vigil until after the end of the feast, refusing all talk of returning to Bethany before then.

Approaching the square of the tribunal beyond which Timon keeps guard, we pause, hearing many angry voices. Even after these thousand days, neither of us ever wishes to see a seething crowd again. Though we have never found words to speak to each other and escape the stones cast hard in our hearts at my sister's death, our eyes meet.

We nod, and then we turn as one to a street that will take us to the eastern entrance instead of approaching our usual way through the main gate. This will make us late for the start of service and sacrifices, but it is a small price, avoiding recent memories that sever our hearts like dogs that tear flesh from bone.

I long for Timon's just but gentle order. Beggars are lining not only the road, but straggling over much of a side gate as we approach. One man's voice shrills above the rest. "Our Lord lifts you up, the rich and the strong ones. But remember the poor, who are cast down!" This man looks up at us and stops speaking.

May the Lord gentle my eyes, for as I see him, I can only think, "This is no man, but a worm." He fails even to sit or crouch like his fellow poor; instead, he lies flat on the stones, belly down and head propped on withered hands.

I must nearly always pass by such beggars, even at a time like this, marked by gift–giving. I live without my sister's scribing, and void of her wisdom to spend money with greatest care. These past years, the days I allow for my writing–goods trade amidst studying with Gamaliel are just enough for my tithe and my needs.

But Saul stops short. "No one has given you a Passover basket?" he asks the figure lying on the lifeless ground. His voice pierces the air like the point of a spear.

The man snorts, hardly raising his head and replying with sharpness equaling Saul's. "A certain friend of yours who guards a certain gate. A certain basket left with him for ones you call 'The worst of all cripples.'" Then, looking Saul fully in the face, "And your next question, sir, is, 'Why are you then here today?'"

To my horror, he has captured my friend's slight stammering of words to the very breath.

"And I will tell you then, though you may not understand. You stand there in your nicely woven robes. Yes, I got a basket. What is that one basket? I am here today because one basket feeds my family for one day. It is gone like the morning dew. Then the sun rises again, and the family's hunger is worse than before."

He lowers his voice to a whisper that I scarcely hear. "And I will tell you another thing, sir. I know why you have given, and I also know why it is the Greek guard who comes to me, and not you yourself."

Saul clenches his hands together. He is pale, whether from astonishment or from fear. All three of us remain motionless.

Then the worm–man hoists his head to look to me. "And as for your tall friend there with the bearing of a Greek god, I know his secret as well."

My feet burn to kick this beggar with his raging rope of retorts. "Be still, my soul," I force into my inner mind, as I look the man in the eyes. His is a face hideous as a hide I once found sunken under a pile of sand while traveling in the desert. "I have no secret, you worm!" Voicing these words relieves the burning in my chest.

"Oh, yes. You have the Mustard Boy."

My mouth is almost too dry to speak, but I force my lips apart. "What do you mean, Mustard Boy?" I have heard songs on the streets with those odd words.

The worm–man begins to sing, and his voice surprises me with its strength.

> *Mustard Boy, oh, Mustard Boy,*
> *Speaking forth your words of joy,*
> *Gave faith and promise you knew well*
> *To hearten men of Israel.*

A woman beggar nearby smiles and joins the song.

> *Roman aqueducts will totter,*
> *But our Lord brings living water!*
> *With a voice so clear, so proud,*
> *Mustard Boy embraced the crowd.*

The man breaks off his singing and speaks on. "The Mustard

Boy was your little sister. I saw her. She was dressed like a boy in a mustard-yellow mantle. She is the one who went up to challenge Pilatus on the day of the massacre, three years ago. She pleaded to protect the corban."

The laugh that tightens my throat and leaves my lips is as harsh as this man's voice. "Do not speak of my sister!" I say through a clenching jaw.

"I am speaking to you of what I know," the worm responds, ignoring me. "That day, your friend stood high on the steps at the other side of the square where I was begging. He is a good man, even if he is only a Greek. I did not know his face or his name, but he paid another beggar a silver coin to drag me upward and save me before the crowd began to run. All the time, he prayed and even wept for this girl he called Irini."

The coldness on my head comes not from the wind, but from a fear of what this worm will say next.

"All of us believed then that the Mustard Boy was a brave young scholar who could not get to the Temple. Later, when I recognized the Greek sitting each day at the main Temple gate, I began to beg there. When he learned enough Hebrew, we spoke, and he told me who you are and how he met you and the girl Irini on your travels in Athens. I figured out who she was once I heard his story."

Saul seems unshaken by the feeling that makes my lips tremble. Instead, he stoops and replies with a soft voice, "But tell us, please, why is it that the people sing of this Mustard Boy?"

The worm-man laughs. His sneer bares the cave of his mouth, and the stink of it. "Because they are as foolish as this man who came into Jerusalem hailed as a king a few days ago, before he cleared out the den of thieves up there." He gestures toward the Temple. "Well, those thieves are back today, growing rich as usual off all your sacrifices."

Saul, too, laughs, to my astonishment. "You speak the truth

of their greed." His softness continues, but now I hear the persistence thronging his voice, so well do I know him. "But you still have not told us, what does all this have to do with mustard?"

The worm-man continues his laughter, bitter as the Passover herbs we eat to recall our captivity in Egypt. "Today that brave little king called Jesus of Nazareth, who spoke of thieves in the Temple, is drawing all the people to the tribunal. That Nazarene says that faith as small as a mustard seed is faith enough to move mountains. And the people remember his words and put them in the mouth of the one from the tribunal three years ago, who spoke small words, but who moved all the people to take heart. That is why they sing of the Mustard Boy."

The worm man spits in his own shadow. But where did all those words disappear to? Just into a song to remember the massacre—and probably to this sweet-worded Nazarene being hung on a Roman cross made from a mustard tree this very day.

I am ready to curse this shrivel-souled beggar when Saul seizes my arm. With strength I did not suspect, he draws me toward the Temple.

But the worm-man's words ring in our ears from behind. "And this is your secret, Pharisee. You are just a limping quail, and I am surely a ground-eating lizard, but you gave the basket because you know well that we are brothers!"

Saul's hand tightens as he pulls me along. Beyond the milling crowd, I can hear words screamed all the way up from the tribunal. "Crucify him! Crucify him!"

In my mind, I cannot dim the picture of that small man on his donkey colt who slowed our walk as the crowd divided us from Gamaliel on our way to Timon's wedding.

"What do you think the man meant when he spoke to us from the donkey, Saul?" The question escapes my lips before I can pull it back.

Saul shrugs. "He was mistaken and full of pride. Now he will pay the price."

But all the days since passing against that crowd, I have remembered the rider's words spoken directly to us both. "You, brothers," he said, "you will know the Son of Man when you next see His face." How Saul would laugh if he knew the peace I felt that day for the first time since my sister's death.

My heart sinks, already over-full with memories of Irini that the worm-man has stirred up. Though he imposed disorder in our Temple, still, it is not a just thing that on our very Passover, this Jesus of Nazareth, a fellow Jew, will surrender his life, even as the beggar predicted.

What bearing of a king did he have then as the people called to him? He had no weapons threatening our oppressors, not even splendor to please the crowd, yet they believed in him. He had only hands that embraced the air and drew their hearts close, and eyes that met ours with a smile.

As we at last arrive near the gate dividing the gentiles' court from our inner worship space, my eyes light on the worn sign forbidding foreigners entry, the same sign that my little sister stopped to read.

Saul, too, has looked up to the Greek words, and then he sways me and pins me to the wall. If his eyes were coals, they would burn my face. "Stephanos, you must tell me the truth today!" he says in Greek.

My heart pounds. How long has it been since he has used our childhood language, or even spoken my name?

"That day—what happened?" His eyes have become as pleading as any beggar's we have seen along our road.

I have no need to ask him, "What day?" Even if I desired to break the pinion of his two hands pressing my sleeves, my shoulder is to the wall, and the crowd pushes all around us. There are only my friend's eyes devouring my gaze. But as my throat tightens, I can make no reply as his grief-lined face lingers close.

Saul pushes chest to chest. To an onlooker, it would appear we are embracing. "These were nearly the last words she said: 'The Temple, the dove, we never told you.'" Though he has whispered, his voice breaks.

I draw breath as from a dagger wound. "It is true, we never told you," I find scant voice to reply. "It was our secret."

The sharpness of Saul's inhalation is his only reply. The crowd seems to remove itself as I recount to him our first day in Jerusalem, when he remained in the Temple to speak with our future teacher, how we went to the court to make sacrifice, and then, how a boy took pity on Irini, how he freed the dove with gentle words for us both. "And one other thing," I conclude. "Though the dove flew free—Irini named her Pegasus—" I gasp a kind of laughter "—both she and I were marked that day with sacrificial blood. How often I have remembered this since Irini was lost to us!"

Saul lowers his hands, releasing his constraint. "You, and Irini," he repeats still in Greek. "And the blood upon you both?" His eyes have cooled, full of wonder.

I lay a hand on his shoulder. "There was a day in Tarsus when you asked for my forgiveness after the races, Saul. Your envy was a thing that harmed only your own spirit. But my sin— I wronged you both, keeping Irini as I did, and we know the result. Her blood returned to the Temple here." I bite back tears as I force my tongue to the next words far too long unspoken. "I have asked forgiveness again and again of our Lord for Irini's passing. I failed to protect her as I should have. Today I also ask for your forgiveness."

Saul's face looking up to me fills my vision. "You and I both set our hearts to protect and save her," he replies slowly. "But our Lord held her in His hands with other designs. Irini became one of the great daughters of Israel remembering the promises of our Lord. Blessed be her memory between us, and let it give us peace to worship together at last as brothers again. The bitterness of what we know should be blessed by the sweetness of what we have loved."

I repeat what I remember of the Hebrew song we have just heard: "Gave faith and promise you knew well, to hearten men of Israel."

Saul covers his face with a sleeve. Then in truth we embrace. Our chests are pounding with the heaviness in our hearts, but today, we have shared this thing and lightened our souls with forgiving.

"Pegasus a dove," he whispers. "Oh, how like your sister's thoughts!"

We can scarcely enter the inner Temple full of praying men, but Saul's status as Pharisee, visible from his garb, makes visitors move aside.

Though we are late for the recounting of the Passover meal, the priest is chanting other words we love just as well, about the parting of the Red Sea for our people. This ancient miracle came to pass upon our haste to escape from Egypt, led by Moses, after the night when every house not marked by blood lost its eldest son. Closing my eyes, I can nearly see the waters waving back before the throng abandoning their slavery. As one, the men of our congregation sway like that very sea as our spirits unite around this story of our deliverance.

The responses I repeat with my brethren rise from a heart renewed. My spirit rests light as a man's shoulders after setting down a heavy burden carried overlong. Saul's embrace and kind words have lifted the barrier between us of these last three years, and my sorrow along with it. At last, we can shoulder the grief of Irini's death together, as he has spoken his love, and I have spoken my sin regarding her.

But our congregational replies are spattered with sounds from outside. Lanterns are being lit, so dark has the sky become, and the wind pulls on the walls and sighs in the upper air of our sanctuary. The crowd shifts, not only from its hours of standing, but from this oddity of the wind and the light, the cold and the restlessness. This weather with its darkness has disrupted the peace and joy that normally mark this holiest of all our feasts. In fact, many people are already preparing to leave.

I renew my attention to the service. But I look at Saul and I smile a little during the next readings, for they involve the man of his own name, King Saul, who sometimes loved the future ruler David, and who sometimes sought to murder him. "Now that is one who had to kick at the pricks!" I feel free to whisper to Saul now that our affection is restored, as we hear the appeals of David to our Lord for safety.

Saul shrugs, but he smiles back. His ancient name recalling a once good but fallen king has never pleased him much, but at least it is a Hebrew name, unlike my own. "The crown is our Lord's to give," he whispers in return, playing on the meaning of my Greek name.

The wind has so increased that I can feel its vibration through the nearby wall. The darkness crawls like a living thing, growing and clustering in our midst. The Temple boys are doing their best to assure oil in the lanterns and protection for the candles, but the light shivers around us and only deepens the darkness. The priest can hardly read from the scroll in these conditions. Rabboni Gamaliel stands close by, ready to assist with his perfect memory.

As the priest falters, I hear prayers around me well beyond traditional words. Many are pleading for change—some for peace amidst the storm—others for protection against the Romans—a few for the Messiah's arrival. It is the only time of year when we can speak freely of what still enslaves us, and the Rome–pocked outer world pays no mind, considering it merely our tradition. Our symbolism fails to pique the Latins who claim governance over Israel.

I remind myself that though once we leave this holy place we will be confronted by our current enslavement, today's repression cannot compare to the plagues of Egypt, nor to the captivity of our forefathers. It cannot even rank with the slavery of my own father whose freedom cap I guard always close at hand. As I try to envision my Baba's face, an inward voice opens my heart once more to the hope and the promise our Lord has shown to my father, to my father's fathers—and as I have learned today, even to the crowd through a little Mustard Boy.

I find my lips shaping only one phrase. "Oh, Lord, remember Your promise. Let me keep it in my heart and never lose it again!"

Many lines of scripture that have sheltered my soul come back to me—their weight and their joy. Saul is swaying with the rest of us. His words have grown soft as he, too, repeats only one phrase now. "Show me Your way and Your law, oh Lord." Joining my motion to his, I lean left, then right, then left and right again. Our prayers and motions renew my spirit like a candle.

My head starts to prickle, as though played by the wind. But raising my hands, I find no motion in the air—none at all. In fact, all the swaying around me is no more. The words of the priest have faded away, if he is speaking at all. How is it that time seems to end its walk here in our congregation? A sharp scent pricks the air like dust before a storm in the desert.

My eyes lift to the front of the sanctuary, toward the great veil. Hanging tall as seven men, it rises from the stones beneath our feet to the ceiling high above our heads. Its wide folds divide us from the holy of holy places where none but our high priest dares enter, and there he can enter just once a year. Though it is a place too sacred to entrust to anyone but the presence of our Lord, yet I am blessed to stand so close. I pray that the words of my heart may pass through the thickness of the purple curtain stitched in gold, that whatever strangeness growing in the darkness is coming to bless us and not to curse us. That there is a strangeness here is beyond dispute, and all of us realize it by now.

Then my locks, my beard, every hair on my flesh rises, as though to salute a bolt of lightning, but nothing is in the air but the strength of some unmoving wind. I recognize the motionlessness of each man around me. How is it that all of them are asleep? I have no time for fear, only a drawing in of breath to wonder. I alone among my brethren raise my eyes to comprehend the ether from which this air is born. But nothing abides here besides the stopping of the wind, and a great stillness.

Stronger than the darkness, and more silent than the thick-hanging atmosphere, huge shadows of aloneness grasp my mind. Why is it that no other man in Temple seems able to move or speak, let alone to behold, not even Saul or Gamaliel? Why in this darkest moment am I the only one to find breath among these far greater men?

Transfixed, I begin to pray aloud. My voice, though a whisper, surrounds the Temple like the wind before. "Let it be in accordance with Your will, Father. Protect Your people on this day." I make bold to turn my face heavenward as I speak this prayer.

Once the echo of my prayer has faded from the sanctuary, a heat beyond the veil, not any light, forces my gaze straight ahead. My eyes forge amidst all this motionlessness, though there is nothing to see. But my ears meet a voice calling from the veil, an inward voice, not one heard aloud.

"Stephanos, Stephanos!" Nearly all the light is gone.

Before my studies with Gamaliel, I would have fled this place. But reassured by what I have learned, the words of many ancestors wrap my heart like a protective mantle. Falling to my knees, "I am here, my Lord," I voice, or perhaps I forge this reply only in my mind.

The silence lingers before further words greet my inner ears. "I am the Son of Man, Messiah, killed today. Fear nothing, for I am with you. But, Stephanos, clasp this burden deep within your heart."

A shining on my eyelids gives me courage to look up. Piercing the darkness stands a Roman cross, on which a figure hangs, dying or dead. Above the shape I read a sign: "King of the Jews."

My eyes fill with tears—not for this vision, but as my aloneness swells deeper in the stillness around that voice. For this I know with certainty. I am the only man here who sees this thing, and I have no desire to be this lone witness. Yet a reverence akin to recalling the waters of baptism in the Jordan sweeps my spirit with peace.

At last my lips part to whisper, "Are you the Son of Man?"

Once more, I hear the inward voice, not a voice echoing like my whisper, but one that burns my inner ears.

"Indeed. I am Jesus of Nazareth, Son of Man, and my blood was shed for all the world today. You, Stephanos, are Protomartyr, the first to witness this, and you will be the first to tell of it. I am the Christ, the one bridging the law, turning to spirit God's great love for you. Your Passover is ended. I am He. Believe; accept My grace. Your soul is free."

A moment before the cross with its figure vanishes, I recognize the face—the eyes of the donkey rider. Once more, they pierce me through. The Temple remains absolutely still, yet the voice echoes with words no other man has heard.

What I have just witnessed racks me with a pain and joy commingled that I have never known. "As You have spoken, Lord, so let it be." The reply I offer wells from my deepest spirit. "I am Your servant; Lord, abide with me!"

Expecting nothing more, my eyes close. But more words come—words which, had I remained standing with the rest of the congregation, would have left me prostrate.

"Hear this, Stephanos of Tarsus. Though you shall not reach the things you most desire, your own life will turn My word to fire."

While what I hear finds its way to my heart, conscience enchains my mind. "Your father gave his liberty for his own father's life. Your sister gave her life in the name of your people's freedom. Who are you, you Greek-tongued son of a freedman and failed protector of a great woman of Israel, to deserve this viewing of the Holy of Holies? You have eaten meat given to idols; around the empire of Rome, you have sat with those not even fit to sit with your brother Jews here! And why do not the rest of them here see this? You could name a hundred men here today more worthy and more pure of heart. Why should you be the one chosen as Protomartyr?"

As the living air maintains its fierceness, a rumbling fills the floor beneath my knees and within the walls. The stones themselves have shaken with this voice. The cold has turned to heat, and with it, a new motion. A savage, shearing noise seizes the Temple veil. Like the Red Sea before our fleeing people, this curtain separating the holy from the unholy parts clean in two.

My eyes behold its splitting, and my ears take in the hiss of its divide. It sweeps back, from the top threads gracing its hanging, to the folds of its hem brushing the floor. I arise, for this rending of our holy veil comes to me not as a shock, but as the confirmation of what I have just seen and heard.

The darkness is too dense to behold the altar and the candlesticks that must stand in such a sacred place, one that no man but a priest dares to enter for any cause. My mind repeats the phrase branding my inner ear: "I am the Christ, the one bridging the law, turning to spirit God's great love for you." As I begin to comprehend the message, my heart beats fast, both with fear and with joy.

When the sundered veil swings wide, time is reborn after all the words, the heat, the shaking storm. The robes of my brethren stir all around me as many turn to flee, while a few fall on their faces and tear their clothes. Yet even amidst the reawakening of all my fellow worshippers and the impending chaos around, the depth of my aloneness as Protomartyr of Christ's image and the memory of His voice all but overwhelm my spirit.

I fail to notice another voice until it is too late. Saul has left my side. While the many kneel and cover their faces, this one man alone has run to hold fast to the veil, pulling it closed as best he can.

His eyes, lit by the remaining candles, shine wide with horror. With a great voice, he cries, "My fathers and my brothers, some great law has surely been horribly broken, above any abomination we have ever known! Some blasphemy, some unforgiven sin, some burden greater than our hearts can bear has fallen upon us today, defiling this place!"

Every priest remains planted to the floor, even Gamaliel. They are torn between dismay at this defacement of our veil and fear at Saul's bravery bordering on madness to approach such a thing.

I can scarcely draw breath as my friend's words pelt my spirit like stones.

Meanwhile, Saul is beating his chest, rending his garments, and calling for all to pray, to cleanse themselves, and to turn our joy to lament. "This is the only chance for our salvation," he cries with a breaking voice.

I find strength to think my prayer only in single words. "Save!" "Deliver!" "Assist!" and finally, "Lord, make me strong!"

As soon as my eyes meet Saul's, I rise and run to his side. He is breathing in shallow gasps. My fingers tingle as they meet his; his hands have turned to ice. Only then, I know what I must do. I work to loosen his clenching together of the torn veil. Slowly he relents and steps aside.

I grasp the cloth in his place, and I pull it wide as I turn toward all the congregation.

"Indeed, abomination," I begin. "This Passover has come to us fulfilled. This day, the very Son of Man has wept, and bled, and torn His body open wide. His spirit has been poured entirely away. He has shed His own blood like the blood of a lamb we know to purge this great iniquity of ours. He is Jesus of Nazareth, our true Messiah, while we..."

All the rest of the words I should speak flee my mind. A force overwhelms me, making my body sway like a ship on angry waves. But meanwhile, my soul rises like a feather on the wind. Though I hear the scraping of stone as I pitch forward, I have no feeling. It is the last sound I hear in the Temple, even as the light around the veil is the last I see.

Now the rightful silence that is true silence, before time or stars or worlds came into being! My heartbeat stills, and all my breath has faded away. I have no hands to move, no robe to brush my shoulders, no locks to wave against bodily ears—not even a tongue to seek abandoned words. The lightness of no fleshly walls to bind my spirit leaves me free and amazed.

Then a vibration of wind fixes some order in my thoughts. Its rushing reminds me of my many lyings down, sheltered in a tent during storms in the desert—and yet, it is unlike this. For there is no fear, no sand. Instead, this wind wraps me in transformation. The darkness before me is a borderless presence, an ocean that picks me up and pushes me forward at a speed I cannot see or imagine, but which I feel carrying me far from the entire earth. The wind's warmth is like the sun, but with no light of the sun. I travel ever in one direction. Clusters of light akin to stars begin emerging before me, beside me, above and below me in this gentle night—shapes of animals, of trees, of things for which I have no words. And yet, these are creations which live, more fantastic even than the creatures our beloved Homer could embody in all his verses. I could open my mouth to call upon our Lord, but the fullness within my heart is sufficient. Enough, my soul, to witness amidst this motion along a gradual lightning.

Any act of my will arranges me in any direction. From a

distance, tones like the hymns of giants begin to build behind my ears, which are in fact no ears, but the knowing of my soul. And before me two tiny lights as stars that I wish to reach, and in the wishing, I reach and pull them toward me—or my soul-self draws itself toward them; I cannot say. These stars fill themselves into the shapes of two figures, and behind them a dimmer third form, beneath which the smaller ones take shelter.

"Who are you?" I ask this without words, but I am sure of my thought's translation. This is surely the state Plato foretold when speaking of the world that is real, beyond the cave in which our earthly bodies and limited minds are imprisoned. My memory of dread in another time is transformed into the purest desire for knowledge. This gentle night has dispersed all fear in its warmth.

The two smaller figures now close by make no reply, but their light converts itself beyond shape, to color. The smaller of them is golden-edged, the larger, wrapped in silver. And I know them. "Baba, sister!" I voice without breath. "How is it that you are here with me?"

My baba's shape trembles, and in its rippling like droplets of water, I hear his laughter. "Better to say this, Stephanos, my son. How is it that you are here with us?"

His phrasing—the rough kindness of his voice, the very fluttering of his accents, are exactly as I recall. But on earth, I forced myself to put all of these far from my mind since his death in Jerusalem. Having no more need to hide the memory from grief now, I reconstruct each line of the beloved face and the strong hands. The learning of our trade and of what traditions he knew and the very scent of my father's breath return to me, just as he imparted all his knowledge to me as his son.

Then I feel my own shape, whatever it is, slipping as though in a chasm. "Father, forgive me!" I voice to him with all my heart and mind. "I did not carry Irini as I needed to; without me, she would still be walking with us on earth. Her blood is upon my soul."

But Instead of fading or shrinking, the shapes descend along with me. The golden-hewed form of Irini moves close and touches me. All my form vibrates with the sunlight of her.

"No, Stephanos! Without you, brother, I would not have lived in the promise of our Lord. Nor would I have seen his goodness to our people. It is a thing far more important to the spirit than the number of our days on earth. It is I who should ask you to forgive me, since you have carried the guilt of my passing with no cause for so long now."

Through these new eyes of mine that neither blink nor sting, I weep. The shapes before me do not twist with the tears, but this grief swells and heats across all I know.

"Forgiveness is not ours to give. It is the Lord's. It is to understand this that you have come here," my sister continues.

Like a candle flame blown strong with the breeze, the third figure once behind joins hands between my father and my sister. So great a presence is here, it could smash my spirit like a lodestone crushing ships. Yet instead, I am surrounded only by a growing, warming, uplifting light that radiates love to the very core of my being. I find no breath, no words, and no air—only this presence wrapping me both within and without whatever existence my soul now occupies, and the profound pardon I have longed for.

"I, too, was marked by blood that day with Irini when the dove went free," the thought entwines my mind. "All three of us were there."

The image of the ruddy boy who spoke reassuring words to us that day in the Temple appears to me, and how he freed the dove with gentle hands. And I understand that this person is one and the same as the man I saw just days ago as he entered Jerusalem on the colt. "Yes, my Lord," I think in return.

"Irini listened to God's voice. She poured out all the courage and the love in her heart, and she walked humbly, and she was gathered to her father and all your father's fathers in joy."

Every tear I had shed has dried in this radiance. "Is it possible to remain together now?" I think in return.

Irini separates herself from the luminous figure to draw close to me again. "You may stay with us here if you wish to, Stephanos. But there are many in Israel awaiting word of our Lord through you and through your marking by the blood. You are called as Protomartyr—as first witness."

My soul is overpowered by longing to remain close to these spirits of love, so gentle and yet so demanding. As I long, I see below me a room, Saul's room, and in the room, I can see Saul kneeling over a prostrate figure on a carpet, another man standing close by. "Any action, any money," he is saying to this standing figure. "Only tell me the truth—is there hope of any kind?"

A trembling fills my spirit as Saul kneels and calls upon God, his voice breaking with heaviness, and he lays hands on the figure lying beneath his fingers. And I recognize the faded gold of Irini's own head wrap beneath his hand.

"Saul's love is incomplete," I hear the inner voice in my mind's ear. "You are the only friend able to assist him on his journey to see the Son of Man again."

The truth underlying this thought—that I must leave this pilgrimage of hope to land again in what I considered my world until this day—is evident to me, but so is the coldness of going back to that room where Saul is praying. Since there seems to be no time here, I allow myself to linger in the presence of my loved ones, a step below my family and my Lord, a step above what now I can call only my earthly remains.

"I am your servant and a very imperfect one, Lord," I think upward. "My father and my sister are far greater than I shall ever be on earth or thereafter. Still, let it be your will."

Irini reaches out one hand, and as she touches the

formlessness that is my soul, again, a vast burning fills me. Then she vanishes behind my Lord, but Baba glides close. "Stephanos, my son on earth, do not fear anything. All the learning from your childhood, all your travels among the Greeks, and all our love will go with you to prepare a way before you. Our Lord will bless your way and show you what you must do."

He has read my heart and its willingness.

Irini's voice cuts past the radiance before me. "When you return there, you will not remember this meeting until you see us once again. But, brother, we await you with our Lord, and his promise binds us together."

"Amen!" Baba thinks, and I receive.

And it comes to pass, like a man thrown from a cliff, I plunge away from all this wonder, diving instead into the enchaining of my body. First it outlines me, then it imprisons my soul like a galley slave seized into hard labor.

"Stephanos!" a voice calls.

Dawn—or is it twilight?—knocks on my eyelids, and my eyes open into emptiness. Like sweet water flowing from a pitcher, a memory pours out of my mind, some fantastic dream fading from my aching head, and with it, a strange sorrowing for distant and wonderful things forgotten. But a sense of relief washes over me, reminding me of my childhood, as though something of the dream remains.

The breathing beside the carpet where I lie is all too familiar; it is the heavy breath of Saul. Recalling his embrace and words of forgiveness spoken before we entered the sanctuary, I smile. I raise my head in the dimness. But why am I here with him, and what is this clutter of ointments stinging the air around us? Why does my right palm burn like fire, and who has called my name?

"Stephanos!" The voice that woke me calls again.

I recognize it this time, the beloved inner voice of our Messiah. Yes! Now that I am awake, sweet dream forgotten, I recall everything clearly—the Temple, the veil, and the voice of our Lord as it spoke to me from the cross. And amidst all the bitter words spoken regarding his death, yet the sweet ones are the ones that embrace my memory closest of all. "Believe; accept my grace. Your soul is free."

My hand plucks at my covering, and my fingers recognize it before my eyes do; it is the head wrapping of my sister Irini, somehow here and descended on me as I slept.

Despite this sweet assurance of holy things around me, a sense of urgency makes me rise. There is no fire, but the smell of it. A lantern near my couch is going out in its own ashes, which have spread like a blanket beneath it. I bind my robe and my sandals, picking up Irini's wrapping and preparing to leave as Saul sleeps on. After what I have seen and known in the great Temple, I must seek out those who knew Jesus of Nazareth, the Christ! But with a soft finger, I leave Saul a message in the ash before blowing the lantern's final flicker into darkness.

10. The Nakedness and the Ash

Witness of Lukas, Jerusalem, A.D. 32

Upon the First Day of Passover

"Dear lady, did not our Lord create such healing rocks, even as He created the fire I have used to warm them and the wool you have given me to wrap them?" I can think of no other reply for this highborn rabbi's widow. From one side of her mouth, she complains bitterly of her aching joints, while from the other, she derides me for proposing a Grecian treatment that I am convinced can relieve her suffering.

Before I ever mixed an ointment or laid hands on an ailing body, my mother, Iphigenia, taught me this. "Lukas, never forget, it is opening the mind that will show you the body. First, you must do no harm, but second, you must open your heart to listen to the shadow–words never spoken."

Recalling these points at every consultation, I read clearly this aging woman's body through her mind. No one of priestly family would summon me on Passover without great agony. But equally, no one of such a family could admit that foreign knowledge might offer more than the traditions they know. So while her desire for healing is strong, and her need for it is great, this patient must be convinced in her mind of the value of my treatment for her body.

Stretching out my hand to the slave girl cowering between the old woman and me, I take the pumice stones that she has first warmed, then wrapped in wool. I smile at the girl. "This heat and wrapping are prepared exactly to my instructions," I tell her. "You have done well."

Rolling my right sleeve to the elbow, I lay a single stone on my forearm and leave it there, while hearing out the woman's lament that this great aching of her joints and tendons in the cold does not even allow her to join the family for the feast. As my arm begins to sweat, I remove the well-packed pumice stone. "See the redness?" I ask her. "It is the sign that my blood has moved in to course all through this spot. Your own pain may come from lack of blood where you need it. The heat of these stones will draw your body's blood to its own protection, and your joints will be loosened with all the motion of the blood passing back and forth."

The woman says nothing, but she lays one finger on my forearm as though she has never touched the heat of human skin before. The finger itself is wrinkled like a dried date, and nearly as sticky with ointments she has tried. "We will see," she replies.

I smile, knowing this patient is ready at last for my remedy. "Indeed," I answer. "I think that if you remain resting this night, you may even be able to sit with the women tomorrow."

Turning to the little slave girl, I speak to her in her native Greek. I start to inform her just how often to keep the stones warm in the two sets I have given her so that there will be no time of cold.

"Do not use your heathen tongue in this room!" my patient snaps after I have spoken only a few phrases.

Now I understand the girl's cringing. Coming from a Greek-speaking province as I did, her Hebrew is not nearly adequate to understand most of the instruction she receives from this woman. Thus, she appears to disobey, though by no act of her own will. I am fortunate that in Antioch where I lived, I could study in synagogue and learn the language of my people from childhood.

Searching my mind, I pray to our Lord for some reply courteous to this suffering woman. Then I find it. "I believe even Naaman's little slave girl did not speak in Hebrew when she told her foreign mistress of the power of Elisha through our Lord to heal leprosy."

The girl has understood nothing of this, but the woman smiles, surprising me. "Well, at least this is not leprosy, thanks be to our Lord," she answers. "Speak on to her as you must, then; she is too dull to understand even simple directions in Hebrew, anyhow."

As I leave the woman's room, promising to return in a day, I hear argument in the courtyard. A slight boy pushes past an older man toward the passage from which I am about to emerge. He appears to be the young Temple boy who ran to my mother's wedding with Timon just a few days ago.

"What, interrupting us again, Ezra?" I intend to jest, but then I see his stricken face. "What is it?" I go on, forsaking my laughter.

"Timon sent me to seek you out, Doctor Lukas," he says, and while these words are unnecessary, they give him time to regain the wind and pump his lungs to feed the fire inside his body.

I lay a hand on his shoulder and breathe deeply, looking straight into his eyes. Sure enough, he begins to calm as his eyes meet mine. Without knowing it, the rhythm of his breath attempts to match my own.

"Timon sent me to tell you this. Our friend has fallen in the Temple, and we cannot tell whether he is alive or dead."

I wonder which elder this news concerns. Since the message comes from Timon, it could be any one of them.

"It is Stephanos, Timon's own Stephanos," Ezra speaks on.

I draw in my breath. A hundred questions leap to the top of my mind like hungry fish when one locust falls into the water. I force my queries into the single point of logika which will open or close the door to everything else. "Did you see this happen yourself, Ezra?"

The boy shakes his head. "There were too many people and too many duties for me to be there."

"No matter," I tell him, grasping his hand and allowing him to pull me. This youth can nurture his sense of honor in using his strength, believing he is hastening me along. Our breath steams before us in the cold.

But we do not go to the Temple. Instead, we reach a gated building nearby.

"This is the home and the school of Rabboni Gamaliel," Ezra tells me. "I am honored to live here and to study with him and to have Saul of Tarsus as my teacher."

Through the courtyard we hurry, and then along some steep stairs to an upper room. Several lanterns surround a couch and hang from the roof, with water both hot and cold in basins set nearby.

With a quick word of thanks and the offer of a coin that the boy refuses, I dismiss Ezra and go straight to Stephanos. His pallid figure is too long even for the soft carpets laid on the floor where he lies. I grasp my new patient's hand, and I feel a penetrating cold. His flesh is soft, with none of the caving in to expect on a fresh corpse. I push away the memory of the warmth and strength of that hand just days ago grasping mine as we sealed my mother's wedding contract.

From my sleeve, I unsheathe a small blade with a tapering point. It is chilled from the air outside. Losing no time, I place the broadest segment just above the prostrate man's lips. After a few seconds, the polished bronze clouds with the heat of his internal fire. Kneeling by his head, and moving my face yet closer, I find no stink of bile that might indicate a poison in his stomach. Nor is there any tell-tale sweetness on his breath that could speak of the need for honey under his tongue, whose wonders I have discovered with a few of my unconscious patients.

"You are alive, my brother, and you must try to stay with us," I murmur both to myself and to him, in case his ears can hear.

"Thanks be to our Lord!"

The sharp voice from behind me startles me so that I nearly drop the blade.

Then the man adds, "Doctor, I thought you saw me, and I had no intent to frighten you."

In my concentration on healings at hand, I often ignore everything around me. Sometimes as now, this is to my woe. While keeping my patient's limp hand clasped in mine, I turn to the voice that has addressed me. It is the guest whose slight limp and stammer at my mother's wedding drew my attention.

"No matter," I respond. "Indeed he is alive. Ezra told me that he fell in the Temple. Did you witness this?"

Some oddness in this Pharisee's countenance cautions me. But he nods readily. "I tried to catch him."

I have noted my patient's heartbeats during this conversation: faint, like a child's, and just as fast. Older doctors pay little attention to the heart, but in my observation, its rhythm is greatly tied to a patient's health.

Now I need to undress my patient, but I must be careful. "Where did he strike the ground?" I ask, before loosening Stephanos' robe. Good. It is not soiled with any urine or the contents of the bowels, another sign of ongoing life.

Again some pause and drawing of breath from this man I am questioning, and I am certain that he bears some discomfort. "He fell hard on my shoulder. I reached for him as I saw him sway forward, and then his knees melted under him, and both of us fell together," the man replies.

"You were both able to fall even amidst all that crowd in the Temple?" Knowing the multitude as I have seen it during the several Passovers we have lived in Bethany near Jerusalem, my doubt builds.

But the man merely answers, "Yes, it was so."

Grasping the shadow words of this witness will be no small task, I fear, but I must take time and thought to know things precisely as they happened.

My patient appears uninjured; in fact, the vitality and grace of his body are striking. Palpation yields no breaking of his bone lines, nor any response on his face or in his limbs when I touch the muscles that should yield.

"Did your friend eat any peculiar food, or drink, or anything else you saw?"

Meanwhile, I open Stephanos' eyes and draw the closest lantern above them. They glimmer, but no response starts from their spheres.

The stammer of Stephanos' friend seems more marked as he answers this time. "You must know that today was no ordinary day, with the darkness and the trembling of the earth. Perhaps this has affected him." Then, clearing his throat, he replies with more deliberation. "I have been with Stephanos since morning, when we walked to the Temple, and he has eaten and drunk nothing. We were to take the feast together tonight."

"Ah, yes," I say. This man's words remind me that indeed, our Passover has begun, and with this sunset, so has our day of Sabbath.

Upon the Second Day of Passover

The night is long and hard and cold. I give scarce notice or greeting to the learned men who venture here to sigh and whisper with the man I have questioned. I finally hear his name; it is Saul. No scholar can look at Stephanos and not weep aloud, but none of these men can raise a single finger to help him, however great their faith and learning. I hear repeated whisperings of "the great veil," and Saul shushing the talk. I have more important things to tend to than peculiar gossip, so I keep my back to the visitors.

The worst affected of anyone is Timon the Greek. His tears are silent, but in my life, I have not seen such rivers of grief until I witness his mourning. I clasp the two hands of this man whom I must now call stepfather. It is all I can do to hold him back from shearing the single good garment he has and which he wears each day at the main gates in honor of the feast. His sorrowing reminds me of the misery of slaves I have tended, men long barred from saying words from their hearts. Timon's tears fall like rain on my patient as he stoops to adjust every piece of cloth around Stephanos, waging war against the cold.

Timon leaves briefly, and then returns somehow with plentiful food. He refuses any of it for himself. I had ignored my hunger, but now the savor of the Passover lamb he produces is welcome.

Saul invites Timon to remain, but the Greek shakes his head, mumbling that he is no scholar like those in this house, that his presence would insult the residents even if he is deemed a Jew. After prayers, Timon leaves, with promise to return early in the morning.

The overnight vigil I keep is marked off by my two ears. The one facing outward is full of the joyful feast songs and the talk echoing from every street and wall outside, while also overflowing with the stammered, murmured prayers of Stephanos' peculiar friend close by. The other ear, close to Stephanos' carpet, begs for sound that does not come, for any breath and movement of this fallen man. Throughout the night, I administer the various waking powders I have with me, placing them beneath Stephanos' tongue. I also brush his nose with fermented urine to force a cough or splutter. Still nothing. To attempt unwatered wine could choke him, so I refrain.

It is a hard thing for me to call this man patient, who five days past was so full of strength, charming us all with his lyra and speaking kind words to my mother. Yet death crouches at the threshold of every man's body, and my duty is merely to hold it distant as long as life allows.

When Timon named this friend of his, this young man Stephanos, his guardian for the purposes of the wedding, it was no more a thing to ridicule than naming myself, giving away my own mother in marriage as though I were her father. I should hate this union, along with the duty it will bring now as this Athenian grows inevitably older and I am obliged to take on his guardianship. But I have witnessed the transformation from sorrow to joy in the woman who brought me to birth. Whether my mother has spoken to Timon of all our past, I do not know, but her newfound joy in itself is enough for me to accept without rancor the man she now calls husband.

All my life, my mother longed for only two things—first, for gaining our freedom, and second, for leaving our birthplace of Antioch and returning to the heart city of our people, the Jews. After all, though she knew then neither our laws nor our language, whom else did we have to call our own? She would speak of these hopes to me as a sweet story at my waking, and as a gentle dream rocking me to sleep.

After the death of my father, a thing I was too young to recall, my mother took on a hard vow. A Greek doctor, knowing her skills as midwife, bought her out of her former servitude. He promised her proper training for me to become a doctor like himself, and freedom for us both at his death. But in return, she would become not only his assistant, to bring him more profit from her skills, but also his mistress and his comforter in old age. My mother agreed, making me believe for a time that they were indeed man and wife, until I was old enough to learn of things for myself. It explained the tears she often shed and her daily prayers for forgiveness to our Lord, which I hardly understood at first.

Our protector kept his word to my mother in not only

teaching me of medicine himself, but allowing me to study with the greatest doctor in our city. This I will say of him. Nor did he forbid me to study at synagogue each Sabbath and learn the traditions of our people, the Jews. But I will say nothing more on his behalf.

My mother failed to hear his shadow words. She was either too trusting, or else afraid to demand more than the gaining of our freedom when our protector died. Thus at his death we gained our liberty, but nothing more.

After arriving in Jerusalem as freedmen, we were greatly tried by the needs of freedom—that is, the earning of enough money to feed and house ourselves. Even a trained physician and a skilled midwife must gather trust and help from others to begin a trade in a new place. Of course, we had none of this as strangers, and my youth worked against me, as most patients respect a doctor with years of experience I could not claim. Thus the first of my success there was hard gained among the poor who could scarcely pay me.

Soon enough, my mother went to the great Temple, feeling called there to pray to our Lord. This Timon of Athens spoke gentle words to her at the gate. He knew her by her dress as a woman from a Greek city, and they discoursed freely. Seeing her sad face, he asked what her purpose was. Through a few questions, he read her want as a lettered man could peruse a scroll.

When my mother came to me with his proposal to help us by sharing word of our medicine with those who could afford to pay us, I was doubtful. When I went to the Temple to speak with him, however, I recognized his face; he was the man rescuing a child from the river Jordan that I treated shortly after our arrival in Palestine. No evil man would have done such a thing, and I agreed to his commerce with my mother, though even then, I remained unsuspecting of the guard's real intent. He spoke of his proposal for marriage only years after, when our practices were well established and he had benefited from the circumcision I administered with my own knife in order for him to join our people. His waiting reveals his honor, as does his honesty in handing over to the Temple every coin my mother brought him. He kept nothing for himself as go–between, though this would be a reasonable thing to expect.

My mind spins from past to present amidst my many risings to attend Stephanos. Like our people of Israel falling away, my family has its shame and its sins to cover. But now, lying in the elbow of darkness before the dawn, I must admit this: Timon of Athens is a good man, a zealous Jew courageous in his conversion. He will be a faithful husband to my mother. For any widow to find not only her desires of freedom and of living in Jerusalem, but yet a third happiness, love, and to receive it as she did, this is a story worthy of a poem—or of the lyra this Stephanos of Tarsus played with such grace at the wedding.

Hearing Stephanos' lyra in my inner ear must have lulled me to sleep, because I am startled sometime later with a whir of motion from the carpet where he lies. Before my eyes open, my heart leaps, believing my patient to stir. But then my gaze reveals a thing that is terrible, and yet, something I have long desired to prove or disprove as patients confide secrets of their sleep.

A small spirit we know as a Lilith, a demon of the night, crouches on Stephanos' chest. It is very still, as I too remain still. My breath must not betray my awakening to witness with my own eyes this thing that I have never before seen but often heard of. Now I can prove through my own senses the presence of such creatures not in the mind, but as part of the night they inhabit. I observe this being as it unrolls a long, slender shroud to cover both itself and my patient. Even in the dimness, this cloth appears to be spun of something golden. After laying the cloth, the night figure extends itself fully to cover my patient's body. Though I know that such sleep visions do patients no harm—they always survive to tell of them, after all—only the softness of this Lilith's motions hold me back from fear.

But soon, stifled gulps I hear from a living throat reveal this Lilith to be something beyond spirit—a woman. If I interrupt too sharply, she could strike my patient or violate his thread of life. Nothing must threaten the slender current of his breath.

"Who are you, and what are you doing?" I whisper into her ear, not loud enough to awaken Saul.

The dim and tear-stained face that turns to me is indeed a woman's, or almost a woman's. "Cassandra!" I hiss. I have not liked her since the wedding day, when I first saw her and she dogged the messenger boy Ezra with needless questions.

Even in the few days since, this child I am obliged to call sister is already like a whirlwind about our home, now peering where she is not needed, now meddling where she is not wanted. How she has appeared here is incredible, and adding to my disappointment is the confusion of thinking her the Lilith whose presence my eyes had seen.

"Get up! You could kill him!" I order, but I keep my whisper under tight control. "His breath is thin as a spider's web!"

"But he is so cold, Lukas—so cold! All I can give him is the heat from my own body."

"Cassandra! Do as I say. You are no doctor!" I place a strong hand between Stephanos' chest and her shoulder.

The girl arises, unresisting, but she folds the yellowish shroud over his chest. And he sighs just a little.

I breathe his breath, feel his heart. Satisfied that nothing is worse than it was already, I draw her down the stairs and into the courtyard. "How did you come here? How did you even know of this?" I demand, my first shock too great for anger.

"With Ezra," she answers.

"Ezra the Temple boy? On Passover? On the night of Sabbath?"

"He promised me," she says with the same simplicity.

"Promised you what?"

"That if Uncle Thaul or Stephanos ever need me, he would come for me."

I force my mind to the essential questions, as with a patient, to divide me from my anger now rising. "And our mother allowed this?"

Cassandra's hesitation speaks her shadow words. "Everyone else in the house was busy feasting and enjoying Passover," she replies.

"So you departed like a thief in the night," I state.

She shakes her head. "I left a message."

"With whom, since you just claimed that everyone was feasting without you?"

"We left a note," she clarifies.

It is my turn to shake my head. "You should know after the wedding that no one in my house can speak Hebrew," I snap, "let alone read what Ezra wrote—though he did well to try."

But she shakes her head again. "The note is in Greek, and I need no Ezra to help me. I wrote it with my own stylus on one of your tablets from your shelf."

I inhale sharp and deep, my amazement at her claim of writing only rivaled by my indignation. "And you think this is enough—to depart with a Temple boy, to say nothing, and to leave a note—if you even write correctly, which I doubt. If you must know, I am the only one in the house able to read."

It is Cassandra's turn to suck in her breath. "First my Aunt Irini, and afterwards, my Uncle Stephanos, saw to it that I can read and write as well as the boys, and I can show you!" she says. "It is not my matter if others cannot read my message." Then she falters. "Can't anyone in our courtyard besides my brother here read Greek?"

As I strive to master myself, I shake my head and seek to put logika into my next words. "Do you even begin to understand the danger, not only for you, but for Ezra, breaking the Sabbath's journey distance allowed us? In days of old, you could both die for this."

"Well, we are alive."

As this half-girl, half-woman shrugs and shuffles her foot, my anger rises out of all constraints. "If this breaking of the Sabbath law means nothing to you, so fine a girl from Athens as you say, so well educated and so intelligent, so eager to sing sweet songs, well, it means everything to my mother and to me. We risked our entire lives and fortunes and destiny to come to Jerusalem to live out our Jewish faith. What notion does such a fine, lofty girl like you possibly have of being a slave and a Jew and longing for freedom, or of trying to learn the proper laws of our Lord? Well, I will tell you this, sister," I hiss the word out. "Your mother will hear of all this as soon as we return to Bethany."

Dawn is just breaking, and I should return to Stephanos. This is the time so many souls take flight. I hope somehow to pin his spirit close with my voice, with my touch. But Cassandra stops me short with her next words. "And when I return to Bethany, brother, our mother shall learn of your nakedness as well!"

My left hand clenches my right to prevent it from striking this—this creature who has come into our house. I am unsure which of my furies is greater, the bile rising within me at her hissing out the holy word "mother," or the flame of my rage at the scorn with which she has called me "brother."

But this is the truth of it. I did run desperate and naked through the streets just the night before this one. There is something unholy in this half-grown girl's ferreting out of every secret. Perhaps indeed she is a demonic Lilith as she first appeared to me this night!

Rapid steps beat from behind us through the courtyard. "It is you, child—thank our Lord that Ezra found you and you have come!" Timon greets Cassandra, knowing her even though our faces are close to invisible in this scarce glimmer of dawn.

Then turning to me as if he reads my mind, "Please do not be angry with her. If anyone can save Stephanos with spirit, it is Cassandra."

Shame boils within me, and I bow my head as I return his greeting. My face burns that the girl knows my unspeakable secret, but far more, my heart burns that I have failed as physician to acknowledge the power of such a loved one to a spirit struggling between our world and the next. How many times have I heard a child or a mother or even a wife sobbing, and with their very breath igniting some spark of will that would otherwise have gone out and ended a life?

"Remain, then," I mutter.

Cassandra nods, but then she leans close to my ear and whispers, "And you will tell me later why you ran home with no clothes." These words are no request; they are a command.

"Please tell me what I must do," Timon continues when Cassandra has entered the chamber and we are left alone on the small stairs leading toward the roof.

My tongue stiffens, for what reply can I give him that will be of any use? One thing I know—I do not want yet another person here to trouble me while I am in the full service of my patient, most of all as my spirit is so perturbed with Cassandra's presence.

"It is best for you to guard the gate even this Sabbath," I respond. "I will send news to you if something is needed."

"Tell me the truth—" Timon begins, and then falters. I hear his shadow words as though he gave them voice.

Laying a steady hand on his shoulder, I press lightly at his flinty musculature, unrelenting in its grief and its worry. My finger pulses with attempt to soften his stance. "I will do everything I can for him. It is a good thing, his surviving through the night. And we know that the prayers of many rest with him."

Then a thought lightens my mind. "And you can help indeed. At the gate, surely you can ask Gamaliel and the others to uphold him in their prayers."

Timon nods with eagerness and replies in so-called Hebrew. "Yes, yes. There I now go before rise sun tell every them all! They me understand, important matter this, pray big all over him!"

How can a man with such fair speech in one language struggle like a gasping fish in another?

"Amen, indeed," I respond in Hebrew. "Go now before they arrive."

"Amen, amen!" Timon calls back as he runs down the stairs with the vigor of a man half his age. Then he turns and looks up. In Greek he adds, "Thank you, my son."

In any other circumstance, I would push this title of son away from my heart like a stray dog. Yet here in the silence of this Sabbath dawn, my throat grows tight at his attempt at kindness amidst his sorrow.

Behind the door, murmurings arise from the room where my patient is lying.

"Stay here, and pray in my place," Saul's words float out. "I will attend the Sabbath prayers at temple, and I will return here." His voice grows stern. "Cassandra, you are in no circumstance to come into the men's court to find me."

"But if there is news, I will let Uncle Timon know!" Always this eagerness in my small adopted sister's voice. "I will pray here the whole time while you are gone, Uncle Thaul. I will pray exactly as you taught me."

Saul's voice softens. "Yes, and you will do so very well. Now leave, and let me dress."

I have given even more thought to my patient during the time it takes Saul to depart. As soon as he leaves, I address Cassandra, who is indeed clasping her hands and praying with eyes closed. I must admit, her Hebrew is as pure as her Greek, and it sounds devout. But I remind myself, so did the songs of sirens that condemned many a sailor to certain death, as Homer assures us. Still, I read the shadow words I heard behind her speech to Saul, her sincerity to help her Uncle Stephanos, and I lay a plan.

"There is one thing you can do for Stephanos," I begin.

Her prayers stop as though cut off by strangulation, and her eyes fly open and fasten to mine.

I need to appease her. "I was wrong to judge you so harshly, though our mother is surely very distressed right now. In fact, it is a good thing that you came here, because your spirit is close with Stephanos. But I have not understood fully the circumstances of his falling. Go to the gate by Timon and learn the truth of what happened in the Temple yesterday, especially as regards the veil."

Cassandra shakes her head. "I will continue to pray here as I promised Uncle Thaul, but I can already tell you all about the veil, because Ezra told me on our way here."

Cassandra relates to me a story that, if I did not see the state of this man, I would hardly believe—not only of the blowing of the wind, the cold, the trembling of the earth that I already know, but of the tearing of the holiest of holy veils at the front of the sanctuary.

"Stephanos and Saul were the only ones who approached," she concludes. "Only Uncle Stephanos looked within the veil before he held it wide for everyone to see, while Uncle Thaul tried to protect our congregation from viewing what would kill them to behold. So you see, this is why he is dying."

Her words have allowed me to comprehend the entire scene, and also Saul's disquiet. No wonder both men could fall in a crowded Temple; the space was open wide before the veil. In fact, it is a wonder that Saul himself is left alive. He is cursed, however, by this knowledge and by his acts, though he does not want to bring the weight of my dismay onto my patient or himself. At last I understand the hesitancy I read in his face and heard in his speech when I questioned him.

I have thought long on a final step I can take to serve my patient. His elements are unbalanced, resulting in the cold, the lack of fire in his veins. Now I must know if he is capable of waking at all, though it brings me grief to do what I must.

"Go to the roof for your prayer," I tell Cassandra, and to my relief, she obeys without question.

When I have looked out the door and am assured that she is gone, I remove the bronze blade on which I tested my patient's breath. I hold it close to a lantern remaining lit, then thrust the tip directly into the flame.

Meanwhile, I softly voice every move, every step, to Stephanos. "I am stirring up the warmth of fire to counter the weight of the opposing water lodged in your body. What I need to do will bring you pain, but it may still serve you well, brother. If you can hear me, if you can respond in any way, squeeze my hand, move your eyes beneath your lids, drop your jaw, sigh. Hold my hand back from this act."

I am speaking as though to a dead man, and yet, "My brother, for what I will do now, I ask forgiveness of you and of our Lord. Truly, I have nothing left to wake you or to help you, as you seem neither to live nor to die."

My eyes close as the heat of the flame and the metal envelopes my hand. "Lord, have mercy upon this man if he beheld unknowing and unwilling the things behind Your holy veil. Remember his years spent in Your learning. His is a soul given to You and a heart seeking only to dwell in Your justice."

With this, I lift the glowing tip of the blade from the flame, and I touch it to the center of my patient's right palm—then press till the flesh sizzles and parts.

And still, there is no shudder—not even the faintest sigh or trembling. Surely this man is bound for death, though the smell of burning flesh recalls his life.

"Lord have mercy," I repeat now in Greek. "Take pity on this poor victim of his over-zealous eyes, and keep and strengthen me. In the service of all my patients, disallow me from witnessing such a thing again or from needing to perform such acts of unwilling destruction."

Yet I long to know what the eyes of this man have taken in beyond our holy veil. If I could know, could I then heal? Surely a vain thought, but also a deep desire.

It is this very eagerness and longing that led to the nakedness that Cassandra knows about. I had heard rumors for months of a great healer called Jesus the Nazarene. These stories came from people claiming to witness things too great for any doctor's skill. Shortly before our Passover, Jesus came to our own adopted town of Bethany, visiting a house where he called a man back from the dead after several days of entombment. This I heard in near identical terms from two Hellenisti who know the man's family. One of them claimed even to have spoken with the man Lazarus who arose from the dead.

It was not difficult for me to inquire and learn some of this healer's habits, including his frequent walks on the Mount of Olives. I wanted to hold discourse with him, but I did not wish to be recognized. It is a delicate thing as physician to talk with someone like this man who claims healing through powers other than our own knowledge of nature and the elements.

Then it came to pass that I was smitten with small, biting insects in the hairs all over my body. To avoid their spreading, I went to the baths and shaved bare to avoid any possibility of carrying the insects on my person to another house. Appearing like a bare-headed Roman instead of a Jew is a small price to pay to avoid the risk of creating more woes for someone already ill. And looking this way for a time is less of a danger to my hard-earned reputation among the wealthy Jews of the city than possible rumors of my own contagion.

It came to my mind just following the bath on the eve of

Passover that I could now approach this healer completely unrecognized. I have a linen toga as payment from a centurion I once treated. Clad in this, I went to the Mount of Olives, where I was told this Nazarene often speaks with his followers.

I did not go there in vain. Shortly, I came across a lone man kneeling in prayer. From his face flowed not only sweat, but tears from his eyes, and from his forehead, I am witness of this, drops of blood with no wound in evidence. His lips moved as though in pleading, but I could hear no words departing his tongue. His face was such a fearful thing, I did not dare approach, but I was certain this was the man I was looking for, since his prayer resembled no natural state.

After some time, this man walked a stone's throw from his place of prayer, and I followed him. Before he had much time to speak with his students, a crowd came up the hill. A man dressed like his students led a large group of Temple followers and soldiers. This man kissed Jesus, and then Jews and Romans alike were surrounding him with swords drawn.

Another student also drew his sword, and with it, he severed the right ear of someone in the crowd as people reassured themselves of the Nazarene's identity. The ear flew through the air to the ground near where Jesus stood. I saw with my own eyes how he reproached this student, picked up the ear, spat on it, and then ran to the white-faced man who had been struck. Jesus whispered something to the afflicted man as he pressed the ear in its rightful place. The man's face flushed in the firelight, and the ear remained attached as the Nazarene removed his palm from the man's face. This stricken man lost no additional blood, though his cloak was red with it. He tried to thank Jesus, but by then, the crowd had regained itself. Many fell on Jesus and began to drag him away. He did not struggle.

Looking back, of course, I was a fool to hope for the chance to speak with this healer. But I found myself following not far behind, thinking only of some way to approach him.

Then young men fell upon me. "A Roman out of his ranks!" they called, and they were ready to beat me. Following my bath, I had been awkward in wrapping myself in the linen toga, since I had never worn one. Now, in trying to capture me, the men seized my cloth and pulled it off my body as I fled.

Their jeers and laughter pursued me as they began arguing as to who would claim it. I had no time to risk my life with these Roman–hating ruffians. I prayed thanks to my Lord for the steepness of the hill, the narrowness of the streets, and my knowledge of these quarters. I rushed away until I could reach a palm tree. I ripped leaves from it and bound my chest and loins, and I slunk in hiding all the way back to Bethany.

I seem to recall some movement of the shadows in the courtyard when I arrived home; it was surely Cassandra in one of her times of sleeplessness of which she has already complained to me.

In my sorrow and exhaustion, I have drowsed again.

Saul startles me as he falls to his knees by my patient. "Any action, any money," he is saying to me. "Only tell me the truth— is there hope of any kind?"

I shake my head. "I have learned of the tearing of the holy veil," I tell him directly. "From here, I can leave things only to the will of our Lord. I have tried every remedy I have ever learned, and even things I have not learned." I still recoil inwardly from the burning of my patient's palm.

Saul's sigh makes the lantern tremble. "Stephanos and I are brothers," he says. "I would give my own life."

"I know," I reply. Then I wish to divert Saul from his grief, and I consider his own situation. "How long have you walked as you do?" I ask. It is not our custom to inquire about such a thing, but my place as doctor erodes our rules for courtesy.

Saul rises with difficulty, but he stands very straight. "From birth." This is as I expected. Saul's throat muscles stretch tight on the bitter words, as I also anticipated.

I kneel before him and touch the hem of his robe. "Please allow me to examine your feet."

Whether from surprise or resignation, Saul loosens his heavy robe and lifts it to his knees.

I palpate the hardness of his calves, and my palms understand beneath his feet the slight rising of one heel to keep in synchrony with the other, stronger limb. "What treatments have been attempted in the past?" I ask, still exploring his muscles and flesh, weaker on the right leg.

Saul's laugh stings my ears. "I am marked by our Lord," he answers. "Besides, what treatment can lengthen a man's limb or make his muscles like the rest?"

Adjusting his robe and clasping his knees, I look upward into his face, and I smile. "Many things that our Lord has given us to try, brother," I respond. "And some of these are quite simple. Here is one example."

Cassandra's shadow appears behind Saul in the door, and she pauses. I do not forbid her, but she stays still. No matter. I remove my bronze blade again and fold the soft leather sheath that protects it. This I lodge into the back of Saul's right sandal lying on the floor just behind him, and then I fasten the shoe on his foot. "Walk some paces," I tell him.

One–sandaled, Saul obeys me, and he nearly falls. "Not this!" he exclaims. "Now it is as though my left foot is the offender."

"Now put on the other sandal." I help him so as to shake him out of any hesitation. With his right heel elevated and without the pressing of his own weakened foot, Saul rotates and paces. With my leather sheath pressing upwards, the unevenness of his tread is nearly gone.

Using my bronze blade, I mark some quick drawing and measures on a small wax tablet bound in wood that I keep with me. "This is a small matter for me to provide you, and it can be done before next Sabbath. With a little exercise and a heavy chain for practice to strengthen your limb..."

Saul shrugs with irritation, and removing my blade sheath, he tosses it onto the floor beside me, striking my hand. "What need do I have for this when I have walked this way all my life, and my brother here is going to die? Do not distract me with your learning!"

Stepping in, Cassandra picks up my sheath, wipes it gently, and turns directly to this unwilling patient. "But Uncle Thaul, my brother wants only to help you. Can you imagine how happy you would be if people stopped staring at you? I want to be happy along with you. It is a very small thing to try it, isn't it?"

Saul's face softens as Cassandra clasps his hand and returns the sheath to me. "It would be as easy as Naaman the leper to bathe in the Jordan for you to have some small leather at your heel."

Saul passes his other hand before his beard, but his eyes have gentled. "What will be the cost for such a thing?" he asks, turning to me.

"If a high sandal relieves your fatigue in walking and makes you well, give a thank offering in the Temple for my family and for me," I tell him. "The treatment is a very small thing."

Cassandra stands between us and looks to me. "Uncle Thaul can sing perfectly well. He never stammers or has a shaking voice when he chants. Can you help him to speak as he sings, too, please, Lukas?"

I have also thought of this man's voice and the words that halt and repeat in his mouth. Now Cassandra has given me an important key to the breath he swallows with his stammering. "Not everything at once, child, but it is possible," I reply.

A scratching at the half–open door interrupts us. "Doctor?"

Saul opens the door, and Ezra the Temple boy steps in. Any fool could see from his face why he promised to help the girl as he did; his blush turns his cheeks from peach to pomegranate upon the sight of her.

"I am here," I answer unnecessarily, but to interrupt his gaze attaching to the girl's unguarded eyes. "Did someone send for me?"

"No one sent, but I heard you promise to return to the house where I found you last night. I saw that you were not paid, and I fear they may give you nothing if you do not return there today. Forgive me, but I have heard things that are not good about this family's greed."

I smile. "I see that many spies are on my side in the Temple."

It is Cassandra's turn to giggle and blush. Saul sighs.

"Today is the Sabbath, and no payment will be taken or given," I remind Ezra. Yet little remains that I can do here, and Ezra has kept excellent faith to hover everywhere and serve. "But I will keep my promise and come in a moment."

Falling to my knees, I clasp the uninjured left hand of Stephanos between my own. This man reminds me more of death that is alive than life that is dying, though I cannot explain my unease. "Staying here with us is easier than leaving us," I whisper. "You are with the ones who love you most, you see."

Only a little shallow breath and that faint, rapid rhythm of his heart remain to him.

Upon the Third Day of Passover

It is no small matter for me to convince Cassandra to come home with me after returning from the house of the rabbi's widow. The old woman's gentler treatment of the Hellenist girl indicates how greatly relieved she is from her former pain. I rejoice as much for the slave girl as for my patient. I succeed in bringing Cassandra to Bethany only when Timon joins my urging. "I will let our mother know that Timon approved your leaving," I reassure her, "but you must never do this again."

Cassandra remains silent, and I do not press her. Instead,

along the way home, I tell the whole story of my nakedness. "So you see," I conclude, "I could as easily tell our mother of this as you could."

For many paces, this sister who is almost a woman says nothing, and I commend myself on a bargain well struck between us. Then she speaks. "Do you believe this Nazarene man had the power to heal anyone he wished?"

I shake my head in surprise at her earnestness and her belief in what I have just told her. "I have no way to tell this, sister. But I know what I have heard, and I saw the man who was healed, as I told you. There is certainly something extraordinary in the Nazarene's praying and in his means of healing."

Cassandra draws short to face me. "You mean, there was something in what he did, but no more," she replies. When I remain silent, she stops on the road in front of me. "Haven't you heard? He was crucified yesterday."

Recalling the angry mob in the garden, I should not be surprised, yet I am.

"He was taken before the governor. Many there called to save him and free a criminal. But the Temple men called more loudly and reminded the governor that anyone who claims to be a king besides our emperor Tiberius must surely die, and that they claim no king but this emperor."

I laugh with scorn, for this level of sophistry is too typical of those in power. "How do you know these things?" I challenge her nonetheless.

Cassandra begins to walk again. "Ezra saw much, and what he did not see, he asked about, and he told me. And I also understand another thing, Lukas. I saw this healer on the way to the wedding. He told me to keep faith, and the entire world fell silent as he passed by Rabboni Gamaliel and me, and he called Rabboni 'teacher' and knew him. Now that you tell me what you saw, I believe even more that he was the chosen one of Israel, as the crowd said."

I lay a hand over my sister's lips. "You are too young to understand these things." Yet I feel this girl's questions writhing in my own heart, full of the quest for truth.

"If I am wrong, I am only a silly girl, as you think I am. But if I am speaking the truth, then we have killed our own Christos," she replies in Greek. "And what will come of this, Lukas? Since you saw even more than I did, why don't you believe as I do? Just use your logika, as I have done."

At her words, two desires burn my soul. I do not want to believe that this was the Christ, but instead, to count him just one of the many faith healers whose peculiar workings die with their memory. In the same breath, I want to believe that this was the Christ, since as a physician, I can attest to the power of his spirit over matter.

Though I am exhausted, I sleep very little.

Through the night, I dream of my patient Stephanos, of his seeing beyond the veil, of his body both alive and dead, of Saul and his dismissal in addressing such a simple thing as his limp. Again I see the Nazarene and his gentleness, his simple yet precise motions of repairing a fallen ear, a thing that should be impossible. My final waking is swallowed only by my prayer to the Lord to guide my hands and to keep my mind fixed on the learning and the healing I know to be my calling, and the faith in the people I know to be my own.

I awaken early, and to my relief, Cassandra is not in the courtyard, nor do I hear her stirring. I leave a wax tablet near the hearth where she will see it. "You are to remain at home, and I will send for you with any needs or news, Cassandra," I scratch, but then, beneath the stern words, I draw as our Lord has allowed my hand, an Asclepius stick with a friendly-looking snake. I hope, then believe, that this nearly ungovernable new little sister of mine will obey a direct command like this one, but that the picture will reassure her that the anger that has passed

[227]

between us is left behind.

The cold has softened, and some faint scent of new life strikes my nose. Before reaching the Jerusalem gates, I recognize Ezra's racing feet, an awkwardness in the sound of his running peculiar to him; I have noted it already. Like many his age, the boy's hands and feet have outstripped his body in their growth, making him clumsy.

I stretch an arm for him to slow, and then he looks up and recognizes me. "I hope you have good sandals," I greet him, "and if you do not, I will need to buy some for you, as much as you are running these days. That, or we must teach you to run a little faster."

The boy tugs at my hand as he did at the rabbi's house. "Come quickly," he gasps.

As my heart beats faster, I am even more convinced of its importance in the body. "Tell me exactly what you know." This time, I neglect to allow him to catch the air he needs. "Cassandra is ordered to remain home, so turn back with me."

Ezra begins to protest, then stops. "But how will she know the news, then?"

"What news?"

"That he is gone," the boy gasps. "Come and see."

It is my turn to gasp. "Gone?" My paces lengthen and we enter the city gates together. "Gone where?" My stupid question fades onto the breeze, and I prepare inwardly for anointing the corpse, while telling myself that my presence there could have done nothing to save Stephanos of Tarsus.

Ezra leads me through alleys that even I have not yet learned back to the scholar's house where Saul resides. He lets me take the upward steps before him.

Saul is standing rigid by the door of his room, his face nearly as pale as Stephanos' was, and mourning ash is white on his dark locks.

"I awoke, and this is all that remained of him," he greets me, his voice breaking. "Only our Lord knows where he has gone. His sandals and his clothing are all he took. He is lost to us, and his mind is lost to himself."

Leading me inside, he points to a pile of ash on the floor. At first, I see nothing, but then my eyes adjust to the flickering light, and then scratchings in the ash form Hebrew letters, and the letters shape themselves into these words:

"Farewell, dear Saul. Pray that your soul shall be unveiled from law. Messiah sets us free!"

11. The Letters and the Miracles Witness of Timon, Jerusalem, A.D. 32-33

Upon the Reading

Here I have remained, rooted like a tree, by the stone posts of the Temple gate each day of Passover. From the glimmer of rosy-fingered dawn, to the tail of fading dusk, some hope waits along with me. But there is no Stephanos, no, not once. Nor for all my asking has one soul seen his face.

I inquire so diligently, that after the second day, Lukas takes pity. He writes a small sign behind my standing place with words. And given as he is to some way of lining with his pen and revealing the shape of things, he draws the face of Stephanos on papyrus below the sign.

But Gamaliel stops to address me that same day. He explains with stern but gentle words that though the sign with words could remain, this face is an image not pleasing at the house of our Lord. I take it down and tear it apart, full of shame for my ignorance allowing a violation, and even for my foster son, drawing such an unholy figure.

In the ways of the Greek gods, we could both undergo great punishment for even an unwitting deed like this one, but Gamaliel reminds me, my prayer to our Lord allows for pardon. This is perhaps the greatest part of becoming a Jew, abiding safe in the law of our Lord which is explained in scripture. We are free of the fear of untimely anger that could destroy us like the lusts of Zeus or the envy of Hera.

I wonder each day, how is it possible that every learned man passing by me can look at the lines on Lukas' sign and understand? Many others like me who cannot take in the meaning of such signs have thanked me for the helpful speaking of the Temple boys I have trained, saving struggle and worry with the many directions posted on walls and gates.

An event occurring shortly after Passover when I returned home to my beloved Iphigenia perplexes me yet further. Cassandra offered to share her knowledge of letters that she learned with Irini and continued with Stephanos. She summoned my wife and me to the courtyard in the cool of one Sabbath. To begin with, she shaped a line in the sand at our feet that looked to us like a fish, pronouncing its voice and asking us to think of words that might include the fish, which is named alpha and whose voice is "Ah."

As we replied, she smiled and laughed, and then she called out to her brother Lukas, "Come see how my students succeed!" She drew a second letter. "This is beta, and its voice is 'Beh,'" she began sternly.

"Beta, Beh," my dearest Iphigenia and I repeated after her.

"Now tell me words like 'bird' that voice this letter 'Beh.'" Her eyes pierced us.

"Hen," I began, and she smiled, so I continued. "Sparrow... stork... dove?"

"You are trying, my uncle, but you are incorrect," Cassandra replied, turning to my wife. "Can you answer better than Uncle Timon?"

Cassandra's very posture recalled to me the stance and tone of many philosopher teachers I used to observe in Athens, overwhelming me with pride and amazement. She did not reproach me for my error, and I knew that soon I would learn the truth from her.

Iphigenia responded bravely. "Feather? Egg? Nest? Wing?"

But with each word, Cassandra shook her head.

Facing Lukas, Cassandra began to laugh. "You see what newfound scholars we have here in our own house, brother?"

But instead of laughing with our little teacher, Lukas rose and struck her across the mouth.

Amazement rendered me speechless.

"How dare you ridicule the woman who gave me birth and the man who pulled you stinking and thieving out of Athens?" he shouted.

I regretted telling my foster son of how I came to know this girl, for I realized now the dignity of even a child could be crushed as Cassandra ran from the courtyard. She had known only her father's greatness, for what good would come from my telling her of her thievery and arrest? Now she would ask me, and I must tell her the rest.

"Why this anger of yours? Why is this a ridicule? She was only teaching us," I then ventured to Lukas.

I will not soon forget the sorrow in my foster son's face as he looked at his mother and me. "This learning of letters is a difficult thing to explain to you. I regret, Mother, that I never tried to teach you myself. Now it is too late." He sighed and shrugged his shoulders. "But you are both far wiser than many who read Greek or even Hebrew."

I rose to face him, and laying one hand on his shoulder, I looked deep into his eyes. "If we are wise as you say, my son, then you shall listen to me. No hand in my house must rise against another person. Our words should be our best guard."

Lukas lowered his gaze, his face reddening.

"And you a doctor—" Iphigenia began.

I turned to her, and she fell silent. "He has heard us," is all I could say. It was my wife's turn to lower her gaze.

"You are right, my father," he replied.

My heart warmed at this new form of address to me, a respect I believed impossible during my bondage.

"I will speak with her to ask pardon for my action."

But since that Sabbath, my fosterlings Lukas and Cassandra have hardly spoken together, avoiding each other whenever they can.

Upon the First Miracle

Again and again since Passover, I have recalled the day of my wedding cut short.

This day is marked forever with my shame at the arrival of the man Jesus of Nazareth into our Temple, when he caused the chaos in my absence. The common people believe in many miracles and healings he performed throughout Judaea. But for all that, he was crucified on the same day of Stephanos' peculiar illness. Rumors blow in all the Jewish world around me that on the third day of Passover, the same day of Stephanos' disappearance, this man arose from the dead. Those claiming to see the Nazarene after his death are not small in number.

Our Temple leaders who are called the Sanhedrin are as uneasy as the sails of a ship in a storm. First the corban and its giving to Rome for the waterways flawed their reputation before the people; now the possibility of something too great to speak, that the Nazarene was killed as an innocent man, as the Messiah himself, under their approval and has returned to judge them, is almost more than the council can bear. The public fails to honor them as before. They begrudge even giving way and allowing them to pass, and they mutter into their sleeves at the leaders' backs.

But as for me, I continue every tradition I have learned from Saul and show every respect. I strive for all the order that is in my power to keep perfect the gates to the House of our Lord. Yet how can I judge the Judeans and their desire to see the kingdom of Israel restored through a messiah? Is it more to ask than dreams in Athens of freedom from Rome?

The Temple boy Ezra comes to me at the main gate early one morning in the eighth week after Stephanos' disappearance. He is the best of any of the boys, because while he devotes his mind to the mighty teachings of Rabboni Gamaliel, he also grasps the practical order I seek to keep with the beggars and the crowds. "Come see a great wonder of our Lord!" he greets me.

I pull one of his lengthening ear locks and smile. "Every day wonder from Great Lord. Maybe you think your own great wonder, do you?"

Ezra does not smile at my fondness, but instead reminds me of the names of three of his friends. "Aaron, Zebedee, and Joshua have agreed to stay here while I take you somewhere. They will help the people with anything they need; they know your order here."

Of course I recognize the other Temple boys, nearly as clever as Ezra. It is no small thing for me to leave my post, but the boy's earnestness convinces me. "You no leave here for nothing, you do agree?" I ask the others.

"Oh, no, not nothing never," they all say together. They laugh as they smile, and I suspect they are using my faulty Hebrew words instead of their good ones. Yet for all their teasing, I love the faith and truth I read in their faces. Unlike many of their elders, these boys accept me as a fellow Jew.

At least, starting this Passover, I have been accepted adequately in Jewish service that each week, I am given a bit of silver from the priests. I found three small gold coins folded into my bag during Passover as well. When I told Gamaliel of this with alarm, he said that perhaps these were to compensate me for my three years of prior service. However, I believe that he himself may have left them as wedding money he knows I would refuse from him. Having no proof, I return one of the coins to the Temple as a thank offering and rejoice that I can now purchase a loom and plenty of fine yarn for my beloved wife, who dreams of weaving cloth in the Greek manner as she did as a girl in Antioch.

When Ezra and I pass the city gates, he leads me to a place I have heard of but not seen before, a small stadium built by Herod and the Romans for racing.

Led by my pricking nose, my mind returns to Athens of its own accord as we near the crowd in the stone–walled structure. Commingled in an entrancing perfume, I detect aromas of spices from every corner of the earth—myrrh from Persia, frankincense from Africa, fragrant mixes from Alexandria—that I recall from the many foreigners I knew when guarding the theater at the Acropolis. And a great calling of voices echoes around this space we have entered. No less than the voices, the colors and textiles of people's garments display all the world in front of me. Arabs clad in white, crimson–covered Persians, silk–clad Asians, and many Romans in short tunics and leather leggings stand and sit side by side, faces turned to a young man dressed no better than a fisherman.

I lay aside my memories of the far greater stages of Athens to listen.

"God has raised up this Jesus, and we all are witnesses. He is exalted by the right hand of God, and the Father gave him the promise of the Holy Spirit, and he has shed his own blood. You are here now to see and hear of all this. Even our King David did not ascend into heaven, but he himself said: 'The LORD said to my Lord, Sit on my right hand, until I make your foes your footstool.' So let all the house of Israel know this absolutely: God has made that same Jesus, whom you have crucified, both Lord and Christ!"

Despite his rough garments, I cannot deny that this orator speaks with such confidence that I raise my hands to applaud; not since Athens have I heard such a voice. But my clapping falls in the crowd only like straying raindrops. The scents rise and the colors part as people turn to one another with distressed faces. Then voices call loudly, but I cannot understand the muddle of languages.

In my fascination, I have neglected young Ezra standing at my shoulder, but true to his nature, he has not overlooked my lacking ears and faltering Hebrew, so he interprets. "They are asking him, 'Brothers, what shall we do?'"

The speaker lifts his voice again. "Repent, and be baptized every one of you in the name of Jesus Christ for the remission of sins, and you shall receive the gift of the Holy Spirit. This promise comes to you, and to your children, and to all that are near or far, even as many as the Lord our God shall call."

A second voice whispers into my ear. "And thanks to our Lord that we share one baptism, and he has called us together, my brother."

Knocking Ezra's arm in my haste, I turn. "Stephanos!"

I can say no more as this man who brought me freedom embraces me long and close.

I turn toward Ezra. "Did you know?"

But the boy is gone.

"I sent him to find you as soon as it was safe," Stephanos answers before I can ask. "But he knows your concern for the gate, and he is already on his way back to the Temple." Clasping my hand, he speaks on. "Come. I will take you to a place where we can talk."

My usual mapping of every direction vanishes in my joy to hear his voice as we walk. Stephanos plies me with questions about my new life in Bethany, rejoicing to learn of my guard pay. When I relate the story of Cassandra's attempt to teach us letters, and then Lukas' rage, he laughs.

But like Lukas, he falls voiceless when I ask him to explain why "dove" or "nest" have nothing like the voice of "bird."

"It is no matter," he replies instead. "Your fosterlings will always be there to read and to write for you."

After a few paces of silence, he continues. "And tell me—is

it still so great to be made a Jew and a husband?"

Recalling the wedding day and my joke regarding circumcision, it is my turn to laugh. "Ah, if you knew! Why don't you try it, Stephanos? You ignore how half the girls at the Temple sigh after your footsteps fade; you race and hold your mind to other things."

I am surprised at the trace of sadness on Stephanos' face. "Yes, other things," Stephanos says. "But love is the greatest thing."

As we leave the stadium crowd far behind, I answer his questions with what I know concerning the council, the priests, and their growing fear of the people.

"They do well to fear," Stephanos replies. "If they would only have faith, they would have no need to fear."

With gentle words, he strikes away my inner protest concerning his silence of these past weeks. "The entire Temple was seeking me because of what happened to me at Passover and because of your questions to everyone at the gate, and I even heard tell that you had the lines of my face inscribed like an idol." He laughs, and then grows serious. "But more important, they would have found the students of Christ if I had come to you, and that would not have gone well for them after the crucifixion."

I know him to be correct.

Once we re-enter the city, we stop at a taverna that stands between the great Temple above and the markets below.

"It is safe for us to speak here," Stephanos says, introducing me to the owner, a fellow Greek named Demetrius. Turning to me, he goes on. "This man welcomes believers in the Messiah to his establishment, both well-paying guests and those unable to give more than a copper penny. It is still unwise for them to appear too boldly in the city."

Demetrius pours us some watered wine, then leaves us to tend to other work.

"But you—will you return to us in the Temple?" The words leave my mouth before I can stop them. I did not realize how much I missed his presence until this question has left my lips.

Stephanos sighs. "In God's time," he answers. "For now, I sit at the feet of Christ's students, and I learn more than even with Rabboni Gamaliel."

Then he tells me things that, if I did not know him, I would disbelieve. The tearing of the veil, he explains, came at the hour of death of this Jesus of Nazareth he calls Christos. "It was also the hour when our Lord spoke to me with His own voice and showed His face to my eyes in a vision," he concludes. "I have sat at the feet of His students all this time, spoken with His mother, listened to all they say. I have met men and women He healed and who believe; He said their faith would heal them. And even you yourself have witnessed a miracle today."

I am accustomed to not understanding many things learned men say, but with Stephanos, I dare to speak my mind. "It is true that finding you is a miracle," I venture.

Stephanos raises his clay wine cup, but he shakes his head. "That was simply an arrangement I made with Ezra, though perhaps his convincing you to leave the gate was a work worthy of our Lord's patience."

I laugh, but his gaze pierces me. "Well, besides this," I say, "I have simply heard a man speaking to a crowd. What miracle is there in this?"

"And tell me, just what did he say to us?" Stephanos asks. He is smiling as though knowing my answer beforehand.

"That King David already foretold Christ's coming, that Jesus of Nazareth is the Christ, that everyone should be baptized," I respond. I am full of the hope I felt when speaking of the voices in Cassandra's letters, but also of the fear to say incorrect things and make him laugh like my fosterlings.

But Stephanos does not laugh. "You are gifted with memory, Timon. This I have seen many times, and it is a far greater thing than reading. Come, tell me more. Perhaps you can even say things you heard in the stadium word for word."

I hear the speaker's voice again in my inner ear, and I repeat. "He is exalted by the right hand of God, and the Father gave him the promise of the Holy Spirit, and he has shed his own blood."

"Amen!" Stephanos replies. "But you need to tell me these words exactly as he spoke them."

I hesitate. "I have told you just as I remember. Shall I say them again?" I am nearly certain that I have spoken truly, yet something is amiss. The same confusion overtakes me as the day when Cassandra began speaking voices of the letters.

"Surely this man was from Galilee," my friend continues. "Don't you agree?"

I nod, recalling the rough robes, but I hesitate. It is even more difficult for me to understand the Galileans than the Jerusalemites.

"Well, then, tell me the words even as he said them," Stephanos urges. "I am waiting."

I shake my head. "It is as though he spoke them to us in Greek."

Stephanos laughs. "In Greek? Is that possible?"

"I suppose it is possible, but—"

"No, it is not possible," Stephanos responds with a voice louder than he would need. "Have you ever seen a fellow like that who knows Greek, most especially the beautiful Greek like what you just uttered? Did you hear a foreign weight on his tongue or misspoken grammar? Did he sound to you like the rough way he appeared? And did you see the Parthians, or the Phrygians, or the Medes, or the Elamites shaking their heads as you are doing now and not hearing his meaning?"

My face burns. "All of us understood," I mumble. "It was clear from their listening."

"This is why I tell you that you witnessed a miracle of our

Lord. Every man there heard the voice of the Holy Spirit in his own tongue, and you are no exception, Athenian."

My speech is useless, because there is no argument against what I have heard. The voice still echoes in my thoughts. "The Father gave him the promise of the Holy Spirit, and he has shed his own blood."

When I have drunk my wine, I reply. "I will return to my house and I will tell everyone of these things, even though they are beyond logika."

Stephanos laughs. "You already have one believer dwelling in your midst."

"Lukas?" I ask. I recall some earlier discussion he has had about the Nazarene and healings he was said to perform in Bethany.

"About Lukas, I do not know. But Cassandra is certain."

"But how do you know? Have you seen her?"

"No, Timon, though if I could do so safely, I would. But Ezra has told me. He also attends our sermons and studies deeply what is prophesied in scripture. I thank our Lord for his presence here, and I think Ezra will come to believe as we do."

Upon the Second Miracle

My unquiet grows day to day concerning the rulers of the Temple. Some followers of Christos have begun meeting on the eastern face, called Solomon's Porch. The portico there is very white, and the front of it looks over a sweeping valley.

This is far from the main Gate of Coponius to the west, where I most often stand. But since a few fellow guards and many Temple boys have learned good order from me, I begin to serve near these peculiar gatherings. Perhaps I will even see Stephanos again.

On a certain day some months after the miracle of language that entered my ears, as I am admiring the beauty of this rugged land for the hundredth time, a great shouting arises from inside the Temple property. I have noted only the usual sort of people going in and out, so the noise startles me.

I reproach my eyes, which were too fixed on the beauty outside and not on the visitors directly in front of me. As I hurry toward the commotion, however, the faces turned my way are full of joy, and the shouts are those of laughter and amazement.

If my eagle eyes ever deceived me, or if my ears abandoned their purpose, I would pass off what I now witness as a mere tale, or as a thing to be heard in scripture. Instead, I can only open my mouth to join the cries of the crowd rushing to gather near the inner gate called Beautiful.

This gate is aptly named, for it is forged by the Greeks. It stands near the women's court, with the height of five men, demanding twenty of us to open or close it. I see what everyone stares at, first reflected in its polished bronze, for the people are thick in front of me.

A man calling out with joy is jumping and holding hands with two others. Though I cannot see this man's face, I know his voice; he is one I have helped with gifts from Saul and others intended for the poorest of the poor, the most wretched of the afflicted. He is a beggar I first met on the day of the massacre— the day of poor Irini's death. He neglects my name, only calling me "Kyrie," which is used for "Sir" or "Lord" in Greek. I call him by no name, but in my mind, I must call him the Worm, since he lies flat on the ground. But his voice always shrills above the rest as now. These words he speaks, I could expect to hear only in a dream: "I can stand! I can walk; my feet and ankles have found themselves. Look, everyone! No, keep your money and offer it to our Lord or to her over there." He points to another beggar.

I step back as word spreads and the crowd thickens around us. Were it any other crowd or any other day, I would call for additional guards. But these people are looking on with fear and joy commingled like water with wine. They will show no unruliness or disrespect to anything in the Temple rules in light of this miracle that has taken place.

The worm man moves first toward the Temple, but then he swings outward toward Solomon's Porch, where I have come from. "You, Kyrie," he shouts as he sees me. "Come teach me some great Greek dance today! Look what these men have done for me!"

He gestures to two shabby figures half dragged by him and following along. I know the face of one of them. This is the man from Galilee whose speech I heard in Greek worthy of any Athenian in the amphitheater the day I was rejoined with Stephanos.

As these men and the Worm step onto the portico, the crowd parts to give them space. The Worm grows calmer, stretching his legs in wonder and admiration, as the man I have already heard begins to orate in the bold voice I remember.

I learn that his name is Peter, and the second man is called John.

"You, men of Israel, why are you so amazed at this? Why do you look so earnestly on us, as if we were the ones making this man walk by our own power or holiness?" Peter asks. "The God of Abraham, and of Isaac, and of Jacob, the God of our fathers, has glorified his Son, Jesus. But you delivered him up, and denied him in the presence of Pilatus, when he was determined to let him go. Yes. You denied a holy, just man, and instead, you desired a murderer to be granted his freedom, and you killed the Prince of Life. But God has raised this man from the dead; we are witnesses of this."

Only the doves cooing above our heads interrupt the silence following these bitter words. Again, though of course I cannot repeat it in Hebrew, yet I understand everything he has just said. The words strike my heart like arrows.

The Worm cannot hold back from more rejoicing as he

twists and turns with his new-found strength. "Praise to our Lord—only praise this day!" he shouts in the face of the crowd.

The speaker lays a gentle hand on this Worm's shoulder. "It is Jesus' name through faith that has made this man strong, whom you see and know well. In truth, it is only faith that has given him this perfect soundness of body before all of you."

Upon the Third Miracle

The Worm is waving and beckoning to a man climbing from below whose face I cannot see. "You, Pharisee! I will never beg another day, and I will never need another Passover basket of yours!" he shouts. "Come here and see me standing, and speak with me face to face!"

As the man he addresses moves closer, I recognize Saul of Tarsus. Something is different in him, yet I cannot define it.

The crowd parts to allow anything the Worm desires, including Saul's approach.

"What is this? You, too, are walking no longer like a quail but almost like a man!" the Worm insists. "Have these men also healed you?"

The Worm is right. Before, the steepness of those steps would have nearly stopped Saul's ascent. Now he has walked them boldly, with hardly a sway in his pacing. I give thanks to our Lord before wondering how this is possible.

Saul speaks quietly to the Worm, who looks toward his feet before returning his attention to the speaker. As he did at the stadium, Peter calls the people to remember the prophets and the past, but to repent in the name of Jesus Christos for the forgiveness of sins.

The pull of eyes fixed on me makes me turn my head from these goings on. "Stephanos!" My heart rejoices as much now to see him as it did at the stadium.

My friend smiles at me, but then he looks beyond me to

Saul. Since his height makes him easy to find in any crowd, Saul has seen him and moves close, the crowd parting for him.

"You are here," he greets Stephanos without a smile. "I feared you were dead, until Timon told me he spoke to you."

By Stephanos' request, I had said nothing more than that he was well, that he would come to Saul when he could.

"You have seen the worm man, and you have heard his question about your healing," is all that Stephanos replies. "How did you answer him?"

Saul does not meet Stephanos' gaze, but all of us turn and walk together to one corner of the crowded portico.

"So, how did you reply?" Stephanos repeats once we are standing close together. He shows the same knowing smile I saw when he convinced me of the miracle of languages.

"I told him I believe in this foster son of Timon's, Doctor Lukas," Saul replies.

Raising one foot, he shows a sandal leveled high.

"He has encouraged me in certain exercises of both walking and speaking that I do not need to explain to you, and he has made me this to allow me to walk like all the rest of you."

Hearing Saul's witness makes my sorrow burn greater than my joy. How is it that I have not recognized the greatness of Lukas as a doctor, regarding him as just another man at work? All these days, Saul has passed me by, and I have greeted him. Yet only now as he shows us do I realize the skill of my foster son and the kind of silent miracle he has created. No crowds will shout and no beggars will dance seeing this, but Saul can walk unhindered, no longer frowned on. He can be seen as a man truly free.

"It is not less wonderful than what we have just seen," Stephanos replies slowly, as though he has read my thoughts. "I am truly glad for it, Saul. But this does not arise from faith."

Saul pulls Stephanos' sleeve tight enough that his arm is raised. "Faith? What faith do you dare speak of? Do not speak to me of faith!" he explodes. "When have I ever broken faith with our law or our Pharisees? You are the one, the newcomer who learned like a graft, even if you are born a Jew. And now with your talk of this 'Christos,'" he splatters the word and chokes a little, "our Timon here is a far better Jew than you, Stephanos." He pauses, drawing breath. "And do not think the words you left written in ash have not burned my heart. 'Farewell, dear Saul. Pray that your soul shall be unveiled from law. Messiah sets us free!'" His voice breaks.

My amazement is only rivaled by my dismay. The two of them face each other, wordless. If they were lesser men, I am certain they would strike each other.

Instead, though no one around us watches as they listen to Peter and the Worm, Saul gently releases Stephanos' sleeve. And then he does a thing I would not believe if I were not the witness. In the Greek manner, he kneels before us. Yes. He kneels and his hands extend, and he clasps Stephanos by the knees.

"Brother, return to us here and set your own spirit in harmony with the traditions. I will help all the rest of our brothers in the Temple to understand the madness that seized you; we all know your state like death after the opening of the veil, and they will take you back." Saul's voice is choked with tears. "Don't you understand the madness of this?—this Christos you have turned your mind to. Surely we can reason together. And if not, if you are under some beguiling enchantment from these men who followed him, I will come with you to the priests to purify you and order your thoughts. After all, who is Jesus of Nazareth beside our fathers, and our father's fathers, our prophets, and our wise ones like Solomon, for whom the great stones of this very porch are named?"

Stephanos draws back just enough to loosen Saul's hands, which he clasps in his. Then he raises his friend with the tenderness of a brother. "Since you speak of stones, I will answer you with stones," he begins, and then hesitates. "Jesus who is Christos said this: 'The stone that the builder set aside has become the very cornerstone.'"

Stephanos pauses, returning Saul's pleading gaze. "Do you remember as children how we laughed and sighed as we spoke of kicking against the pricks of our law? You know as well as I do just how difficult—no, how impossible—it is for a man, however willing, to follow every last point, each jot and tittle of this law laid down by our forefathers. Yet this is what we are commanded to do, is it not?"

Saul sighs and nods.

"But the Christos frees us from kicking at these pricks. It is the law of love that is our new law, and the word of truth is to go out not only to our brother Jews, but to every nation."

Saul has heard enough, and he snorts. "What are you speaking of? There is no freedom but following the ways of our fathers, and Gentiles have no place and nothing to do with this!"

Then Stephanos looks my way, and he sighs. "The Gentiles are already among us, as you know." He lays a hand on my shoulder and goes on. "I am afraid for you, Saul, that you cannot see the truth as I have been given to see by our Lord in the Temple and later as I learn with the people who knew Jesus of Nazareth. But surely you heard the words of this Peter that he was merely the instrument of healing the worm man—that the actual power comes from the name of Christos."

When Saul turns his face to me, I wish to walk away. Yet it is as though my feet are deep planted in the stone. Suffering is etched deep on both men's faces like lines gouged into the clay pots of Athens. I am unworthy to be privy to what these two men believe in their hearts. How can I understand which man is right? It is only from courtesy for me that they are using Greek now.

Seeming to ignore Stephanos' reply, Saul continues. "Gamaliel will also defend you, and after you purify yourself, surely we can return to what came before."

Stephanos sighs so deeply that the breath of it moves Saul's beard just in front of him. "My friend, there is no return to the past," he says slowly. "The past would bind the worm man to his begging. The past kept you and me kicking and kicking against the pricks of our tradition to keep to every rule and custom. The past only recalls being set free from Egypt. It is the present that sets our hearts free from sin as we keep faith that Christos died, that He is risen, and that He will come again. Healings like what you saw are only proof for people of little learning and faith who need to see with their eyes what is true in our hearts."

Saul hesitates for a long time, and then he turns to me. "Timon, know this. All forgiveness does is to set you free; it lets you think just about yourself. Honor is a different thing. You know it as a Greek, not only as a Jew. Honor is what makes you strong. It binds you to your past. It shapes your life with form and meaning."

I open my lips, but it is as though a wind has torn away any words I would say—as fathomless as the Alpha fish and the other letters Cassandra tried to show me. "All I know, sirs, is this. I seek to honor our Lord with all my heart, and all my strength and all my mind, as both of you taught me," I finally manage.

Upon the Final and Greatest Miracle

But now my ears, and also my eyes, are forced toward other things. It is close to sunset, and only the marble whiteness of this place keeps darkness from closing in. The crowd has grown immense, but the sound of measured feet breaks through even the milling crowd. A row of torches advances straight toward the portico.

"Stop this babbling!"

Calls from behind interrupt the speaker, the dancing Worm,

and the massive crowd. I recognize the captain of the Temple, a man who respects me, and some priests, along with scholars I know as Sadducees from their robes.

The crowd parts, but it begins to rumble. The captain has brought soldiers along.

My inattention amidst the words from my friends' hearts has finally served to distract me fatally. My breath comes fast. But even if I had seen the armed approach, here at this porch, I have no junior guards to read my signals. A sickness weights my stomach like a stone; it is the same foreboding as the day of the massacre, when the crowd approached the governor closer and closer, until he raised a single finger and the disguised soldiers moved in. Only now, it is Peter who is like the governor. The crowd is ready and willing, some of them all too glad, to strike even men who are armed and even men who are priests.

"Kyrie eleison!" (Lord, have mercy!) I breathe in, even as I did when I last saw the yellow robe of Irini approaching the Temple.

Words of anger are hissing and swelling, rising from below the steps and moving toward the intruders newly arrived.

"Why are you here with guards?"

"Has Peter or John done any violence or made you angry?"

"You are the ones who need healing now, you fools!"

"Why don't you stop your noise and listen and repent?"

"Oh, my brothers! Do not rise or lay a single hand against these men!" Peter calls, and though I see his regret, the Worm repeats this loudly enough to be heard by everyone.

And to my ignorant eyes, what I see next is the miracle most amazing of anything I have witnessed. These holy men neither fight nor struggle. Surely if they can heal a man, they could also call down the fires of heaven. Instead, in the presence of the captain, the speaker, Peter, and his fellow student of Christos present their arms to the officials advancing on them, and they are bound fast.

I hear more than murmuring now against the priests, and I know my duties will be long and hard if these men are harmed in any way. But why should they be harmed? As the speakers are led away, they begin to sing.

Blessed are the peacemakers: for they shall be called the children of God.

Blessed are they that mourn: for they shall be comforted.

Blessed are they which are persecuted for righteousness' sake: for theirs is the kingdom of heaven.

Blessed are you, when men shall revile you, and persecute you, and shall say all manner of evil against you falsely, for my sake. Rejoice, and be very glad: for great is your reward in heaven: for they persecuted the prophets this way who came before you.

The crowd begins to sing with the men. The Worm follows close, calling, "I will not leave these men, and I will not leave our Lord!" Even the captain has no heart to lay a hand on him, and he follows unimpeded.

I recall words from the argument just held between Saul and Stephanos. The song of these men has proclaimed not only their freedom, but also their honor. Of this I am certain. A single gesture from them would have turned the crowd against the soldiers and the Sadducees, marking our Temple once more with blood. Instead, Peter and John and even the Worm are risking their own lives and offering their freedom for their belief in this Christos.

"If this singing does not speak of honor, what does?" I turn to ask Saul. But he has vanished.

"It is a song of Christos they sang," Stephanos' voice comes from behind me. "Is it this that gives your eyes their shine,

Timon?"

I raise my garment hard to wipe my eyes. "They do not fight, but they sing instead. Even the priests and their captivity do not bar their praise," I manage.

Stephanos draws close to lay a hand on my shoulder. "Yes, Timon. You see now that we who follow Christos have not lost our sense of honor as Saul claims. So, now, can you join us in our belief?"

12. The Scroll and the Questionings Witness of Gamaliel, Jerusalem, A.D. 33-34

Opening Prayer

My Lord and my God, will the trembling of the sanctuary flagstones beneath my feet forever torment my dreams by night? And by day, will the arguments of our priests continually make me want to rend my garments like Your great veil split last Passover before our very eyes? Though You have seen our generations disputing such questions as the existence of the soul or the resurrection of the body, never have we been split to the core as we are now.

My ears are tired of my name repeated, "Rabboni, oh, Rabboni Gamaliel!" as students and elders alike seek to turn me from Your word, entreating me instead to side with their own opinions. While on the one hand I smile to see the Rome-pleasers brought down in the eyes of the people, what a fearful thing it is, my Lord, to consider the unity that we, the Jews of Jerusalem, have lost within Your very sanctuary!

A First Questioning

The very day of this breaking of unity I remember well, for it begins on the heels of a great wonder, the curing of a beggar who came for many years to our Temple. All of us know him by sight.

Ezra comes to me trembling with joy at bearing the news that very hour.

Later in the evening, Saul also approaches me, but he is full of anger. He tells me how two men named Peter and John of Galilee, claiming to work this miracle, were arrested from amidst a crowd of thousands. "And Stephanos was with them," Saul adds. "Along with the magicians who brought this thing to pass, he claims this Jesus of Nazareth as Messiah."

Hearing of the oddity of this new sect, and mourning the utter disappearance of Stephanos from our ranks, I comprehend the sorrow in Saul's troubled face.

We lose no time in learning more from Peter and John. The next day, we of the Sanhedrin council, along with many others who are of the highest learning, all gather in our Temple council hall. The arrested men are brought in to us. The man who was healed follows with a loud voice, praising our Lord and insisting on standing beside the Galileans being questioned.

Caiaphas is our high priest, since he is a Sadducee and thus among the greater number of men of the Sanhedrin. But our fellow Pharisee Annas joins him in standing. This Sadducee Caiaphas and his family keep close ties with the Romans, with the understanding that even as the Temple will not be tarnished with pagan emblems beyond the eagle on the gate, neither shall the people of Jerusalem be turned against Pilatus and his underlings by our own contriving.

We have much to discuss, and Caiaphas loses no time. As scorn sharpens his voice directed at these country folk, he asks our central question. "By what power have you done this healing?"

Peter and John bow their heads as though in prayer.

"Or by what name?" Caiaphas adds, breaking the new silence.

It is Peter who replies, with a voice as bold as that of Caiaphas. But his eyes do not fix on our two priests standing before him. Instead, he looks out to the scores of us seated around. "All of you, rulers of the people and elders of Israel, if you are inquiring today about the good deed done to this weak man, and how he is now strong, know this. Every one of you, and all the people of Israel, it is by the name of Jesus Christ of Nazareth, the man you crucified, the man God raised from the dead, it is by him that this man stands here before you whole."

When Annas and Caiaphas do not reply, Peter's voice rises higher. "This Jesus is the stone that, as our builders, you rejected, but He is now our cornerstone. Salvation lies in no one else."

Saul's indrawn breath hisses behind me, along with many others all around. How can this simple-tongued man none of us would even greet in the street, a man not invited in for holy festivals, find the gall to throw the teachings of our forefathers under our feet? He is all but directly accusing those in power of murder! My Lord, surely he is aware of things that could be done to him as a result, actions I desire not even to contemplate in the beauty of Your sanctuary.

"Praise God! He speaks the truth!" This voice rings out from the man who has been healed.

Though the divide of my thoughts is great, I cannot help whispering an echoing prayer of thanks to You, oh Lord. It is not only this man walking upright that I see, but a transformation of his face, like the desert from the bleakest frosting of winter to the brightest flowering of spring. In the many years of his lying on the ground like a worm, how could I have imagined his smile of today?

Upon a gesture from Caiaphas, the Temple captain and his guards escort all three men out of the room.

Our voices stir like angry wind as soon as they are gone. This much is true. A man all of us know, a man whom half the city has seen on the ground, is completely healed. But now, my Lord, what must be our response to such a mighty act, but one not performed in Your name?

Annas raises his hand, and three men enter from another door. One of them I recognize. He is the young doctor Lukas who greeted Saul, Stephanos, and me with the fullness of Greek courtesy at the wedding of his mother and the guard Timon.

"Do you know the man who was healed?" Caiaphas asks the three men. His omission of any preliminary greeting of respect reveals the extent of his agitation.

Each doctor nods. "At least we have seen him in passing," the oldest man replies. "His condition is unforgettable to a doctor."

"And have you made a full examination?" Annas continues, piercing each physician with his gaze.

With a smile, Lukas, youngest by far, steps forward to speak. "Sir, this morning he consented to our examination and to all the questions we had," he begins.

"We have no need of a physician's report," Caiaphas snaps.

As Lukas' face falls, I realize that his delight in what he has seen is tempered by his disappointment in not being allowed to speak of what he knows better than we, the scholars.

The doctor in middle age steps forward to join the conversation. "I assure you, the man's feet and legs are normal. His whole body is as full of vitality as that of a young man."

Annas sighs. "Does he fully convince you?"

Lukas speaks again, his smile returning. "Sir, if I did not know differently, I would say that this man was among the healthiest men of his age I have seen. He is probably well beyond forty years old, but no one knows, since he says he was passed from family to family as a child and neglected, and left to beg here."

"Enough!" The echo of Caiaphas' voice bites from the wall. He fixes the men before him with his gaze, almost as though they are guilty. "Tell me this. Is there any chance that this one whom you have examined is another man and not the beggar we know?"

As the physicians look first at each other, then to the ground, high laughter breaks forth from the back of the room. Young Ezra has come in, uninvited and unnoticed. But his laugh has bounced forward from throat to throat. Everyone younger than the elders joins in.

Lukas does not lose his poise. As though deaf to the derision, he meets the high priest's gaze and speaks out. "Sir, if this is another man and not the worm man, as he has been called all these years, then finding such an impostor would be even a greater miracle than what we have witnessed."

Caiaphas and Annas look to each other. Both are equally angry, but neither can dismiss the doctor's words. Not by his witness, but by his final reply, this young Doctor Lukas has made them both look like fools, though he has no experience dealing with our leaders. After such a retort, his increasing reputation among the wealthy of this city may suffer.

Caiaphas frowns, then dismisses the doctors. Ezra's mirth is still reflected in many faces around me, for despite all the fear and the anger in this room, everyone has heard Lukas' clever reply, revealing the leaders' efforts to dismiss the healing for the ploy it is.

A general murmuring surrounds the physicians' exit. Then Saul stands and raises his voice. "Brothers, come. Let us use our own reason," he begins.

All eyes turn to him. Something in his bearing makes me look steadfastly at my student, something different than before. Is it a straightness in his shoulders, or a solidity in his stance? Certainly he appears confident before all the able–bodied men around us in a way I have never noticed before, my Lord, and if it is a thing from You, I give You praise!

This difference I have noted in a few heartbeats, as all other voices grow silent before Saul speaks again. "A living man can sometimes heal in the name of our Lord, this is true."

All of us nod in recognition of our prophets like Elijah who have done such things.

Then Saul goes on. "But not in all our scripture could a dead man's name do anything but make widows cry and sisters weep! What do you say?"

Again, we murmur and nod.

"Therefore, it stands to reason that those Galileans used some evil power to make him strong. Calling on a dead man as this John and Peter claim will only bring death, death to the very soul," he concludes. "We must make the healed man come purify himself at once."

Seeing the disturbance of our fellow Pharisees at Saul's referring to the death of the soul, I think swiftly how to preserve any vestige of unity remaining among us. Saul has not thought well on the choice of his words, a thing to avoid even in the anger he feels. Or is he trying to throw a reconciliation to draw the Sadducees to his own mind, with their disbelief in the afterlife? A flame is in my throat. Saul is failing to use his reason, but rather he is building on the feelings already hot around us.

I have no time to ponder this as I raise my own voice and stand. As soon as Annas recognizes me, I begin. "But what evil power would seek to heal a man? And what gain do these Galileans take in confessing the name of Jesus of Nazareth? You saw them. These are fishermen and tradesmen, hardly above slaves. They have no money, and they want no fame for themselves. They spoke to us today at their own peril."

"Except that the people would storm the Temple if anything were to happen to them," Saul mutters.

But the disturbed Pharisees nod in agreement on this common ground I wish to establish.

"They went peacefully when they were arrested," I continue.

Saul snorts and turns away.

My throat tightens with anger, for never before has this brightest of my students degraded his power to listen and to reason to mere derision. Even if I am in error—may our Lord be merciful—still, both he and I are worthy of better answer than this.

Annas raises his voice to override the discussion swirling around us. "The key of the matter is this, brothers. Whether this man was healed by good or by evil, the preaching of this Jesus is blasphemy."

I join the voices saying "Amen" in agreement all around. With this, the guards return with Peter and John, along with the man who was healed.

Standing directly in front of them, but on a higher space from which our speakers commonly address us, Annas looks down at the three of them. "You are free to go," he begins. "But know this: If you teach in the name of this man you have named, or if you speak of him at all to the people, you will be brought back to us. It will not go so easily with you the next time."

As Peter and John turn to each other with brows knitted, the healed man continues to smile.

John speaks in a soft voice, but one that enters every ear in the room. "Is it right for us to obey you more than to obey God? We can, and we must, speak of the things we have seen and heard, or we would be false prophets indeed."

The healed man shakes his head. "There are many who hope for healing, like me. Who would turn them away if he is able to help with words like Peter and John, here? Why do you speak to them with such anger, sir? Is it so important how they have done it?"

Again, voices sweep all around the air of this room. Saul begins to rise, but I turn to him, and he resettles, sighing.

Caiaphas raises his voice a final time as he signals to the guards to release the men. He does not meet the gaze of the man who was healed as he speaks to Peter and John. "You have been warned, and your ears have heard our judgment." Turning to the man healed, he invites him in a gentler voice. "You should come for your ritual purification."

John and Peter smile to him, understanding this tradition of priestly examination. Then the healed man trails Annas and Caiaphas out one door as the followers of Jesus exit by another. Behind them, I perceive Timon the guard, following close by.

Upon the Reading of the Scroll

Not long after this day, Ezra comes to me after dinner on the Sabbath.

"I wanted to wait until you were rested to show you something from a friend," he greets me.

I am pleased that Ezra has considered his timing. I chastised him for his misplaced laughter in the Sanhedrin during the questioning of the doctors. After hearing his apology and taking him to the high priest, I explain to him in private in the words of Solomon, wisest of our scripture writers, that to everything there is a season. As one so young, he must learn to wait until he is certain before acting. This Ezra is as upright and keen as any student I have taught since Saul, and it is a pleasure to keep him by me in the house as he grows in body and spirit.

But oh, give me wisdom to equal his zeal, my Lord! He has asked, and I have granted, that he may occasionally visit the followers of Peter and John, though I doubt that what they say will bring anything new to his mind, given the men's simplicity. Still, as long as I have taught, I know that the best way to minds of students like Ezra or Saul is to allow them to explore and open for themselves.

Before even unwrapping what Ezra hands me, I recognize its quality. Inside a fragrant box oiled with cedar lies a bound scroll. The scroll itself is finished with red tabs and wrappers, its ending rods shaved smooth with pumice. And indeed, unrolling the beautiful skin in private, the even lettering of my student strikes my eyes almost like his own voice.

Stephanos begins with these words: "It seemed the best thing, honored Gamaliel, for me to write to you what I have learned regarding Jesus of Nazareth and how he fulfills our scriptures, so that you may read, and in so doing, use the reason and the wisdom with which our Lord has blessed you to understand the truth."

What shall I make of this scroll, my Lord?

Stephanos begins by indicating the birth of Jesus in Bethlehem, as your prophet Isaiah foretold for our Messiah.

As I read onward, I hear my father's voice at the end of his life lifting up the very words Stephanos has laid flat on the parchment: "Lord, now Thy servant may depart in peace, according to Thy word, for my eyes have seen Thy salvation, which Thou hast prepared before the face of all people, a light to illumine the Gentiles, and the glory of Thy people, Israel."

Stephanos could not know, indeed, no one could know my father's words or his final story.

In his last year of life, my father spoke of a promise he received from our Lord that he would not die until he had seen the Lord's Christ. We had kept these words, along with many other things he said then, bound in the secrecy of our family. As for my father, we sheltered him safe in our home in his final months, given his tendency to wander and speak to strangers.

But it came to pass that on a certain day my father was left unattended. He made his way to the Temple, as he had done all his life as rabbi and son of a rabbi. When I heard from my school the loud calling of voices, I hurried away from my studies in preparation to become a rabbi like my father and his fathers. As I approached the room where boys are dedicated, I understood the shouting not as fear or sorrow, but as cries arising from joy. And the image of my ancient father cradling an infant will never leave my inner eye. As I rushed to his side, a woman as old as my father came and took the child from his arms.

As soon as he safely surrendered the sleeping boy, my father turned to a poor young couple from Galilee. Though I cannot remember all he said in my dismay at his presence, one phrase he said to the mother I still recall. "But a sword shall pierce your own soul for the sake of many." This phrase, too, appears in Stephanos' writing as he tells of this very blessing in the Temple and notes my father by name.

On that day in my youth, I babbled apologies to this unoffending couple, attempting to explain my father's extreme age and confusion. But they hardly paid attention to me as they thanked this ancient rabbi, even blessing him.

I half carried my aging father back to our home, but despite his fatigue, he was full of song and rejoicing. "Today our Lord has indeed shown his mercy to Israel! Today my eyes have seen our Christ!" he said continually until I could make him lie down to rest.

That very night, my father, Simeon, son of Hillel, was called to our forefathers. I had long put away those crazed words of his final day of life, only now, they rise up like an unquiet spirit that hounds my heart.

When I regain my composure, I take up the beautiful scroll once more. Much is there that Stephanos has sent me, thoughts that I must read over many times. For the most part, my student has gathered the words of the Nazarene as spoken to him by his students. And many are these words, indeed: he and his students harvesting corn on the Sabbath and comparing this misdeed to David's taking of the holy bread meant only for the priests when they were hungry; also the healing of many in temples on the Sabbath; commending a widow for her tiny, secret offering that he calls greater than those of the rich; and numerous proclamations condemning us, the Pharisees, as sternly as we judge others.

The Nazarene likens the truth of our Lord to seed scattered throughout the path, the field, the land—planted, growing, and awaiting harvest. Furthermore, he compares the love of God to a shepherd seeking a single sheep gone astray when all the rest are safe. Such sayings are too peculiar for me to fathom.

But the story ending the scroll leaves me nearly as shaken as that first account of my father.

> *A certain man planted a vineyard, and let caretakers rent it, and went into a faraway country for a long time. And at the right season, he sent a servant to the caretakers for them to give over a portion of the fruit of the vineyard. But the caretakers beat him, and sent him away empty handed. And he sent another servant, and they beat him also, and treated him shamefully, and also sent him away empty handed. And again he sent a third, and they wounded him also, and they cast him out. Then said the lord of the vineyard, what shall I do? I will send my beloved son. It may be they will respect him when they see him.*
>
> *But when the caretakers saw him, they reasoned among themselves, saying, "This is the heir. Come, let us kill him and make the inheritance our own!" So they cast him out of the vineyard, and they killed him.*
>
> *So what shall the lord of the vineyard do to them? He shall come and destroy these caretakers, and he shall give the vineyard to others. Remember, as it is written, "The stone which the builders rejected, the same is become the cornerstone."*

"From that day, the leaders of the Temple laid plans of how to ensnare Jesus of Nazareth," Stephanos concludes. "And as you know, Gamaliel, these plots bore their fruit."

My Lord, what is best? Should I reveal this scroll to my fellow Pharisees? Show me Your way and Your time.

After days of thought, I call Saul aside and ask him to dinner following the next Sabbath. Once we have eaten and drunk, I invite him to my library, where I have stored the writing.

"Here are some words about this man who is dividing us," I say, and I stretch out the scroll.

Like me, Saul recognizes the exquisite writing as something from his friend, but as I hold it out to him, he withdraws his hand as though from a fire or from a thing impure.

"You should see how Stephanos himself writes words here as he has spoken with people who knew the man," I add, trying to reassure my student.

Saul glares down at the scroll as though he longs to spit on it. "Jesus of Nazareth has already stolen the reason of my dearest friend," he says through a clenching jaw. "A curse on the heads of both this Nazarene and on Stephanos if such teachings steal your own sound mind as well!"

As Saul turns his back on me and stamps from the room, his robe swings wide. I see for the first time that his sandals are of two heights. Now I understand the recent sureness in his gait. Moreover, this explains to me the confidence he has gained before our assembly. I breathe thanks to You, my Lord, for delivering this man from the captivity of his infirmity, the needless scoffing of our fellow scribes and students.

But glad as I am for this, I also pray to You, my Lord, for other things as I lay the scroll on its proper shelf. "Let Your servant Saul regain his own reason concerning these things, to discern and not to strike everything down before a proper hearing."

True to their word at our first questioning, Peter and John returned to Solomon's Porch. It has become a meeting place for the Jews who believe them, or at least for those who long for healing. I have spoken with young Ezra, whose feet are everywhere and whose eyes miss nothing, as well as with Lukas. Of this the boy and the doctor assure me: These followers of

Jesus seek neither wealth nor fame. Rather, they speak plainly of the need for baptism and the forgiveness of sins, calling upon the name of Jesus of Nazareth as Christos to heal in the same breath.

So far does the fame of these healings travel that our countrymen hemming all Jerusalem visit the Temple, now, though it is not the time of gathering or of feasting. Day by day, I hear voices raised outside the walls of my school and wending through the windows of the sanctuary. The cries of joy and singing and praise remind me of the spirit of what I heard the day of my father's final visit to the Temple. My heart is wrung with their gladness, though I do not wish it so.

Ezra claims that at times, even the shadow of Christos' students falling on a sick man, or the grasping of one of their garments, brings relief from the kind of suffering we see each day among our sick and poor. He adds that not only do those afflicted in body find cure, but even those stricken with demons of the mind come to peace.

It is a difficult choice, and perhaps not a just one, that I do not venture out to see these cures for myself. My Lord, it is for this reason: Stronger than my desire to witness come wonder and fear.

I have read the story of Simeon's blessing of the baby Jesus in the Temple until it torches my soul. Is it possible that my father's supposed madness of old age was indeed the voice of our Lord calling out like a prophet? And if this is true, if we have not opposed the death of our own Messiah—No! Lord hold me back from completing this line of reasoning!

Yet the final story told by Jesus of the vineyard reminds me too well of the prophets who spoke to our nation like the Lord's servants visiting the caretakers of the vineyards. Their shameful treatment sometimes even ended in death, and now, the preaching and the crucifixion of a man who spoke like one of those prophets divides our people to their very souls.

A Second Questioning

On a certain day, I no longer hear the usual cries of "Hosanna!" or "Praise to our Lord and to his Christ!" I resolve finally to approach Solomon's Porch, but I find it all but empty. In fact, the only man there is Timon, and not Timon as I know him standing guard. He is walking slowly in a circle, his staff tapping the marble of the porch floor as though to dig a hole.

"Shalom, Timon," I greet him. My voice trained with the assurance of teaching does not show my concern at his peculiar bearing.

The guard turns around and stands with the same straightness usual for him. "Oh, shalom, Rabboni, shalom," he returns my greeting. "You find me here crazy Greek do funny thing."

As I contrast this man's labored Hebrew words with the flowing Greek of his invitation to attend his wedding, pity washes over me. My Lord, I thank You that you have set me here in my native Jerusalem where I live peaceably, with no need to struggle like this striving convert.

When I do not reply but only smile, he continues. "I do something today like big old Greek story help me remind it. You want I tell you?"

"I am sure that even your Greek stories are sometimes very nice," I reply.

"This one very funny also very true, Rabboni. You listen me."

"I am listening," I say clearly to be sure that he understands.

"So, Rabboni, one time big, long time past, we have king. He name Midas King. This king, he make very, very angry one Greek god."

Timon lowers his eyes, which had been full of eagerness until now, transforming his face almost like an actor. "Sorry, Rabboni. I tell you this sure. I know now, this here not be real god like our Lord, but this just story, all right?"

"All right," I respond, willing to listen on. And to encourage him, I add, "You tell stories well, Timon. I did not know you were such an actor."

"Oh, sir, more twenty year I serve theater, big theater on Athens. I them see actors all time every year, I love what do they."

"I see," I reply. "Well, do say on, then."

Past his rightful shame at the mention of a pagan god in our Temple, Timon clears his throat and reverts to his story with gusto. "So, Rabboni, you see, this god, he make Midas King ears big like donkey ears. He angry cause Midas King say him that god music no very good. Greek not real god give Midas King big ears cause he angry, you see?"

"I see." I nod with pleasure to hear the guard speaking boldly, like many shy students I remember over the years finally grasping voice for a thought.

"So, this Midas King you know no want nobody his people find out his big donkey ears. Only one man know this. It man give cut his hair, you understand?"

"His barber?" I encourage.

"Oh, yes, that man, barber man. Thank you, Rabboni. So barber every time cut hair and every time no tell nobody nothing on this. But you see, Rabboni, that barber man need somebody know. Truth too big for only him know. You know what he do?"

I shake my head, my smile growing wider. "Tell me, Timon. What did the barber do?"

"So, he go to river, big, long river where water go, and..." His voice falls. "Rabboni, sorry. Always I never know words in Hebrew enough for to say good. What you call big tall things what grow by water you write with them sometime?"

"Reeds," I answer.

"Oh, yes. Rits. So barber make like this," and he repeats the digging motion I saw him begin on the porch. "He make deep place by rits. He put mouth down by deep place and he say truth. He say 'Midas King have donkey ears.' Rabboni, you know this story?"

I shake my head, the same amazement around me as during his wedding when I heard the ancient poetry. "What happened?" I ask, for now I am as curious as my own young scripture students.

"Oh, Rabboni, big, big thing what happen next. I tell you. So, barber go home. He feel peace and happy cause he tell secret but you know, no tell nobody like promise Midas King, only deep place by river, in rits, you see?"

"Yes, I see," I answer. "He kept his promise, but he was able to tell the truth. To the hole in the reeds."

"Yes, just yes, this exact yes, Rabboni. You always wise man very understand, I know." Timon laughs.

Again he clears his throat. "But well, these rits around hole, they also hear secret. You know rits have voice. Wind come, rits her voice like this." He whispers.

"The reeds whisper," I interpret what he intends to say.

"Yes, right. Rits whispers. And they say it. They say 'Midas King have donkey ears. Midas King have donkey ears.' So then these birds hear, and fishes hear, and people hear it, too. So you see meaning, Rabboni?"

My face is beginning to burn. This story that the guard has told me has completely passed my understanding, though I am almost certain I have heard the meaning of his words correctly. "What does it mean, Timon?" I ask. Then I laugh. "You know, we Jews might think differently from you Greeks."

Timon joins my laughter. "No, Rabboni. This story, I think you also think we Jews here. It means truth. Truth always come. Even you no tell nobody, she come. People know. Then everything all right in world, as people know truth, right?"

"The truth comes out," I repeat. "Yes, I can see this meaning in your Greek story. But why were you thinking of it right now and acting like the barber?"

Timon sighs. "I say goodbye Temple and wish her truth. You know what today was happened?"

When I shake my head, he goes on. "Again the Temple captain and those Sadducee priests come take and Peter and John right away, but I ask and know today they go to common prison."

"Were others also arrested?" I ask. In my concern, the story of truth's triumph falls to the back of my mind, since I can see no connection between this and his odd behavior.

Timon shakes his head. "All people just gone away like sheeps. Stephanos with us here, he say very very, 'Peace, peace! No need hurt priests, our Lord make good everything.' And people they just go away like never nobody remember nothing on Peter and John, sir."

"So there was no fighting?"

Timon shakes his head. "No fight, sir."

"You and Stephanos did well to keep the peace."

I have no doubt that his being here is not mere coincidence. The guard must not be able to understand my question about the meaning of his former strange bearing. Perhaps it is of little matter, and I do not want to embarrass him by asking again.

Timon looks straight in my face as though he reads my thoughts, and he continues. "It also why I think of Midas King and story. That teachers tell truth. Many people no want hear truth say no true. But I want truth come here, and I remember myself on this story. Also I know, truth come even in wind and rits, Rabboni. Truth always come, even after today things."

As this guard stands before me in the sunlight, I see the lines of age on his face. He continues to look at me earnestly, and then he sighs. "But I here no more, you see, sir. Also when he take Christos' students, Temple captain me ask, also I believe this Christos? And I say him truth, yes, I do very believe like

Peter and John and Stephanos. Truth, she come out, sir. I tell captain that, too. And captain get anger. He say me no need come back Solomon Porch and no back nowhere here, he no want guard like me what thinking on Jesus is Christos. So today I go home, sir, but also I say you everything I do for Temple always with open heart, and I always friend, you ever need big thing, little thing. You understand, sir?"

Though it takes me a moment to assemble Timon's broken words into thought, I meet his gaze. "Would you like me to speak with the captain?" I ask slowly.

The Greek shakes his head. "No, Rabboni. He know I guard like soldier, but he no want people believe Jesus is our Christos and you live after you die. He make me no more come here for this truth believe."

I hesitate, then find myself speaking another question in the voice of one of my own students. "Timon, why do you believe that the power of Jesus of Nazareth is the truth?"

The guard raises one hand as though he would touch me, and he sighs. "Sir, you no here to see that, what I see. You see only one man no walk be walk now. I see much, much people what walk now, what see now, what hear now, what believe in Jesus the Christos. If you see, sir, you also believe."

As I hesitate, he draws a breath to continue. "And also this, Rabboni. You think, just think. Why one man, why any man say he die for all our bad—my bad, you bad, everybody bad? Why one man live good life and then come again after that he die? Only Christos do that thing. Only God man love neighbor and love Israel and love world do that thing. I cannot be such man, but I can to love such man believe he true God man. You understand my meaning, sir? This big truth to believe even more importanter than this people what today can see and to hear and to walk again."

Without thought, I find my hand reaching out to this guard as my tongue voices an ancient prayer. "The Lord make His face to shine upon thee, and be gracious unto thee. The Lord lift up His countenance upon thee and give thee peace, thee and thine house," I pronounce. "I will not forget you in my prayers, or if I can find a place for you."

A look crosses this man's face that I know well from my students, a smile that pretends to comprehend and that is ashamed to question. With an inward prayer to You, my Lord, I search for every vestige of Greek I might summon, though I am certain that it is worse even than Timon's Hebrew. "Timon, I want that God walk long, long with you, and face like sun to you and give shalom you and you house," I attempt. "And if I find of good work, I tell them you good man, you do it."

The Greek clasps my hands and whispers "Efharisto, efharisto!" which is his native "Thank you."

A Final Questioning

As I expect after Timon's words, all the council reconvenes the next day. While we speak of this riot of divided faith and splitting of feeling between the Jews who love our one and only God and the Jews who call on the dead Jesus of Nazareth for healing, my perplexity grows. I have not heard of such healings and other good works full of love and peace if they do not come from our Lord, yet the Lord our God is one, not two–fold. Many eyes turn to me throughout the morning, but I remain silent.

The only word I voice is to Ezra, who comes to me quietly. "They are already here in the Temple again, preaching," he whispers.

"Who?" I whisper back, my mind not fixed on his meaning.

Ezra's laugh, though hushed, makes my locks tremble. "Peter and John, who were imprisoned last night. An angel led them, and they escaped with no violence or harm to the guards."

Word of this magical escape sweeps through all the men in our assembly.

Our high priests, hearing the murmuring, stop their deposition of possible crime or punishment to ask what is the matter. Annas and Caiaphas grow equally pale when one of the guarding officers repeats part of Ezra's news.

"Does anyone know where they have fled?" Annas asks the guard.

Ezra has not yet exited our hall full of elders. To my chagrin, I hear his youthful voice rise to answer. "Sir, the men whom you put in prison are standing in the Temple and teaching the people."

This boy has committed a double fault. Not only has he raised his voice in the presence of everyone here who is his elder, but in his zeal always to be the first to know things, he has once more embarrassed the highest leaders in public, and now even the Temple guards, who should know such things. With his being a member of my school and of my household, I, too, bear some failure in my duty to instruct him better, my Lord.

Silence reigns until Caiaphas draws several deep breaths. The anger in his regard shifts from Ezra who, after all, is just the messenger, even if a proud one, to the Temple captain and his officers. "Go bring them here," he says, the quiet in his voice more fearful than his previous anger.

As they hasten to obey, he adds, "And invite them. Use no violence against them. You know what the result could be."

Murmurings and shuffling accompany the departing guards, continuing through all the time it takes for them to return.

Now, when I would have spoken with Ezra, of course he has disappeared. I shall warn him sternly to come only to me with his announcements, however amazing he thinks such news could be for others.

When the party returns, additional murmuring arises, not only for Peter and John's appearance, but as the tall figure of Stephanos strides behind the rest, Ezra at his side.

As in the prior questioning, Annas and Caiaphas waste no

preliminaries on the men under scrutiny.

"Are your ears deaf that you cannot hear? Did we not straitly command you not to teach in this name?"

When the men remain silent, Caiaphas continues, voicing the accusation that is with us all. "Instead, you two have filled Jerusalem with your doctrine. You intend to bring this man's blood upon our heads!"

The Galileans turn toward each other. Is it dismay I see on one of their faces? Is it incomprehension of the fear behind the high priests' words that makes the other lower his gaze? My Lord, I cannot read their hearts.

Then the one called Peter—the leader, as I understand it—repeats the words he closed with in the prior hearing, words branded on my memory. "Sir, we must obey God rather than men."

There is no falling short of this man's courage before men who could have him killed. This I cannot help but admire.

Then John continues. "The God of our fathers raised up Jesus, whom you killed and hung on a cross."

That name Jesus again, the name which our high priest has not even permitted himself to say aloud.

In the growing silence and glaring, Stephanos steps forward to stand nearly side by side with the high priests, facing our assembly like a congregation. He raises a hand, and Caiaphas acknowledges his right to speak.

"Brothers, God has exalted Christ with his right hand to be a Prince and a Savior, to give repentance to Israel and forgiveness of sins. We are all his witnesses of these things, and so is the Holy Ghost. God has given this spirit to the people who obey him."

Is this "holy ghost" the power by which they claim to heal, I wonder. There are many questions I wish that I could ask Stephanos instead of the Galileans, for even if he is wrong, he has the power to explain this treachery of spirit in their midst.

And again, my Lord, I am cut to the heart by the whisper deep within my mind. "What if it is not they, but we ourselves who are in error?"

"For these words, we should kill you," Caiaphas replies in a voice cold as the stones beneath our feet.

Rumblings of assent begin to swell around me. Stephanos and the students of Jesus look on, their gazes unfaltering.

As some of the leading Sadducees rise with voices growling, I, too, stand quickly. I do not know what I must say, and my heart breathes a prayer to You, my Lord, to guide me.

Looking toward the captain of the guard, I meet his eyes and find my voice. "We would do well to speak together without these men present," I say.

The Temple captain nods, the worry on my face doubtless mirrored in his own thoughts.

Meanwhile, my mind runs like a hunted beast, flailing for words to calm my brethren. Already the blood lust of hunters appears to shake some of them as they rub their palms. I am thankful for the slowness of the men's departure with the soldiers as I breathe deeply and the doors are pulled closed behind them.

As with my students in difficult discussion, I modulate my voice to make it clear but low, forcing attention from those wishing to hear it. "Men of Israel, be very careful concerning what you plan to do to these men," I begin.

I search over my knowledge of our recent history with the Romans and even with others inhabiting our holy land. And it is as though the voice of my father and his generation is in my ear in what I say next, a story my father told me from his own childhood of a supposed wonder worker. "Remember long ago how a man named Theudas became famous boasting about himself as a great man?"

Faint murmurs and a few nods surround me. I go on. "For those whose memory fails, in the days of our fathers, about four hundred men joined him; then he was slain. Then every one of them who followed him was scattered, and brought to nothing. But you see, hardly a generation later, we scarcely remember a man all Israel used to speak of."

As my argument grows, I see how it can bear fruit as a new image comes to mind. "And after this man, there was Judas of Galilee, in the days of the first Roman taxing, and he attracted many people after him. But he also perished; and again, all of the ones who obeyed him were dispersed."

Here the nods of recognition come from every side, since this event of money demanded from the people is one so recent that even Saul and Stephanos could recall talk of it in childhood.

Now that I have grasped these men's minds, perhaps I can speak to their hearts, and I think an upward prayer to You, my Lord, as I am compelled by the point I have to tell in conclusion. "We are only dust without our Lord and forgotten by the children of our children. And now I must advise you, leave these men alone. If their words or their works are merely human, it will all come to nothing."

Nearly every man is looking at me with subtle nods, even a few smiles. They think I have concluded, but I do not yield my place. Instead, I raise my voice so that every man must hear me clearly. For an instant, the echo of Timon's truth tale crosses my mind. "But if this is a thing of God, you cannot overthrow it, and if you try, you may be found guilty even of fighting against God," I conclude. Only then do I take my seat.

Again, the men are divided. Some look at me in anger, but none of them can find a point to counter what You, my Lord, have just laid upon my tongue to speak. Instead, Annas signals for the doors to be opened, and as soon as they swing wide, the soldiers return with Peter and John, followed by Stephanos and a few others.

"There are no crowds in this place to protect you from your disobedience!" Annas greets them. "This will show you to speak in the name of your Jesus and put your elders to shame!"

Then he signals to the soldiers. Peter's and John's arms are pinned behind them by two men each, and in front of them, other guards strike their faces. Following, those who held them from behind twist their arms forward to bare their backs. The guards strike strong and bold, but with no letting of blood, which would be an abomination in this place.

The Galileans are almost too winded and shaken to remain standing. However, first John and then Peter look fully on our high priests before turning to the congregation, as another begins to sing: "Blessed are you when they persecute you for the sake of righteousness, for yours is the kingdom of heaven."

Then John speaks softly, but with the same kind of carrying voice I have just used to address my fellow council members. "Oh Lord our God, I thank You that You have found us worthy to suffer shame for Your Son, and for our sake, that He took upon himself so much more than shame."

With this, both Peter and John do their best to join in the singing as they are half shoved, half carried from our presence.

As with his earlier entrance, Stephanos holds the rear of the group. The light shines on his face when he turns at the door to face us. He appears older since Passover, graver around the mouth. He gazes steadfastly on Saul and me as he speaks his final words to our assembly, and his voice rings out with the same kind of newfound confidence I have just witnessed with Saul. Alas, alas for them both, my Lord!

"I wish it were as easy to heal your hearts as to heal a man's legs. But the shame you intend is in fact the honoring of our Christ."

Stephanos' words sear through the air to rend my soul, and the souls of many of us. From this day forward, the peer once known and loved as Stephanos of Tarsus is dead.

A Final Prayer

You have given me to understand two things this day, oh my Lord, and recognizing them, I beseech Your protection upon all our milling and divided people.

First, I know our Stephanos will never return to us. Lay Your mantle of protection over his body and his mind.

And second, despite the thin shielding You gave me to contrive safety over the Galileans today, I beg You, hold our leaders back. For if there comes a next questioning, it will surely bear fruits of blood!

Part III
The Deliverance

13. The Prayers and the Pledges Witness of Stephanos, Bethany, A.D. 33–34

Upon the First Prayers

Though I long to accompany Peter and John from Solomon's Porch as they are apprehended, instead I set my face like flint and return to tell my fellow believers in Bethany what has come to pass. My heart is full of praise after the worm man's healing, and surely with a peaceful arrest, no harm will befall these followers of Christos.

Nonetheless, I leave Jerusalem not as a happy messenger, but as a soul-stricken brother. For the Son of Man alone knows what I keep deep in my heart, and the matter is this. Today, I have lost brotherhood with Saul of Tarsus, my dearest friend.

All along my way out of Jerusalem, my knees still burn with the memory of Saul's clasping. My eyes still swim with the tears of his pleading as we spoke there on Solomon's Porch. Recognizing my steadfastness in faith fulfilled by our Messiah, Saul left me with whispered words as Timon's heavy gaze turned to the advancing Temple guard: "If you believe in this magic as you say, Stephanos, then you are dead to me."

With that, he turned his back and walked away, his new gait sure and steady. And though this was an act I could expect from Saul, yet how can I bear it? His words have struck my ears like the pelting of stones, to my inmost heart. The constant rhythm of my beloved running is all that can lend my spirit the strength to carry on.

Arriving at the assembly of the women and men who dare to follow our Messiah, I am no stranger. I have come each day since Passover to the believers in Christos. But today is different. Until now, I have never spoken before these brothers and sisters, who gather in private rooms when not at temple. Many of them saw Jesus of Nazareth face to face and broke bread with him. Some even share his bloodline. Who am I, after all, beside these believers? Yet today I introduce myself as Stephanos of Tarsus to those who know only my face. Even my Hellenist name is unfamiliar and difficult to pronounce for many.

But I lose no time in telling the news from Jerusalem. My fellow followers of our Messiah rejoice in the worm man's healing, to know that the Lord laid it on the lips of such a well-known beggar, one of such monstrous deformity, to speak to Peter and John, and that in turn, the name of Jesus once again gave my teachers the power to heal.

Some laugh around me as I answer their questions.

"A beautiful thing to think of Peter and John outwitting even the priests and performing miracles completely barred from them," some voices murmur.

"Having eyes, they do not perceive, and having ears, they do not understand," others reply, using words like those our Lord spoke during His teaching on earth.

But though our faith runs strong, my listeners fall to their knees in fear to beseech the Most High for the wellbeing of the men who were closest to Christos. I continue the story and recount the arrests. Peter and John speak the only words we know from our Messiah, for He neither wrote nor composed His teachings for others to read. Without our leaders and the words of eternal life they bear, to whom can we turn?

The next day, I rejoice with the assembly to see the teachers return to our midst. My joy is even greater to behold Timon following them.

"I do now believe," he greets me before taking a place in the very back of the room. "Now my baptism is complete!"

But the "Hallelujah!" and "Hosanna!" arising from our midst and greeting Peter and John are short lived. Their sober bearing speaks more of fear than of triumph. Even the most ardent of us who seek to persuade the great Temple and its assembly of Christos' truth can see the fatigue lining the men's faces, the tightness of their lips.

This is what our leaders tell us. With the worm man standing in their midst, and with news of his healing sweeping Jerusalem, the priests and elders could do nothing against them. The boldness of spirit given to them as they prayed for wisdom angered our Pharisees and Sadducees even more than the teaching, John says. Knowing the Temple order as I do, I can imagine this all too well.

"The leaders of the Temple have commanded us in no uncertain terms to stop the preaching of Christos' resurrection," Peter concludes.

Upon these words of his, I know a fear akin to what I first felt in my vision at the tearing of the veil, but I voice the question that many around me whisper. "Did you make any reply?"

"Of course we had to reply," John answers. "We told them what we know to be true. We cannot obey man saying one thing, when God has clearly shown us another thing. Otherwise, how could His truth live within us?"

Hearing John's plain-spoken words, I imagine the shock on faces like those of Gamaliel and the high priests. And in my mind, the eyes of Saul burn as though he were standing before me.

How I wish that I could have been the one arrested on

Solomon's Porch in place of these men. Twice blessed, by my education as a Hellenist and by my upbringing as a fellow Jew, I know well how to argue and to persuade; surely I could prove our Messiah through scripture and by what we already know of Moses and the prophets. But my role here is student, not teacher, and I remain silent before these rough-tongued tradesmen.

In the world, they are barely above the son of a freedman. But I remind myself, these unlearned Israelites are those whom Jesus of Nazareth chose as his students. It was these men who took upon themselves his following, not the men of our Temple—myself included, though we had the chance. Now it is their words alone that can turn the mind of our people to the truth before the second coming of Christos.

Many in this room also witnessed the swaying of the crowds before the crucifixion of our Messiah. Today, in light of this healing, all Jerusalem claims Peter and John as the apple of its eye, but tomorrow, words of the authorities could turn the people aside with equal ease.

"What they said to us is what they spoke to Jesus when they plotted his death, and he preached yet a while, but in the end, the leaders arrested him, and you know the result," Peter adds in a bitter voice. "Even the ones who loved him, left him. I myself was the greatest traitor of us all."

"Oh, Lord, hasten Your coming!" arise murmurings from every side.

Understanding the frailty of our lives as servants of Christos, we also know that John and Peter are not the only ones to fall under scrutiny. Any one of us now speaking the truth of Jesus' birth, life, death, and resurrection is in equal peril. The earlier murmurings of concern turn into statements of outright fear. When a number of followers slip from the room, no one has heart to implore them to remain.

Amidst our confusion, Peter urges us to fall on our knees in prayer. Many words rise heavenward around me as I seek some hope, opening my heart in silence. "Lord, You are God, and You have made heaven, and earth, and sea, and all that is in them. We remember how by the mouth of Your servant David, You have said, 'Why did the heathen rage, and the people imagine vain things?' Today we have seen how the kings of the earth stand up, and the rulers are gathered together against the Lord, and against his Christ. For truly against Your holy, anointed child, Jesus, Herod and Pontius Pilatus, with the Gentiles and the people of Israel—everyone was gathered together. And now, Lord, You know too well their threats. Grant Your servants great courage to speak Your word. Allow us to stretch forth our hands to heal. May Your signs and wonders be done through the name of Your holy child, Jesus."

I have heard that early in the morning, before the miracle when Timon heard Peter speaking like an Athenian, the room where many believers gathered to pray was swept with wind. I can well imagine it. Surely it was akin to the living air I felt at the rending of the veil, the day Christos transformed my fear and shame into love and understanding of who He is. On this present day, as the mingled fears and hopes in our prayers ascend toward the throne of God and the son of man, His Christ, I understand a quickening in our midst. It is not the air, nor the wind or light that sways us. Rather, as we raise our hands, one by one, together, we tremble with a motionless wind, a power entering into our hearts.

I turn my mind to wrap it in God's truth, truth so much greater and higher than ourselves. For God's word, we are mere vessels. And yet, small as we are, we have opened our very hearts and souls to witness the power of this meaning surging within us. The pulse of it is like that day long ago as I ran in Tarsus before Saul and Irini. All my youthful mind and body, and my heart as well, fixed steadfast on the goal, on the truth that I would win. There could be no other winner, no different result.

Even when my foot was grazed with the sharpened flint that sought to harm me, I did not let my spirit stray from the certainty of triumph. It was this meaning, running within me, even more than my feet, that made me victor.

Just so, the truth seizes us, each one. Where before, our minds and intellect were persuaded of Christos as Messiah, now that conviction crosses the finish line to touch our hearts. We are at last convinced that as willing vessels of this truth, we, and not the authorities, are the ones who hold power to change the world, preparing it for Christ's return.

Upon the First Pledges

To mark our unity, we make the decision this day to live as a family. Those who have property or money pledge to give what they have to the students of Jesus; those who lack worldly goods sigh in relief at the promise that they will receive what they need. From this day on, we agree to call nothing our own. This decision will serve not only to relieve the poverty of many, but also to knit us together, in case even one of us feels temptation to go astray to other things.

As we state our promises or requests, one by one, I listen to wealthy men like Barnabas of Cyprus. He is a fellow Hellenist, able to give the believers enough support for many months through sale of his property.

"I have only a few empty books and scrolls and my writing things," I admit when it is my turn. "Today I do not even have a room to call my own, but I thank some believers in our Messiah who have allowed me to sleep in their courtyards."

Surprise lights the faces of many, who believe me to be a wealthy man, since they have seen me sitting with leaders in the Temple or heard my confident speech. So I add this. "Though before this time, I could have surrendered more."

The prior strong demand for the fine writing goods I have

through my connections with the merchants of Greece and Tarsus has come to an end. Even most former customers from outside the Temple have stopped buying from me, so strong is the pressure from the Temple leaders to cut all ties with those of us who use our logika and understand that the Messiah has come, died, risen, and is seated at the right hand of our Lord.

"They say you are impure," Timon told me when I pressed him. "Hands of a man who saw behind the veil and who touched it are not the hands they want to touch things intended for their houses."

"It is the way we Jews often think, and it is not a surprise for me, Timon," I replied, almost laughing with grief. "You do me no insult; you merely speak the truth."

For the only time I heard Timon stand against anything Jewish, he replied with these words, unknowingly speaking almost as Christos once spoke: "It is what is inside a man that makes him pure."

"Do you have need of support?" Peter asks me directly now, interrupting what I remember.

A well-known voice replies from behind me. "Stephanos not never need no support. If he no got place, let he come live my house, sir. We no eat meat so much, but we enough have."

I can hardly look Timon in the face as our roles are so reversed now—I, the one in want; he, the provider. I give thanks to our Lord that Lukas' practice of healing grows, and with the diligence of all of them, they are surviving well even as Hellenisti, and strangers in this strange land.

"It is good," Peter says to Timon, and then to the rest, "This Greek kept guard on the Porch of Solomon and greatly calmed the crowd when we were arrested. He returned with us today from the Temple and professes his faith. He was even recognized earlier by John the Baptizer."

My face burns as I turn to Peter. "But there is one thing I can give our family of believers," I pledge. "I shall write the story of Christos, with your permission."

Several of the followers laugh as they stare at me, particularly an elder standing close by. "A fine, tall fellow like you, and look, just fit for sitting and writing? Why don't you do real work?" this man asks. Turning, I note powdery flecks on his tunic. "If you cut stones the way I do, you could change the world with things that last forever instead of ink that runs and skins that rot."

What do I have left? Perhaps the sorrow of losing Saul blunts the taunt of this man by comparison, for I feel no anger at his words, only sadness. "Sir," I reply in the most polite Hebrew I know, "if it is the will of our family in Christos, please let me learn from you, and I will join you in your work. I have no fear of labor. I have merely offered what I can give."

The man laughs again, this time with open scorn. "Do you think a mason can teach a man like you enough to cut and support others in a week or a month? Even your query is an insult to my trade!"

Then he continues as the laughter falls short and others begin to murmur. "But what need do we have for scribes like you? You are probably even friends with many who persecuted the Messiah and brought him to death. How do we know you yourself are clean in heart?"

Peter frowns. "Will you speak of your faith, Stephanos of Tarsus?"

But how can I claim a vision of the Son of Man while standing in the presence of those who knew him in the flesh? And what language could I find to describe the rending of the veil? "Yes, it is true that I know many members of the Sanhedrin," I begin. "But I was baptized by John the Baptizer, and your Lord is also my Lord." Turning from Peter and John back to the mason, I cannot resist voicing words of Greek irony. "He is a finer cornerstone than you could ever cut."

The mason glares at me as he casts words back at Peter and

John. "But, even if it is as this man says, I repeat myself. What need do we have for books and scrolls? Our business is to preach and to heal in the name of Jesus of Nazareth. What importance could it have for some scribe to labor on books or ponder mystery when Christos is coming at any time to reclaim the world? And who would read it as we await our Lord's return? There is far too much real work to do, and the harvest is great."

John sighs. "Though you yourself cannot read, there are many who can," he answers the man. "And if writing is the gift our Lord has given this man, then surely he has also given you other gifts. We can use both gifts with one accord to build our family of faith."

"Yes," Peter agrees. "Yours is a worthy pledge, Stephanos of Tarsus, and we give our Lord thanks for your willingness to be our scribe."

Over the next weeks and months, I speak not only with John and Peter, but I pursue others, such as Jesus' mother and other women who knew him, as well as asking many who followed from afar to test and compare their memories. It is no small task to assemble such thoughts, and I call on our Lord for wisdom. My tablets of wax and of soft clay are filled with the memories of others that I plan to join together to create a unified book.

But even as such witnesses come only one by one, so the preparing to write is no rapid matter. The skills required to create holy writing that I began in Tarsus and perfected in Jerusalem are fresh in my mind. The ink used for writing the word of our Lord I mastered when using it for the Torah. Its lasting blackness can only be obtained by boiling together certain oils, pitch, and wax, and then distilling their vapors for use. Afterwards, I combine that mixture with tree sap and honey, then dry and store it for a setting time, before finally mixing this compound with gall-nut juice for its hydration. Any scribe performs such labor with the same degree of prayer and diligence with which he later writes.

This shaping and preparation for things to come recalls the memory of one boyhood day, a day while things were right in my world, while Baba was still alive.

Near our great library of Tarsus, a man chiseled at a huge boulder of white marble over many months. But he was no common mason, like the man whose words here in Jerusalem are so bitter. He was a sculptor, and the finest in Cilicia, so it was said. A small crowd always gathered around him as at first he pounded with heavy iron, then later scraped with files and knives. Perhaps on this certain day my regard was so earnest that it brought him to speak, or perhaps my closeness standing there simply made him aware of my presence, for amidst his work, he neither ate nor drank, nor sat nor spoke, nor looked to anyone around.

But on that day, this master artist turned from his work and spoke to me. "This is a story I tell. It is a stone waiting to be freed of its unneeded portions and its flaws to shape itself into the true form I feel hidden inside it."

That form emerged as Pegasus, alert and proud, his flanks ready to quiver, his nostrils flaring no less than in true life, his feathered wings poised to rise.

I do not know why the great man spoke to me that day, yet his words remain with me; indeed, I was reminded of them later in my youth as I first struggled to create a kosher scroll. I failed a hundred times, even with the sacred copy before my eyes, but I always tried again. Then one day, as though my regard were unveiled, I saw the words on the colorless parchment as though they existed there already. My part became merely to render them visible.

Therefore I find deep refreshment in spirit in making such beloved preparations for the writing of words from our Lord. I rejoice to contemplate the lining and the lettering I will perform—the size, the shape, the lovely crowning of certain letters and fixed numbers of lines and columns on a page, each in its order proscribed by our forefathers.

Still, before I begin my permanent work, I wish to discuss a certain problem with my teachers. "The letters of holy writing are put down in Assyrian script," I say. "But now that I am prepared to begin, I know that only a few will be able to read my work, and certainly not most of the followers of our Messiah."

To my dismay, Peter's laughter cuts me short. He lays a hand on my shoulder and continues his mirth as I stand uncomprehending before him. "Stephanos, oh, you fine and true scribe and son of the Temple!" He can hardly speak for his laughter as other leaders attach their eyes to my burning face. "Haven't you paid attention to the things you have written here?" he manages at last, gesturing to my pile of temporary tablets.

For the first time, I taste on my tongue the wordless and stuttering heaviness of which Moses complained. But unlike our great leader who brought us out of Egypt, I have no brother Aaron to be appointed my voice to the people. My heart curves within me as I also remember the halting words of Saul and how his own breath embarrassed him with its faltering, and my love for him gives me just enough courage to speak in my turn. "There is nothing I wish for more than to perfect this writing," I manage.

Smiling, John lays his hand on mine. "It is our Messiah who is perfect, and not any writing that your hand can create concerning him. This is a new scripture, and you, Stephanos, are a scribe of the new order."

John proceeds to tell me of the reproach dealt to Jesus and the students when they did not wash their hands in the ritual manner prescribed before a meal.

"And you complain of difficult script and you brag of your holy ink. This new law demands one thing, your love, and that your writing may appear in love to those who wish to read the truth. What need is there of all these ancient rites of the law that you speak of with such sorrow on your face? Write well, and write quickly!"

It is at the same time a bitter and a sweet thing to think of myself as this "scribe of the new order." Since those words from John, I have written every day when I can, every night when I must. However, I have done so in the manner of a common, quick-penned Greek scribe, setting aside our traditions of cleanliness and of fasting when committing errors surrounding holy writing. Nonetheless, I find the quietest and most peaceful place to work, no small task given Timon's active household, and always I kneel in prayer before and after my writing. I also pause to give thanks at each penning of the name of our Lord and of His Christ.

The demand is far more than I can provide, yet provide I must. I remind myself of the urgency of this task. And perhaps those who never know us will keep these words of our Lord to teach them until His return, if He is merciful and postpones His judgment of all the world yet a little while.

Many readers long for the words of Jesus of Nazareth as recalled by His students. Thus this work of scribing serves a double purpose: It allows for the telling of the works and the words of our Lord to many who have never seen Him, and it provides steady sustenance for our common needs as the writings are sold.

The severity of this task of scribing is recalled to me in my own body as my eyes tingle, my wrist throbs, my fingers burn, and I desire a little hot oil for my hands. Sometimes, Irini would also beg oil of me, but it was something which I could not always provide her. I remember how I would say to her, "Just a little more, and it is finished."

But now, while I allow my memory to grieve, and my pain is its own punishment, yet I know that even this sin of failed compassion for my little sister is hidden beneath the river of baptism. I am free by our Lord's mercy. I bless her spirit each night as I finalize my work for the day, along with the memory of sweet diligence in scribing, the witness she has left to me. The more I strain under the burden of composing and copying, the more I seem to hear her gentle laughter. If a tiny girl growing to womanhood could write so well and for so long, surely, after all, I am capable of the same. Somehow, this thought always gives my eyes their vigor and my hand its precision to finalize one more line... one more column... at last, another page.

And though I entreat her to pursue the hobbies and the work of a young girl, small Cassandra insists on providing for me as she can. Learning that I have soon exhausted my supply of holy ink, she comes each day with what is always just enough ink for my use. And this I must say: It is ink of the rarest quality and binding to the page.

When I ask her how she procures it, she merely smiles. "I see what you have done, Uncle, and do you think I was so young that I could not remember how Aunt Irini did certain things?"

I do not know which is greater, my dismay at a child so small seeing a thing and remembering it, or my admiration of her skills.

I sacrifice my remaining fine Roman scroll for the most complete writing I compile. This I send as a gift to Rabboni Gamaliel. I pray for its acceptance, for my teacher to look carefully at what I have written with reason and not to push it away with fear or rage. Who knows, but perhaps our Lord may lay it on his heart even to show Christos' teachings to Saul and the rest? I breathe this prayer onto every line of words shaped by my hand.

This finished scroll I send to Gamaliel with Ezra. "You will look carefully at Rabboni's face, and you will report to me his mood if he accepts my gift," I tell him.

This boy often visits us and asks questions that show his desire to understand the truth. Even Timon The Eagle praises his shrewdness.

Ezra returns to me after the next Sabbath without the scroll, but with a smile as he recounts Gamaliel's joy. Then I know what the hope was for Noah when he saw the dove returning to his ark after the flood, the day when it flew to him bearing in its frail beak a leaf from a shore—distant, but dry.

Upon the Second Prayers and Pledges

Then an occurrence with Timon arises that, though I should have foreseen, yet I did not suspect amidst my toil of words.

Timon performs day labor as he can but continues his visits to listen to Peter and John. No man pays particular heed to him, nor does the Athenian in any way draw attention. In fact, he is a model of courtesy and service as he pours water for one coughing here, carries a sleeping child to its mother there, and in all other matters shows the eye of diligent guardianship that is his way.

After many months, however, it comes to pass that Timon speaks.

It is a usual thing for the teachers to ask us if any stand in need of prayer. When Timon rises, he is recognized. "Sirs, you pray every day. You say widow names; I hear them names like Naomi and Rachel and Esther. These important, fine Jew names and your widow women you care about and when you pray, you do after you pray to give food, money them. Thank you for this giving, sirs."

"Amen," say many around him, ignoring the poverty of Timon's speech, hearing his meaning.

But Timon waves the amens away like gadflies, and he sighs. "Me, sirs, also I pray, too. I pray for widow women their names like Penelope and Pandora and Daphne. You see my meaning, sirs?"

Timon's question is greeted with silence. I grasp his

meaning immediately, but I wait for him to go on.

"These Greek women names, sirs. You know, maybe you no see in synagogue, but you hear many Hellenisti come here. They Jew people, too, just they not know Jew things what like you know. But they was slaves or slaves' kids. Give up own cities, own family sometime, own life come Israel for to find our Lord. Maybe like you all come many, many year before from Egypt, yes?"

Nods of agreement greet Timon's continuation. I think of the teachers I saw in Athens in his serious pose, his hand gestures, and I smile.

"Only problem thing is, such women, sometime even such men, they not know you. They not talk cause even more bad than my Hebrew their Hebrew, sirs. I know you not believe that there even possible, but it truth, you believe me!"

Many laugh around me, even Peter.

"But thing is this, bad thing this. Widow Penelope or Daphne, she need food just like widow Rachel or Esther. But she not know how ask you or tell you. My dear wife help many them babies, them sick, them hungry. Why Hebrew Jew no help them, too? They need just like Hebrew Jew widows, you see?"

Now the silence around Timon's words is not one of hesitation or incomprehension, but of shame. Many men and women look at one another, and they nod, pursing their lips.

But Timon appears not to comprehend the reaction. "Sirs, you maybe no believe me, I bring in them. They tell you as Stephanos help speak them Hebrew from Greek, all right?"

He turns to me, a question in his eyes.

For only the second time now, I address the assembly. "Timon is quite correct in what he says, even if he does not say it correctly," I affirm. "These Hellenisti are as foreign here as we ever were in Egypt, and then, when we left Egypt to return to our promised land. Their dream is the same dream as ours."

Peter replies, not only to his fellow disciples, but to all of us in the room. "It is not reasonable for us to leave the teaching of God's word to serve tables."

Timon bows and shakes his head. "No, God word more importanter, sirs, but eat also real important. And also, no different, soul talk Greek, soul talk Hebrew; this not important before our Lord."

Peter raises his hand, stopping Timon amidst his broken, truth–filled attempts at words. "So, brethren, look to yourselves and find honest men, men full of the Holy Ghost and wisdom, whom we may appoint for this."

"Thank you! That right thing you do!" Timon exclaims, and many in the crowd nod in agreement.

We make short work of nominating fellow Hellenisti who will conduct the daily sharing of alms and of food with integrity. Phillipos, Prochorus, Nicanor, Parmenas, and Nicolas of Antioch, a friend of Lukas, spring to our tongues. Standing beside me, Timon is so full of gusto in naming such men that he does not notice the gentle laughter and all the eyes looking directly at us. I take heed no more than Timon.

"I believe the messenger should also be included in this task, though we will miss Timon in our midst," Peter finally says.

Timon looks up, coughs, blushes like a boy, then nods consent. And then he turns to me. "I glad do this every day, sirs, but we need leader, good man. Stephanos can to lead like nobody never lead after Moses!"

I wish to cover my face with my robe. If only Timon had consulted with me, I could have told him no in private. Each day, it is my joy to listen to our teachers, to write whatever I can, and to speak only what I must in doing so. I have no power or skill like Timon to organize crowds or oversee the faintest need his eyes always perceive, as is his gift from our Lord.

Meanwhile, one harsh laugh barks from our assembly. "How can this scribe be expected to wait on tables, either, sirs? You yourselves assigned him the task of recording the life of

Christos, after all."

Peter regards the stonecutter who has spoken. "God's work is never finished. But Stephanos has written enough that those less lettered than himself can copy his writings down and distribute them."

A sinking of my heart nearly chokes me, as though I am a man used up and cast down like a cracked vessel. How can I abide to be away from the women and men who knew the Messiah, now that I know them and the truth they speak? Being beside them is as close as I can ever approach to Christos, after all.

Then John walks close to me and lays a hand on my shoulder. "Your gifts are diverse, Stephanos of Tarsus, and you yourself cannot see all of them. Nevertheless, the Lord has need of you as you are now called among the Hellenisti. So go, take your place with them."

The next day, along with Phillipos, Prochorus, Nicanor, Parmenas, and Nicolas of Antioch, Timon and I are compelled to the front of our crowded assembly room. None of us speak as we form a circle, surrounded by the main teachers who have been our counselors since Christos' crucifixion and resurrection. My mouth contains no air at all as I feel hands laid on my head, oil anointing my brow, and words of blessing uttered all around.

"Prosper Your will in these Hellenisti as they care for our brothers and sisters, Lord."

"Grant them justice and wisdom in Your labor."

"Remember these least of our brethren as we distribute to their need and as they come to Your truth, oh Christos!"

The ink staining my hands seems to mock me; it is the used-up remnant of my former pledge. When I close my eyes against seeing it and knowing it will fade to nothing, it is as though my ears again hear the first word of our Lord as he called my name in the Temple. "Stephanos!"

My breath catches tight, and I whisper, "Here am I."

Timon clasps my hand. "Amen, amen; I have long believed this is your ministry, Stephanos!" he whispers, his voice taut with feeling. "As for the rest of our brothers, they will serve well under our direction together. Do not be afraid; I will do everything to help you, and you will pray and speak to the priests and the people to assure the fair distribution, that is all."

I bow my head, tears behind my eyes. This ministry will take me even further from my lost friend Saul, who has no contact with the Hellenisti, though by his schooling he could be one of us. Then as though whispered in my ear, I hear a phrase that I had forgotten from my vision in the Temple:

You shall not reach the things you most desire,
But your own life will turn My word to fire.

"Amen," my mouth shapes the word. "Let it be so."

14. The Requests and the Truths Witness of Believers, East Jerusalem, A.D. 34-35

First Request of Ezra

How my feet fling pebbles in the dust, pounding and throbbing, and how my tongue burns as I run gasping. But my mouth is overflowing with good news, good news! Before I can speak it, bursting into the courtyard from the gate of Timon's household, Cassandra's laughter breaks out from beneath the cedar tree where she is sitting with her uncle, Stephanos the scribe.

"Oh, Ezra! You are just like a flapping crow, the way you run!"

I collapse beside them, too winded after my hot run to voice a single word of protest.

Cassandra ends her laughing and goes on in her voice so sweet to my ears. But is it mockery or compassion? "Poor Ezra!" She frowns. "You run all the way from Jerusalem to Bethany, and you are always a man half dead when you arrive."

Oh, she has called me a man! I dare to look Cassandra in the face with my next words. "But my feet always find their way to you well enough, don't they?"

Cassandra ignores my question and avoids my gaze, but at least she answers. "Did you know that Uncle Stephanos was a great runner in Cilicia?"

I turn to him. "Is it true that you ran so well?"

"Not for long," Stephanos replies. Picking up a small lyra that I did not notice in my hasty entrance, he begins to strum.

"But Uncle! You won the great race as the fastest boy in Cilicia when you were not much older than we are."

Stephanos nods.

"Well, why don't you show Ezra how to run? He has the look of a bear pursued by hounds every time he arrives. I've seen you travel twice the distance without even being winded."

By now I have recaptured some of my breath. "I am just an awkward scholar boy, not a graceful Hellenist runner."

As soon as these words fall from my lips, I fear that I have insulted my host by overshadowing his own scholarship with his Greek ways.

But Stephanos laughs. "To run well, it is not one's height or build that is so important, and certainly not one's native land."

Then he turns. "Cassandra, aren't you going to bring some water for Ezra? Just look at him."

Cassandra glares at me, but I know her. She is reproaching herself for failing to offer hospitality before her uncle must ask her to welcome me. And having seen my face, she understands there is news. Well, let her miss these words my tongue carries, since they are meant for Stephanos' ears alone. Besides, I am surrounded right now by the stink of my sweat, the curse of becoming older. May the Lord send a breeze to make this stench depart before she returns. I force myself outside the shade of the tree in hopes that the sun will dry me.

Now I can speak my heart! But I must keep everything in its good time, as Rabboni Gamaliel constantly reminds me. Therefore, I begin with the news I have to tell that may put Stephanos in good spirits to hear the request that gave my feet their speed.

"Most of your fellow scribes are reading the scroll you gave me for Rabboni Gamaliel. He has encouraged them to do so."

"Praise to our Lord!" Stephanos replies, smiling.

My breath comes fast. My words have had the desired effect.

"But I do not think you have run here with such speed to tell me this, have you, Ezra?"

Even in the heat, my face grows hotter, and I hope my start at a beard may hide this as I shake my head.

"Well, speak on, then." The scribe's words are gentle, but I feel amusement behind his smile.

"Your friend Saul has asked to see Cassandra."

It is strange to me that Saul has not written or come himself to make such an odd request. But my business is to convey matters, not to question.

Stephanos' smile disappears like spring rains into the desert sands. "Saul," he says, then, "oh, Saul."

Then, as though speaking words to himself, he continues. "He counts his knowledge of our Lord and of His law better than ours, of course."

My heart sinks, but I make no response to his last words. Perhaps my next words will make him smile again.

"Yes. Saul has consented to teach Cassandra along with me, each eve of the Sabbath."

The breath Stephanos draws recalls my long journey from Jericho to Jerusalem to study in Gamaliel's house. I heard the piteous wheezing of an old man as I passed him, struggling along a narrow path on a steep mountain.

A faint smile reappears on Stephanos' lips. "But tell me, then, why did you run here so fast to deliver this request? Why does this favor hold such value for you?"

Despite my attempt at subtlety, I am sure that this man has seen through me, and I can do nothing to hide. And since this is so, and Cassandra will return any moment, I must hasten the speaking of my heart's desire. I am a man with no shield before an oncoming soldier, but I think of young David before Goliath, and I gather myself.

"May I take Cassandra to and from Jerusalem? I will surely bring her home each week before the Sabbath starts in the evening."

"Cassandra!" Stephanos calls. Then he utters words in Greek.

Even if I had studied the Hellenisti and their tongue, I am certain I would not understand his rapid speech. My heart sinks.

Then he frowns as though recognizing his discourtesy. "I have told her to bring you some food."

Does he guess my hunger, or is this clever Stephanos giving us more time to speak together alone? I must remember this action, for perhaps I will use it someday myself. My throat is too tight to trust my voice to speak, so I simply nod in gratitude.

"Gamaliel and Timon both speak well of you," Stephanos continues.

The nodding has stiffened my neck, already aching from the breathing and shaking of my recent run.

"I believe you are honorable, Ezra. I also believe that Saul has honor in wanting to teach Cassandra. He does not want me to be her teacher anymore." His face grows pale. "No, not me," he repeats. And then as though talking to himself, he adds this. "Perhaps it is Cassandra that Christos will use to persuade him of the truth."

Cassandra emerges, bearing not only water, but a tray full of strange but fragrant food. Besides olives of an unusual size, there are pancakes rolled with something white inside them, and separate, sweet, fresh figs.

Stephanos looks up as she sets the food before me. "Cassandra, you have been invited for weekly scripture lessons in Jerusalem with Saul. What do you think of this?"

The heavy pitcher she has brought along with my water cup sways in Cassandra's hand. "Is it true?" she asks him, and then turning, she repeats this to me directly. "Oh, is this true, Ezra?"

"Yes," I manage after gulping down half the water in the cup. It has the taste of something tart and refreshing.

"Then you will go," Stephanos replies. "Lukas or I will accompany you." Then turning to me, he adds, "There is no rule preventing you from walking the same road with us."

"Oh, pick up your lyra, Uncle! Please pluck it the way you do when I sing poems of Orpheus. I am so happy I need to sing, and I have a new song for you both to hear," Cassandra says. As Stephanos begins, she stands straight as a lantern flame in a room with no windows for air to pass through.

This music surrounding us in the courtyard is like a warm and fragrant wind. My heart throbs with the beauty of her voice, but hearing her words, my ears shrink close to my head. The singing of Greek and the strumming of a lyra in Jerusalem are things left to whores and foreigners, to conquering Romans longing for what they call civilization, and evil actors and lusty poets who write of vanity. Why can't Cassandra sing in Hebrew with a flute or a trumpet, which are more traditional to our people? Then perhaps I could rejoice in her song instead of fearing the gods and idols it must be invoking.

Stephanos stops playing when Cassandra looks down. "What is this poem, Cassandra, and where have you learned it?" His voice is too gentle for the idolatry that has shot around us like poisoned arrows

"Oh, just a little song," Cassandra says, rubbing her foot in the dust.

I cannot utter one single word.

"Now I will tell you its meaning, Ezra," Cassandra says. My heart trembles in fear of what is about to pollute the mouth of this beautiful, wonderful girl in my own language. But she stands straight and looks me in the face. Forgive me, Lord, my desiring eyes! Then she speaks so that I understand:

Oh earth with your stones, Oh water with your waves,
Oh wind with your air and fire with your heat,
Forever you live, but only as slaves
As footstools to Christos upon his high seat,
Who lived and who died, who rose from the dead,
Who stone of all cornerstones rules over earth,
Who soon will appear even as he has said,
Whose name of all names gives our souls second birth!

Rendered speechless by the beauty of the verse, I draw in my breath, as much in relief as in admiration. If only our Lord had given me the gift of poetry! I believe that if I could write even one such verse, I would be a happy man.

Cassandra's eyes burn into mine. "And you thought I was singing about the gods of Mount Olympus, didn't you?"

"I—I..."

"Yes, Ezra, I saw your lips murmur a prayer as you listened. Well, it is not only Hebrew that has beautiful words. Greeks can praise our Lord as you do."

Stephanos interrupts. "Cassandra, I have not heard this beautiful song in our worship place."

I cast him a thankful glance.

Cassandra laughs. "Of course you haven't. First, it is in Greek, so we would not sing it there. But second, I wrote it myself. Why do you think that everything lovely has to be written by old men?"

Stephanos and I look each other full in the face, and we laugh. From that day, Stephanos trains me during our weekly trip to Jerusalem to run not as a crow, but as a man!

Request of Cassandra

Each day before Sabbath is my joy, but it comes to pass so slowly. On other days, I learn the ways of women, both well and sick, with Aunt Iphigenia.

Her sternness is like the masks my father Alexander of Crete wore on stage that I can still see with my inner eye. When I told her my lineage, she only blew air from her mouth, saying, "It is better to be a slave born a Jew than a free Greek. You must thank our Lord for his mercy on you."

But from her I learn many things, I must admit. For example, I have no fear of the monthly courses that show me to be a woman. She has told me what to expect, and she has also told me that after this time, I may not venture out much, and never alone, and that my studies should end. But for me, the essential thing is this: Nothing must bar me from my learning.

It is simple enough for me to get what I need, making almost any man's face soften as I turn my eyes to liquid. This is too easy to do if I think of losing my time with Ezra and Uncle Thaul. Tears gather of themselves. So when I smile at the market, I can always beg a few handfuls of wool here or scraps of rags there, which I burn after using to keep my monthly secret.

This is the prayer I speak at such times: "My Lord, You have made me woman. You have given me eyes to see and hands to write and rhymes inside my heart. Surely You will be with me as I learn Your word. I am Your handmaiden as certainly as my uncle Thaul is Your servant, and my uncle Stephanos is Your scribe and preacher, and Ezra is Your faithful messenger."

Ezra shares joy with me week after week when we proceed to the school in Jerusalem. When he is not running under Uncle Stephanos' instruction—"Straight, like a javelin!"—then he is walking all around us.

Sometimes, as we sing hymns or laugh together, my uncle does not forbid us from wandering a stone's throw ahead or behind him. At such times, Ezra also speaks to me about his native city of Jericho, and his hopes to return there someday as a rabbi. He claims that the Dead Sea close to his city is so blessed by our Lord that no man can drown in its waters, but every man floats like a basket. However, in the same breath, he claims that the bitterness of its waters can poison a strong man in a single mouthful.

I long to make a retort, before remembering a thing Iphigenia said to me: "Allow a man to talk and to consider himself the smarter one, so that when you need to use your mind, he will not notice." Therefore, I hold my peace.

And when I remain silent on a certain day, Ezra even tells me that since he has met me, Jerusalem and Bethany feel closer to home for him.

Along our way this day, as is our wont, we take turns asking each other the names of the sons of Israel, of prophets and miracles, of cities built and enemies slaughtered by our people entering the Promised Land. Uncle Stephanos needs to correct us only rarely, though we agree that his word is final.

Ezra says that reading a scroll, he can later picture it in his mind, which explains how he can recite back even long passages. But he admits that he can never think up rhymes or verses as I can.

On this certain day, Ezra has turned back several stones' throws away and is charging toward us. The sweat on his brow catches the sun.

I begin our weekly game of playing parts from our scripture, amusing each other with our ways of creating life as another person. As his back was turned, I inflated a limp goat's bladder kept hidden in my sleeve while Ezra gasped and panted ahead. Now I clasp the full bladder under my tunic. When he turns about to race toward us, I see how much he has learned. How sure his strides have become as he tucks flailing arms inward and rises to his toes in landing.

"You are surely Rebekah as she awaits the birth of Jacob and Esau," he gasps through lips parted with laughter.

I shake my head, but my face burns imagining a woman

heavy with twins. I slow my gait to lumber, tilting my head as though beneath a great weight. The twinkle in my uncle's eye makes me believe he has guessed my part. I shrug my shoulders and hold my arms stiff out from my body, as though blocked from returning to my side. I slow my pace to lumber and shift like any fat man.

"Why don't you bow to this great personage?" my uncle asks. Yes, he knows.

But after bowing, Ezra remains perplexed.

I wrinkle my nose.

Uncle Stephanos joins in. "Oh, the air here, surely we must leave this person to his intent!" he mocks.

Still Ezra remains baffled.

Finally, I grasp his left hand, smashing it into the goat bladder beneath my robe. "Oh, oh, oy!" I cry, slumping forward over his trapped arm.

"Cassandra!" My uncle's voice is stern now, and blushing,

Ezra removes his hand, which by accident has been enfolded near my bosom. But he is laughing. "Your majesty, King Eglon," he proclaims. "Now have I slain thee, and long thy servants will await to find thee, as thou sittest with my sword in thy gut and thy bowels stinking the palace."

"Thou hast spoken well, wise and brave Ehud," I reply, in my deepest and most commanding voice. "But why did not my guards perceive thy treachery upon thy coming into my presence?"

"Though my left hand was reviled and slapped as a child, yet it served me well to disguise my sword and to kill thee as the guards inspected only that side where a normal man's sword would be girded," Ezra replies.

"And thy father's name, and thy tribe, thou traitor bearing gifts as false as the horse outside Troy?" I demand, stamping my foot.

Though Stephanos laughs, Ezra's face is as blank as new

parchment. Suddenly I pity him, knowing the ways of only one people, of us the Jews, but not the Greeks and our wonderful stories such as that of the Trojan horse.

But Ezra is oblivious to my thought as he cries, "My father's name is Gera, and I am a Benjamite! As to false gifts, they were true in serving my purpose!"

"Well done!" Uncle Stephanos exclaims.

Ezra snatches the goat bladder from my hand, which I have let drop from under my robe. "You will never guess who I am now!" he laughs.

Though his hands do not touch me, yet I feel every pulse of heat as his fingers nearly embrace my shoulders, then lower to my arms.

"You are surely Elijah wishing me the mantle you have cast from your chariot as the Lord brings you to heaven. I am your student Elisha," I say.

But Ezra shakes his head, smiling. "Here, let me give you this," he goes on. His voice is without breath despite his recent running, a small, gentle voice that I have never heard from him. Then he raises the bladder above my face to tilt downward. Turning to me, he goes on. "Rest now. You are safe here."

Looking to my uncle, I am uncertain from his face whether he has guessed the message or not.

Finally, Ezra throws his right hand high, and with a shout that makes fellow travelers turn around, he slams a stick into the road. It breaks with the thrust. "Now I have killed you, my enemy!" he shouts into my face. "With my tent peg, I have nailed your head to the floor!"

My uncle and I laugh.

"Jael, oh wife of Heber the Kenite, you are a brave woman indeed!" I cry.

Ezra, still in the high voice intended to be womanly, calls on. "You asked for water, but I gave you milk. You asked to hide like a woman in my tent, and I wrapped you in my own cloak.

But as the army of Israel sought you, it was by my hand, and not by any soldier's, that you lie dead while you sleep, by my own hand, with my own tent peg! The Lord our God delivered you, a general fighting our people, to a mere woman like me!"

All three of us choke with laughter.

Then my uncle turns to acting. I see it immediately as Ezra does not. His pace changes to that of an older man; his shoulders stoop as though with a heavy weight. His eyes sink to his chest, his hands rise to cradle an object close to his heart. When my friend notices me watching my uncle, his eyes also turn.

"Surely you are the Christ, sheltering the single lamb that has been lost from the flock," Ezra says.

Stephanos nods. "Perhaps. Perhaps." Then he turns straight to Ezra. "But how is it that you know of this teaching of his? Studying with Rabboni, you do not attend our congregation so often."

"I have been among the first to obey the suggestion of Rabboni Gamaliel. I read the scroll you sent several times, and carefully," Ezra replies.

Stephanos nods, then turns to me. "What do you think, Cassandra?"

"I am certain you are Prometheus!" These words burst forth from my lips before I can stop them.

Ezra looks at me hard. "Who is this Promitus, or whatever you have named him, Cassandra?" And turning to my uncle he adds, "Why do you let her speak about false Greek ways and stories?"

Before I find a fitting retort, my uncle turns to me and lays a hand on my shoulder. A mix of gentleness and of warning tingles in his voice. "It would be a good thing for our Hebrew friend here to know this story so that he can appreciate its truth."

I bite back my anger. "Prometheus is his name. Prometheus." I am intent in pronouncing the 'th—' sound found in Greek but not in Hebrew. "He was a great hero in the days before Israel was even a nation."

"Oh?" Ezra says loudly. "And how do you know it?"

"Because without him, we would have no fire for mankind to warm itself, and cook, and heal, and be comforted."

"In fact, it is written that Adam was made of clay," my uncle adds. "But nowhere in scripture do we learn of the origin of fire. Cassandra's story will tell you, so listen well, Ezra."

Encouraged by my uncle's words, I go on. "Prometheus was a Titan. This is what Greeks call giants who are immortal. Most of them went around fighting and living not much better than animals. But Prometheus thought and thought; his name means taking thought, in fact."

"Then why was he walking with something in his hand?"

I am not sure if Ezra is challenging me or if he is interested. "Have you heard of Zeus? Zeus?" I say the name slowly and repeat.

Ezra shrugs. "It's some pagan god, I think."

I shake my head. "Not just any god, but the chief god that is worshipped in Greece. He is king of the gods who live on Mount Olympus."

Ezra nods. "I thought so," he admits.

"But of course all of us know these are not real gods. That is why we are living here in Jerusalem, and why the Hellenisti have come," I add.

"Thanks be to God!" Ezra retorts.

"Well, Ezra, the gods in Greece are like people with all their anger and jealousy and thoughts."

"Prometheus, too, I suppose," he says. But I note the proper pronunciation he has now given to the name.

I shake my head. "Prometheus was not exactly a god, though he did live with the gods for a time. But in Greece, many people believe it was Prometheus who created man."

"Truly? They believe this?" Ezra asks.

"This, and much more, Ezra." I smile. "You should see the

many plays in our theaters. Then you would learn what we believe."

"But this is not the point," my uncle says. "Tell him what I was doing, Cassandra—if I was Prometheus, that is."

"The gods do not love mortals as our Lord protects and loves us, Ezra. And so, mortals were created, but they were cold and hungry and miserable."

"Many are that way today, even here," Ezra says.

"Yes, I know. But even the poorest mortal has some way to become warm if he can find a fire."

"The Greeks have no fire?" Ezra asks. "Now you are testing my belief."

I laugh. "Of course we have fire in Greece. But in the ancient time, we did not. It was Prometheus who gave us this fire; he stole it from Zeus, the king of the gods. Then he carried it to earth inside a hollow reed. He gave it to humans and showed how it could be used to bring all the good things we know about."

Ezra shrugs. "This is impossible."

Stephanos lays his other hand on Ezra's back. "But listen to the continuation, Ezra."

"Zeus was very angry, because he saw it brought power to mankind to eat and live in comfort and not to call on the gods like before. So he learned how it came to man and that Prometheus had stolen it."

"What did he do then? Kill him, like Christ?"

The scorn in Ezra's words is enough to scorch the air between us—if the air could burn, that is.

I shake my head. "I wish it could be so easy. But you have forgotten an important thing I said, which is that Prometheus was immortal."

"Christos is also immortal and he will come back to the world very soon," Ezra answers.

My uncle laughs amidst his "Amen."

"Yes, I agree," I add. "But the gods and the Titans cannot die at all."

Ezra sighs.

"Instead, Zeus had Prometheus captured and dragged far away to a high mountain in the cold north where he could have no fire. He lay in chains. Each day an eagle came and devoured his liver, but each night, the liver grew back, since he could not die."

Ezra turns to my uncle, then to me. He appears less sure than before. "Forever?" he asks, voice quieting.

I reply, "It should have been forever. But our great Greek hero Hercules heard of Prometheus' suffering for all mankind. He came to the mountain, he killed the eagle, and he set the Titan free."

Ezra looks relieved, then turns to my uncle. "So who were you pretending to be?" Something akin to pleading laces his voice.

My uncle smiles. "I am only Stephanos of Tarsus. But perhaps a Greek sees a myth, and a Jew sees a Messiah. It is as it should be to spread the truth of our Lord. To prepare for faith."

"Enough!" Ezra says. "I will run now. We are almost there."

When he has left us, I open something held long in my heart. "I have a request of you, Uncle." I hate the formality that edges my voice.

"Why so serious?" he asks. "You look like you want to demand half a kingdom."

I grasp my uncle's hand. "I request not half, but a whole kingdom, Uncle. I want to enter into God's kingdom as you and Aunt Irini did. I wish to be baptized, and I want you to be my baptizer."

Request of Stephanos

Like Prometheus, I give much thought to the request

Cassandra has laid on me. It is no small matter for one so young to claim baptism. And while many students besides Peter and John actively baptize now, I am not among them. Since my calling, in Peter's words, to "serve tables," I have scarcely had time to continue study of the teachings of our Lord. Timon and I often arrive home in the courtyard late in the evening, so tired from the day's work and preaching that we can scarcely eat or speak.

Yet as the poor among the Hellenisti gather around, receiving daily portions, I thank our Lord for their faith. I speak to them of the truth we know through the words of Christos. There is only one rule, to love our Lord with all our heart and to love our neighbors as ourselves. Christos has taken upon himself the entire weight of our laws and duties, I explain.

But with this new teaching, many are made angry, including some of our rabbis who minister to the Grecians. These priests reproach me with the very reason our freedmen have come here. Like Timon of Athens, the men have counted it a joy to be circumcised, and like Iphigenia, even some women strain to loosen their tongues in Hebrew, though seldom with success.

Still, my words often prevail in local synagogues where many freedmen come to worship, as well as in other places. Perhaps it is because knowing both the scripture and the Grecian ways, I can cross the barriers between our peoples.

Many days, following my organization of ministry and my prayer, Timon claims that I work miracles. I charge him not to tell anyone of such things that people say. Yet I cannot deny the working of my own body. A great tiredness fills my soul, a heaviness on the days when he comes to me reporting one man hearing who was deaf, another speaking who was silent, a woman relieved of pain that crippled her legs. If this is a thing of God, I am the smallest and most distant vessel of his mercy. I am a man who would better be left to his studies and his writing. But it is not the way of our Lord to lead us in paths we know, and so I minister on, prayer–tongued, honor–bound, grateful for any moment of peace or of truth given to others through my existence.

But there is not enough love and peace within our own household. I note a coldness between Cassandra and her foster brother. True, Lukas sometimes instructs her in healing things, and I have even heard her ask him a question regarding the way to wrap a wound in such a way that a patient feels less pain. But at table and on the road, silence reigns between them.

Thus I return to Cassandra's request for baptism only after much thought and prayer. "There is a thing you must do before your baptism."

When she asks me, I explain. "Our Lord does not mean for any battle to go on in our hearts, or between our heart and that of another. We must cast aside all hatred and embrace the love of all mankind. Is there in your mind a thing that you can do to relieve your anger and make peace?"

Cassandra does not hesitate, though she sighs. "You know the thing," she responds.

"Then you can tell me without fear," I answer.

"I will embrace my brother Lukas and invite him to witness the baptism," she replies.

The three of us depart the next morning to arrive in a place Lukas himself suggested. Running through the valley of Kidron, east of Jerusalem, is a brook, amidst which there is a beautiful pool, deep and still.

"It is quite near the place where I saw Jesus of Nazareth," Lukas says.

"Have you dressed with care, brother?" Cassandra looks at him, and they laugh.

"Do not call me a Roman," Lukas replies, and they smile together.

Though I have no idea of the cause of their shared amusement, I thank our Lord in my heart that the wall between them has fallen away.

The spring-fed water is chilly as I wade in. When Cassandra

hesitates, I look back. "I am afraid of this water, Uncle," she says.

"I am with you, and I will not let you go," I reply, remembering Timon's rescuing her from the near drowning in the Jordan on the day of my own baptism with Irini. With this, I clasp Cassandra's hand to assure that she does not slip on the stones.

Near the pool in the middle, I stop to ask her the usual question before baptism. "Is there any sin for you to confess before we enter the deeper water?"

Cassandra's eyes fill with tears. "Yes," she whispers. "Yes."

I return her regard without comment, waiting.

"At Timon's wedding, you told me to take Iphigenia like a mother. But I have dishonored her. I have not told her the truth about a certain matter."

"How so?"

Our voices are low enough that Lukas, standing on the bank above, cannot overhear. Then Cassandra tells me that for many months now, she has had her womanly courses, that she has kept this hidden in order to continue her studies with Saul.

I clasp her hands in mine. "We must speak to your stepmother about this, Cassandra. I do not know the reply, but she must know two truths, not just the truth of your womanhood, but the truth of your seeking our Lord through your love of scripture."

Cassandra sighs. "Now I am ready for this baptism, even if it means that I can no longer come with Ezra to Jerusalem."

So, it is not only Ezra who longs for these walks, I see. This was not a matter I would ask her, yet as I contemplate her future life, my heart is much lightened to know it.

I guide Cassandra deeper, not hurrying, keeping hold of both her hands as we descend toward the pool. In my heart, I speak a prayer of gladness, blessing this daughter of Athens.

Both of us look up toward Lukas, and her eyes light with joy as she lifts her arm to wave to a distant, hurrying figure high behind him. "Lukas says he sent a message to Ezra yesterday, and now here he is, too!" she exclaims.

But as she waved, I have seen another thing. The weight of Cassandra's watery garment allowed her entire sleeve to fall back, exposing her arm almost to the shoulder. Like bones of a fish, scars both small and large rib all her flesh.

"Cassandra, what is this?" I ask.

When she sees where my eyes are focused, she snatches her sleeve to draw the cloth down.

"It is nothing!"

"No, Cassandra. You must tell me. Who has done this to you?"

My heart beats with fear for her and with the remembered sorrow of Irini's similar scars exposed to me in the moonlight on the night when she begged freedom from the house of Saul's family. But in Cassandra's case, I know this certainly did not happen during her years living with me, nor can I imagine it in the house of Timon.

Again Cassandra shakes her head. "I tell you, it is nothing," she repeats.

Meanwhile, Lukas has taken off his sandals, descending the bank and wading into the water.

As he approaches, Cassandra raises her other arm and hides her face.

Eyes fixed on Cassandra, Lukas advances, then rolls back the sleeve of her striped arm. Though he draws sharp breath, his hands reach to cradle Cassandra's face, coaxing it upward.

"This is no disease or disorder of the flesh," he says in a soft voice. "From what I know, I fear this is a deliberate and methodical cutting with a sharp blade. Only you can explain this to us, sister."

Cassandra wrenches out of Lukas' gentle clasp and throws herself deep to the middle of the pool. Her arms and legs flail, but the weight of her garments, her fear, and her distress draw her downward.

Lukas seems too shocked to move, but my own voice

speaks nearly without my knowing. "She is even more afraid of the truth than of the water." Stepping in front of Lukas, I hasten in and draw her toward me.

Cassandra clasps her arms and legs about me, shuddering and weeping. "The pain is too great!" she whispers. "Oh, I cannot bear it!"

"What pain?" I whisper back.

"I remember everything, uncle. When Aunt Irini made her ink, she would pierce her arm to draw blood. I was afraid at first, but she explained to me that this was the binding power of the ink, and a piece of her soul to give to anything she wrote. When I make the ink for you, my heart wants to break inside me, remembering her. But when I pierce my skin and draw the blood out in order to add to the writing, the pain becomes less, I feel her spirit beside me, and I can go on until the agony returns."

These words have come scarcely louder than the breeze rippling the water's surface. Though my soul shudders, the spirit within me blows the breath of God in my lips.

I pull back her sleeve once again, and I draw the shape of a cross upon the hatching of her scars, touching each one. "I baptize thee, Cassandra, and I call upon our Lord himself, who has suffered, shed His own precious blood, and even died for thy pain and mine, to assume this sorrow in His own spirit, to leave thee free of all this burden. Do you believe our Lord capable of taking away the terrible sorrow devouring your soul?"

"I believe," she replies. "Oh, Christos, help my faith!"

I lower Cassandra into the depths of the water, hold her there a moment as I avoid the gaze of Lukas, focusing all my prayer on her spirit, and then I lift her up.

"Remember always that you are a daughter of our Lord, free of the sorrow our world brings, through the power of His spirit living within you," I whisper.

Cassandra's hands relax. Then a smile transforms her face. She touches my cheek. "You look like an angel, Uncle!" she whispers back. "May our Lord allow me never to forget your words, as I will never forget your face."

Second Request of Ezra

Even a full stone's throw away as I stumble down the path, my eyes widen beyond their own will. If I had breath to spare, I would call praise to our Lord and beg pardon for my lateness to this baptism. Never have I seen such joy in Cassandra's smile. And as for Stephanos, I can only remind myself that he is no angel, but a man. Their faces are as translucent as the precious stones surrounding our high altar! Has all the sunlight in Jerusalem exhaled onto their figures? Meanwhile, Lukas stands like an opaque statue before them. Oh, if only I could will my stumbling feet to take root, and make the terrible words I must say swallow themselves as Cassandra and Stephanos stroll so lightly to the bank, arm in arm.

An inner voice shakes me: "You will never see such happiness again."

Indeed, the message I must speak now will shatter their joy as a rock crudely thrown destroys fine glass in the twinkling of an eye. But I make myself shout with the Temple voice I have practiced to read our scripture aloud. "Stephanos, come quickly!"

A treacherous step turns my foot, nearly breaking my sandal, and I hurtle downward. Lukas braces me as I tumble into the water.

All three of them begin to laugh until I lift my head, and they see my face.

I can only meet Stephanos' eyes and gasp out the rest. "Timon is arrested! Some Athenians accuse him of escaping as a slave. Saul says you are the only man who can save him!"

15. The Words and the Walls
Witness of Many, Jerusalem, A.D. 35

Healing Words of Lukas

Ezra's message of my stepfather's arrest rains brimstone on the joy we have just shared. Indeed, it seems to darken the midday sun blazing down upon us in the valley.

The girding of my doctor's bag slows me. Then, as I stride upward behind the others, my ears catch a sound not a stone's throw from the path. It is a woman's call, but no louder than the mewling of an Egypt cat.

My mother's words, "You are always a doctor, and not only when you want to be," echo in my mind as I call upward. "Stephanos, I must stop here. Leave word for me at Demetrius' taverna."

Stephanos turns, and pointing from above to the human form I cannot yet discern, he nods.

Though a girl lying in her own blood is nothing new to my eyes, nonetheless, my heart turns at the sight of her weakness and shame. Before kneeling to examine her more closely, I lift her hand stretched limp along the dirt like a useless wing. "I am a doctor," I say in my gentlest voice. "Let me help you."

The girl's face is half covered with matted hair. Even so, the freshness of her flesh shows her as hardly older than Cassandra. To my surprise, she murmurs her reply in a Greek graced with the softness of my native Antioch. "He told me he wanted me to teach him proper Greek. He told me we would leave Jerusalem together, and I could live as a free woman. He told me—"

Drawing the hair away from her face, I gaze into her eyes. They are dark and dilated, but they seem not to see my form. "He told me he loved me." Her breath stinks of wine.

"Shhh, let me take you to where you can bathe," I answer. As I lean closer, my nose detects another odor beneath the wine, the bitter-sweet breath of mandrake. This is a drug I have used myself to bring on sleep before surgery, but it can also cause death. Anger throbs in my throat. This girl was not only violated, but poisoned and left to die!

"Please trust me," I whisper, and the girl's head nods as though in a dream. "I must rid you of the poison you have swallowed."

With no patience to fumble through my bag for my usual purgative, I pluck a branch from the nearest bush. Lifting her so that we are seated side by side, I open her mouth and insert the leafy tips to touch the back of her throat. She does not shrink from me in fear, but her gaze is distant and unfocused. As I hoped, she retches nearly immediately.

"Good, very good," I reassure her.

Attempting to rise, the girl begins to retch again. I steady her shoulders with one hand and with the other, I hold aside her hair, though in her current filth, what difference could it make?

"Now you will feel some relief. Let us go down to the brook for you to wash and drink," I say. "You have no more evil in your bile battling for your life. Your blood will turn to its proper course."

The girl is trembling with such violence that I lift her. Forsaking my staff and bag, I carry her down to the stream. Even before her immersion, my tunic is red with her blood. Some virgins have this unfortunate symptom even on the wedding night, but the bleeding is nothing that the cold of water cannot stop in most cases.

After laying her on the bank and cupping several handfuls of water for her to drink, I draw her into the current. "Here, now, it is cold, but it is clean. Wash yourself and hold to me as much as you need to."

The gleam of awareness returns to the girl's eyes once the water surrounds her. Her hands move up and down her legs and inside to do as I have told her. Her breathing becomes less labored, and her face calms.

For the first time, her eyes focus on me as I steady her. "Oh, sir, there are no hot stones we can wrap that will ever take away this pain of mine!" she moans.

Thinking that the poison and the wine still own her mind, I say nothing, but she repeats herself. "No hot stones. No pumice rocks like you used to treat my mistress, the rabbi's widow."

My memory returns to the Passover of Stephanos' near death, and in my mind's eye, I see the old woman scolding a cowering little slave girl for her incomprehension of the Hebrew tongue.

"You spoke gentle words to me in Greek instead of Hebrew. You praised my preparing of the stones then, sir, but today you are kinder to me than I deserve!" The girl breaks into sobs. Then she flails toward the deep pool amidst the stream.

I lack the height and grace of Stephanos as he reached for Cassandra, but I have health and speed on my side. I pull her back by the end of her torn robe. "What are you doing, throwing yourself to death after I have just pulled you back from its reach?" I shout.

The girl does not resist as I draw her from the depths.

"Are you still bleeding?" I ask.

Whether from modesty or from the drugs still in her body, she ignores my question and says, "My name is Penelope. But Penelope is beloved of the Greeks because she was faithful wife to Odysseus. I am just a stupid and worthless girl now, and I will never be free again or worthy of her name!"

Her breath comes so short that I almost fear for her again.

"Shhh," I reply. "Save your strength for this trail upwards." We pull ourselves from the water together, both of us wringing our clothes. Most of the blood has fled our garments.

Fortunately, in her haste to leave, Cassandra left an item of use on the bank. It is just an old strip of faded yellow cloth, but it will serve well enough for Penelope to dry herself and then to bind her hair.

"My father was in debt when he died," she answers. "We were hungry, and I was the only thing left for my family to sell." Her unspoken shadow words are clear even to a fool. "I have no way to repay you."

"You will rest in the widow's house, and my mother will visit you with ointments tomorrow, and there will be no need for either you or the house there to pay us," I say, seeking to reassure her.

"Please do not make me return to them, doctor," Penelope answers. "It was her son who—"

I picture the entire scene: Penelope's foolish hope, her loneliness, her faith in men somehow kept despite her enslavement. Perhaps I, born a slave, was more fortunate to keep to my own counsel and trust no one without good cause. But I say nothing as we advance up the path, and she clings tightly to my arm for support.

Beside my abandoned staff and doctor's bag, I spot another object. It is a purse, and this purse is full of silver coins. This man who left Penelope after violating her was not only a murderer and a coward, but also a fool. Returning to her, I show her the bag. "Do you know this purse?"

She shrinks away and nods.

"You will never need to visit that house again, but I will, and this man will be too afraid of what I could tell his colleagues to force your return. He will realize that my bringing of this purse is proof against his reputation, and I will demand your papers of manumission at once."

"Oh, sir!" Penelope's words hang on the wind as her shadow struggles behind her.

By the time we reach less steep and more inhabited places, the sun has moved two or three hand's breadths downward. My patient Penelope is so exhausted after our lonely ascent that I procure a cart for us to cross the valley full of markets and the poor.

The great Temple on Jerusalem's east side gleams toward the homes of the wealthy on its far west. On our way, I form a plan and tell her. "You will rest in the home of a Hellenist woman I know until my mother can come to treat you properly. Then we will find a place for you to live."

My mother's recent delivery of healthy twins to this merchant's wife guarantees safekeeping and perhaps even work for Penelope with the new babies.

After I make my introductions and request at the prosperous home, I tell her to lie down and rest immediately, but she follows me back to the gate. "For the rest of my life, sir, every day I will remember you to our Lord."

Behind my patient's gratitude, I hear more shadow words that make me smile. "What happened today will remain between you and me alone, Penelope. To the world, from this day onward, you are simply a deserving woman set free."

Penelope raises her eyes to meet mine, and now they are eyes under her own control, beautiful and gentle. But she seems unable to speak.

"Your prayers will reach our Lord more than those of many who consider themselves far better than you," I add.

Then she looks down. "You seem like one of the Jews who calls Jesus of Nazareth Messiah. I know they are very kind to the poorest and the neediest people."

For reasons I cannot explain to myself, I speak my heart to this patient. "It was right for me to find you and care for you. I, too, was once a slave, and I know the sweetness freedom will bring you."

She smiles. "Are you one of the Jews who follow the Christ?"

I shake my head with a slight laugh. "No, I am not such a Jew, but many of them I know would be happy if I were."

As I turn to go, Penelope clings to my arm. I rejoice at the strength I can feel in her grasp now, but her smile vanishes. "Oh, sir, if you know them, then you must warn them of things in the Temple."

"What do you mean?"

"In the house where I will never live again, sir, there was talk of apprehending one of them. His name is Stephanos of Tarsus. He is a former student and scribe. This is one reason the men of the Temple desire his blood so bitterly."

I stop short. "Are you certain of this?"

She nods.

"May the Lord bless you for telling me this news!" I reply before turning on my heel.

Greek Words of Saul

To make public the arrest of Stephanos would bring on the same outrage that arose after the treatment of Peter and John. The people still condemn us for accusing these men of magic. This is why the leaders have turned a blind eye to these spirit worshipers, at least until the people tire of them. But I am bound to address this contagious madness as I must. Thus to the leaders in our Temple, I persist in speaking of the chaos Stephanos of Tarsus instills in the hearts of those returning to our land and seeking the traditions of our ancestors.

Stephanos' deliverance into my hands comes in a manner worthy of a Hellenist.

Our governmental rulers hold contests of racing every fifth year, and also competitions of music and of drama. The winners will boast prizes worth the work of a lifetime.

Reading Greek signs announcing these events, I note a certain acting company has hazarded its way here all the way from Athens.

It is a small thing for me to find these men. I pay a certain sum and arrange a private meeting.

On this appointed day, as we stand on Solomon's Porch, my lips water the ears of these pagan Athenians with words about the construction of our great Temple, but my mind tenses like an artisan holding the final block to set in a mighty wall. Behind their smiles, the actors are merely pretending to listen to me. Of course, they know nothing of our Jewish ways, nor do they care. No matter. It is right for such godless Greeks to remain ignorant of how our Lord will use them to complete his design today.

Meanwhile, Timon is chatting with some guards—near, but out of sight. He knows only that his presence is required for a matter at the Temple. Yet he came straight away at my request, as I knew he would.

My design was further confirmed as yesterday Ezra spoke of Cassandra's request for baptism, where he will surely find Stephanos and deliver my summons.

It is easy to spot the tall figure of the madman hurrying up the valley road toward our portico. But I am dismayed to see Cassandra struggling up behind. I curse my foolishness in not admonishing Ezra to keep his news for Stephanos' ears alone.

Cassandra runs ahead to greet me. "Uncle Thaul! What has happened to Uncle Timon that he is arrested?" she calls out in breathless Hebrew.

I lay a hand on her shoulder, trying to reassure her. "It is only a Temple matter, one involving his witness and not his harm."

But I cannot meet her eyes.

Relief warms me as my little weed smiles.

"Thanks to our Lord. For you should know, Uncle Thaul, I

am baptized into the kingdom of our Lord this day. Let it be a day of dancing and joy!"

It is not enough that Stephanos beguiles illiterate freedmen with baptism and this treachery of a Messiah; he has also managed to instill this poison in the minds of Ezra and Cassandra. But in light of the matters at hand, I master my spirit to divert not only Cassandra, but also my own rage at this child's baptism.

I gesture to the company of the three men behind me. "Cassandra, these are men from Athens," I say, lapsing into Greek.

"Good day, sirs," she responds with the politeness she always shows at will. "I come from your city."

"More than this, they are actors," I continue.

The girl's eyes widen, then fasten on the three men. "Is this true?"

They nod, amused, no doubt, by what they think is her provincial wonder. I could not stop her from voicing the next question if I tried. "Did you know my uncle or my father?"

One of the men laughs, but the others look at her seriously. "Why should we know your uncle or your father?" the oldest asks. "But I will say, your father could indeed come from Athens, judging from your lovely speech."

"My father was an actor in Athens, too. His name was Alexander of Crete, and he was the greatest actor of any of you—" Cassandra's face falls. "At least, so it is told to me by Uncle Timon."

"Alexander of Crete was indeed a great thespian," the oldest man exclaims. "I directed the actors there at the time when he died. There was a child he kept, it is true. And a young man and a woman dressed as a man took the child away on the day of his death. So you are this daughter of his?"

Cassandra tugs at a cord around her neck to produce a gold ring I have seen before. "This was my father's ring. You allowed me to take it when my Uncle Stephanos and Aunt Irini left Athens, sir. I am the daughter of Alexander."

The man sighs, gazing at the ring and reaching a hand to touch it. Then he clasps her hand. "You are always welcome with us in Athens," he replies, his voice hoarse with emotion beyond that of a thespian.

Cassandra keeps hold of the senior actor's hand, gazing into his face. "My father sang poems to me that I still know. Do you remember that, too? Please, sir, can you tell me more about him?"

The purity of Cassandra's Greek words and gentle voice wring my heart, given what I have left to do.

Meanwhile, the other two actors devour her girl's face not with the tender regard of this eldest man, but as greedy men appraising a woman. My own eyes widen as I recognize now how the little weed I remember has sprouted into a brilliant flower. Soon she will be lost to me. Not even my affection can override our tradition or permit her to remain in our scripture studies as a woman.

The man meets Cassandra's gaze, and then he nods. "Yes, I remember it," he replies softly. "And I know your name. It is Cassandra, isn't it?"

Cassandra nods.

"Let me tell you why this is so. Alexander chose that sorrowful name in order for you to bear all the sadness of life with strength. He said you would call it nothing as compared to the name of a prophetess whom men despised. No man would say this about his daughter without great love and desire to protect her. And this name of yours, Cassandra, is also nearly like his own, Alexander. He also wished this."

Meanwhile, Stephanos has ascended close enough to hear us.

"This is the Stephanos of whom the girl speaks," I say, turning to indicate my dead-souled former friend.

"What is this matter with Timon?" Stephanos asks, ignoring the Greeks. Thanks be that he has used Hebrew, perhaps in deference to Ezra, who is close to his side.

I do not meet his eyes, nor do I reply or proffer my hand in greeting as Cassandra reluctantly steps back.

Instead, I whisper to Ezra, who goes to the inner gate to summon the man most important in what will come next. Timon emerges behind the actors. As his ears detect the pure Athenian speech, he smiles.

"Perhaps you will recognize another fellow Athenian here," I say to the actors, gesturing to Timon to step forward.

All three men look into his face, then at one another for reassurance.

"The Eagle," the senior actor whispers.

He turns his back, as though ready to run. The second freezes like a statue. The third man's knees shake with a violence worthy of replication on any stage. Each man turns as white as the marble wall behind him.

"By the trident of Poseidon, I have never seen a spirit until now!" the youngest man exclaims. Turning to me he whispers, "Is this the power of your god and your Temple, to bring a dead man to life before our very eyes?"

All three of them recoil from Timon, who has advanced within a few paces.

Turning around to face us again, the senior actor, who is by far the boldest of these three, looks at the floor to avoid Timon's gaze. "If you are not the theater guard all of us know as The Eagle, then I am no thespian and no Athenian," he manages.

"My name is Timon, and I am from Athens," Timon replies.

Stephanos walks close to stand beside his friend.

The Temple guards have surrounded us, though loosely, as I requested of the captain. But they are close enough to witness all that will transpire.

"Sirs," I say, facing the actors and using the confident breath

Lukas has shown me, "we have indeed a great mystery today. I believe there are two possible explanations," I continue. "First, it is quite possible that our Lord who can do all things raised a man from the dead. Second, it is possible that Timon of Athens, your Eagle, has never died, but rather that he is a runaway slave in need of claiming back," I lower my voice, "for a great profit to the claimers, as you can guess."

Timon and Stephanos lock gazes, but they are trapped.

"Shall we ask Timon the guard of Athens and Stephanos the scribe of Tarsus about the truth of this matter?" I conclude.

The actors nod, eyes still wide not only with terror, but also with curiosity.

I continue with the self-assurance of a judge. "And will you tell us all the truth you know, Timon of Athens and Stephanos of Tarsus? You are after all standing on the porch of the Jewish Temple of the one true God."

"We need no temple for truth, for our Lord is your Lord," Stephanos replies, "but we will tell you what is true."

Timon nods his assent.

One of the other actors has regained a small measure of confidence, seeing me conversing with Stephanos and Timon. "You give your name as Timon. But were you not also called The Eagle by everyone who knew you in Athens? Are you not this same man?" he ventures.

Timon nods. "I am the man you say," he states in the voice of a defeated man. "I am the guard you remember."

"But you...are...dead," the same actor manages. "All of us knew of the thing. The order in our theater has not been the same ever since your death. Do these Jewish spirits bring you to us as some kind of proof of the power of their one god who they say holds sway over all the universe?"

Oh, our Lord could not have put better words in the mouth of this pagan for the Temple guards to hear! But before the reluctant Timon can answer, I turn to him and divert the course of questioning to the real matter at hand. "I have heard many things about what you and Stephanos do in Jerusalem and in Bethany. Would you care to say more?"

Timon throws me a grateful glance for what he considers my diversion from his past, but he hesitates. Only when Stephanos nods does he answer. "After leaving my work as Temple guard, Saul, I joined the students of the Christ, along with many Jews and rabbis who came to realize the truth of his being the Messiah. After some months, Peter and John, whom you saw healing people on this very porch, asked Stephanos to lead in ministering to our poor Jews who are Hellenisti. Now I stand by his side and assist in everything he does."

I interrupt him, hoping to keep the interest of the actors. "I have heard that Stephanos gives out not only food and coins, but other things."

In his pride or his relief at this turn of conversation, Timon fails to see the alarm in Stephanos' eyes. "Yes, it is true," he replies, smiling. "He has made many miracles come to pass."

"And among these miracles, tell us, Timon, has he also raised people from the dead?" My eyes dwell on his face.

Timon looks to Stephanos, who has clasped his hands as though in prayer. "It is possible that this is true," he answers cautiously. "I do not know all the works that our Lord Jesus Christ has done through him."

As I turn to Stephanos, my tongue is so heavy that I can neither speak to him nor meet his gaze.

"If such wonders have taken place," Stephanos says, as though reading my thoughts, "it is indeed as Timon says, only by the power and the name of our Lord Jesus the Christos, and not by power or might of my own works."

"So you do not deny it?" I manage. My voice is so tight with fury and distress that it hardly emerges, yet all can hear it.

Timon surprises me by interrupting. He is not a tall man, and by no means young. Yet he stands straight, and if he were not just a Greek, his next words would almost match the bravery of our prophets of old.

"Men of the stage, I remember with pride and pleasure hearing your words, observing your masks, assuring that all went well at the plays. That I am even thought of now is a thing I hardly believe."

He pauses. "But even as I was a faithful guard, I am as you see, also a criminal and a renegade. It is surely the fate of such a wrongdoer to be found out. In Jerusalem, I first found work in this Temple, and later a ministry among the Hellenisti who live here. I have also," and his voice trembles here, "I have also been blessed to love the greatest woman in this city, and to be loved by her and to make her my wife."

Every eye rests on Timon's face. It is as though a play of our own is being acted here at the Temple as Timon composes himself.

"I will see no harm come to Stephanos of Tarsus for any role in assisting my exit from Athens." He proffers his hands toward both the actors and the guards standing behind them. "Therefore, take me home with you. I can bear whatever punishment the civil authorities will give me for my escape, and you will divide among yourselves the coins proffered when an escaped slave is returned."

As the captain of the guard moves to bind Timon's hands, Cassandra begins to weep. Ezra stands unsure, comprehending nothing, but he draws closer to the girl, his gaze one of comfort that she ignores.

I raise my hand as Timon looks directly at me, and he turns from Greek to Hebrew.

"You want Stephanos get bad things from this, Saul. This thing, no good, and I did think you more better man. Why you blame good man for bad thing what I do, not him do it? I go back to Athens, but you no can say any bad thing what Stephanos do. He just only help people and say them truth about Christos!"

The irony that this illiterate runaway has been the first to see to the bottom of my motives and speak them aloud enrages me.

Meanwhile, the actors have all looked at one another and come to one accord. The senior actor speaks again. "If you are a spirit, no chains will hold you, and reward money will never compensate us in Athens. And taking you, we may be cursed by the gods. If you are simply a runaway slave who somehow arrived here, it is no matter of ours to arrest you. But your speaking as though this were true and as no slave of flesh and blood would speak is further evidence that it is scarcely likely. We will go our way, now, and have nothing more to do with this matter."

With this, all three men turn their backs on us.

For the first day in my life, I thank those bitter years of Grecian schooling in Tarsus, where I was forced in with the Greek boys of the academy. Those years have allowed me to anticipate these men's fear and superstition, which I have foreseen with complete accuracy.

"Please, sirs! You are the only ones who know things of my father!" Cassandra calls after the men hastening away.

But not one of them turns his head back toward the scene that has terrified them. Nor will their feet ever bring them back to me for the second half of the money I promised them.

Cassandra lowers her head in defeat as Ezra begins to question her urgently about what has just transpired. I turn my eyes back to Stephanos and Timon, nearly unable to bear this sorrow I have forced upon her.

When I gesture to the captain of the guard, he steps back to join the other soldiers. "See, no one will arrest you or cast you back into slavery now," I say to Timon, smiling.

The guards behind him nod.

"It was merely a matter of procedure to have you brought here to answer this charge. From today forward, you are a free man indeed. Take Cassandra with you, and return to Bethany, and rejoice to pursue your life there."

"But, sir," Timon begins. He no longer uses my name, as he would have before.

Now that both my acts and his words have made me distant from him, I speak to him as though indeed he were a slave. "I told you to go. You have a free life to live, so go home and begin it now!"

Stephanos nods consent.

"But I cannot...." Timon protests.

The guards have turned their backs on Timon and begin walking toward Stephanos.

Timon turns to me once again, but a look from Stephanos keeps him silent.

"Go in peace. You have my blessing and that of the Holy Spirit," Stephanos says. His words come out like those not of a master, but of a friend.

But the starkness of fear on Stephanos' face leads me to even more bitter words, which burst from my lips. "What, Stephanos, no song of praise today, like the one you sang with John and Peter when they were arrested here? Has the Messiah forsaken you?"

Too late, I follow his gaze, which is fixed on Cassandra. "Timon, for the love of our Lord, take Cassandra away quickly and protect her," Stephanos commands. "Seeing this is a thing too heavy for her heart to bear."

The look of disbelief that Cassandra fixes on me will scorch my inner eye until the day of my death. But looking one more time into the eyes of Stephanos, neither protesting nor stopping, she clasps the arm of Timon, and together they walk away, toward the outside Temple walls.

My soul shrinks within me as Stephanos' eyes fix on me and their footsteps die out. Looking at the captain of the guard, who is a Roman, a poem enters my mind unbidden, something memorized from my school days in Tarsus in the start of Latin. And though the words were written a century ago by the Roman degenerate Gaius Valerius Catullus, the lines strike my inner ears like an Egyptian's rod against our people:

I hate, and I love,
And if you ask me how,
I do not know.
I only feel it, and I am torn in two.

Drawing a deep breath in order to brace my spirit for what I must do next, I turn to the senior guard standing behind Stephanos, who knows enough Greek to understand our former talk.

"All of you have heard today what is said about this man Stephanos, that he uses unholy names to create magic among the people. And he is from our very midst. This matter surely deserves further questioning, do you not agree?"

"Yes, sir," the guard answers, as several of the others nod.

Disregarding the approaching soldiers, Stephanos speaks directly to my ears. "Saul, why did you use trickery to bring me here? This is our Father's house. You know well, I would have come without any of this."

"Your own words show your madness," I reply.

But though the guards have surrounded Stephanos on every side, not a man lays hands on him. He paces toward our Hall of Stone, surrounded.

Interpreted Words for Ezra

As soon as Cassandra tells me how these departing Athenians knew her father, I hasten away from Solomon's Porch to follow them. The peculiar weave of their chitons and the brightness of the square cloaks over these outlandish garments should make them easy to spot, but as usual, crowds are everywhere, and the streets are narrow. A glimpse of the red cloth worn by the oldest man sparks my attention as I descend just in time to see them turn a corner.

There is a gate of sin lurking at the very base of our Temple. It is a bath frequented by Gentiles, a place that breeds iniquity and filth beneath the supposed cleansing of the waters. And this is where the men have disappeared. It is such an evil place that our Torah scholars would never claim to visit, even in jest.

Yet in my zeal to mend Cassandra's grief and beg their return, what choice do I have but to follow them?

The very breath of this place, full of sweat and steam and something I cannot define, the scents of men, curls around me like poison. One of the men is passing coins to a woman attending.

"Sirs!" I call out, relieved that I need go no further than the threshold.

As the woman's eyes take me in, she laughs. But the actors turn and gaze on me with earnestness.

"Please, tell me where you are staying, sirs, so that the girl can find you and you can speak to her more about her father!"

I am a fool! The men's faces are as blank as the limestone wall behind them. One of the younger men says something to the other, and they nod and laugh.

"He does not understand you, boy, but he welcomes you to join them," the woman says. Her own Hebrew is none too good. "They will gladly pay for your comfort in the bath with them."

I shake my head. "I need you to tell them what I said, please."

The woman smiles. "They will pay plenty of attention to you if you go in with them. You will have no need of language."

Then the oldest actor speaks to the woman. He has such a strong and beautiful voice that it is like Gamaliel when he teaches scripture of greatest importance. I try to hear him, but it is as though I am a deaf man in this babble of theirs. Yet I do recognize one word, "Pavlos," which I have learned is the name that Saul of Tarsus uses in dealing with the Grecians.

"This man says the man called Pavlos owes them some money," the woman continues. "Is this why you have come, to give it to them?"

I shake my head, but then I remember the small piece of gold which was the last thing my father gave me in parting from Jericho. I have kept it these seven years. "I can give them my own coin," I reply, extending my hand. "I need to speak with them, but not here."

The youngest actor steps forward. He draws to himself not my coin, but my hand, and he begins to stroke it as I have imagined Cassandra brushing her hair a hundred times. His eyes cling to mine as his lips intone his foreign words, soft words.

"He says you will have twice this sum if you join them," the woman interprets.

Like a bird in the gaze of a serpent, I can neither breathe nor remove my fingers from his clasp.

Hebrew Words of Stephanos

I, Stephanos, former scholar and scribe in this temple, enter our familiar Hall of Stone, the council chamber. Only today, the place seems new to me, for I walk surrounded by the guards. Facing me as though lying in wait sits the entire Sanhedrin, the high council. Most of them are men I know. But no man's face smiles to see me, and no man's hand rises to greet me.

Saul takes a seat near Gamaliel.

Three men file in after me, two Hellenisti who have heard me at the synagogue of the freedmen, and a fellow student of Gamaliel. As soon as the first Hellenist begins stammering in Hebrew, Saul rises, and the man is grateful to revert to his native Greek.

As the men look on and fall silent around us, I am pierced through by a memory from our youth, Saul's and mine. How is it possible, my Lord, that this man who once stood in the circle of runners and celebrants at the academy to protect me with his logika when I was called not a whole man, unworthy to receive the racing victory, this same man now hastens to voice for those accusing me? Saul is an able interpreter, voicing even the subtleties correctly into Hebrew, but the words themselves are those of a false witness.

"I have heard him say that this Jesus of Nazareth shall destroy this place and shall change the customs which Moses delivered us," the man says. "But it is for learning these customs that I gave up my entire life in Corinth and sacrificed everything I knew there. I count that not a loss, but a gain. I sold the little I had, I said farewell to all my family, and I came to Israel to learn the ways of our people. You know our people well, but for me, until now, calling myself a Jew was only raising the shadow of my ancestors to me. If this Stephanos speaks the truth, which he does not, of course, he makes mockery of everything I have come here to learn from you, the elders who know best. If he speaks the truth, our entire world is lost."

As I bite my tongue to remain silent, many listeners nod.

The second Hellenist claims my designs against the teachings of Moses. "More than this, Stephanos speaks blasphemy against our own Temple," he adds.

Yet when this man is asked of what I say of Moses, he properly replies with actual scripture that I have translated for the understanding of the Hellenisti, along with my explanation of the Hebrew people and their history, of which he knew nothing before this.

Finally, my fellow student of Gamaliel waves a piece of parchment. "These are Stephanos' own words, and they are no words of Moses!" he begins. "See here what he thinks of our Temple!"

Then he reads these fearful words of our Lord copied from my own scroll, of what our Messiah spoke according to what many witnesses told me:

> *A certain man planted a vineyard, and let caretakers rent it, and went into a faraway country for a long time. And at the right season, he sent a servant to the caretakers for them to give over a portion of the fruit of the vineyard. But the caretakers beat him, and sent him away empty handed. And he sent another servant, and they beat him also, and treated him shamefully, and also sent him away empty handed. And again he sent a third, and they wounded him also, and they cast him out. Then said the lord of the vineyard, what shall I do? I will send my beloved son; it may be they will respect him when they see him.*
>
> *But when the caretakers saw him, they reasoned among themselves, saying, "This is the heir. Come, let us kill him and make the inheritance our own!" So they cast him out of the vineyard, and they killed him.*
>
> *So what shall the lord of the vineyard do to them? He shall come and destroy these caretakers, and he shall give the vineyard to others. Remember, as it is written, "The stone which the builders rejected, the same is become the cornerstone. Whoever falls on that stone shall be broken, but whoever it falls on, it will grind into powder."*

When Saul draws a sharp breath, I know that these words are new to him. But why should I be surprised, given that I am a man dead to him, by his own words. Surely he would not care to read anything I sent, not even with Gamaliel's admonition.

Members of the Sanhedrin whisper to one another after this reading. Then Caiaphas, the high priest, interrupts their disturbance and asks me directly, "Are these things so?"

Many of my former fellow scribes appear to be curious or perplexed, but expectant. Only Rabboni Gamaliel meets my gaze, but in so doing, he gives me strength, and the Lord leads me to my next words.

"Men, brethren, and fathers, listen now," I greet them. The hollowness of my own voice echoing from the stone walls around us surprises me. I must speak slowly and well to prevent a single word from being lost.

But as I draw my next breath, all fear flies from my soul. It is as though I am a boy again, sitting on the stones and listening to Gamaliel himself as he told scripture to Saul, to me, and to Irini in this very Temple when we first entered Jerusalem. What a small thing now for me to repeat his words, but what a great thing to demand the power for my brothers to hear them with their hearts.

"The God of glory appeared to our father Abraham when he still lived in Mesopotamia and said to him, 'Get out of your country and from your relatives, and come to a land that I will show you.' Then he came out of the land of the Chaldeans and dwelt in Haran. And from there, when his father was dead, He moved him to our land. But God gave him no inheritance in it, not even enough to set his foot on."

As though cast into my ears, I hear all the shifting, each sigh from the men seated before me. Now every eye is on my face; their regard burns me. I thank our Lord for the recent sermons I have given in front of many, both the believing and the scornful, for without these, I would surely lose faith in my tongue to convince the men in front of me, men I know and love. Combined pity and hatred line their faces.

I must go on in order not to lose courage, so I proceed with the familiar story.

"But even when Abraham had no child, He promised to give it to him for a possession and to his descendants after him. Then He gave him the covenant of circumcision; and so Abraham begot Isaac and circumcised him on the eighth day; Jacob begot the twelve patriarchs. And the patriarchs, becoming envious, sold Joseph into Egypt. But God was with him and delivered him out of all his troubles, and gave him favor and wisdom in the presence of Pharaoh, king of Egypt; and he made him governor over Egypt and all his house.

"Now a famine and great trouble came over all the land of Egypt and Canaan, and our fathers found no sustenance. But when Jacob heard that there was grain in Egypt, he sent out our fathers first. And the second time Joseph made himself known to his brothers, and Joseph's family became known to the Pharaoh. Then Joseph sent and called his father Jacob and all his relatives to him, seventy–five people."

These words I have felt leaving my heart like the dove set free by our Messiah, Irini's dove and mine. It is not the detail or the depth of my knowledge, but rather, the solidity of the covenant and the promise of our Lord moving me to continue. The former restlessness amidst my listeners has ceased.

"When the time of the promise that God had sworn to Abraham drew near, the people grew and multiplied in Egypt till another king arose who did not know Joseph. This man dealt treacherously with our people and oppressed our forefathers, making them expose their baby sons, so that they might not live. At this time Moses was born, and he was well pleasing to God. But when he was set out, Pharaoh's daughter took him away and brought him up as her own son. And Moses was learned in all the wisdom of the Egyptians."

A cough too familiar to my ears interrupts my monologue. It is the cough of Saul when he is angry or distressed. I pause, not only to allow my friend to catch his breath, but to let my mind rest on what I must say next. How heavy the burden of my upcoming words feels on my lips. But I set my full mind on illustrating this promise of our Lord that I must defend, and how our beloved Moses played his part in it.

"Now, when Moses was forty years old, it came into his heart to visit his brethren, the children of Israel. And seeing one of them suffer wrong, he defended and avenged the one who was oppressed, and he struck down the Egyptian. For he supposed that his brethren would have understood that God would deliver them by his hand, but they did not understand."

The phrase catches in my mouth, and my voice breaks. "They did not understand," I repeat.

For I can nearly see before my eyes this figure of Moses, and in my heart, I am stricken with grief, feeling for the first time the sorrow that was his bitter drink. I continue in order for my fellow scholars to know my knowledge and my belief in Moses, which matches their own. Now only silence stands between these brethren and me while I compose myself.

"And the next day he appeared to two of them as they were fighting, and tried to reconcile them, saying, 'Men, you are brethren; why do you wrong one another?' But the Hebrew who did his neighbor wrong pushed him away, saying, 'Who made you a ruler and a judge over us? Do you want to kill me, as you did the Egyptian yesterday?'"

These last words sting my throat and stick in my mouth. Indeed, I can hardly speak them.

Despite myself, my gaze turns straight upon Saul, this Saul who is my fellow Tarsian, Saul who is my fellow Jew and scholar, and still before our Lord, Saul who is my dearest friend. The full weight of Moses' words resounds in my spirit.

"Do you want to kill me, as you did the Egyptian yesterday?" I repeat.

For now it is no longer pity or anger that I feel from my childhood friend; hatred blazes in his eyes. Anyone looking at the two of us would surely call him the madman, and not me, as I know I have been called here since my seizing of the torn veil at Passover, three years ago.

Oh, hasten, Lord Jesus Christ in your return. The truth of

this story, the speaking of our Lord the Christ to our brothers here, and now my own words to them echo and empty into nothing. The refrain of my words sighs through the council as men turn to one another during my pause for composure. Saul looks everywhere except at me. With the strength given by our Lord, I must go on.

"Then Moses fled and became a dweller in the land of Midian, where he had two sons. And when forty years had passed, an Angel of the Lord appeared to him in a flame of fire in a bush, in the wilderness of Mount Sinai. When Moses saw it, he marveled at the sight; and as he drew near to observe, the voice of the Lord came to him, saying, 'I am the God of your fathers—the God of Abraham, the God of Isaac, and the God of Jacob.' And Moses trembled and dared not look. Then the Lord said to him, 'Take your sandals off your feet, for the place where you stand is holy ground. I have surely seen the oppression of my people who are in Egypt; I have heard their groaning and have come down to deliver them. And now come, I will send you to Egypt.'"

Rabboni Gamaliel nods slightly. This reciting of scripture is child's play, nearly as much so to me as to my beloved teacher.

Yet I feel with certainty that now my memory and my beliefs hold the power of life for my listening brothers; surely our Lord has placed me with my knowledge akin to theirs here to speak to them, to turn their disbelief to understanding. And so I continue, encouraged, and lifting my heart in prayer.

"This Moses whom they rejected, saying, 'Who made you a ruler and a judge?' is the one whom God sent to be a ruler and a deliverer by the hand of the Angel who appeared to him in the bush. It was he who brought them out, after he had shown wonders and signs in the land of Egypt, and in the Red Sea, and in the wilderness for forty years.

"This is that Moses who was in the congregation in the wilderness with the Angel who spoke to him on Mount Sinai, and with our fathers, the one who received the living oracles to give to us, whom our fathers would not obey, but whom they rejected."

I have demonstrated at last that my faith in Moses is uncorrupted. Gamaliel is smiling. He grasps before the rest of them the sway of my words. For as I tell the story of Moses untarnished and straight from our beloved scripture, at the same time, I demonstrate that these current scribes and priests and elders, like the caretakers of the vineyard as told by our Messiah, are far from the first men to turn their hearts and minds to reject the Lord.

It is time to address their second accusation now, that of my slander of the Temple.

"Our fathers had the tabernacle of witness in the wilderness, as He appointed, instructing Moses to make it according to the pattern that he had seen. David, who found favor before God, asked to find a dwelling for the God of Jacob. But it was Solomon who built Him a house."

I look around. Even as just a small side room of this new Temple, the hall in which we sit speaks of wealth and treasure. While its simplicity contrasts with much of the splendor around, still, I think of its purpose, of Peter and John, who stood here before this same council, and of Jesus of Nazareth, who suffered a thousand days before and a thousand times more than any of us could suffer, being a man who was blameless. And my heart wrenches within me.

"However, the Most High does not dwell in temples made with human hands," I continue. Since this phrase "by human hands" recalls the way we describe idol worshipers with their crafting of false gods, I go on quickly.

"As the prophet says: 'Heaven is My throne, and earth is My footstool. What house will you build for Me?' says the Lord. 'Or what is the place of My rest? Has My hand not made all these things?'"

As Saul shifts, preparing to rise, Gamaliel raises a hand

toward my friend to silence him. But others begin to mutter, enraged at my quoting of Isaiah, whose words regarding the Temple they have perhaps forgotten, but which they cannot deny.

For the first time in all our studies, Saul defies the moderation our teacher has instilled in us. He rises. "Perhaps it is the time to test the work of human hands on one who was our brother here!" he cries out in a voice foreign to me.

I cannot move, cannot pray, can no longer understand. Instead, I feel the entire heaviness of what I have spoken of our laws, our promises, and our people, heavy as though the ceiling of the entire room were descending onto my shoulders. But while a man as good as Gamaliel might withstand this, I cannot. No, I cannot. Here, gathered close, in every day of life, in each breath of my beloved fellow scholars, in their troubled faces, I feel the pricks at which we have kicked and kicked since childhood, the full weight of the law from which our Lord has freed us. But I see no respite, no desire on their part to comprehend the new order, as my brothers assembled here cling to things proven to be in error. Oh, my God, it is too much for me!

Whispers bubble the air around me: "Madman!" "False-tongued liar!" And even "Traitor!" And these words emerge from the lips of men with whom I have sweated in study, eaten at table, and compared scripture for all our years together.

So I retort to Saul and the rest of them in anger, with all my breath and spirit, pointing from our many generations before the coming of our Lord Jesus Christ directly to this small crowd of studious men, who should know better.

"You stiff-necked and uncircumcised men in heart and ears!" I cry out. "You always resist the Holy Spirit. Just as your fathers did, so do you. Which of the prophets did your fathers not persecute? And they killed those who foretold the coming of the Just One. You have now become His betrayers and murderers, you, who have received the law by the direction of angels and have not kept it!"

Prayer Words of Gamaliel

I bow my head and close my eyes before you, oh Mighty One. The man whose mind I have loved above all the rest has broken with his reason today by calling his brothers here to violence. But the man whose heart I have loved has now spoken words to bring on even greater anger.

Had Stephanos only continued to speak the scripture known well to all of us, he could have stayed the raging of the ones gathered here against him, and perhaps allowed them to partake of the knowledge he brings of this Jesus of Nazareth. But instead of addressing our minds, he has just cut us to the heart, a thing the council cannot endure from him.

My eyes have closed not only in prayer, but in fear. I cannot take the witness of my eyes for evidence of truth, yet how can I explain his looks to my mind? As this man first listened to the witnesses and now stands before us, the face he shows is not the face of Stephanos of Tarsus as I have known it. He seems transformed by his own words, by the love of whatever remained to him to say to us before Saul's interruption.

Now some gasp of air I hear but do not feel surrounds me, like motionless wind. And behind my eyelids, there shines a brightness as though the walls themselves are rolling back as a scroll, the sunlight entering in upon us. Warmth touches my back like a benediction, and every lock of my head and beard rises. A fragrance pulses the atmosphere and prickles my nose with its freshness.

As I open my eyes, Stephanos is gazing above our heads, toward the light and warmth at our backs. His mouth drops like a man receiving unexpected news, his eyes shine, and then raising his hand to gesture where his eyes are turned, he tries to speak but finds no words.

The weight of this moment is the same as the day when the veil was split.

But not a man among us can turn to the direction of his hand, for we are fastened to his gaze and to his face reflecting joy beyond any earthly gladness. At last he returns to motion as we cannot. And speaking in a voice as filled with wonder as Saul's had been with rage, his words fill the hall.

"Look! I see the heavens opened and the Son of Man standing at the right hand of God!"

Alas, oh my Lord, alas!

Curse Words of Saul

"No man can see God and live!" I scream. My legs lift me like eagle's wings after these final mad words from Stephanos' mouth, so poisoned with pride. Since I alone am unafraid, I alone am called to action amidst my peers, who sit motionless with shock and dismay.

The rest of our council cover their ears and begin shouting with one voice, "Blasphemer!" "Possessed fool!" And even "Insane Hellenist!"

As I approach Stephanos, my brothers rise up behind me. But along with my fury, a hopeless desire struggles within me to guard him from his own demonic vision. Yet it is this sorcerer, this blasphemer who has opened his mouth like a mad dog; how can it be that he is the one who lifts his arms when I draw close, as though to shelter me, Saul of Tarsus, an undisputed keeper of our law?

His next words pierce like arrows, and they are words that I alone can hear. "Pavlo, dear Pavlo, the Lord has heard my prayer that you will be my fellow protomartyr, for we here are first to witness the return of our Lord Jesus Christ this day. Oh, turn to look behind you! Alleluia!"

My blood tingles at the breath of this even greater blasphemy. Meanwhile Stephanos' eyes plead earnestly as a sailor spotting land. And despite his sheer insanity, those eyes of his are full of peace and love. Only one act remains for me.

With a three-word prayer, "Deliver us, Lord!" I force my body to Stephanos' heaving chest. With all my strength, I press him backward toward the wall. Not expecting the force of my weight, his body yields, until his shoulders strike stone with a sharpness that jars his breath.

The pain ignites his eyes as lightning, but then, that accursed delirium of joy returns. "I knew that you would indeed be protomartyr with me for the sake of all who love our Lord!" he whispers. Then grasping my hand extended to ward him off, gently, as though I were a child, he turns me round.

His look almost made me believe his truth for that moment. If this man comes close to deceiving even me, surely his insanity will infect every man in Jerusalem. And so I cry out words that must bring him to himself even as a slap in the face revives one who is fainting. "Stephanos! You are no Christ! For you, no trial!"

But with eyes fixed on mine, Stephanos takes no notice. Instead, his brow lowering with pity becomes the very spirit and image of the face of his sister, my beloved Irini. It is as though I hear again her final words, forever on my heart. Her voice knocks at my inner ear with a weight that only now I comprehend: "Oh, what a hard thing—to kick against the pricks as you do!"

I cannot withstand this regard from her brother, God's enemy. With relief, I see that the rest of the men have taken heart, drawing up in a circle, closing in. Those who know the ritual are rubbing their hands to roughen them for the casting of stones. But my gaze draws away from their motion when Stephanos looks upward again and gasps.

Swiping his tears like flies, Stephanos stares only at what the rest of us behold, a wall of solid stone, rising and blank.

It is my turn to pity. Yes. Were I not born of God's people, and had I not set my heart since childhood on honoring the Most High, surely this man would remain my friend forever. But not in light of our laws. Despite my indrawing of breath to steady my soul under its burden of duty to our people, my own eyes burn.

I turn away from the circle around us to guard the other men from seeing my emotion, and I face Stephanos once more. "You know that I can do nothing to save you or ourselves against the unclean spirit that has infested you. The greatest mercy is putting an end to your life," I hear myself say.

I long to look away as Stephanos' gaze turns from sorrow to pleading. "Saul, only this: Do not let them bind my hands," he whispers. "I must go of my own free will."

16. The Witnesses and the Stones

Witness of Many, Jerusalem, A.D. 35

Witness of Cassandra

With every step we take away from the Temple, my heart sinks like a stone, lower even than I plunged in the pool of baptism. For as long as I may live, and as many years as our Lord gives me breath, I will never speak to Saul again. I will hate the name of Little Weed that once made me smile every day. And though I know it is against the teachings of Christos to call a man our enemy, I bite back burning words that I wish I could speak aloud to Uncle Timon, who walks in silence toward the taverna where Lukas asked us to meet him.

When the owner, Demetrius, sees Uncle Timon's face, he laughs. "You look like someone who has seen a dead man!"

My uncle does not laugh in return, and the tavern owner goes on. "Well, let's greet this face with a large cup of wine."

Timon tries to smile as Demetrius also even pours some watered wine for me in a lesser vessel.

"Uncle," I begin, "I know that you did not die in Athens, and I also know that you are a free man. Why did these actors believe something different?"

Uncle Timon takes a long drink. He sighs, moving close to the wall where I am sitting to join me in the shade. "There is some truth in what they told us," he begins.

Remembering again the advice of Aunt Iphigenia to remain

quiet as a woman, I stare deep into the clay bowl where my wine is swirling. I try to imagine the color of the fruits, the grace of vines that bore them. The pulp shifts in the bottom with small motions of my fingers. This is the only way I can wait without seeming impatient.

Uncle Timon drains his entire cup before answering, and then Demetrius pours him more. I have never before seen him drink unwatered wine.

Finally, he goes on. "There are many things, Cassandra, that are difficult for you to understand here in Jerusalem, because even though all of us live under the laws of Rome, it is another matter in Greece. As a guard in Athens, even though I witnessed every great play, I was in fact a slave, yes. I never even had the hope of a free man to hold life in my own hands. I had hardly enough to eat, and no man to call a friend."

"You really were a slave? No wonder you cannot even tell me the voice of alpha, Uncle," I exclaim.

If I could bite off the end of my tongue to unsay this sentence, I would.

But Uncle Timon cuts off my apology. He bends his head to level with mine. "I am afraid, very afraid."

Perhaps the wine he has drunk has made him speak these strange words, or my own wine has made my ears ring. "But even Saul called you a free man today," I reply. "What do you have to fear?"

My uncle leans close. "The guards were not there to arrest me, Cassandra. They were there for your Uncle Stephanos. They have surely already brought him for questioning in the Temple regarding his curing of those in need through the name of Jesus of Nazareth. What he says will fill them with even more anger than they already have in their hearts. Peter and John were beaten after their questioning, but for your uncle, it could be even worse."

I jump to my feet, sweeping aside my empty wine cup.

"Then we must return to the Temple and help him!"

My uncle also rises, clasping my shoulder. "No, Cassandra. We shall not go against his wishes, neither you nor I," he says. I know this voice of his, quiet as the breeze, but once contradicted, then strong as a gale.

But I care nothing for his words, because I remember a horrible day long ago, the day when Timon begged me to surpass the angry throng and to enter the Temple to find Saul. My slowness then cost the life of my Aunt Irini. I must not allow such tragedy to come again. Instead, I gather my robe between my thighs, and I run.

Witness of Timon

Under my breath I curse the drinking of those two cups of strong wine from the generous Demetrius, for they have made my hands too awkward to act with a guardsman's agility.

It is no difficult matter to catch Cassandra before she reaches the street corner, struggling to run in her tangled robe. But she shrieks and strikes and scratches my face before I can withdraw the rope I always carry hidden in my tunic, a relic of my guardsman's days. As I draw the knot tight enough to capture her hands, she freezes like a man turned to stone upon seeing the gorgon Medusa.

Despite myself, I laugh, and again it is the accursed effect of the wine. "It is not the first time I have knotted your hands, my girl, but I hope it is the last!"

Then Cassandra weeps—not the loud cry of one seeking attention, but the silent and shaking sobs of a woman. "Let me go, let me go! We must go to help Uncle Stephanos."

Inwardly I call out with all my heart to our Lord. For what words or teaching do I have to give to this unfortunate girl, first stripped of father, then of guardian aunt, and now, this final grief, the arrest of Stephanos, her dearest uncle?

I do not loosen my grip one fraction, afraid of what her wildness could bring upon her. At last I clasp her shoulders in my hands and draw her back from my chest where her tears and spittle have soaked the top of my tunic. "Will you run if I release you?" I ask.

The child–almost–woman nods. "But I am sorry to hurt you, Uncle."

This Cassandra. She has the courage of a born Athenian, but the acquired honesty of a Jew admitting her resolve to flee!

"I thought as much," I reply, wiping the blood from my face that she has scratched. But it is no matter; she was fighting not me, but her own fear and memories. This I know. "You and I will sit together here and wait."

Lifting her beneath the arms, I place her atop a stone wall so that we are face to face in height. As I look into her eyes, our Lord puts words on my lips to say to her. "The main thing is this, Cassandra: We must raise your uncle up in prayer before our Lord and before the Christ," I begin in Greek. Then because what I have to say to her burns too painful in my mouth, I turn to the language I have adopted with the help of our Lord, this blessed tongue of Abraham and of Isaac, of Jacob and of Moses. "And we must remember also, God have place for you, for me, dear Cassandra. He put us in His hand still far in Athens. You remember this thing?"

I hoist myself onto the wall beside her. The weight of my own body and my heavy breath remind me that I will never be a young man again.

As Cassandra shakes her head, I wipe the tears from her face, since her hands are not free to do so.

"Then I help remember you," I go on. "It is why I say not first time to tie your hands, you see. Our Lord find you in theater where your father Alexander of Crete wonderful, big actor. But you, very small, no wonderful girl. Day I know you, you take purse all money away from you Aunt Irini. But I see like eagle, so soon my eye see you, and so pick you up, tie you hand just like now."

Cassandra says nothing, but her eyes do not leave mine, and I go on with the story that perhaps I should have told her long ago.

"Yes. All you know till now is your father, big, famous, great actor, and this is truth. You very proud your father, and you right be happy and proud. But it is not all truth. So here is more for you to listen. Then that day when you so small tiny girl, I ask every man, who have this child? No man come, but I see Stephanos, see Irini, stop them for to give back the purse of Irini you take away from her. Then you take us where your father that day die, you no know he die yet, but just you know you cry, be with him, and then Irini, she say this."

My own eyes are sharp with the tears I remember from that day. "She say, me, my brother, we orphans, too. We take this girl, even stinky, thief, nobody girl, we make her life together with our life."

I would like to untie Cassandra's hands now, which have grown limp on her knees, but I do not trust her yet. At least her anger has passed.

"So, next day, we together go meet, talk, you, them, me. I ask help me go away from Athens, and your Aunt Irini say right away, she want help me."

"So she freed you from slavery?" Cassandra's voice is full of wonder.

I smile despite myself. "She allow money so they write me dead, and I leave Athens with you. This why actors think I am dead, but I am real slave, never free there."

For a while, we sit in silence as passersby turn away, perhaps thinking that I am there to arrest Cassandra.

I wait until Cassandra meets my eyes again. "Same day they call me dead man, we all together leave Athens, and we travel, travel, travel, and we come Jerusalem."

"Yes, and you were baptized before we arrived," she replies.

I nod. "Baptized river Jordan, from man John, yes. I baptized, but it because you. I go inside river only cause to save you. You remember?"

Cassandra nods.

"That day, I know Jew God my God, too, and I say my life need be Jew life."

"I believe you, Uncle," Cassandra replies. "I know you are truly a Jew, more than many Hebrews from Israel."

Then she begins to cry again. "But what will happen to my Uncle Stephanos? We must do something, anything!"

"We can do no something," I answer, though the words pain my lips.

"Please speak in Greek, Uncle," she replies, looking left and right to the Jerusalemites passing by.

I sigh and revert to the words that are natural in my mouth as I come to the heart of the matter.

"Do not cry, Cassandra. One of two things can happen, and whichever road opens, our Lord will oversee the result. First, perhaps with the help of our Lord, as Stephanos speaks there in the Temple, the scribes and scholars there will understand through his words the truth of Jesus the Christos. But it is equally possible that they will turn his words against him. Then he will see the face of our Lord this very day in His kingdom, Cassandra. He may give his life even as your Aunt Irini gave her life to give people faith and hope. By going there, you would bring him no help, and you could certainly bring harm to yourself, and that is all."

Though Cassandra remains silent, she nods.

"But you and I are witnesses to pass on hope from our Lord. We must live on to speak this truth, especially to our Hellenisti."

"His face was like an angel," she says, and her tears fall again, but silently. "I cannot forget his face or his words."

I nod. "And I cannot forget his truth. If Stephanos does not return to us today, then always remember this: Your uncle's crown today will be far greater than the laurel he won at the race in his youth at Tarsus."

Witness of Gamaliel

As my Sanhedrin peers burst forward to surround Saul and Stephanos, I turn away.

My student who read the words of Jesus of Nazareth describing the vineyard and its evil caretakers rips apart the precious parchment copied from Stephanos' scroll, preparing to burn it in the lantern kept near the front of the room.

I hurry from the seething hall unnoticed, for I cannot allow Stephanos' scroll to remain in my house. But as I leave the Temple, I cannot set my heart to destroy it as I should. Before my eyes as I walk, the words of my father Simeon's final day pursue me. Though these writings are engraved in my memory, how can I destroy them?

Burdened with sorrow for what I must do, and with grief for what my eyes have just seen and my ears have just heard from the two students I once considered my finest, I enter my house with a troubled and heavy spirit. No one is in the courtyard, and I am glad of the chance to be alone, at least for a final moment. Soon enough I will be rending not only my scroll, but also my garments.

I welcome the cool stillness of my beloved library after the late-afternoon heat. I inhale the musk of the scrolls, the sharpness of the ink, and as I pick up Stephanos' cedar box, it, too, exhales a fragrance. Even if it is the foreign fragrance of evil Rome, surely our Lord created the cedar for such things as this. My lips move to speak to the Most High as I remove Stephanos' writing from its case.

Then a familiar voice, unheard by my ears but resounding in my heart, whispers within me. "Be still. I will show you what you must do."

My hands drop from the scroll to clasp in prayer. "Oh, may the words of my mouth and the meditations of my heart forever please You, my Lord," I whisper, repeating words of King David, poetry beloved to my spirit. Laying the scroll back on its shelf, I sink to my knees. Time loses its measure as I pray without words.

And it comes to pass that a scratching at the library door interrupts my meditations. "Rabboni?" comes a young man's whisper.

I turn my head but do not rise. "I am here, but how do you know it?"

A shape appears that must be one of my students, but his posture is like that of an old man.

"I have seen where you hide the key behind the molding on a plinth, Rabboni, but I have told no one. Since it was gone, I came here to find you."

Looking fully upon my student's face, I make haste to rise from my knees. "Ezra! What troubles you? Are you ill?"

It is my student's turn to fall upon his knees and wring his hands. "Oh, Rabboni, I am an unclean man of unclean lips today! You must tell me my punishment, for I have seen the very gates of Hades and was nearly dragged down!"

I have never seen this student Ezra weep, not even as a boy of ten summers when his father left him here and returned to Jericho. In his tears I read repentance enough. But the inner voice I have awaited has spoken to me, both in his words and in his struggle.

When I do not question him, he continues in a choked voice. "It was my intent to return to Jericho and to become a rabbi there. Only now I think it is impossible, Rabboni."

I lay a hand on his shoulder as he looks up at me. "Our Lord never despises a penitent spirit," I say.

I await his calming with no hurry, holding him in the

shadow of my spirit, but I prepare the words I must say next, once he regains his composure. "Tell me, Ezra, what do you believe about this Jesus of Nazareth?" I gesture to the scroll. "Do you think the things Stephanos of Tarsus wrote here are true? I must tell you as your rabboni, your answer today will allow you to stay in my house, or it will divide us from living together."

Still on his knees, Ezra wipes his tears on a sleeve, but he looks up to meet my eyes. Then he rises. When did he become as tall as I am?

"Rabboni, as you are aware, I know the writer of this scroll. He would not willingly deceive any man. I have not hidden from you that I have also gone many times to hear the teaching of Peter and John. I have not yet been baptized in the name of Jesus of Nazareth, but I am certain in my heart he is the Christ we awaited."

"Do you know what has happened to Stephanos of Tarsus?"

Ezra shakes his head, as I expected. Looking into his eyes, I speak with the quiet authority of my position. "Then I must tell you. This evening, even as we are speaking, your friend the scribe is being stoned for the belief you have just confessed aloud. It is for this reason and not for any sin of yours that I must order you to leave my house of study. You may go now, pack your things, and then you will return to me here. If you have no place to stay until we can arrange your return to Jericho, I will assure you a family with whom you may remain until you can leave for your father's house. If you lack money, I will give you enough today for your needs. But we will not meet again after this day, Ezra. Do you understand?"

Ezra bows his head. "Your words are just, Rabboni. But as for Stephanos' death—it is as unfair as the crucifixion of our Messiah!" he says, before exiting my library.

In less than the time it takes me to recite two brief Psalms, he returns to me with his small bag of possessions. "I am ready, Rabboni," he says. "I will find a place to stay."

"In Bethany?" I ask him, smiling just a little.

"Yes. At the house of Timon, the former Temple guard. You know him."

I nod. "He is a good man." Then, lifting the scroll in its box, I place it in his hands. "You brought this to me as messenger from Stephanos. It is right that you should continue to guard these words you believe in."

Ezra sighs, and he looks into my face. "I will hold fast this writing as I will also keep every memory of what you and Saul have taught me here. But before I depart, Rabboni, will you bless me?"

I clasp his hands in mine. "Ezra, farewell. The weight of whatever impurity stains you is overcome by your love of our Lord. Stay strong in your boldness, like Joshua entering the Promised Land. And may our Lord forever bless you and keep you."

Ezra's lips shape the words "Thank you," but his voice cannot open to breathe them out.

Quiet as a dove's wing, he turns, adjusts his burden with the heaviness of the scroll, and departs.

Witness of Lukas

The sun is red with evening as I approach the Temple, turning her white face to blood. My eyes grasp what I fear most.

A mob of shouting men proceeds well ahead. They are not bound south or west to the inhabited city, nor east to the outlying towns like our Bethany. No. They are crossing to the north, to the barren and rock–strewn face of the hills that have protected our city from invaders. But on this evening, the slopes offer only a secret place to perform murder beyond the scrutiny of the Romans.

Out the Sheep Gate I follow them as they advance, and in their midst is a tall man, and it is indeed Stephanos. How strange that he is neither bound nor carried, but he walks of his own accord. I gain ground on them as they push him to the deep corral where our Temple animals are led before slaughter. It is a place of no escape.

As they pursue him to the edge of the drop–off, one of his sandals scrapes from his foot to the dirt; the other tumbles two men's height down the steep wall. They intend to throw him downward, face first. But displaying his remaining agility, Stephanos slips from their hands, only to leap down the embankment of loose stones. Had the ground not already bloodied his feet, perhaps he could even escape, by the grace of our Lord. But he seems to take no thought of this as he turns. Yes, he raises his face from the depths of that pit, and he looks up into our midst. Surely these are the eyes of Joseph when his brothers sought his life.

After he scrutinizes every face glaring down at him, he calls heavenward. "Into Your hands I commend my spirit, Lord!"

Despite the hastening to loosen their garments in the remaining heat of the evening, to flour their hands with dust in order for the stones not to slip free, every man among us freezes for a moment.

Then Saul's cry breaks the silence. "Come, brothers, lay your garments here with me. Be strong and of good faith. Set your stones free!"

There is a frailty of the bone just behind the corner of the human eye. The place is so thin, even a tap can sometimes break it. I stoop to locate the stone I want; it is oblong, with a point at one end. It will execute perfectly. Yes, with my steady hand, it will indeed execute.

I breathe a prayer to our Lord in lifting it to my chest, to my shoulder, to the height of my own temple. "Steady my aim, oh Lord, and sanctify your servant below me, and forgive me this one trespass of my doctor's vow to do no harm. You must know, to end my friend's torment before it begins is the only mercy I can offer him."

Words arrest me as I steady my stone. Standing so close before me that I can smell his sweat, Saul is hissing in Greek. "I'll bind up every one of them, men and women. I'll pursue them house to house. Prison will be their new home, and this pit will be their grave! A curse on Stephanos and all his plague of believers!"

The face whose bone I would have broken a moment before turns up to me. The eyes which will dim with the life beaten forth from them meet mine. The arm which would have had no gestures left if I had struck according to my intent now motions to me. The hand points southward, fingers splitting to encompass all Jerusalem and Bethany. He is pointing me away, to warn the Jews and the Gentiles and the Hellenisti who believe in the Christ. They know nothing of the imminent danger they will face, perhaps this very night.

No heavier than an apple, the death stone drops from my hand, coming to rest on the pile of garments Saul is set to guard.

Witness of Ezra

I am banished.

But louder than the blessing and all else left behind, in my mind, I hear again the woman's voice interpreting in the bath. It came to me as from a distance when the elder actor slapped the hand of his colleague away from mine, pressing my gold coin back into my palm. "This man will come again to the Temple two days from this morning, after their competition, which is tomorrow. He will meet you there, and he will speak with you and the girl."

Can my heart for Cassandra cancel out my defilement? My hand still burns where the young man clasped it, even as I walk away from Rabboni Gamaliel's house, exiled from all I have learned and known these seven years. Though my heart burns with shame, yet I rejoice that I have the actor's promise to speak with Cassandra, surely to bring her happiness.

Recognizing the physician's bag of Doctor Lukas ahead of me, I call out, and he turns. His face is drawn with worry and sorrow. He must not have succeeded in saving the patient he stopped to help along the path near the brook. "We must hurry to Demetrius' tavern," he says in greeting. These are his only words.

As we turn a steep corner to reach the tavern, what I see freezes my blood. Not twenty paces ahead, Timon—Timon the guard whom I have known since childhood, Timon the Greek with his many stories in his ridiculous, broken speech, Timon, whom I respected and trusted—has pinned Cassandra sitting atop a low wall. He stands facing her. Her arms are tied firmly, and she is helpless to escape.

As I call her name and Cassandra turns her face to me, the pain in her eyes shoots directly into my heart.

I run to confront the guard. "What have you done, tying Cassandra's hands as if she were a common criminal?" I scream.

Timon sighs, removing the knot at her wrists. "You no run away now Ezra and Lukas here," he says to her. "Truth?"

"Truth," Cassandra replies. but then her eyes fill with tears that spill down her cheeks.

Timon turns to face me. "Ezra, this girl, crazy girl, think to go follow Stephanos in Temple, maybe help him. He tell me no, tell me keep her away, but she no want understand and listen. It's just only why I did this."

Cassandra nods, rubbing her wrists a little. "It is true." Looking at both Lukas and me, she whispers, "What has happened to Stephanos?"

Lukas has drawn close, but he appears unable to speak. Instead, he extends his arms to her shoulders. "Sister," he says, and then, "Oh, my sister." He can only whisper. "Cassandra, you will not see him walking on this earth again."

With a single motion, Timon shears his tunic from shoulder to hip.

At the same moment, Cassandra shrieks once, with a soul–severing height to her voice. But then, she stops. She turns to all three of us, as we surround her. "Indeed, now there is no one left to love me," she whispers. And the whisper is more frightening than the shriek.

I look, not at her, but rather at Timon. He knows how my heart beats for Cassandra. Now Timon nods at me with a faint smile.

"Cassandra, I have loved you since the day I first saw you at the Temple," I dare to say, as Timon looks on.

"This true thing, Cassandra, and this I did see with Ezra's face to you. It is look just like that I did love your Aunt Iphigenia first day see her face at Temple, too," Timon adds, laying a hand on Cassandra's shoulder. "Now I take care you, talk father of Ezra and help you be together, with help our Lord."

Cassandra shakes her head. "No. My uncle is dead. Now no man remains to love me. No man will love me," she repeats in a rising voice. "Not when they see this!"

As she lifts her left hand, the sleeve of her robe falls back. My curious glances have snatched glimpses of the swaying wrists of women as they knead bread, or spin, or cook. But even in my most blessed or my most cursed of dreams, of course not a single woman has ever shown me any part of her body! My eyes are helpless to remove themselves from the beauty of this wonder; I can hardly breathe. The early dusk coats Cassandra's skin with the sheen of young grapes in our vineyards in Jericho. For a few days, they shed their greenness, transforming toward their final depth of bronze that proclaims them ripe. It is exactly this smoothness and luster that my eyes drink in.

Cassandra gasps, and so does Lukas behind her. Just like me, she is staring at the inner skin of her forearm as though she has never seen it before. She turns to Lukas.

The doctor's eyes are filled, not with shock or dismay at her action, but with tears. "Give thanks to our Lord, Cassandra," he whispers.

Drawing breath with difficulty, wrenching my eyes from her arm, I can only sigh an inner, "Amen!"

Lukas takes Cassandra's hand. "Not a mark remains, not one, Cassandra! This comes from your faith."

Cassandra once more extends her arm. "But I have believed that Jesus is the Christos since I met him on the road to Uncle Timon's wedding, because he told me to keep faith. This—this perfect skin is my uncle's final miracle. It is all he could give me at my baptism," she whispers. "Nothing more remains of—of my past actions. I can remember both my baptism and my uncle now, every day, in my own body."

Lukas looks into Cassandra's eyes, then toward the sky where the first stars are piercing the dusk. At last, he sighs, and he nods. "Indeed, this day, Cassandra, your Messiah is my Messiah, too," he breathes. "Your miracle will remain in my heart forever."

Though I am ignorant of whatever miracle they speak of, I rejoice in Lukas' new belief and amazement. "I also confess him as Messiah," I reply. "I have believed through reading this scroll." I pull out the box from the top of my bag. "Look. I have left the home of Gamaliel, and he has blessed me, and he has returned this writing to me from Stephanos."

Lukas nods. "May I take this scroll to read later, Ezra? I long to make copies and to expand on his words to keep across our generations. But now we must hurry to warn our people of what has happened."

"Amen," I reply.

"Now just only one thing more what I can do for Stephanos," Timon whispers. "I will go together with Greek men here in taverna what know him take body for to bury. Tomorrow many many soul carry sorrow, but never like our sorrow here with you."

"Shall I come with you?" I ask Timon, suddenly unsure what I should do.

For a long breath, Timon looks at me, and then he shakes his head. "No, Ezra, no. Our girl here need not to be alone. I think she need you be strong man help her."

I turn to Cassandra. Though my heart breaks for Stephanos of Tarsus, other words burn my mouth with wonder that I must speak aloud. In fact, they form the poem I have longed to compose ever since hearing hers.

"Cassandra, I will always believe in two things. I will stand in the greatness of our Messiah who gives us life, and I will lie down in the beauty of your soul that brings me gladness!"

And to my joy, Cassandra smiles through her tears. Yes, she smiles, and she clasps my two hands in hers! "We shall see whether you spoke the truth to me about this Dead Sea of yours in Jericho, whether a man really cannot sink in its waves!"

Witness of Stephanos

Half dragged, half carried from our dear Jerusalem, I weep with failure, begging God's pardon. Others may think that I recant the words I have just uttered at the Sanhedrin, or that my tears attend my coming death. But they are wrong. Not one soul understands the sorrow weighting me, pounding my heart.

I am calling to mind Christ's final words He spoke to me at Passover, when I saw Him in my vision before the torn veil, the day He died:

You shall not reach the things you most desire,
but your own life will turn my word to fire.

True, I converted my desire to write, to pray, to listen to Christ's students, taking instead hard ministries, Your will. My own recent labor amidst the poor has strengthened me, hands steady, eyes alert to dangers, opportunities, and friends.

But Your word turned to fire? Forgive! Forgive! My anger eclipsed my witness, left it unfinished there in the Temple today—and then resulting, Your own true face came only to my eyes and not to theirs. What so-called first witness, what Protomartyr can I be? Your holy fire cannot ignite a single soul from this poor life soon to be beaten out of me.

They are not strong, these minds of Israel. Of course, they are well trained to law, but not to worldly things like making heavy stones target their mark. Their rocks, so awkwardly and crudely flung, will hardly reach me, afraid as they are to stray too close, frightened to meet my gaze. Coming from them, this is no easy death.

But after I spoke my final prayer to save my spirit from my lack of ministry this day, a final scourging of my soul comes hardest of all. Saul's voice strikes worse than any blow of theirs.

"Come, brothers, lay your garments here with me. Be strong and of good faith. Set your stones free!"

Thank God that Lukas has arrived somehow. He sees me, understands my fear. He will keep faith to warn those who are in danger. His doctor's wish to protect will allow him to do no less.

As soon as he leaves, one stone obeys its mark, my chest. I want to fall, to sleep. But I kneel instead, hearing Messiah's words as I was told, and as I wrote them of how He redeemed us from His cross of death. Trying to meet each man's flinching regard, I hear myself repeat them, facing Saul.

"Lord, into Your hands I give my spirit!"

I see what the circle facing me cannot perceive: Saul's eyes are filled with tears. Now he is bowing his head, as if unsure. This will be his last glimpse of me alive.

My eyes turn upward to the azure sky, the color of truth, I've thought since childhood. One star, a single ray, beckons my sight. Soon the great Lyra will surround its light, but I will not be here to hear its song.

I have voiced my final suffering, and so I fix my thoughts toward its rays, return my soul to God. And I rejoice, not feeling anything. No rocks erupting higher in my bones, no curses sparking to my inner ears. Nothing remains but wonder; nothing more.

Fixed on the star, my spirit finds its breath fluttering, loosening, and ready to rise. I pour my love on Saul, my prayers on God, wishing to know, will he ever believe? Can he be freed of kicking at "the pricks" that thorn through every facet of our law?

And once again, that well–loved, inner voice transfixes me, releases me, lives on.

"Saul is a chosen vessel of my own to bear my name before the world around. Great suffering shall be his for my name's sake. But you, my Protomartyr, first to see, receive your crown. Come now. Abide with me."

Praise God! My friend shall be the one to fly this newborn faith to our awaiting world! As you have spoken, Lord, so let it be.

One final phrase of Jesus strikes my tongue. I force my breath to cry it loudly now, and speaking it, I raise prayers for them all.

"Lord, do not count this act to them as sin!"

The single star spins closer, shining high, as I release my blessing to the sky.

Not the end,
Alleluia!

Questions for Thought
and Discussion

Questions—Part 1

Which Biblical and Greek myth references in this part of the novel were familiar to you? Which ones were new?

Did reading any of the Biblical and classical references as depicted here make you look at them in a new way?

What does Irini's decision to cross dress have in common with those who cross dress today? What elements of her decision are different from today's reasoning?

What symbolism do you draw from the marking by blood in Chapter 1, and how does this run through the events of Chapter 7?

What do you make of the relationship between Jesus and Irini as she gives him bread and he cleanses her from the spattering of sacrificial blood?

The battle described in Chapter 2 is a historic event from 31 B.C.. Why do you think Baba made his decision to offer himself as a slave? How does this parallel and not parallel Passover traditions, as he calls himself "a lamb"?

In Chapter 3, Stephanos makes a difficult decision to take responsibility for Irini's direct welfare. Discuss your thoughts on family role models and how his decision was made.

How does the description of the race in Chapter 4 parallel or differ from your image of Olympic races?

In exposing his family history and faith, Stephanos separates himself from his fellow runners. What do you think made him speak in public of his personal past?

Do you think Saul's concern for Irini's lifestyle was more a matter of keeping her in the Jewish faith tradition, or because of his concern for her as a person?

Which of the boys had more reason for envy, Saul desiring physical wholeness, or Stephanos longing for the deep scripture studies Saul followed in Jerusalem?

What differences do you note in descriptions of life in Athens as noted in Chapter 5 and in Jerusalem from Chapter 1?

Are you surprised that Athens' executive police consisted of slaves? How would you characterize Timon's relationship to his work and his life as a slave?

What makes Stephanos and Irini decide to adopt Cassandra? What about their later help to Timon?

Given her past, what do you expect of Cassandra and her future faith?

How is the depiction of John the "river man" similar or different from your own?

Do you think that John would have invited a man obviously not Jewish, like Timon, to be baptized in the Jordan?

Chapter 7 is based on a historic incident from non–Biblical sources during Pontius Pilate's early rule. How would you compare and contrast this protest to events occurring today?

Who is and is not to blame for the death at the end of Part 1?

Questions—Part II

What dividings, large or small, do you find in this section of the book?

What statement of faith would you give to Rabboni Gamaliel? What do you make of his cross-cultural relationships with the Hellenisti?

Why does this author choose to show Jesus only in brief scenes, or, as in Chapter 8, by the crowd's chanting? Would you like to see more depictions of Jesus in literature of this kind?

In Chapter 8, why do you think Cassandra was carrying Irini's yellow scarf? What significance did it have that she showed it to Jesus, and then to Saul and Stephanos?

While the splitting of the Temple veil is mentioned only briefly in the Bible, how does this writer use the event in the action in Chapter 9? How likely do you think the reaction described in this novel was in the congregation of worshipers witnessing this event?

In Chapter 10, we learn a few things about medical practice in the time and culture of the Roman Empire. What does such practice have and not have in common with medical thinking of today?

Concepts of the Hellenisti returning to Palestine emerge in Chapter 10. How does this compare to finding our roots for Americans and others today?

What contrasts do you find between miracles as indicated in Acts Chapters 3-5 and those depicted by this author in Chapter 11?

Which of these events do you consider the greatest exception to the rule? Have you ever witnessed what you believe to be a miracle?

As Gamaliel describes the politics and the arrests in Chapter 12, the tension among characters builds. How can we compare this with today's religious and political situations?

Questions—Part III

What role if any does language play in this and preceding parts in communication between Timon and the Hebrew-speaking characters?

Chapter 13 of this novel reflects statements in Acts Chapters 3-5 concerning communal giving in the pre-Christian Jewish community. How realistic was it to expect people to share everything they had?

Do you know of any examples of where this has been successful in other times or cultures?

Do you think Saul would have continued relations with a girl like Cassandra after his division from Stephanos? Why or why not?

Why do you think that Ezra is drawn to Cassandra, despite her non-Hebrew background?

In Chapter 15, how fair do you think it was for Stephanos to speak and to be questioned?

Why did Stephanos resort to such an extensive listing of the early history of the Jewish tradition?

Could Saul have done anything to save Stephanos from the stoning awaiting him? If so, what?

What is possible to say to those who believe that differences in faith will make the difference between death and eternal life?

What made Lukas drop his stone in Chapter 16?

What faith steps can you trace from Lukas' skepticism

toward belief in Jesus and his ultimate acceptance of belief in him as Messiah?

Was Gamaliel's handling of Ezra fair, given the situation? Why or why not?

Why did Ezra speak of something so joyful in the tragedy unfolding before the friends of Stephanos?

What effects of Stephanos' death can you trace affecting others in this novel? What do you know of the effect of his martyrdom in the larger course of events leading to Christianity and to Saul's conversion? (See Acts Chapter 8 and early part of Chapter 9.)

About the Author

Elizabeth L. Sammons' love of both scripture and Greek mythology dates back to childhood. So does her fascination with the story of Stephen the Protomartyr and his world. She holds an M.A. in journalism from The Ohio State University. She has lived in six countries, served in the Peace Corps, and taught a course called "The Art and Science of Simultaneous Interpreting." A highlight of her international life included interpreting for several traveling clergy of diverse faith backgrounds and finding the key to conveying their thoughts in cross–cultural settings. She has also done advocacy interpreting in the disability community. The author is open to conducting lectures and sharing thoughts almost anywhere, whether in English, French, or Russian.

This author intends the release of a second novel, *With Best Intent*, questioning the moral value of genetic testing, and is mapping a third, *Translation of Bones*, whose primary focus involves the spiritual dilemma of an interpreter who finds out too much about a cross–national cult.

You may find her literary blog at
WindowsOfThought.wordpress.com
and may contact her through *IAmAntigone@att.net*

Her book-related website is
http://www.dldbooks.com/elizabethsammons/

Made in the USA
Columbia, SC
09 April 2018